Turning, she looked at the distant dock light. She looked down at the money in her hand and then stuffed it into the front pocket of her white shorts. She had to make a decision: stay where she was or go to the light. She raised her right leg and the sneaker was sucked from her foot. Raising her other foot she lost the other sneaker. She took three awkward steps across the muddy section of land she was on, but then stopped and took a deep breath, the stagnant odor of the marsh causing her to gag. Covering her nose with her hand, she considered going back a few steps and venturing out into the water. She felt she could make better time and cover more ground by swimming, but the thought of the gators, snakes and sharks caused her to hesitate. She heard a splashing sound to her left and then a swishing noise to her right. *Gators!* she thought. She felt something rub up against her bare leg. *A snake?* Quickly, she stepped from the mud until she could feel herself entering the water. She walked out, still stepping in the muddy bottom, when she felt a sharp pain in the bottom of her foot. Had she been bitten by a snake or had she stepped on a broken shell? Utilizing the breast stroke, she quickly made her way out a few yards into the dark water and then stopped. She found she was able to still touch the muddy bottom, the mud covering her ankles. Looking toward the distant light, she screamed at the top of her lungs, "Please... someone help me!" The moonlight returned as the clouds drifted away. As far as she could see there was nothing but black water and the gloomy salt marsh. She screamed again, "Help me... please!"

LOWCOUNTRY BURN

BURN

by Gary Yeagle

a BlackWyrm book
Louisville, Kentucky

LOWCOUNTRY BURN

A BlackWyrm Book
BlackWyrm Publishing
10307 Chimney Ridge Ct, Louisville, KY 40299

Printed in the United States of America.

ISBN: 978-1-61318-167-5

First edition: August 2014

Dedicated to
Credit, Debit, and Ledger
my three cats, who are always
curled up by my side in the room
where I write

Chapter One

SHE COULD FEEL THE HARD DIRT BENEATH HER BACK. Blinking her eyes twice, she felt fatigued, the way she always felt when she slept too long. But this feeling was different. She was confused. She wasn't in her comfortable bed; she was lying on the ground. Tilting her head slightly forward, she saw a number of old oak trees draped with Spanish moss, the towering trees flanked with tall weeds and grass. An old rutted dirt road disappeared in a stand of Palmetto trees. Looking to the west, the blazing sun was low and partially shadowed by the overcast sky. A large, black rain cloud hovered above her as the first few waves of raindrops gently caressed her face. Shaking her head, she tried to get to her feet by using her hands to support her body, but it was then she discovered her feet were secured with what appeared to be black electrical tape. Coming to full consciousness, she realized her mouth was taped shut. Reaching up to remove the tape, she was interrupted by a voice and then a masked face, "I can't allow you to remove the tape."

The man firmly forced her bare arms back to the ground and continued, "The reason the tape cannot be removed is I can't afford to have you screaming. If I were to ask you not to scream if I removed the tape you would no doubt promise you wouldn't, but I've had experience with young girls your age and I can assure you when a seventeen-year-old girl informs you she will not scream, that it is not the truth, so we'll just leave the tape where it is. Besides that, there is no reason for you to speak. You can answer any questions I have by simply nodding yes or no. Do you understand?"

The girl remained silent and stared up into the dark blue ski mask. The only part of the man's frightening face that was exposed were chapped lips and dark eyes. The man repeated himself, "Do you understand?"

The girl turned her head to the side and refused to answer.

The man reached out and turned her head roughly so she was looking directly up at him as he stated harshly, "Look, you need to cooperate with me if you expect to get through this ordeal. So, one more time: do you understand?"

The girl, despite the intense fear building inside her, nodded yes.

"Very good," said the man. He then stood over her, his hands on his hips. Looking up at the man, the girl felt helpless. Aside from the foreboding mask, his tall, slim body was encased in a dark blue sweat suit; a set of white plastic painter's gloves covered his hands. Pointing at her hands, he explained, "I'm going to permit your hands to be free because in a few moments you'll need them so we can play the game. Your feet and mouth will remain taped."

The man changed the subject and sat on the ground next to her and gazed up at the sky. "I hope we get a good rain. We could really use it. It's been so hot lately. I think it reached ninety-five today. The tomatoes in my garden are not doing too well this year."

The girl was not paying attention to what he was saying, but remained focused on his previous statement about playing the game. *What did he mean?*

Her question was soon answered when he got up on one knee and looked down into her face. "Do you by any chance know how to play Rock, paper, scissors?"

The girl was familiar with the game but didn't want to answer the man's question. Then she remembered what he had said about co-operating with him. She nodded, yes.

"Good. But before we begin let's go over the rules so we can be sure we're on the same page. I want the game to be fair."

Standing, he walked in front of the girl and held out his right hand. "Here's the way it goes. We each pump our right fist three times as we say, Rock, paper, scissors. On the third and final fist pump we each indicate our individual choice: a clenched fist indicates rock, your palm held out flat means paper and your index and middle fingers separated is scissors. Any one of the choices can defeat the others. For instance: rock smashes scissors, paper covers rock and scissors cuts paper. In case of a tie we go again and again until there is a winner. Do you agree with the rules?"

The girl agreed with a slow nod of her head.

"Great," remarked the man. "Now that we both understand the ground rules, let's determine what the winner receives. If you win, I will release you and you'll be free to go. On the other hand, if I should win, then I get what I want. I know it must seem unfair for me to not tell you what it is I want, but that's just the way it has to be. Besides, if you win, what I want won't make any difference anyway. Are you ready to begin?"

The girl, realizing she had no other choice but to play along, once again, nodded yes.

"I'm going to remove the tape from your mouth, so that you can participate in the game properly, however if you scream, I'll kill you on the spot."

The man slowly loosened the tape and warned her once again, "Remember... no screaming. On the count of three we'll begin. One, two, three!" He pumped his fist twice and spoke confidently, "Rock, paper..." He stopped and with a look of anger, pointed down at the girl. "You're not following the rules! You're pumping your fist but you're not saying the words. You *have to* say the words or the game is not valid. Now, let's try again and remember what I said before about not cooperating."

Clearing his voice, he coughed and then started again pumping his fist and reciting his lines, "Rock, paper, scissors."

The girl reluctantly followed his example, slowly pumping her fist and saying through a choked voice, "Rock... paper... scissors."

On the last pump she kept her fist clenched, indicating rock. The man stood over her, his fist also clenched. He laughed and then spoke joyfully, "Looks like a tie. Let's go again."

The girl had played the game many times with her sister and friends. Sometimes she had won, other times she had lost. The outcome of the game had determined simple things: who got the last piece of pie, who got to take out the garbage or just like last week where she was at a party and had lost the game and therefore had to dance with Leonard Fink, the creepiest kid in their school. Dancing with Leonard at the time seemed humiliating and embarrassing, but at the moment she'd give anything to dance with pock-faced Leonard rather than be in the current dire situation she was in, not being aware of what would happen to her if she should lose.

The man started again and she followed his lead, "Rock, paper, scissors."

They once again both displayed a clenched fist. This time the man did not laugh, but he frowned as if *she* were getting the best of *him*. He looked down at her angrily. Tears filled her eyes. The last thing she wanted to do was irritate the unknown man. Bending down, he brought his covered face within inches of hers. She could smell his stale cigarette breath. Pointing a bony finger at her, he strongly suggested, "It looks like we think alike. I like that, but the thing is we don't have all night to determine the winner, so here's what we're going to do. We're going to cut down the odds. This time when we play only one of us can indicate Rock. If there is another tie I'm really going to be upset!"

The girl was now crying, but responded with a nod of yes.

The man pumped his fist, looked down at her defiantly and through gritted teeth, spoke, "Rock, paper, scissors!"

She did the same, but in a sad tone as if she were being forced to participate in a game she had no desire to play. At the exact same time they made their choice. The girl indicated scissors and the man paper. The man's head sank in defeat and he remained silent. He stared at the girl's fingers that were separated and then at his flat palm. Looking off into the distance, he let out a long breath then turned back to the girl and forced a smile. "Looks like you win. Scissors cuts paper. I was sure you would choose rock a third time and that my paper would cover it, but you out-guessed me."

Seemingly frustrated at having lost, the man walked out a few yards from her, placing both hands on his head and mumbling to himself, "I can't believe I lost the game." Kicking at the ground, he turned and walked back to her, an odd smile on his face. Reaching into a pouch on the front of his sweat shirt, he removed a roll of electrical tape and bent over the girl. "I may be a lot of things but one of them is not being dishonest. I told you if you won I'd release you... and free you shall go. The thing is I can't release you here. First, I have to bind your hands, tape your mouth and blindfold you. Then we'll be taking a car ride and a short boat cruise. Then I'll release you with instructions on what direction you should go. There is no longer any reason to be afraid or to fear me. Trust me. A few hours from now and you'll be on your way to freedom."

The girl fought her every instinct to strike out at the man but she knew with her feet bound she could do little to escape. The man said she could trust him. But, *could she?* She was at his mercy. She remained perfectly still while the man wrapped a cloth around her head, covering her eyes. He then rolled her onto her stomach and bound her hands with the tape. Jerking her to a standing position, he ordered her to stand still while he cut the binding around her ankles. He taped her mouth and then, taking her by the right arm, he started to lead her away and spoke, "Just keep walking straight ahead. I'll make sure you don't stumble. Don't try to run. You won't get far. Just remain calm. Everything will be alright."

The girl could feel the uneven ground beneath the soles of her fashionable pink sneakers. The rain was now coming down harder. Her heart was pounding. She felt like she was going to faint and her legs started to give way. The man's strong arms prevented her from going down. Picking her up in his arms, he moved forward and commented, "Looks like I'll have to carry you. We'll be at the car in a few minutes." .

Helpless to do anything, the girl went completely limp in the man's arms. She felt the rain on her face, arms and legs. Occasionally a branch brushed the side of her face. She had no idea where she was being taken.

A few minutes, which seemed like an eternity passed when she was laid on the damp ground as the man went about binding her feet once again. She heard a metallic sound that resembled a door being opened. The next thing she knew she was being picked up while he spoke, "I'm sorry I have to put you in the trunk of my car. I hope you won't be too uncomfortable in here. It'll just be a short ride to where we need to go. When we get there I'll let you out and explain what's next."

Laying her in the confines of the trunk, he continued to speak, "Here, just let me move this spare tire to the side so you won't be so cramped. Now, don't try to move around too much. You might injure yourself. If you remain calm, then soon you'll be walking toward the light." With that, she heard the slamming of the trunk. She moved slightly to the right and bumped her head on the side of the spare tire. She listened intently for anything she could hear. There was complete silence then the sound of the engine when the ignition key brought the car to life. The car moved forward and she was jostled to the side when the vehicle went through a deep rut. She vaguely heard the man's voice as he apologized, "Sorry, just hold on. We'll be there soon."

For the next few minutes the car continued to bounce in and out of ruts in the rough, uneven road, but there were no more apologies from the man. She took a deep breath and tried her best to relax. At the moment she was still alive. Since she was blindfolded and unable to cry out, she had to rely on her other senses to control her emotions. She could still hear, which at the moment, didn't seem like much of an advantage. The only sounds she could decipher were the sounds of the tires on the dirt road and the constant noise of the car's motor. Then, there was a new sound; music. The man had turned on the car radio. She listened intently, hoping that a newsman or a weatherman would reveal a location. She turned her head toward the front of the car and listened to the different sounds and voices while the channels changed: a Country and Western song, a brief conversation between two men discussing the economy, an advertisement for a restaurant. She perked up, hoping the restaurant's name would be mentioned, but the station was changed before the name was divulged. Next, there was an announcer who was talking about a baseball game and following a few more short snippets of various songs, the man driving the car finally settled on a sports talk show, that at the moment, was talking about an international tennis match.

Taking another breath to relax herself, she noticed the different smells her nose detected: It was a combination of odors: the new rubber from the spare tire, a slight hint of gasoline or oil and the lingering, what to her was the sickening odor of stale cigarette smoke. She remembered the stench of cigarette smoke on the man's breath. He was either smoking now or smoked quite often in the car. There was a mustiness that seemed to overpower the other odors. Her sense of smell was working fine, but this was not an advantage to her.

She ran her fingers over the rough carpeting beneath her and felt the dust and dirt that had accumulated over time. The only real advantage she still had was she could think. As she laid in the darkness of the trunk, she started to put things together. The last thing she remembered before waking up back in the woods had been walking out of the shopping mall. It had happened so quickly. She felt a sharp stabbing pain in her side and then things went blank. The next thing she knew, she woke up on the ground. It was obvious the man had accosted her. She hoped it wasn't the man they had talked about on the radio for the past two years, but from what he had said about the game, she was pretty sure it was him. The news media hadn't gone into much detail about the past killings but did express the fact that the killer was still out there somewhere. *How many girls had he killed?* She couldn't remember, but she did recall two different girls reported he had let them go. She prayed she would be the third.

Suddenly, the car stopped then made a right hand turn onto a smooth road as the man changed the radio to another sports station. The car picked up speed and she could hear the humming sound of the tires on the pavement. She was on her way to the next stop wherever that was. Then, she thought about something the man had said: 'If you remain calm, then soon you'll be walking toward the light.' Laying her head to the side, she tried to compose herself as she thought, *Stay cool, and just follow the man's instructions and maybe you'll get out of this alright.*

As best as she could tell, they had driven for what seemed like a half hour, but she couldn't be sure. Being blindfolded and lying in the trunk of the car seemed to have a way of distorting time. During the short trip, the car made a number of stops, obviously red lights or stop signs. Despite the sound of the radio she could hear an occasional truck or car pass by. They made a number of turns, but for the last ten minutes or so seemed to be heading in a straight direction. She closed her eyes and tried to prepare herself for what was to come next. She no sooner closed her eyes when the car slowed down and made a right hand turn onto a rough road which she thought was probably dirt. After a few minutes the car stopped and the radio was turned off. She heard the slamming of the driver's side door then there was silence.

She knew, within a few seconds the trunk would be opened. What happened after that she was completely unsure of, except for the fact the man had said he was going to release her and she could walk toward the light. *What light?* she thought.

She was startled when the man banged on the back of the car and spoke to her, "I've got to go check on something. I'll be right back and let you out."

This was followed by an eerie silence. Then, it suddenly dawned on the girl. Maybe the man was not coming back. Maybe she would die right there in the trunk of the car. It seemed like she had plenty of air, but if she was left in the trunk for days she would die of thirst or hunger. She wasn't a religious person, but from time to time in the past she had called upon God when she felt she was in trouble. This was one of those rare moments. *"Dear God,"* she whispered softly, *"I have no idea what the intentions of this man are, but please God. Do not let me die here... in this car."*

She wasn't that great when it came to praying. It had been a short prayer. She didn't know what else to say. Behind the blindfold her eyes welled up in tears. *Is this it?* she thought. *Is this how my life is going to end?* Lying in the pitch black she thought about what she had always heard about people that were on the verge of death: how their life passed before them in a few seconds. She thought how blessed she was to be born in the United States, the great parents she had. She thought about her sister and how she would miss her. For some strange reason her past years as a girl scout came to mind, then she thought about how she would never get married or have children or be a grandmother. A deep feeling of sadness settled in over her demeanor and she felt like giving up.

The dreadful feelings of her life being over were interrupted when the trunk suddenly opened, followed by the man's now familiar voice, "Alright; let's get you out of there and on your feet."

She felt herself being hoisted from the trunk and then laid on wet ground. She could feel the still falling rain on her face, arms and legs. "Relax," said the man. "Let me get that blindfold."

The first thing she noticed was the beam from a flashlight lying on the closed trunk of the car. It was dark out, but a dim light hanging from a pole next to an old dock allowed her to barely make out the man who began to untie her feet. When her feet were free, the man walked over and grabbed the flashlight. He looked at the glowing face of his wristwatch and spoke, "It's just after ten o'clock. We have to wait until later for the boat ride. We'll shove off around one in the morning. Since it's raining we'll wait in the car." He shined the light in her face. "You're so close to being set free. Don't mess things up by doing something stupid... like trying to escape before I actually release you. Don't worry, you'll be set free, but not until the time is right. Now, let's go sit in the car where you'll be dry."

After placing her in the front passenger seat, he fastened her in with the safety belt. Once again she could smell the noxious odor of stale cigarette breath, the man only inches away from her. Tugging on the belt to make sure it was secure he patted her on the side of her face. "That's just in case you get a crazy notion about bolting from the car." The man slammed the passenger door shut, then a few seconds later the driver side door was opened, the man climbed in and then the door slammed shut. He hung the blindfold from the rearview mirror. "There, that must feel better," he said. "I can't untie your hands until after the boat ride. Your mouth has to remain taped until that time also. You might as well relax and try to catch some sleep. You're going to need all the strength you have for your early morning walk toward the light." Removing a wrinkled pack of cigarettes from the console, he took out a cigarette and pushed in the car lighter. Seconds later, he lit the cigarette and took a long deep draw and blew a stream of smoke toward the roof of the car. Snapping his fingers, he apologized, "I'm so sorry, would you care for a smoke? It might help you relax." The girl shook her head no and stared out the front windshield into the darkness.

Rolling down the driver's side window a crack, he placed the burning cigarette in the console ashtray and then removed a small tube of Chapstick from the console. Opening the tube, he ran the ointment over his chapped lips and commented, "I stayed out in the sun too long yesterday. Chapped my lips. Should have known better. I have very fair skin. Can't take too much sun." Nodding toward her bare legs, he remarked, "You have a nice tan. It becomes you."

Throwing the Chapstick back in the console, he picked up the cigarette by his ring and little fingers. She had never seen a person hold a cigarette in that fashion before. He took another long drag and then coughed twice. Looking across the seat at the girl, he opened the door and commented, "I need to get some air. I'm going to lock you in the car. Try and get some rest. I'll be just outside."

The girl watched the man while he paced back and forth in front of the car. She thought about what he said about her getting some sleep since she was going to need all her strength for her upcoming walk toward the light. She still had no idea what he was referring to. She wasn't the least bit tired at the moment, but she did try to relax, hoping an opportunity for escape was in her near future. Maybe escaping was not necessary. The man said he was going to release her, but not until he was ready. He told her they had to wait until one o'clock in the morning before they took the boat ride. She didn't understand the logic behind leaving at one o'clock, but if by some chance the man allowed her feet and hands to be free at the same time when she was in the boat she might have an opportunity to jump out. She was on the school swim team and a strong swimmer. If she got in the water she stood a better than average chance of getting away. She wanted to close her eyes and rest but she was afraid to take her eyes from her captor. As long as she had him in sight, she could prepare herself for whatever he had in mind. If she closed her eyes for a second, she could just imagine the man ripping the door open and doing horrible things to her. *No,* she thought. *I'll stay awake and on guard.*

She watched the man for the next two and a half hours walk back and forth, smoking one cigarette after another, the red glow at the tip of each cigarette and the occasional flame from the man's lighter a constant reminder that he was in fact still out there. At times, the man would lean on the hood of the car or walk to the passenger side window and look in at her, at which point the girl would close her eyes and fake sleep. Finally, the man glanced down at his watch, pitched an unfinished smoke to the ground and walked to the passenger side door. Unlocking the car, he ordered softly, "Okay, it's one o'clock. Time to go. Come on."

The girl reluctantly stepped out of the car and for a moment considered running off into the nearby darkness, but thought better of it. He had told her to cooperate and that she would be released. If she tried to escape, he might change his mind and the results could be fatal. She wanted so much to run, but refrained from doing so. She was going to have to go with her gut feeling, that the man was sincere about leaving her go.

Leading her toward the dim light next to the wooden dock, he spoke, "When we get in the boat I'm going to bind your feet and your hands will remain secured. When we arrive at our final destination, I'll remove the bindings from your hands and feet and the tape over your mouth."

As they stepped onto the wooden dock, the man warned her, "Be careful where you step. This dock is very old and seldom used. Many of the boards are rotted." Venturing out onto the rickety dock she could see soft rain hitting the water on either side. Ten yards further out, they came to a small eight foot wooden boat. The man remained silent and positioned her at the front of the boat then secured her feet with the electrical tape. Without turning his back to her he went to the rear of the boat and started the attached motor. It sputtered, then with a puff of smoke started. Sitting next to the motor, the man guided the boat out into the dark water then made a right turn, the boat picking up speed.

Placing another cigarette in his mouth, he lit it and then looked at his watch. "We'll be pulling over in about a half hour."

From a small running light attached to the rear of the boat she could see the man's mask. He appeared so evil, sitting there taking that cigarette to the slit in the mask where his mouth was located. He looked up into the dark sky and remarked as if he were some sort of professional and that he was sharing his expertise with her, "The rain has stopped. It's really not that big of a deal but it's going to make your upcoming journey a little more difficult." Removing the cigarette from his mouth, he pointed it at her and explained, "Out here in the salt marsh the insects are really bad, especially in the summer when it's hot out like it's been for the past two to three weeks. If you're out here for any extended amount of time, they can just about eat you alive. That's just a colorful metaphor for saying they can drive you crazy. Swat them away as you will, but they just keep coming. The rain tends to keep their mundane activity down, but now that it has stopped they'll be out in droves later this morning." Waving some irritating insects away from his face, he commented, "See what I mean? They're out already and it's only going to get worse."

Waving more insects away from his face, he apologized, "I'm sorry your hands are not free to combat the little bastards, but we'll be where we need to be in a few minutes." Looking at his watch again, he hit the throttle and the front of the boat lifted slightly and cut smoothly through the black water. The girl looked up at the sky. The rain clouds were beginning to move off, allowing the light from the bright moon to occasionally pierce the darkness. The dim light from the dock had long since disappeared and she felt like they were going into a black void.

For the next ten minutes the man sat in silence, the only noise he made was the coughing, obviously caused by his constant smoking. Pitching the third cigarette he had since they had gotten into the boat over the side, he cut the engine back, and then completely off as they drifted slowly forward and then to the left. A few seconds later she felt the boat when it bumped into something and then stopped. Glancing at his watch, the man stated proudly, "Not bad! It's one thirty-three. We're only three minutes off schedule." Picking up the flashlight laying in the bottom of the boat, he flipped it on and shined it in her face. "Alright," said the man. "Here's where we part ways. Just let me free your hands and feet then I'll get that tape off your mouth. When the tape comes off you can scream to your heart's content. At this time of night no one will hear you out here."

After removing all the bindings, the man reached up and ripped the tape from her mouth and laughed. "There, that wasn't too bad, was it?" He then moved back to where he had been seated and held the flashlight on her and spoke sarcastically, "Now you have a choice to make. You can jump out of the boat and start swimming or step out onto the salt marsh and start walking toward the light." The girl turned to see what he was talking about and the mysterious light he had referred to a number of times during the past few hours came into view.

The man went on to explain, "That light is from a dock area on a nearby island. It's a good two miles away. Either way, whether you decide to jump out of the boat and swim or walk to the light, I'll not try to stop you. Like I promised; you won the game so you're going free. I'm not happy about you winning the game, but rules are rules. I'm a man of my word. I will say this; you dodged a bullet this evening. If I would have won you'd be dead by now. When, and if you make it to safety, you'll be asked all kinds of questions about me. Just so you know, they've dubbed me the RPS Killer. Stands for Rock, paper, scissors. Consider yourself very lucky. Normally, I don't lose the game. If you survive your hike out of here, later on, probably a few days from now you might just be reading or hearing about another girl, who by the way, I haven't even met yet, who lost the game... and because of that... her life. Now, you need to get out of the boat. Land or water? It's your choice."

The girl wanted to say something to the man but thought better of it. Stepping over the side of the boat, her right foot found semi-solid ground that quickly engulfed her foot, the marsh mud coming nearly up to her calf. The girl looked at the man and spoke for the first time, "Oh, my God."

The man stood and went to the front of the boat and shined the light in her face. "You've made your choice. Step completely out of the boat. Don't piss me off by not following my instructions or you could wind up being a statistic."

The girl placed her other foot down into the oozing substance. She felt like there was a thousand insects buzzing around her head as she wildly waved her hands and arms to ward them off. The man placed his hand on her shoulder. "Believe me, the insects are the least of your worries." Looking at his watch again, he went on to explain, "The tide is out at the moment but will be back here in the marsh in approximately three hours, so that being said... you need to get moving. At this time of year, especially with a tropical storm brewing off the coast means the water here in the marsh will rise six to seven feet and the land you are now standing on will be flooded for hours until the tide goes back out. If you decide to just remain out here and wait until daylight for some meandering fisherman or boat enthusiast to come drifting by... forget that. You could drown out here."

Pointing the flashlight in the direction of the light, he continued, "That light is your goal. But here's the thing. Aside from the pesky insects and the eventual rising water there are some other concerns. The salt marsh is home to occasional alligators and countless snakes, many which happen to be poisonous. The gators, for the most part like it closer to shore, but the snakes could be anywhere. Hell, as we stand here there could be a snake just a few yards away. It's all up to you if you are to survive. As you head for the light make as much noise as possible. Gators, if they are aware of you will more than likely swim off. Believe it or not, they are more afraid of humans than we are of them. Snakes, on the other hand don't have ears as we know them, but from vibrations they can sense our presence. The one thing you don't want to do is walk up on an alligator or a snake and startle them. Their instinct in a situation like that is to attack to protect themselves. And, if you decide to try and swim toward the lights, I should inform you that you are surrounded by salt water. There have been numerous shark sightings out here in the marsh. One other thing: this marsh is like a gigantic jigsaw puzzle crisscrossed with a great number of small inlets, some a few feet wide, others much larger. So, prepare yourself to do some swimming. Try not to swallow much of the water. Aside from it being primarily salt water it, in some places, will be brackish. If you swallow too much of it you can get quite sick." Reaching into the front of his sweat shirt he pulled out some money and handed it to her. "Here's three dollars, another perk for winning the game. I don't have time to reveal the significance of the money. Just take it and be on your way."

The man reached down and picked up an oar that had been lying in the bottom of the boat. Using the oar, he pushed off from the muddy bank leaving the girl standing alone. She watched as the boat drifted off, bathed in the pale moonlight. A few yards out, the man placed the flashlight beneath his chin, the beam of light casting a chilling glow over the masked face. Placing the flashlight on the bottom of the boat, suddenly there was darkness then the girl saw the flash of his lighter and the red glow of a lit cigarette. It was then that a group of clouds blocked out the moonlight and the girl was surrounded by total darkness. She heard the sound of the motor when the man started it up, the boat slowly turned and started back the way she thought they had come. She stood and watched the rear running light until both it and the sound of the motor vanished.

Turning, she looked at the distant dock light. She looked down at the money in her hand and then stuffed it into the front pocket of her white shorts. She had to make a decision: stay where she was or go to the light. She raised her right leg and the sneaker was sucked from her foot. Raising her other foot she lost the other sneaker. She took three awkward steps across the muddy section of land she was on, but then stopped and took a deep breath, the stagnant odor of the marsh causing her to gag. Covering her nose with her hand, she considered going back a few steps and venturing out into the water. She felt she could make better time and cover more ground by swimming, but the thought of the gators, snakes and sharks caused her to hesitate. She heard a splashing sound to her left and then a swishing noise to her right. *Gators!* she thought. She felt something rub up against her bare leg. *A snake?* Quickly, she stepped from the mud until she could feel herself entering the water. She walked out, still stepping in the muddy bottom, when she felt a sharp pain in the bottom of her foot. Had she been bitten by a snake or had she stepped on a broken shell? Utilizing the breast stroke, she quickly made her way out a few yards into the dark water and then stopped. She found she was able to still touch the muddy bottom, the mud covering her ankles. Looking toward the distant light, she screamed at the top of her lungs, "Please... someone help me!" The moonlight returned as the clouds drifted away. As far as she could see there was nothing but black water and the gloomy salt marsh. She screamed again, "Help me... please!"

Chapter Two

MOVING THE SIXTEEN FOOT EXTENTON LADDER THREE feet to the right, Nicholas Falco adjusted the height, then secured the safety lock, grabbed a one-gallon bucket of white house and trim paint and a China bristle brush and started up. Stopping just beneath the second story bedroom window, he placed the bucket and the brush on the attached metal paint tray, turned and looked out over the city. Far below, on the Ohio side of the river, Cincinnati sprawled out before him: the mid-morning sun reflecting off windows of the tall office buildings downtown, the traffic where Routes 71 and 75 merged, snarled as usual, the always muddy Ohio River flowing past Riverfront Stadium, home of the Cincinnati Reds. Despite the fact he was an avid Red's fan, he hadn't attended a game since the season ended last year. Here it was July and the new season was half over and he hadn't been to a single game. Disgusted, he turned back to the window, dipped the brush into the bucket and with long, even strokes began to coat the sill with the thick white paint.

For the past three months he had been questioning his current station in life. Today was no different. His thoughts drifted over the past five years he had been in business as an independent painting contractor in greater Cincinnati. His first year in business, what with the all the equipment he had to purchase, plus the fact he was an unknown contractor and new to the business world, he estimated he would lose money. Following his second year, he broke even and the third year, he finally started to bank some cash. His fourth year in the business had been quite profitable; he purchased a newer van and was on his way. Toward the end of that year he had thoughts of purchasing a second van and maybe putting on a couple of employees as it had become difficult to keep up with all the work that had come his way. But this last year had been difficult. It seemed like the bottom had fallen out. The economy in Cincinnati had taken a nose dive and not only he, but contractors all over the city and the surrounding area were experiencing a massive decline in available work.

Dipping the brush back into the bucket, Nick shook his head in wonder as he found himself in a position of nearly being broke. It was hard to believe. He was a college graduate with a business degree, he was better that average at his profession and yet here he was; twenty-seven years old and what he considered—a loser. Many of his high school and college friends, which he would run into on occasion around town, were married and raising families. They owned homes in the suburbs with white picket fences and flower gardens. They had pets, insurance policies, retirement programs; a relatively new car.

Being married was the farthest thing from his mind. He hadn't dated anyone in the past five years and held no desire to do so now. He had never owned a car. Between his work van and the motorcycle he had owned since high school he got around town okay, despite the fact that his van desperately needed a tune up and his motorcycle was nearly ten years old. Currently, he was behind one month on his van payment and nearly two months in arrears on his apartment rent. The $2100.00 check he would receive later in the morning from the Middleton's, whose house he had been painting for the past two weeks would bail him out as far as the van payment and his rent but when it was all said and done, he'd be lucky to have two hundred dollars left in his pocket. It was simply a matter of bad mathematics; another month would pass by and he would still be on the verge of being broke. He had just over two hundred dollars in his checking and savings accounts. Of course, there was the $1350.00 he had in a safety deposit box at the bank, but he promised his Grandmother, Amelia who had mailed or given him a crisp, brand new fifty dollar bill each year on his birthday not to use the money unless it was a dire emergency. Running the brush down the left side of the window, Nick realized if things kept going the way they were he would have to dip into his emergency fund.

Descending the ladder, he moved it to the left and then climbed back up and resumed his painting. Thoughts about his emergency account caused him to think about his grandmother. She and her husband, Edward Falco were his grandparents on his father's side. Actually, they were the only grandparents he had as far as he was concerned. He had never met his mother's parents and according to her it was just as well. Her father had left her and her mother when she was two years old and her mother eventually ran off with a used car salesman. It didn't really bother him that he didn't know his grandparents on his mother's side because Amelia and Big Ed, as he was referred to, were wonderful people.

Every year for the first ten years of his life, his parents had taken him on a weekly vacation down to Fripp Island, a barrier island at the end of a string of connecting islands just below Beaufort, South Carolina. He couldn't remember much about the first few years vacationing at Fripp because he was simply too young to recall those early years. When he turned seven, Amelia called and asked if Nick could stay for the entire summer and then she and Edward would fly him back to Cincinnati. His parents agreed with his grandmother's request, so between the ages of seven and ten he spent the summers on Fripp.

As a youngster, and still today, he viewed his grandparents as rich people, or at the least, very well off. They lived on a private island in a large five bedroom home right off the beach. Their home was lavishly furnished with antiques and expensive oriental rugs, the bathrooms were marble adorned with exquisite brass fixtures. Edward owned an old restored '49 Buick and they bought a brand new car every two years, normally a Cadillac. They were always taking expensive vacations: going on safaris in Africa or skiing in the Swiss Alps. Edward dressed impeccably, always in a three piece custom suit. As Nick recalled, his grandfather was away from home quite a bit. On one occasion when he had gone down to Fripp for the summer, he had asked Amelia what Big Ed did for a living. She answered by saying he was a businessman and his work required him to travel a lot.

Big Ed was the perfect nickname for his grandfather; the man stood 6'5" and weighed in at close to 275 pounds. There didn't appear to be an ounce of fat on the man. For an older man he was in excellent physical condition. When he wasn't on the road on business, or on one of their many expensive vacations, he relaxed by playing golf or tennis. His favorite pastime was fishing with his good and faithful friend, Carson, a professional fisherman who lived on Fripp. Amelia had mentioned to young Nick during one of his vacations that Carson actually worked for Edward from time to time and was considered a dear friend and member of their family. Nick had met Carson at cookouts at his grandmother's house and had always thought he was a strange sort of person. He was rather quiet and always seemed very protective of Edward and Amelia.

Moving the ladder around to the right side of the house, he refilled the bucket and back up he went to finish painting the two windows on the east side of the home. His thoughts returned to the four summers he spent in the lowcountry on the island. Big Ed wasn't around that much, his work taking him away to New York,

Atlanta, Charleston, Savannah and even down to Tampa. Nick spent a great deal of time with Amelia who was quite the sportswoman. She'd take him out fishing and taught him how to go crabbing in the salt marshes that were quite prevalent on Fripp. His grandmother was involved in everything that went on at the island. She was a member of the Fripp Island Home Owner's Association and belonged to the Preservation of Loggerhead Turtles Club. There was many an occasion when he'd get up bright and early and with bucket and small shovel in hand, he'd walk the dunes on the three and a half mile beach as he and Amelia rescued countless tiny black sea turtles, releasing them into the ocean before they became prey for seagulls or other ocean birds that searched the beach for food.

Still, today, he remembered every nook and cranny of the six-square mile island. Amelia had taken him down every road and path via their golf cart that was kept in their garage. She showed him how to play golf and tennis and taught him everything about the beach, the plant and animal life that existed there, how storms and the weather affected the tides. When he wasn't with his grandmother, he'd walk the beach in search of seashells. Amelia had informed him that Fripp was not much of a shell beach and shells of any significance that could be found were rare to say the least. Despite the lack of shells on the beach, he always managed to find a small sand dollar or conch shell on the remote ends of the beach. He always kept his shell collection in a large mayonnaise jar his grandmother had given him. Over the years that jar turned into four jars that were filled with shells. He kept the jars by the window on the dresser in the bedroom where he always slept. It was the perfect room. How many summer nights had he fallen to sleep from the sound of the rolling waves of the Atlantic? Dipping the brush back into the can for another supply of paint, he thought about his grandmother and smiled. She always referred to him as her little beach bum: *a curious little boy with sand in his shoes and a shell in his pocket.*

Putting the brush on the edge of the tray, he gazed up into the blazing sun and then at his watch. Not even ten o'clock in the morning and it felt like the temperature was already in the high eighties. It had been one of the hottest summers he could remember, the sweltering heat causing everyone to move at a slower pace. The air conditioner at his apartment had gone out two days ago. He had considered going down to the office and complaining but he felt his request for them to repair the unit would no doubt fall on deaf ears, since he was two months behind on his rent. He had purchased a small rotating floor fan that did little to relieve the heat; it just simply blew hot air around whatever room he placed it in. Removing a handkerchief from his coveralls he mopped his brow. He needed a break, and a cool drink.

Climbing down the ladder, he walked to the front of the house where his van was parked in the driveway. He opened the rear doors and flipped up the lid of his old dented cooler and removed a bottle of water wedged down in a bed of ice. Sitting on the back of the van he held the cold plastic bottle to his forehead and then his neck. He opened the bottle and took a long, refreshing swig, when he noticed a dark blue, late model sedan parked across the street. A completely baldheaded man seated in the driver's seat appeared to be staring directly at him. He ignored the hairless man and blew it off. It was probably just his imagination. Seconds passed when he looked in the man's direction again. The man was still staring at him. The man reached up and adjusted his sunglasses, then lit a cigarette, but never once took his eyes from the van. Nick, thinking it was unusual wondered if maybe the man needed directions. Getting up from the back of the van, he started across the street, but got no more than three steps when the car was started and the man drove off. There appeared to be another man in the passenger seat. For some reason, Nick tried to read the license plate, but the car was too far up the street. It definitely was an out of state plate, but he couldn't make it out. At the end of the street the car speeded up then made a right hand turn.

Nick stood in the middle of the street and took another drink of water. He was startled by the loud honking of a car horn. Turning, he saw a Ford Mustang just inches away from running him over. Moving to the curb, Nick raised his bottle in a silent apology for blocking the street. The frustrated driver gave him the finger and yelled out the driver's side window, "What the hell's wrong with you? Stay the hell out of the street!"

Watching the Mustang take the corner of the street too quickly, he heard the screeching of rubber on the hot pavement. *It must be the heat,* thought Nick. *It's putting everyone on edge.*

Leaning on the side of the van, he watched a girl about his age walking an Irish setter up the street. Her build and long auburn hair reminded him of Jenna. There didn't seem to be a day since she had broken it off with him that he hadn't thought about her. It was five years since she had given him his engagement ring back and he was still full of resentment. He still loved her. He couldn't imagine ever finding a girl like her again. Finishing off the water, he walked around the side of the house. If he expected to finish up by noon, he needed to get off his butt.

Grabbing the paint and his brush he went to the rear of the home where he had three windows and a patio door frame to trim out. Stirring the paint, he looked up into the hot ball of sun that beat down on the city. It seemed like it had gotten hotter in the last hour. On the way into work that morning the weatherman had forecast a high of ninety-eight degrees with little or no wind. The heat index was estimated to be a high of 102 degrees. The news people had warned listeners to stay indoors if at all possible or to make sure wherever they were going there was air conditioning. *Stay indoors!* Sarcastically, he laughed to himself. He didn't have a choice. He needed that check for $2100.00 desperately.

Draping a canvas drop cloth over some hedges, Nick thought about Jenna once again. It had been his sophomore year in college when he first met her. The Bearcats had just defeated Rutgers at a home football game and the students were out and about Cincinnati celebrating their latest victory. It was early in the season but the team was 3-0 and it looked like the way they were playing that they might take the conference title. He remembered it was just after midnight when he was seated at O'Malley's bar, a quaint neighborhood tavern, just off campus. Jenna walked in with three of her friends laughing and joking. Instantly, he was captivated. There was just something about her: the long hair, the smile, the way she carried herself. He had never been much of a ladies man and when it came to talking with the opposite sex he was all thumbs, but Jenna seemed to have a magnetism that drew him in.

Before he even realized what was happening, he found himself standing next to her table, asking her if she'd like to dance. Amazingly, she accepted. He'd danced before with girls, but this was different. She seemed to melt in his arms. It felt so right. They danced, drank a few beers and laughed into the wee hours until the final call was given. Before she left, he asked if he could see her again. That was the beginning of a three-year relationship that he considered the best three years of his young life.

Jenna was from Cleveland and as he later discovered was from a wealthy family. She was studying for the medical profession and was very career minded. She was a freshman and well on her way to becoming a member of a prestigious fraternity on campus, while he was virtually a nobody. He wasn't involved in any sports, didn't belong to any of the campus clubs or societies. He considered himself just a plain old student. Nonetheless, he and Jenna seemed to hit it off. They went to concerts, football games, the movies and out to eat. That summer when she went back home to Cleveland they contacted each other weekly.

They continued to date for the next two years and things got quite serious. She said she loved him and had never met such a nice, mannerly and hardworking young man. Immediately following his graduation from The University of Cincinnati, he took her out to dinner and asked her to marry him. She accepted, but said they'd have to wait until after she graduated, which was a year down the road.

At the time of his graduation from college he had already been working for Neimier's Painting Contractors for four years; part-time during school and then full time over the summers. He had saved enough money to set out on his own. So, with his business degree under his belt, the knowledge he had learned while working for ol' man Neimier and a few thousand dollars, he opened Falco Painting Company. He had previously discussed his plans of owning his own painting business with Jenna who seemed enthused about the concept of her soon to be husband owning his own company. By the time the next year rolled around and Jenna graduated he had survived his first year in the business world, but unfortunately had lost money, which he had planned on. He figured it would take at least two years before he'd get his head above water.

A few months after Jenna graduated she secured a good paying job in Cleveland. It was at this point that she became less than supportive about Nick operating his own business. She began to question his ability to become successful. After all, the way she looked at it; he was doing all the work, and even at that not making a profit. How was he going to be able to contribute to the success of their future family if he kept going in the direction he was going? He tried to explain to her it would take a while to establish himself in the market place, but she continued to disagree with his business plan. Their numerous conversations about his failing painting business turned into mild arguments and eventually one evening at dinner, she said she had evaluated their future together and things didn't add up. She laid his ring on the table and said she thought it best if they put the wedding off until he got *his life* straightened out. As far as he was concerned *his life* was right on schedule. He was confident that his next year in business would be profitable. She refused to listen to any reasoning he could muster up in defense of his failed business attempt, got up from the table and told him it was over. He never saw her again.

Later that week, he tried to contact her via her cell and home number. She never answered or returned his calls. Her mother or father always answered their home phone and politely explained to him that she was out or not available to come to the phone. He wrote a number of letters, but they were returned unopened. Finally, after months of trying to reconcile with her, he threw in the towel; a towel that was still lying on the floor after five years of bitterness. He vowed he would never date or fall in love ever again. It just wasn't worth the pain. He had given his heart to Jenna and she had not only ripped it out, but had trampled it to bits. Even after all this time, the pain still lingered.

The morning passed quickly and by the time he was finished he discovered he had completed the trim fifteen minutes before he planned. It was 11:45 a.m. and with any luck he'd be sitting in the downtown air-conditioned Skyline Chili, wolfing down a three-way, a couple of cheese coneys and a large iced tea by two o'clock. But before that was going to happen he had to get to the bank with the Middleton's check, pay his van payment, then drive to his apartment complex and catch up on his rent.

While Mrs. Middleton did a final walk around to inspect his work, he went about folding up his drop cloths, lowering his ladder, cleaning his brushes and organizing all of his equipment in the back of the van. Sitting on the back of the van, sipping on another cold bottle of water, he was interrupted by the voice of Mrs. Middleton, "Mr. Falco, my husband and I are very pleased with the job you have done painting our home. If you'll recall, you painted my sister's home over in Ft. Wright last year. She recommended you and I'm glad she did. Here's your check. And thank you so much. I think we now have the best looking home on the street."

Accepting the check, Nick folded it and placed it in his wallet, handed her a few of his business cards and responded, "Thank you Mrs. Middleton, and if you hear of anyone who needs some painting done just give them one of my cards. The biggest percentage of my business comes from referrals." With that, he stood up and closed the rear doors of the van, turned and saluted the woman. "Gotta run!"

Forty-five minutes later, after crossing the Ohio River and fighting the downtown traffic, Nick pulled into the Fifth-Third Bank in Colerain, entered the bank and after a short wait in line, cashed the check and made his van payment. Following a short conversation with the teller about the lingering heat wave they were experiencing, Nick made his way back out into the parking lot. Just before he arrived at his van, he noticed a dark blue sedan parked at the end of the lot near the street. It looked like the same car the man had been in back at the Middleton's. The thought left his mind, but then his curiosity got the best of him. On closer inspection, he saw that no one was in or near the vehicle. Looking around to see if anyone was watching, he slowly walked toward the car. The car had been backed in so he was going to have to walk around the vehicle to see the license plate. Checking again to see if anyone was paying him any attention, he walked between the sedan and the car parked next to it. At the back of the car, he hesitated and looked down at the plate. It *was* the same car. It was an out of state plate from New York. *Strange,* he thought. *Am I being followed?*

Realizing that what he was thinking bordered on ridiculous, he walked back in between the two cars, but then stopped, leaned over and peered in the driver's side window. The interior of the car was immaculate: not a shred of paper, food wrappers, empty drink cups; none of the items normally left in a vehicle were evident. Scanning the interior, his eyes fell on a piece of paper clipped to the passenger side sun visor. He leaned closer to the window and read the printed writing:

NICK FALCO
314 TERRACE PLAZA APARTMENTS
CINCINNATI, OHIO

Shocked to see his name and address clipped to the sun visor of the strange car caused him to straighten up and look to the right, the left, then back toward the bank. *Someone is watching me!* he thought. *Someone is following me! But who... and why?* Then he recalled the man who had watched him from across the street back at the Middleton's, the man wearing the sunglasses. He had been wearing a dark shirt. *Who the hell was the man? Why was he watching me? Who was the man with him in the car? Did they follow me into the bank?* He thought about the time he spent inside the bank. Ten minutes at best. He couldn't remember seeing anyone wearing sunglasses, or who was bald or that was wearing a dark shirt. Looking back in the window, he wondered, *Why do they have my name and address written down? What do these men want?*

He felt the tee shirt beneath his coveralls tighten around his neck as he was dragged backward off his feet, then pushed face first roughly to the pavement, his left upper arm scraping against the rear bumper. Rolling over and coming up into a sitting position, he stared up into a face that looked like it had been through a meat grinder: a nose that at one time had no doubt been broken, old scars over the right eye and down the left side of the unshaved face, two gaps in the snarled mouth where there had at one time been teeth. Before Nick could say a word the huge man picked him up by the front of his coveralls and slammed him up against the side of the car. The man had to be well over six foot in height. The unbuttoned bright red and yellow flowered Hawaiian shirt partially covered a black tee shirt adorned with three separate gold chains. The man's muscular, tattoo covered arms lifted Nick up off the ground, his feet dangling inches above the pavement. The man, just inches from his face, yelled, "What the hell do ya mean snoopin' around our car?"

Suddenly, out of nowhere, the sunglass wearing man ran between the cars and grabbed the big man by his arm. The man Nick had previously seen in the car was much shorter and quite thin compared to the man who had him suspended in mid-air, but he seemed to be the one who was in control as he yelled at his large companion, "Derek! Let him go... now!"

The big man jerked his arm away from the other man and objected, "But he was messin' with our car!"

The other man boldly ordered, "Derek, I'm not going to tell you again. Put the man down!"

Derek released Nick and he crumbled to the ground, the back of his head banging against the rear car door. The other man pushed Derek and suggested quite strongly, "Derek, I think it would be best if you go sit in the car."

Derek, still upset, walked around the back of the car and gave Nick a look that sent a shiver through his body. The other man helped Nick to his feet and apologized, "I'm sorry. Derek has a bad habit of overreacting at times." Straightening out Nick's wrinkled and twisted tee shirt, the man looked down at the blood dripping from Nick's arm and remarked, "You might want to have that wound looked at. You might need stitches."

Nick, at the moment wasn't all that concerned about his arm. Nodding toward the window of the car, he asked, "Who are you and why do you have my name and address clipped to your sun visor?"

The man held up his index finger indicating that Nick had asked an inappropriate question. "It's not important that you know who I am or that we know who you are. You'll find out soon enough. In the next few days you're going to have to make some decisions. I want you to know you're not in any danger as long as you don't go to the police about this little incident. Are we clear on that?"

Nick didn't understand what the man was talking about and he most definitely didn't agree with him about not going to the police, but realized that he was not in a position to argue the point. Looking at his bloody arm, he answered the man, "Yes, it's clear."

"Good," said the man. "You may see us again in a week or so. That depends on how things go for the next few days. Like I said... relax, you're not in any danger. Now, I suggest you get to the hospital and have that arm examined." The man patted him lightly on the cheek, opened the car door and drove off, leaving Nick standing in the parking lot.

Nick looked around the lot to see if anyone had witnessed the altercation. There was a man entering the bank and a car pulling out, but other than that, apparently no one had been around during the short attack and conversation. He wiped the blood from his arm on the side of his coveralls and noticed what looked like a deep cut. He quickly walked to the van, wrapped his arm in a clean shop towel and drove out of the lot, his next stop, the immediate care center two blocks from where he lived.

An hour and fifteen minutes later, his arm stitched and bandaged, he pulled into the Terrace Plaza Rental Office where he could pay his last two month's rent. Entering the small office, he waved at the girl who Monday through Friday manned the main desk. "Hey Veronica. I've got some money for you. And by the way, do you think you could get maintenance to drop by my place and fix the AC?"

Veronica didn't return his smile. She didn't seem to be her old self. She lowered her head and ran her fingers across the keyboard of the computer in front of her. "Let's see. It looks like you owe us a total of $1500.00."

"Not a problem," said Nick, reaching for his wallet. "Got the entire amount right here." Peeling off one hundred dollar bills, he counted, "There's one hundred, two hundred, three, four, five, six, seven hundred..." When he got to $1400.00, he realized he was short. "Crap, I forgot!" Holding up his arm, he explained, "I had to go to the immediate care center and have my arm stitched. Had a little accident this afternoon. Can you believe it? It cost me almost two hundred just to get patched up. Listen, I need to run back to the bank and make a withdrawal. I'll be back in about twenty minutes or so."

Veronica glanced back at the glass wall separating her from the main office then she signaled him to her desk. Standing up, she spoke in a low tone, "Look, I probably shouldn't be telling you this. We have new management here at Terrace Plaza. You didn't hear this from me, but the new owner is a complete jerk. He's a kind of by the book sort of individual. He doesn't have a shred of compassion about him. He's going to evict you after you pay your back rent."

"Evict me!" stammered Nick. "Hell, I've lived here at the Terrace for, what, almost nine years? He can't evict me!"

She walked around the desk and held her index finger to her mouth, a signal for him to quiet down. "Maybe evict was the wrong way to put it. He told me that you could move out immediately or apply your first month's security deposit toward next month. That will give you time to locate another place. There's no sense arguing about it. He's a tough character. You're lucky he's allowing you to use your security deposit." Looking back at the glass wall once again, she walked him to the door. "You need to decide what you want to do. Me, well, I'm quitting next week. I can't work for this man. I got a great offer from a complex on the other side of town. Maybe I could get you in there."

Their conversation was interrupted by a gruff, demanding voice coming from the opposite side of the wall, "Miss Kinser, have you made those phone calls yet?"

Shouting across the room, she answered, "Yes sir, all but two. I'll get right on that."

Nick looked toward the unseen voice and remarked, "That guy does sound like a jerk. Listen, I'll be back like I said to give you the rest of the rent."

Sitting in the van, he leaned back and took a deep breath. *God, what a morning,* he thought. *What else could possibly go wrong?* Putting the key in the ignition, he turned it: Click... click... click. Lowering his head, he knew exactly what that sound meant. The starter was out. He tried the key again: Click... click... click. He slammed his fist down on the steering wheel and cursed, "Damn it! I didn't need this to happen... not now!"

Getting out of the van, he walked past the office, then two large buildings to the last building where his apartment was located. Taking his set of keys from his coveralls, he climbed on his motorcycle, started the machine, backed out and sped out of the complex to the bank.

Plopping down in the familiar seat: Section 36, Row D, Seat 12, Nick placed a cardboard tray that contained two hotdogs, nachos and a bag of salted peanuts on the seat next to his. Taking three swigs from a cold bottle of beer, he looked across the manicured grass of Riverfront Stadium. It was the perfect night for baseball, a tad on the warm side, but still a good night to be at the ballpark. The Pirates were in town to challenge the Reds in a three-game home stand that would determine the sole owner of first place in the National League Central. Looking around at the stands, it was a large crowd. He didn't realize how much he missed coming to the park: the noise of the crowd, the smell of hotdogs and popcorn and watching the teams take infield practice. He was glad he had decided to attend the game. It had been a rough day and he was tired of feeling like a loser.

Taking a bite out of one of the hotdogs, he tried not to think about everything that had happened. He needed some time to think things out. After going to the bank and withdrawing $500.00 from his reserve fund, he went back to the apartment complex and paid the remainder of his rent. Between his meager checking and savings account which was now down to $210.00 and his remaining emergency fund which now stood at $850.00, he had a little over a grand to his name. He only had one more month to live at the Terrace Plaza. He had enough money to get another apartment and funds so he could eat. He didn't have the money to get his van repaired, so even if he did get a painting job in the next couple of weeks he wouldn't be able to get himself and his equipment to the location. Maybe he'd go back to work for Neimier's. He was in good standing with ol' man Neimier and was told when he had left them years ago that he was welcome back if things didn't work out. The doctor at the immediate care center said that his arm would heal in about two to three weeks. He always painted with his right hand anyway, so that was not an issue. He could still work.

The worst of his problems was something he didn't even understand; the two men who had his name and address. What the hell was that all about? Nothing the man with the sunglasses said made any sense: what decisions was he going to have to make in the next few days? The man said he was in no danger as long as he didn't go to the police. He had no intentions of going to the police. What could he possibly tell them? The whole thing didn't make any sense. The police would ask him standard questions which he wouldn't be able to answer. What could they do with the vague information he had?

His thoughts were interrupted when the crowd roared as the Red's took the field. Just when the crowd settled down, his cell phone rang. Reaching into his pocket he flipped it open and answered, "Hello."

When the person on the other end went about introducing themselves another roar of the crowd blocked out what was being said. Standing, Nick spoke into the phone, "Can you hold on a second? I need to get out of this noise so I can hear you."

He could barely hear the response, "Of course."

Climbing the concrete stairs, he stepped through a short tunnel and entered the men's room. Leaning against the far wall, he spoke into the phone, "Okay, I think I'll be able to hear you now."

The voice on the other end responded, "Is this Nicholas Falco?"

"Yes it is."

"Mr. Falco, my name is Khelen Ridley and I'm calling you from Beaufort, South Carolina. I'm an attorney. I've been representing your grandparents for years, probably before you were born. Believe it or not I met you at their home when you were eight years old."

"If you say so," said Nick. "I really don't remember."

"The reason for my call," explained Ridley, "is that I need to know if you're coming down for the service."

Confused, Nick asked, "What service?"

There was a brief moment of silence, followed by an apology, "I'm sorry, I just assumed your mother told you about Amelia, your grandmother."

"What about my grandmother?"

"Your grandmother passed away in her sleep two days ago. The only contact I had for you was your mother's home number. We telephoned her and asked her to let you know about Amelia's passing."

"I haven't talked with my mother in months, so this is the first I've heard this."

"I'm sorry you had the get the sad news in this fashion. According to Amelia's will you are to spread her ashes out on Ocean Point on Fripp Island."

Nick was at a loss for words, but he finally spoke, "I never knew she had intentions of being cremated."

"Well, she didn't, but after Edward died, she changed the will. The service is to be held in two days at the community center on Fripp at ten in the morning. If you can't make it or decline, we have an alternate that can stand in for the memorial proceedings."

Nick didn't even hesitate. "Yes, I'll be there. I love my grandmother very much. She's a special person. She was always there for me when I was growing up. I won't let her down. I'll drive down tomorrow, stay overnight and be on Fripp the next morning by nine o'clock."

"One more thing, Mr. Falco. After the memorial service you need to meet with me at my office in Beaufort. There are some items in Amelia's will I need to discuss with you in person."

"Items... what items?"

"I cannot divulge anything about the will to you unless it is in person. I'm sorry, but that's just the way Amelia wanted it. I'll see you at the service, Mr. Falco." The next thing Nick heard was silence. Ridley had ended the call.

Turning to leave the men's room, Nick was confronted by two what appeared to be rough looking younger boys in their early twenties. One of the boys went to the entrance to guard the door and the other pulled a knife. Moving the weapon back and forth, the youth spoke with confidence, "Give me your wallet and then step into the last stall. Wait a few minutes *and then* you can leave."

Nick wasn't in the mood for any more bad situations. It had been a tough day and he was at the end of his patience with the world in general. He had grown up on the outskirts of the roughest part of Cincinnati. He had learned at an early age not to back down to bullies. Before the young boy knew what was happening Nick kicked the boy in the groin, kicked the knife to the side and then punched the youth in the stomach. The youth guarding the doorway, seeing that his partner in crime had not succeeded in gaining the wallet opened the door and ran out. Nick was livid. He dragged the youth across the floor and threw him into the last stall, turned him around and slapped him twice. Inches from the boy's face, he spoke sternly, "Look I've had it! You picked on the wrong person today. I'm getting kicked out of my apartment, my van won't run, this is the second time today I've been assaulted and I just got news that my grandmother died. Besides that... I'm broke. In short, I'm the last person you want to mess with today!"

He punched the boy again in the stomach at which point the boy turned his head and vomited.

Nick left him lying on the floor of the stall and walked out the exit. A few feet away an officer was walking by. Nick approached the man and commented, "Excuse me, officer, but there is a young boy in the men's room who seems to have a problem. You might want to check him out."

The officer no sooner entered the restroom when Nick ran down the wide hallway, down the escalator and out to the parking lot.

Once on Route 75, he thought to himself, *What on earth could Amelia's lawyer want to discuss with me about her will?*

Chapter Three

TRAVELING DOWN ROUTE 75 AT SEVENTY MILES PER hour took the edge off the early morning heat, but the constant bugs bouncing off his face and arms wasn't a very good tradeoff. Nick left Cincinnati at six in the morning and after an hour and a half on his Harley he was leaving the outskirts of Lexington, Kentucky. It was a ten hour trip down to Beaufort, then another half hour to Fripp. He glanced at his watch and estimated that he'd arrive in Beaufort around five in the evening. He'd have to stop for gas at least once and then for a quick bite. He had packed lightly, the only suit he owned folded neatly in his saddle bags along with dress shoes, a white shirt, burgundy tie and some toiletries. With any luck, after attending the service, spreading his grandmother's ashes over the water at Ocean Point and meeting with Khelen Ridley in Beaufort, he'd be back to Cincinnati and all the problems facing him there by Tuesday night.

The way his life was heading seemed insignificant at the moment, the unexpected death of his grandmother superseding any problems he currently had. Despite the fact he and his mother were not on the best of terms and hadn't been since he graduated from high school, he still couldn't believe she hadn't passed on the information to him about Amelia's death. She had never gotten along that well with Amelia, but for her not to tell him about his grandmother's passing away was downright wrong.

Passing the off ramp for Richmond, Kentucky, he thought about the last summer when he was ten that he had spent on Fripp with Edward and Amelia. Little did he know it at the time, but that was to be the last summer he would ever spend on Fripp during his school years. That was the year his mother and father got a divorce, his father moving to Canada. He had always been of the opinion that his parents got along as well as any other married couple, but the day his father left he told him that his mother was a hard woman to live with. After his father was gone, Nick realized what the man had been talking about when his mother informed him as long as he lived under her roof he would never be allowed to visit Edward and Amelia or even go down to Fripp. After he graduated, and was no longer her responsibility, he could go wherever he wanted—including Fripp. So, for the next eight years he didn't spend the summer or for that matter a single day on the lowcountry island with his grandparents.

Needless to say, Edward, and especially, Amelia, were quite upset and phoned his mother saying if it was a matter of money they would fly him down and back, but it went much deeper than that. His mother resented the fact that Edward and Amelia had money, something she never had. Over the next few years Nick figured his mother also resented that her ex-husband had parents that cared about him, something in life she had missed out on. The fact that his mother would not allow him to go down to Fripp did not keep Amelia from seeing her grandson. Each summer, Edward flew her to Cincinnati for a week. Amelia was not allowed in his mother's home as his mother didn't relish the idea of his grandmother coming to visit him. Amelia would take him out for meals and shopping for clothes. Of course, just like always she presented him on his birthday with a fifty dollar bill, which he immediately placed in the bank.

His thoughts about his past years were interrupted as he passed the exit for the Great Smoky Mountains at exit 407. He decided to stop for gas and maybe a drink before crossing the upcoming mountain range of North Carolina. He hated crossing the mountains, especially on a motorcycle. People reacted differently to the highway as they traveled through the peaks and valleys of the winding road. The truckers slowed down to at times a speed that could only be described as a crawl which caused other motorists to pass them, clogging up the passing lanes. Other motorists always gawked at the wonder of the cuts through the mountains or down into the deep ravines. This was especially dangerous for motorcyclists who were at a disadvantage to begin with.

Two hours and fifteen minutes later, he crossed the North Carolina, South Carolina border, the mountains now behind him. It would be smooth sailing from here to Beaufort. Pulling over at a rest stop on the outskirts of Columbia, he used the restroom and then purchased a sandwich and a drink from the long line of vending machines in the visitor's center. The temperature on an outside thermometer read: ninety-seven degrees. Now that he was off the highway and the wind was not blowing in his face, he realized how hot it was. Sitting at a covered picnic table near the back of a grassy area, Nick quietly ate his sandwich.

Throwing the empty cellophane wrapper in a nearby trash receptacle, tears suddenly welled up in his eyes. The fact that his grandmother was truly gone finally hit him hard. He smiled through his tears and thought about that first summer after his high school graduation. He moved out of his mother's house and shared a rundown apartment over top of a grocery store with one of his school chums. Now that he no longer lived under his mother's roof, he was bound and determined to hop on his bike and head down to Fripp to visit Edward and Amelia.

That was the first time he made the trip by himself. Previous to that, as a young boy he always sat in the back of his father's station wagon and watched the scenery pass by during the ten and a half hour trip. It was the longest trip he had ever taken on his cycle. He hadn't seen Edward for eight years and he was still in great shape but seemed to have aged in his face. Amelia was spry as ever. He stayed a week and the day before he was to return, she said there was something she wanted to discuss with him. They walked on the beach and she told him she was sorry her son had divorced his mother. She also mentioned she was aware of the fact that his mother didn't like her. Amelia wanted him to go to college and get a business degree. He told her he couldn't afford college, but that he was working part-time for a painting contractor in Cincinnati. The one thing he always admired about Amelia was when she set her mind to do something it was a done deal. She was determined to make up for all the summers he didn't get to come to Fripp and she wouldn't take no for an answer. That summer, when he returned, he moved into Terrace Plaza and enrolled at The University of Cincinnati, the entire tab covered by his grandmother. The one concession she did make was that she would agree to only foot the bill for his apartment for the first year, then it was on his dime, but as far as the four years of schooling was concerned, she was paying for that. Every year after that, he'd hop on his cycle and head down to Fripp to spend a week during the summer with his grandparents. It was nearly a year since he had been down. Getting up, he walked to his cycle. Next stop: Beaufort. Sadly, he realized this would no doubt be his last trip to Fripp. It was a nice place to spend a week, but without his grandmother there, it was just another island.

Four hours later, he made the turn from Route 95 South onto Route 17 that would lead him to Route 21. This final twenty-mile stretch to Beaufort had always been his favorite part of the drive down, the two-lane highway often flanked with Spanish moss covered oak trees and salt marshes. He passed the corner grocery store where he and Amelia always stopped for a snack on their many trips over to Walterboro where she would shop for antiques. Further on down the road, he smiled when he saw the old refurbished gas station where he and his grandmother would always stop for peaches and cherry cider. Then there were the numerous pop up, ten by ten tents where old black men sat and sold the catch of the day. How many times had he and Amelia stopped by the tents and purchased fresh shrimp or whatever fish they happened to have that day?

Entering the Beaufort city limits, he soon found himself cruising down Carteret Street where he passed The Chocolate Tree. Amelia always stopped to purchase chocolate truffles for Edward who as he recalled, had a sweet tooth. It had always seemed odd to Nick that such a tough looking character enjoyed chocolate. He remembered the night Amelia called him, just six months ago. Big Ed had apparently lost control of his car and ran off the Sea Island Parkway just north of Harbor Island into a salt marsh during high tide. When he was discovered the next morning during low tide, there he sat in his car, drown to death. Amelia said it wasn't necessary for him to come down for the funeral. Edward had never gone in for all the sadness that surrounded funerals. She was going to have a private, very small service and then Edward would be buried in Beaufort. Nick had persisted and said he wanted to be there for her, but she insisted he respect her wishes. At the time, he remembered thinking the next time he drove down to Fripp it would only be his grandmother he would be visiting. Little did he realize it at the time, but the next time he stepped foot on Fripp, she too would be gone.

Checking his watch, he discovered he had made better than average time. It was five-fifteen. Pulling over at an Econo Lodge Inn, he checked in, ordered a pizza and a two liter bottle of soda. Following a refreshing, cool shower he felt better after the sweaty, ten hour ride covering four states. He sat on the second floor veranda outside his room and enjoyed his delivered dinner. The ride had exhausted him and he fell asleep on a plastic chair, listened to the rain from a sudden downpour and thought about what a sad day tomorrow was going to be.

The phone rang tree times before it was answered, "Fripp Island Security, May speaking."

The voice on the other end was calm, but to the point. "May, this is Carson. I just discovered a body. It's a teen age girl. Looks like she washed up in the salt marsh about a mile down from the marina. It's pretty bad. You need to get the Chief out here... pronto!"

"What's your exact location?"

"Like I said; about a mile out from the marina, just off Old Harbor Creek. It's raining like hell out here right now. How soon do you think the Chief will be out here?"

"He just left the office about fifteen minutes ago to head home for the day. He's probably all the way to St. Helena Island by now. By the time I contact him and he drives back to the marina to get the patrol boat, it could be an hour or so."

"Alright, I'll just stay put. Make sure he calls the Medical Examiner from Beaufort as well."

"Okay, but the Chief will have to wait for him to drive down from Beaufort, so you might be waiting out there for an hour and a half to two hours."

"Well, just tell them to get here as fast as they can. With the overcast sky and the rain it's going to be difficult for them to pinpoint me. I'll wait for an hour and then I'll send up a warning flare every ten minutes. Tell them to be on the watch for the flares."

Carson Pike checked the time on his cell phone: 6:10. Placing the small phone in his jacket pocket, he lit up a cigarette and looked up at the foreboding sky as a mixture of black and dark grey clouds moved quickly across the salt marsh. Normally, from where he was on a clear day, he could make out the buildings of the marina in the distance, but at least for now, for as far as he could see there was nothing but pouring rain. He looked over the side of his twelve foot fishing boat at the girl who was bobbing up and down in the gentle low waves being created from the wind which had picked up considerably in the last ten minutes. She was face down, the upper portion of her body mired in the deep marsh mud, the lower half floating in the black water. He watched as three small crabs ran across her right arm and then disappeared in the tall grass. The girl was shoeless, her white shorts and pink top caked with mud. Her hair was matted to the back and sides of her head. Over the years he had witnessed a lot of strange things out in the tidal marshes, but nothing like this. He didn't want to touch or move the body until the authorities arrived, but depending on how long it took them to get to where he was, the incoming tide might cause her to drift off. Taking a section of one inch rope from the bottom of the boat he tied her ankle and anchored it to the side. It had been a sweltering day. He hadn't caught all that many fish and had been looking forward to a cold shower and then a good dinner at the marina. It didn't look like that was going to happen now.

Jeff Lysinger, Chief of Fripp Island Security picked up the receiver from the metal holder attached to the console of his car, and answered, "May, what's up?"

May's voice spewed out the bad news, "I just got a call from Carson Pike. He discovered a body of a teen age girl out in the salt marsh about a mile north of the marina. Looks like you need to turn around and drive back out here. I'll call the M.E. and have him meet you at the marina."

Making a U-turn, Jeff switched on his flashing lights and sped back down the Sea Island Parkway. "Did Carson give you any other details?"

"No," said May, "except that he said it's pretty bad. He also said if it keeps raining hard, he'll send up a flare every ten minutes. I hope this isn't what I think it is, Chief?"

Turning the wipers on high, Jeff responded, "Me too, May. One more thing: is Travis there in the office?"

"No, he took the Jeep for his evening pass down the beach."

"Well, call him and have him drive over to the marina and get the boat ready. I should be there in about fifteen minutes."

Hanging up the receiver, Jeff pulled out his cell phone and called his wife. She didn't pick up, so he left a message, "I'm sorry, Lil, but it looks like our planned dinner out is going to have to go on the back burner for tonight. A body of a young girl was found out in the marsh. I'll probably be up most of the night. I'll call you later. Keep this to yourself until I talk with you."

Stopping at the guard shack, after crossing the Fripp Island Bridge, he signaled the security guard over to his car. The young man, surprised to see the Chief back so soon, commented, "Thought you were going to have dinner with the wife."

"Was," said Jeff, "but something came up. Listen, Ted. The medical examiner from Beaufort should be rolling in here in the next half hour or so. Someone from the Beaufort Police Department might be coming by also."

Ted gave the Chief a strange look. "You said the medical examiner. That means there's been a death."

"Yes, there has been. Things could get a little hairy around here later on tonight. I don't want you to say anything to anyone just yet. Folks here on the island are already on edge. If any news people show up, call me before you let them in. I don't want this to turn into a circus."

It wasn't even seven minutes, when Jeff pulled into the marina and stopped next to the boat dock. Putting on his raincoat and hat, he climbed out and ran down the dock were he saw Travis taking the tarp from the top of the boat. Bending down, he helped Travis with the tarp and asked, "We got plenty of fuel?"

Travis motioned toward the twin Johnson engines attached to the rear of the motor craft and answered, "Yep, filled her up last week. May said we have another body on our hands."

"I reckon so," said Jeff. "Let's get out of the rain. We can't leave until Bob Levine gets here."

Huddled under a small metal roof next to the Bonito Boathouse, Travis looked out into the pouring rain and then to the north. "May said ol' Carson found the body. Said he was out there about a mile or so." Turning back to Jeff, he asked, "Do we know if the girl was murdered or what?"

"No, we don't know that. We don't have any details." Jeff put his hands inside his coat and stared out across the marsh into the rain. Except for the rain beating on the roof, there was silence.

Travis broke the silence and asked, "I know what you're probably thinking, boss. Has the RPS Killer struck again?"

Jeff removed a handkerchief from his pocket and blew his nose. "I think I'm coming down with a summer cold. Happens every year; during the winter months I'm fine, then come summer, I start coughing and my nose runs."

"Maybe you just have allergies."

"No, the doctor said I'm healthy as an ox. He said it was a summer cold." Walking to the edge of the dock he stared down into the water and remarked, "I am concerned that the RPS Killer might be responsible for our latest victim."

"It sounds so strange for you to use the term, 'latest victim,'" said Travis. "That sounds like big city talk; something you may hear someone from Boston or Chicago say; places where someone gets murdered weekly. This is Fripp Island and up until two years ago we didn't have a murder for as far back as I can recall, even when I was a kid growing up over on Ladies Island. If this does turn out to be the work of the RPS Killer that puts the total death count at eight girls, and that's what we know of. Did Pike give any indication that the girl's death is related to any of the RPS killings?"

"No, he just said it was pretty bad. In the next hour or so, we'll know. The RPS Killer has a very distinct method of killing. As soon as we see the body... we'll know."

Travis started down the dock toward the paved parking lot. "I'm going to walk over to the store and grab a sandwich or something. It could turn out to be a long night. Want anything?"

Removing his hat from his head, Jeff ran his fingers through his short hair. "Cup of coffee sounds good."

Travis looked up at the sky then ran across the lot.

Jeff took a seat on a nearby old wooden bench and adjusted the brim of his hat. He hoped the body of the young girl out there in the marsh was not the killer's eighth victim. A dead girl was a dead girl, but it would be a relief if it wasn't the work of the RPS Killer. He thought back to that night almost two years ago when they found the killer's first victim on the edge of the marsh next to Fripp Inlet. That was the beginning of a string of brutal murders Months later, they discovered a young girl in the salt marsh on the opposite side of the inlet, on Hunting Island.

His thoughts were interrupted when two fishermen walked around the edge of the large building and started up the dock. The man in the lead, stopped when he saw Jeff and asked sarcastically, "Chief Lysinger, what on earth brings you out to the marina on such a pleasant late afternoon?"

Jeff replaced his hat back on his head and responded, "Just routine business. How you fellows do today? Catch anything out there?"

The second man answered, "Not much. It was a pretty lousy day for fishing." Looking into the window of the restaurant, he angled his thumb, "We're going inside to drown our sorrows with a few beers. Care to join us?"

"Love to, but I'm still on duty."

Looking at the uncovered Fripp Island Rescue Boat, the first man asked, "You coming in or getting ready to head out?"

Jeff hesitated. It was going to be a difficult question to answer without raising any suspicion. Lying, he answered the man, "Believe it or not... going out. Someone reported an abandoned boat out in the marsh. We're just going to check it out."

Fortunately, the awkward conversation was interrupted when Travis walked up, a steaming cup of coffee in his hand. Before Travis could say a word, Jeff stood, reached for the coffee and ordered, "Come on, Travis, we better get moving."

The two men, anxious to get inside nodded at Travis then walked down the dock and entered the restaurant.

Travis confused, asked, "I thought we were going to wait for the M.E. before we left."

"We are," said Jeff. "Those two started asking too many questions. It got sticky so I told them we were going out to check on an abandoned boat."

Travis looked in the window and saw the two men seated at the bar. "Well, that's all well and fine until they notice the medical examiner when he rolls in here."

Jeff sipped his coffee and replied, "We'll just have to make sure we head out before they come out here and start asking questions. One thing for sure; we don't need any rumors being spread around the island."

Travis agreed, "At least until word gets out about the girl out there in the marsh. Whether it turns out to be a victim of the RPS Killer or not, it's still another dead body found on Fripp. Once the word gets out, it'll be the talk on the island. Tourism is down already. Another person reported as dead isn't going to help matters any."

Glancing out to the parking lot into the rain, Jeff pointed his cup at the white van with bold black lettering as it pulled in: BEAUFORT COUNTY MEDICAL EXAMINER. "Start up the boat," said Jeff. "I'll go tell Bob we need to pull out immediately."

When he arrived at the van, he noticed a man seated in the passenger seat.

Bob Levine, County Medical Examiner rolled down the window as Jeff approached the van. "Evening, Jeff." Turning to the passenger, he continued, "You know Detective Graham from Beaufort."

Jeff nodded through the open window and responded, "Sure do. Paul and I graduated high school together."

Bob turned off the van, grabbed his medical case and a black body bag and stepped out into the rain and looked toward the dock. "May said you've got a body out there somewhere."

"That's right," emphasized Jeff. "One of our local fishermen discovered the body on his way in. He's out there right now keeping an eye on things until we show up."

Paul, now out of the van joined them and inquired, "How far out is the body?"

"Not far... about a mile give or take."

Holding out his hands and looking up at the sky, the detective remarked, "If this rain keeps up it could be like searching for the proverbial needle in the haystack."

"We've got two things going for us," said Jeff. "Our fisherman friend said he'd wait for about an hour and then start sending up a flare every ten minutes. It's been just under fifty minutes since he called the body in. In approximately ten minutes we should see the first flare. The other thing he told us was the body is in the salt marsh, right on the bank of the river. The only problem with that is he didn't say which side."

Bob started toward the dock and looked at the dark sky, commenting, "It's going to be a wet ride out there, so let's get started." Passing the restaurant, Jeff glanced nonchalantly in the window. The two fishermen he had talked with were too busy talking with the bartender to notice the trio walking down the dock. After everyone boarded, Travis shook hands with Bob and Paul, backed the boat out, then turned north and sped out into the rainy river.

Carson huddled uncomfortably at the rear of his fishing boat and pulled the collar of his torn and faded yellow rain slicker up around his neck. A distant roll of thunder was followed by a flash of lightning on the opposite side of the river. It felt like it had cooled down a few degrees, the rain now falling even harder. The wet weather was a welcome reprieve to the lowcountry but he realized when the rain stopped, the heat would return and more than likely be hotter than before the rain started. Leaning over the side of the boat he checked on the body again. The pelting rain had started to erase the mud from the girl's arms and clothing. He figured it had been almost an hour since he discovered the body. He couldn't be sure if the authorities were in the water on their way or even at the marina as of yet. *Time for the first flare.*

Reaching underneath the wooden seat, he pulled out a metal chest and unlatched the top. Removing his flare gun, he inserted a flare and closed the chest. Aiming out over the river, he pulled the trigger and the flare was catapulted up into the dark sky. A bright red trail was followed as the warning signal reached its maximum height, then like a miniature fireworks, exploded into a blinding orange and red ball of fire. Following a few seconds the flare fizzled out. Carson placed the gun back in the chest. He would wait ten minutes before the next warning.

Travis guided the boat out into the river, then by means of a nautical floodlight on the front of the craft, maneuvered the boat over next to the western shore. Hugging the bank that bordered the edge of the large salt marsh, he cut the engine to a slow idle while Jeff aimed the brightly directed beam of light along the bank. Peering through the gloomy rain, he pointed at an alligator lying half in and half out of the water. He spoke calmly, "Gator out there, about ten o'clock." Suddenly, the sound of the engine startled the creature, who in a fraction of a second slithered out of the water and into the tall marsh grass.

Bob turned to Jeff and asked, "You did bring that rifle of yours along, right?"

Giving the medical examiner a reassuring smile, Jeff knocked his knuckles on a built-in low cabinet attached to the inside of the boat. "Don't fret, Bob. Got it right here."

Looking at the area where they had spotted the gator, Bob inquired, "How big do you think that one was?"

"That was just a small one. I'd say about three to four foot."

"Well, small or not, I don't like alligators," said Bob. "I'm pretty much a landlubber. I've been the medical examiner for the last seven years and I've got to tell you. I don't like being on the water, especially out here in the marsh."

Travis guided the boat around a section of the marsh that jutted outward and commented, "Don't worry, Bob. Most of the gators here on the island tend to stay closer in."

"That's easy for you to say. I'm the one who has to leave the safety of the boat and examine the body when we get there. You just make sure you have that rifle trained on the surrounding area."

Detective Graham patted the unseen holster holding his revolver beneath his coat. "If Jeff misses any aggressive reptiles, I'll get 'em."

Bob placed the folded body bag over his head as he was getting soaked. "That's all well and fine, but it doesn't make me feel any better about getting out and walking around in the marsh mud."

Travis made a gradual right, but then discovered they were heading into one of the many interconnecting inlets. Turning the boat toward the left hand bank, he went back toward the river.

"Time for another flare," said Carson to himself. Loading the gun, he fired directly above the boat, the reddish glare lighting up the surrounding area.

Graham, who was looking in the distance, noticed the warning signal and pointed north. "Looks like a signal flare up ahead."

The others turned and saw the red glow in the rain swept sky. Jeff removed the rifle from the cabinet and checked to see if he had a full load as Travis increased the boat's speed. Within seconds the light from the flare disappeared. Moving out a few feet from the river bank, Travis remarked, "Should be just up ahead."

Carson heard the sound of the approaching boat before he saw the craft emerge from the rain. Quickly, he fired a third flare into the air, fearing that they might pass him by. Grabbing a flashlight from the console, he waved it back and forth. "There!" said Travis. He turned in toward the bank and cut the engine, the boat drifting forward.

Relieved, Carson reached out with his foot and prevented the boats from bumping into each other and shouted, "Thought you guys were never going to get here. The body is right over here on the bank. Got her anchored to the boat."

Taking a handheld lantern from the cabinet and his rifle, Jeff stepped over into Carson's boat and shined the beam down on the body. Joining the two, Bob looked down at the bobbing corpse and remarked, "I best get to it." Stepping onto the soft mud he sank down to just above his ankles. Looking around, he went on, "Horrible place to be murdered, that's if she was murdered."

Detective Graham, now in Carson's boat, surmised, "I can't imagine anyone, dressed especially the way she is taking a leisurely stroll out here in the marsh. More than likely, somebody dumped her out here."

Unfolding the body bag, Bob then opened his medical kit and placed, with some difficulty, a pair of plastic surgical gloves on his wet hands. Without looking at Carson, he asked, "Is this exactly the way you found her?"

"Yes," explained Carson, "Except for the fact that I secured her to the side of the boat."

"Cut her loose. I need to roll her over and have a look see at her face."

Once the girl's ankle was untied, Levine carefully rolled her over onto her back. He opened her right eye, then her left, placed his forefinger and index finger on the side of her neck, then parted her bluish lips.

"How long do you think she's been out here?" asked Jeff.

Examining her scalp, Levine answered, "It's hard to tell exactly, but I'd say less than forty-eight hours?"

Detective Graham, chimed in and inquired, "Cause of death?"

"It could be a number of things. I probably won't be able to give you a definite answer until I get back to town and give the body a good going over." Shining a small flashlight on her left leg, Levine pointed out. "These marks on her lower leg are consistent with a snake bite. There's another set of marks just above her knee. If it was a poisonous snake, she wouldn't have had time to walk or swim to where she could get help. Another thing:" He raised the left arm and indicated, "All the fingers on her right hand are missing except for the thumb. Look at how the skin is ripped. Her fingers were not amputated, but rather torn off. If I had to guess I'd say one of the local gators or possibly a shark ripped them off which means she could have bled out causing her death."

"What about all those tiny marks on her arms and legs?" asked Travis.

"Fish," answered, Levine. "The fish out here are not capable of eating an entire body, but it appears they had a good time nibbling at our victim."

Jeff wiped the rain away from his face and asked, "Okay, I've got to ask what's on everyone's mind. Is this the work of the RPS Killer?"

Examining the girl's feet, Levine shined the light on the girl's chest, then her head, elbows and knees. "Doesn't appear so. The RPS Killer has a pattern he follows. None of those traits are found here: no chest wound caused by scissors, or the scissors themselves which he always leaves in his victim's chest. Her head has not been tampered with and her elbows and knees do not appear to be broken from being beaten with large rocks. This girl, if she died out here in the marsh, either drowned, bled out from the gator or shark bite or from the poison in her system from a snake bite. Then, again, she might have been dumped here, already dead, at which point an attack from out here can be ruled out as the cause of death. I'll know more after I get her on the table."

Travis noticed something that seemed out of place in the mud. Jumping out of the boat, he knelt down and pointed at the edge of something pink. Gesturing at Jeff, he held out his hand. "Give me that small shovel we have in the cabinet."

The shovel in hand, he dug down carefully and extracted a pink sneaker. Holding it up for all to see, he questioned, "Think this belongs to the girl?"

Reaching for the sneaker, Bob remarked, "Let's see."

Untying the shoe, he picked up the left bare foot and slid the sneaker on. "Perfect fit I'd say. Doesn't mean it's hers but I'd be willing to bet it is. That being said, she probably died right around here. It's just too ironic that the sneaker belongs to someone else. It no doubt got sucked off her foot from the deep mud. The other one might be nearby."

Jeff pointed to the white shorts and suggested, "Check and see if she has any I.D. on her."

Bob removed the sneaker and placed it inside an evidence bag, then began to search her front pockets. In the right hand pocket he found a wrinkled receipt for a bracelet that she apparently purchased. Reading the soaked paper, Bob stated, "Anybody hear of a store called DuQuonn Jewelers?"

Detective Graham snapped his fingers and blurted out, "I know exactly where that is. It's over in Savannah. It's a specialty store down by the river. My wife and I were just over there doing some shopping last week. I remember the place because we had dinner at a seafood joint next door to DuQuonn Jewelers."

Jeff shot the detective a strange look and stated, "If I remember correctly aren't all the girls the RPS Killer murdered from Savannah?"

"True," said Levine. "But that doesn't mean this girl is from Savannah."

"We can find out easy enough," said Travis. "When we get back to the office I'll call the Savannah Police Department and see if they have a recent missing girl over there."

Levine, continuing to search the girl's pockets, extracted three folded one dollar bills and sat down in the mud with a look of hopelessness on his face. Holding up the money, he said sadly, "Gentlemen, this changes everything. Our thoughts about this girl being the RPS Killer's eighth victim is probably true. If you will recall, the killer let two girls go, giving each one, three one dollar bills. He probably dumped this girl out here in the marsh and told her to walk out just like the others he released. She didn't make it." Placing the money in the evidence bag, Bob stood and motioned to Travis. "Let's get her bagged up and then I can get her back to town where I can give her a thorough examination."

Jeff looked off into the rain, sneezed, then commented, "I'll have to call this into Beaufort tonight when we get back in. Paul, how long do you think you can keep a lid on this?"

"Few hours at the most. It's difficult to keep something like this under wraps, especially when you consider the related murders we've had the past two years. The press, believe it or not has an uncanny way of finding out about this sort of thing before anybody else does. Once that happens, they'll be people out here in boats wanting to see where the girl died. If I were you Jeff, I'd cordon off this area. It's still a working crime scene. You might want to post an officer out here for a day or two, until we get everything wrapped up. When the news gets out, it's going to get nuts out here on Fripp.

Chapter Four

NICK WOKE UP AT THREE O'CLOCK IN THE MORNING AND found the rain had finally come to a stop. Walking back inside his room, he lay on the bed, but after fifteen minutes realized he was wide awake. He sat in a worn out easy chair and flipped on the small twenty-one inch television. Running through the local channel selections, he settled for a sports talk show. Five minutes into the program, he discovered that the Reds had lost the first two games of three against the Pirates. Despite the fact that a few hours ago he had wolfed down a large pizza for dinner, he was famished. The continental breakfast the inn offered wouldn't be set up for another three hours. Grabbing the room key, he decided on a short walk around the inn. He was too keyed up to try and sleep. He passed the lobby, walked out into the parking lot and strolled over to where his bike was parked. The seat was still soaked from the recent overnight rain. Opening one of his saddlebags, he removed a clean shop towel he always traveled with and wiped down not only the seat, but the handlebars, gas tank, front and rear body. He looked up at the star dotted sky. It was a clear night, the big and little dippers easy to make out in the overhead blackness.

Satisfied his bike was alright, he walked around the left side of the inn and started down the back of the two-story building and thought about the day that lay ahead. It would only take him about twenty-five to thirty minutes to ride out to Fripp. He hoped it didn't start raining again. He certainly didn't want to walk into the memorial service looking like a drowned rat. What would people think of him?

Suddenly, he felt alone. Amelia was the last bastion of true friendship he had in his life and now she was gone. His father, who he hadn't seen in years, as far as he knew was still living in Canada somewhere, his mother was just a pain in the ass, Big Ed had been killed in an automobile accident and now his grandmother had passed away. He didn't have a female companion he could turn too, either. But that was his fault. He was the one who decided not to date for the past half-decade. He really didn't have all that many friends as over the past few years he had immersed himself in his work. His business was failing, he was practically broke and in less than a month he would have no place to live. Shaking his head in disgust, he felt like the world was a monopoly board and he was Mediterranean Avenue. He couldn't imagine his life being any worse than it was at the moment. Turning the corner of the building, he saw something that caused his shoulders to slump and he realized that he wasn't completely at the bottom rung of the ladder, but still had a ways to go.

There, parked beneath a dim parking light sat the dark blue sedan with New York tags. *It can't be the same car,* he thought. *It just can't be!* Leery about getting too close to the car based upon his experience in Cincinnati at the bank, he looked around the lot to see if anyone was nearby. He looked at his watch: 3:30 in the morning. No one was going to be outside. Everyone in the inn was no doubt sleeping. Bending down, he read the license number: New York; SGW – 779: the same number as the car in the lot of the bank back home. He checked the lot again and then went to the driver's side and looked in at the sun visor where his name and address had been written on the slip of paper. The paper was gone, but he knew it was the same car. He thought back to the moment he had been assaulted by the man named Derek. He thought about the other man, the one with the sunglasses and how he had taken control of the situation; how he had ordered Derek to go sit in the car, how he had been concerned about his bleeding arm. The man told him he wasn't in any danger as long as he didn't contact the police. He had also been told he might see them again based on the decisions he made over the next few days. He *had* no decisions to make. Everything was laid out for him. He had to go to the memorial service, then empty his grandmother's ashes out on Ocean Point. He couldn't imagine what any of that had to do with the two mysterious men from New York. One thing was for sure. The men had followed him down to Beaufort all the way from Cincinnati. It was obvious they wanted something—but what? He had nothing to offer anyone.

Getting an idea, he walked around to the front entrance and entered the lobby. There was no one at the front desk so he hit the bell ringer which sent a resounding metallic sound throughout the room. Within seconds, a sleepy-eyed young man wearing horn rimmed glasses appeared from behind a paneled wall, looked Nick up and down, then asked, "May I help you sir?"

Nick, leaning on the desk, politely asked, "Yes, you might be able to. I was wondering if you have any guests from the state of New York staying here this evening?"

The young man gave Nick a strange look and replied, "I have no idea. We're full up tonight."

Nick didn't understand the young man's answer and spoke again, "What does being full up have to do with knowing where those staying here are from?"

The young man frowned and answered, "I just came on after midnight. Most of the people staying here had already checked in. I only had two couples check in after I came on."

Nick inquired, "Were they from New York?"

The clerk was becoming frustrated. "Let me check." Going to a computer on the counter, he brought up a screen and scanned the information displayed. "They were both married couples. One from North Carolina and the other from Pennsylvania."

"No, this would have been two men," said Nick. "One was wearing sunglasses and the other one was quite large; a rough looking character."

"I have no idea if anyone fitting that description is staying here tonight or not."

"Well, can you check the people who checked in before you came on to see what room the New York people are staying in?"

The young man turned the computer off and looked directly at Nick. "Sir, we are really not required to give out information about those who choose to stay here. Are you with the police or something? Why are you asking all these questions?"

Now Nick was getting frustrated. "No I'm not with the police, but I am one of your guests. I'm staying in room 43 on the second floor. I think someone is following me. I might be in danger."

The clerk shrugged and answered, "You're welcome to call the police if you want *or* I can call them if you wish." The young man reached for a phone on the counter.

Nick panicked, "No, don't do that! I was told by the men not to call the police. Look, just forget I mentioned anything. I'm going back to my room. I'll be checking out in a couple of hours anyway."

The clerk replaced the receiver back on the phone and held out his hands, "Alright then, will that be all for tonight."

Without answering, Nick turned and walked to the elevator and thought to himself, *What the hell am I doing? The clerk probably thinks I'm nuts.*

Getting off on the second floor, it suddenly occurred to him that he needed to check out before the two men either went down for breakfast or to their car to follow him. Who knows? The desk clerk might even mention to the men that someone had been asking about them. He'd skip the continental breakfast at the inn and grab something on his way to Fripp.

Following a quick shower and shave he put on his dress shoes and suit, combed his hair, hopped on the elevator, went to the front desk and checked out. The clerk never said a word to him about his previous strange behavior, which was a relief to Nick. He just wanted to get out of there before the men left for the day. He was sure they would be up early, looking for him. *Maybe they know I'm going to Fripp,* he thought. *Maybe they don't.*

Outside, he put on his helmet, lifted the kickstand, started the bike and backed out. It was just after four in the morning. Surely the two men were not out of the sack yet. Turning the bike back off, he had an idea. Removing a small screwdriver from a tool pouch in his saddle bag, he walked around to where the blue sedan was parked. He checked the area. No one seemed to be around. Quickly, he walked to the front of the car, knelt down and unscrewed the air cap. He then inserted the tip of the screwdriver into the interior of the cap until he heard a low hissing noise; the sound of air escaping the tire. It was a slow process, but following five minutes, the tire was deflated to the point where the car could not be safely driven. He replaced the cap, looked toward the inn and casually walked back to the bike, started the machine, backed out, made a left, passed the blue car and smiled as he pulled out of the lot into the street.

Five minutes later he made a right on Bay Street. He passed the ice cream parlor where he and his grandmother always stopped for ice cream. He always got peach, she got strawberry. It was far too early for any of the quaint restaurants or coffee shops to be open so he turned around, went back down the street, made a right turn and crossed the Woods Memorial Bridge that would lead to Ladies Island. Looking down at the Beaufort River he recalled the many dolphin sightseeing excursions he and Amelia had taken on the river. It seemed that wherever he looked there were memories of his grandmother.

There were hardly any cars on the road and soon he pulled up at the red light at the main intersection of Ladies Island. On the right he saw Steamers Restaurant, where Big Ed and Amelia had taken him quite often for lunch. He thought about the seafood bisque they served. It was one of his favorite things to eat when he came to Fripp. The light changed and he pulled out and noticed the Publix Grocery Store on the left; another place where he had spent a lot of time with his grandmother.

It didn't seem all that long before he was passing through Frogmore, with its lowcountry gift shops and eateries. Crossing St. Helena Island all of the old homes that occasionally lined the side of the road were dark, except for an all-night gas station on the left. Pulling in, he gassed up and then walked inside where he purchased a bag of day old donuts and a large coffee. Looking at a clock above the counter, he noticed the time: 5:09. The memorial service on Fripp didn't start, according to Ridley until ten. He had planned on getting to the island around nine, but still, he had a little more than four hours to wait. Parking his bike on the side of the building, he sat on an old picnic table next to some boxes and crates.

Dunking one of three donuts into the coffee, he thought about the men back at the Econo Lodge and how they would react to the flat tire. When they discovered he was gone and the fact that they now had a flat tire would they put two and two together and blame him for their temporary setback? As the time slowly drifted by, Nick sat on the bench and watched the ever increasing traffic pass by on the Sea Island Parkway. At exactly eight thirty, he used the restroom, purchased a pack of gum, fired up his Harley and headed for Fripp.

A few minutes later he passed Pasture Shed Farm where his grandmother always stopped for fruit and soon found himself crossing the Harbor Island Bridge, the bright morning sun shining on St. Helena Sound on his left. Speeding down the tree-lined road of Hunting Island he remembered the many picnics his grandmother and he had just down from the island's lighthouse. It was on Hunting Island that Amelia had taught him how to swim.

It seemed like no time at all until he pulled to the side of the road off into a small parking area. He was ten minutes early and besides that he needed to get himself together. He had no idea if he was required to do anything other than spread his grandmother's ashes at Ocean Point. He wondered if anyone would recognize him. He knew it was going to be a big turnout since Amelia was one of the most popular residents on the island. Walking out to the edge of the dirt lot he gazed out at the Atlantic to his left and then out over Fripp Island Inlet, where he and Amelia had caught many a fish in his younger years.

On his way once again, he made a right and began to cross the Fripp Island Bridge that spanned the inlet. On the opposite shoreline he saw the thin natural strip of sand that bordered the beginning of the vast salt marsh on the north side of the island. Looking to the east, he saw the lengthily fishing pier that jutted out into the choppy water, a number of early morning fishermen scattered here and there. Farther out to the east he saw the large rocks that designated the spot where Ocean Point began. Occasional seagulls, which always seemed to be perched on the side wall of the bridge, spread their wings or flew out to sea as the noisy Harley sped by.

Exiting the bridge, Nick smiled when he saw the entrance to Fripp Island: the manicured grass that lined both sides of the two lane road, the lavender sage, the Palmetto trees and assorted ornamental grasses. He pulled up to the stone guard shack and was instantly confronted by a security guard dressed in the standard beige and white uniform. The female guard, holding a chart that was fastened to a clipboard gave Nick a friendly smile and asked, "Are you a guest here on the island today sir?"

Balancing the bike with his legs, Nick answered, "My name is Nicholas Falco. I'm here this morning to attend my grandmother's memorial service."

The girl smiled pleasantly and scanned the clipboard. "Yes, we've been expecting you, Mr. Falco. Here it is… right here on the list." Stepping back into the shack for a moment she reappeared and handed Nick a pink slip of paper. "Here's your day pass. How long do you anticipate staying here on the island?"

"Not that long," answered Nick. "I imagine that after the service, I'll be heading back home."

Placing the clipboard under her left arm pit, the guard gave Nick a look of compassion and explained, "I really didn't know your grandmother all that well. I've only been employed here on the island for about three months. I'd see her when she'd come and go from the island. I do recall my first day on the job. I was quite nervous. Your grandmother, Amelia showed up here at the shack with orange juice and donuts and welcomed me to the island. Just two weeks ago she brought a thermos of fresh lemonade down here to the shack for the guards. She seemed like such a nice person. For the last half hour or so every car that came across the bridge is someone who wants to pay their respects to your grandmother." Turning and looking up the road, she continued, "The service is being held at the community center which is just up the road on the right. I'm sorry for your loss."

Nick folded the pass, placed it inside his coat pocket, nodded at the girl then moved off, slowly passing the Mango Gift Shop, the Spring Tide Convenient Store and a real estate office. He had to stop when three deer ambled across the road, a common sight on Fripp. Pulling into the dirt lot of the All Faiths Chapel and Community Center, he parked his bike at the back of the lot as the front was full of cars and golf carts. A number of people were walking into the community center. Hanging his helmet on the handlebar, he climbed off and gave himself the once over, rubbing his shoes on the back of his trousers. He felt uncomfortable wearing a suit and the only reason he was now was out of respect for his grandmother. He ran his fingers through his semi-short hair, adjusted his necktie and headed for the building opposite the chapel.

Climbing the wooden steps in three quick bounds, he took a deep breath then pushed open the community center door. The large room was crammed with people, two men stood just inside the doorway talking. Nick excused himself and forced his way between the men. He got no further than a few feet when he was stopped by a voice on his left. "Well, well, if it isn't Nicholas Falco."

Turning, Nick saw the familiar face of Mrs. Reign who had been Amelia and Edward's neighbor as long as he could remember. Relieved that he ran into someone he knew, Nick reached for her wrinkled hand. "Hello, Genevieve. The last time I saw you was last year walking on the beach. Do you still have Rex?"

Sadly, Genevieve answered, "No, I had to have him put to sleep last month." A tear came to her eye as she went on to explain, "He was a good dog. Lived fourteen years. Had him since he was just a pup. Your grandfather, Edward found him on the side of the road over on Ladies Island. I had just lost Felix; that's the dog I had before Rex. I really wasn't ready for another dog but Big Ed said he couldn't stand to see me walking on the beach without a companion." Squeezing his hand, she whispered softly, "I'll be eighty-six this summer. I'd like to get another friend; another dog to walk with me on the beach but I think I might be too old. If I passed on who would take care of the dog?" Waving off her emotions, she nodded toward the front of the room. "Enough of my problems. Today isn't about me. It's all about your grandmother. Edward and Amelia were like family to me. It's sad when I think both of them are gone now. How long are you staying?"

"Just for the service," said Nick. "Then I have to meet with Amelia's attorney in Beaufort then head back to Cincinnati. I wish I could stay longer but I have quite a few things I need to take care of back home."

Genevieve perked up at the mention of Amelia's attorney. "That would be Khelen Ridley. He happens to be my attorney as well. You probably don't remember him, but you met him years ago when you were just a youngster when you were down one summer." Taking him by the hand she led him across the room. "Come on, he's right over there. I'll introduce you."

Nick was embarrassed as Genevieve pushed her way through the crowd, dragging him along, not apologizing to a single person for forcing her way forward. Nick could only nod or smile and follow the old woman.

Approaching two men, Genevieve stopped and pulled Nick close to the men and made the introductions, "Khelen Ridley, Carson Pike, this is Nicholas Falco, Amelia's grandson." Ridley, a tall man, was dressed impeccably in a three-piece, black, pin-striped suit, starched white shirt and conservative light blue tie with a gold tie clasp. Matching gold cufflinks could be seen just below the cuffs of his suit coat. He looked to be in his seventies, white mustache and a shock of long white hair sat atop his lean tan face. The other man was not quite as tall as Ridley but appeared to be on the muscular side, his huge biceps and legs straining at the thin material of a dark blue leisure suit. His large fingers were covered with various ornamental rings and he was completely bald. Beneath his suit, Nick could see a lime green shirt buttoned at the top.

Ridley reached for Nick's hand and spoke, "We've been expecting you, Mr. Falco. How was the trip down?"

Shaking the lawyer's hand, Nick looked at the other man and commented, "Fine, just fine. Didn't start raining until I got in last night."

The baldheaded man offered his hand. "We've met before. But that was a long time ago. I've known your grandparents for more years than I can recall. I've done a lot of work for Edward and Amelia over the years. They'll both be missed here on the island."

Placing his hand on Carson's shoulder, Ridley broke in on the conversation, "Carson here was the assigned alternate for spreading Amelia's ashes in case you couldn't make it to the service."

Somewhat confused, Nick looked around the room and asked, "I'm afraid you've got me at a disadvantage. I've never done anything like this before... I mean with the ashes. Do I have to get up in front of these people and say anything?"

Ridley, seeing Nick was nervous, responded, "No, not at all, that is unless you wish to get up and say something nice about your grandmother."

Nick shook his head. "There are a lot of nice things I could say about Amelia, things they probably already know about her. Actually, I'd rather not. I'm not all that good at public speaking. So, that being said... what's next?"

Pulling up the sleeve of his shirt Ridley looked at his Rolex and spoke, "The actual service won't start for another thirty-five minutes. I guess you just need to mingle and tell folks who you are. You've probably met some of the people here who attended parties during the summer at Amelia's house over the years. Even if they don't know you they'll know who you are once you introduce yourself. Amelia talked about you a lot. Many of these folks are no doubt looking forward to meeting you and to give you their condolences. You can sit right up front with me once the service begins. When it comes time for you to receive the ashes I'll tell you what to do."

Nick followed Ridley's advice and shook the hands of a few people, but aside from not being that good at public speaking Nick was rather uncomfortable around a lot of people. Slipping out a side door, he found himself in a long hallway where there were a number of chairs and couches. There was a couple seated at the far end of the hall but other than that it was empty. Taking a seat on the end of a green couch, he tried to relax. He couldn't figure out why he was so nervous. All he had to do was get through the service and then spread his grandmother's ashes out on Ocean Point. Maybe it was just everything else that was going on in his life at the moment. His business was failing, his van was on the fritz, he was losing his apartment and then there were those two men who had been dogging him for some reason. He had no one to talk to about these things. In the past he had always confided in Amelia, who always told him things always had a way of working out. Sitting back on the couch he brushed some lint off his suit pants when he noticed the sunglass wearing man and his large partner enter through the front door. The man wearing the glasses removed them and then looked to his left where he spotted Nick.

Tapping his partner on his shoulder he nodded in Nick's direction and then said something to the man he had called Derek. Before Nick could get up and go back inside to disappear in the crowd the men approached. Nick took a deep breath and thought, *They can't do anything to me here inside the building. Just stay put and try to remain calm.*

Walking down the hallway, Derek leaned against a water cooler and got a cupful while the other man sat next to Nick on the couch. Both men were dressed in dark suits which were appropriate for the occasion. The man on the couch adjusted the crease on his trousers and then spoke in a quiet tone, "Ah... Mr. Falco. I see you made it safely. We on the other hand were not as fortunate. Derek and I had the misfortune of getting a mysterious flat tire at the motel where we stayed last night, ironically the same place where you spent the night. I don't suppose you know anything about our tire... would you?"

Nick, making a face of confusion responded, "How would I know anything about a flat tire that you got? I didn't even know until this very moment you were even in Beaufort. Why are you bothering me? I haven't gone to the police. And, why are you following me?"

The man on the couch signaled silently for Derek to go have a look inside the room, then he turned back to Nick. "I don't think you're being completely honest with me, Nick. When we went down to the lobby to check out this morning, we found the Beaufort police waiting to talk to us. According to them some young man; a man from Cincinnati questioned the night clerk about some folks from New York State and said that someone might be following him and that he might be in danger. It seems rather obvious you went against my orders and went ahead and contacted the police which I told you not to do."

In a subtle act of defiance, Nick sat forward on the couch and looked directly at the man. "Alright, I did discover you were staying at the inn, but I did not contact the police. That night clerk must have called them. I told him to forget about the whole thing."

"Apparently, he didn't forget the whole thing. You made things difficult for Derek and myself. After explaining that we were on our way to a memorial service on Fripp Island and answering a bunch of other personal questions, the police finally went on their way. You need to do what I tell you... understand?"

"No, I don't understand. You're goon partner there roughs me up back in Cincinnati and then you tell me that I may see you again in a few days depending on the decisions I make. Then, on top of that you follow me down here to South Carolina. What am I supposed to think... and do?"

"You don't have to think or do anything other than what I tell you to. Is that clear?"

Derek walked back to the couch and addressed the man, "Looks like we have company."

Nick looked toward the side entrance of the community center where he saw Carson Pike walking briskly toward them. Derek stepped directly in front of him, but Carson pushed him to the side with little effort. "Get the hell out of my way!" Standing in front of the couch, he looked down at the seated man and stated firmly, "Charley Sparks... what brings you down to Fripp?"

Sparks remained calm despite Carson's strong tone. "Same as you Pike. Derek and I came down to pay our respects to Big Ed's wife. You have a problem with that?"

"That's bullshit and you know it," snapped Carson. "You might be some big deal up there in New York but now you're in my stomping grounds. You get out of line down here and you'll have to answer to me."

Sparks blew off Carson's demanding meaning, stood and smiled. "Nice to see you again, Pike. I think the service is starting. Come on Derek. Let's go in and get a seat."

Nick stared blankly while the two men walked away. After a few seconds of silence, he turned to Carson and asked two successive questions, "What the hell was that all about?" Do you know those men?"

Motioning toward the main room, Carson waved off the questions as unimportant. "Yes, I do know those men. They work for the same company that Amelia's husband worked for. It's nothing to be concerned about right now." Gesturing once again toward the door, he added, "Like I said it's no big deal, but if they approach you or bother you again make sure you let me know. Come on, let's go on in."

When they entered the room, Nick looked for the two men who happened to be seated in a second row of folded chairs. Nick and Carson joined Ridley in the front row on the opposite side. When they passed the two men, the man who Carson had called Charley gave Nick a sarcastic grin then looked toward the front of the room. Derek simply gave him the same type of discomforting stare that he had in Cincinnati.

It was the strangest memorial service Nick had ever attended. Rather than a closed or open coffin which contained the deceased, there was a brass urn centered on a green velvet covered table. In front of the urn there was a stand which held an old photograph of his grandmother, Amelia. The only thing that resembled what he considered to be a normal memorial service was the background of pleasant piano music and the large number of plants and flowers with attached cards.

Following a short lead-in from the Catholic priest from Beaufort where Amelia and Edward had attended church for years, what seemed like an unending procession of Amelia's friends shared wonderful moments and memories of Amelia's past life with those in attendance: comical stories or favors she had done for folks, charities she had been involved with or when she had just been there for someone in need. On three different occasions, Nick turned and glanced over at Charley Sparks and his associate Derek. Derek glared at him while Sparks would nod and gently smile as if he truly felt compassion for Amelia's passing. What was it that Carson had told him? *The two men worked for the same company that Edward had.* Based on how Carson had reacted to the men being at the service and what he had said to them which wasn't exactly a pleasant conversation, Nick knew something wasn't right. He had no idea what was going on as far as the two men were concerned but did know he was involved somehow. To what extent or for what reason he was in the dark.

The priest finally took over the podium. Nick gave another look over at Sparks. Carson gently tapped him on his wrist and whispered, "Like I said, you don't need to be concerned about those two now. If they bother you again... just let me know. Right now all you need to be concerned about is getting through the service and then proceed with your grandmother's final wishes in regard to spreading her ashes."

Following a few more short heartwarming stories from some of Amelia's friends, the priest went into a fifteen minute eulogy, recapping Amelia's life as he knew it to be. The service finally ended and he signaled Nick up to the podium where he received the urn. Nick was asked in a whisper from the priest if he wanted to say anything. He was starting to get emotional as he held the urn containing his grandmother's ashes. He didn't feel like saying anything but fought back his tears and spoke into the microphone, "Thank you all for coming today. I know my grandmother would have appreciated it."

After a few seconds of silence the priest came to his rescue and announced, "That concludes our service. The spreading of the ashes is a private and personal family matter, so at this point Amelia's grandson and a few others that Amelia requested will proceed out to Ocean Point. Thank you all for coming."

A few individuals approached Nick, and stood next to the podium, offering their condolences. The last to speak with him was Genevieve who approached him in the parking lot with tears in her eyes. "Nicholas, this will probably be the last time I ever get to see you. I hope you have a good life up there in Cincinnati. I'll think of you when I'm walking on the beach." Sadly, she turned and walked away, right next to the blue sedan where Sparks and Derek were talking.

Nodding his head toward the two men, Nick asked Carson, "What about them?"

Carson opened the side door of his Land Rover and motioned for Nick to jump in. "Don't sweat them. There're not going to give you any trouble as long as I'm around."

"That's great!" commented Nick, "but what about when you're *not around?*"

After you talk with Ridley later today, you're heading back up north, right?"

"Yeah, I am."

"They won't be following you back up there because their business is down here. There's no reason for them to follow you back to Ohio."

Nick shook his head in confusion and settled into the seat while Khelen Ridley and the priest got in the back. As Carson started the vehicle, Nick watched a deer cross Tarpon Boulevard, then asked, "Why are the clergy and the attorney going along for the spreading of the ashes?"

Making a right hand turn onto the main road, Carson answered the question, "Because that's the way Amelia wanted things done. All nice and tidy... no loose ends. Besides that, the will can't be read until she is at rest at Ocean Point."

Passing the road on the right that led to Fiddlers Ridge Nick thought about all the times when he and his grandmother had taken the golf cart over to the salt marsh and how they would watch the many birds that congregated out on the marsh: snowy white egrets and wood storks patiently waiting for their next meal. Further up the road a fawn stayed close to its mother while they quietly fed on the lush grass when a group of tourists stopped for some photos of the local wide life. Carson guided the Land Rover down the first road on the left and soon they were rolling down Remora Drive, flanked on either side by numerous homes.

It was the height of the tourist season and people from the surrounding states of Georgia, Tennessee, Alabama and Florida had flooded onto the 3,000 acre island. The normally quiet street in the off-season was now bustling with activity: a man mowing his front yard, another watering his grass, a group of children playing ball next to their house, a construction crew replacing a roof on a home. Within minutes they were passing the greens of the Ocean Point Golf Course on the right.

Passing the clubhouse and the restaurant, Carson maneuvered his vehicle down a sand covered path that led to a small parking area. Climbing out of the Rover, Carson pointed toward a small walking path through the large rocks that bordered the north end of the island from the Atlantic. Leading the way, he remarked, "My boat is anchored just on the other side of the rocks. We can board and then head out to the point. We'll have to do some climbing to get down to the water but it shouldn't be all that bad."

Nick, who was bringing up the rear, thought it must have been a strange sight to anyone who was nearby watching: three men in suits and a priest climbing over the rock wall barrier, one man carrying an urn. Carson scrambled over the rocks with little difficulty, but the priest and Ridley, obviously out of their element were quite apprehensive about where they placed their feet and hands. Carson assisted them over the last few rocks and then held out his hand for the urn. "Give me that. We don't want to spread Amelia's ashes just yet."

At the edge of the water, Carson handed the urn back to Nick and climbed in his fishing boat, started the motor and looked out over the ocean. "Father, you and Khelen can sit in the rear. Nick, you need to be right up here near the front. We'll go out a couple of hundred yards and then we'll put Amelia to rest." Checking to make sure the priest and Ridley were seated, he backed the boat out into the choppy water of the inlet, then made a left toward the ocean. Standing at the front of the boat he pointed to the large area where the inlet merged with the Atlantic. "Amelia loved it out here. She came up here in the mornings two or three times a week to watch the dolphins play at the edge of the inlet." Looking down at Nick, he asked, "Did your grandmother ever bring you out here to see the dolphins?"

Nick clutched the urn tightly as the boat was rocking from the low waves and answered, "Yes she did. We came here quite often whenever I came down to the island."

Scanning the surrounding water, Carson commented, "Probably won't see any today. There's a hurricane brewing out at sea. It's about two hundred miles out but the waters here are still affected."

Ridley looked out across the vast water. "The weather people haven't said all that much about the storm. I take it that it's not going to affect the South Carolina coastline."

Pointing north, Carson confirmed the lawyer's statement. "It's supposed to run up the coastline but stay out at sea until it gets up into New England where it may or may not come ashore. All we'll get is some rough water and maybe some light wind and rain." Cutting the motor, he circled around and brought the boat to a slow drift. "I guess this will do. Nick, come up to the very front of the boat. After Father says a few words you can proceed."

Holding onto the side of the rocking boat, Nick carefully slid to the front where he positioned himself with the urn secured in his lap. Looking at the priest, Carson gestured for him to begin.

The priest raised his hands and spoke softly, "Let us pray." Following a brief moment of hesitation he spoke again. "There is not a person now, in the past or ever will be that can determine the amount of drops of water in the sea, nor can they determine the number of grains of sand on the beach or the stars in the heavens, but you Lord, know these things. The last time Amelia was at church after the service she and I discussed that very topic and how you know the number of hairs on our head. Amelia Falco was a good Christian woman and I am confident that while she was on this earth she had a relationship with you Lord. We, here on Fripp, will miss her. We can also be reassured that even though the island will not be as good a place without her presence, that heaven is getting a good woman. We now commit her to the sea." Smiling at Nick, he held out his right hand. "It's time Nick. You can now put your grandmother to rest."

Taking a deep breath, Nick unscrewed the metallic lid, and without looking in at the contents reached over the side and dumped the grey-white ashes down into the water. The priest, making the sign of the cross, said "Amen," as Carson pointed north at a group of dolphins about thirty yards out from the boat.

Looking back at the priest, Carson remarked, "It is the fool who says there is no God!"

Placing his hand on Nick's shoulder, he gently asked, "Do you want to stay out here for a bit or just head back in?"

Looking out at the dolphins, he smiled. "No, let's go back. My grandmother is in good hands now."

Minutes later they were back at the rocky shoreline. Climbing out of the boat, Ridley turned and addressed Nick. "So, how long do you think it will be until we can get together at my office in Beaufort?"

Stepping out of the boat, Nick responded, "I was planning on heading into town as soon as we finished up here, if that's alright."

Ridley bent down and brushed some sand from his pant leg. "Sounds good. I'll see you then in about an hour or so at my office. I'll have my receptionist order lunch in for us."

As the lawyer and the priest started back up the path, Nick turned and saw Carson looking through a set of binoculars toward the Fripp Island Bridge. Lowering the binoculars, Carson shook his head in disgust and looked out at the Atlantic.

Nick walked back toward the boat and asked, "Something wrong, Mr. Pike?"

"Nothing you need to be concerned over." Starting the motor Carson backed the boat out and ordered, "Go on back to the chapel with Ridley and Father. I have to take my boat back to the marina."

Waving at Carson, Nick yelled. "Thanks for everything. I probably won't be coming back to Fripp. It was nice to meet you."

Carson saluted and shouted, "Oh, I wouldn't place too much stock in that. We might be seeing a lot of each other. Remember, I worked for your grandmother for years. She was a sharp lady, always ahead of the curve. Just because she's buried out there in the Atlantic doesn't mean she can't have an effect on your life."

Nick, not understanding what the man was talking about, looked down at the urn in his hands and then out across the ocean.

Chapter Five

KHELEN RIDLEY'S OFFICE WAS LOCATED ON BAY STREET in what appeared to be a restored antebellum mini mansion: three story, white brick facade, black hurricane shutters, stained glass double oak doors flanked with expensive coachman lights. Four thick white sculpted columns fronted a comfortable looking porch while two large banana plants in white stone planters guarded either side of the main entrance.

Parking his motorcycle in a side lot off Church Street, Nick looked out across the Beaufort river and the numerous watercraft that drifted slowly by. A sign on a door at the side of the house read: PLEASE USE FRONT DOOR. Making his way around to the front he passed well-trimmed hedges fronted by an assortment of silver Dusty Millers and bright red begonias. Taking the steps quickly he debated on whether he should knock or ring the doorbell and just go on in. It wasn't like they weren't expecting him. He was about to knock on the heavy oak door, but then the door suddenly opened. On the other side stood a very prim and proper woman in her forties: short black hair with a touch of grey; reading glasses hanging from her neck, black skirt and conservative white blouse. Nick thought she could have passed for a librarian.

The woman introduced herself, "Hello, my name is Gwen. I work for Mr. Ridley. I saw you when you pulled in. Thought I'd meet you at the front door. Please come in."

Nick politely followed the woman through a mahogany paneled foyer into a reception office, the walls tastefully decorated with paintings depicting Civil War battles and moments of importance. Gwen offered him a seat in a padded dark blue leather chair then spoke into an intercom located on her neat as a pin desk. "Khelen, Mr. Falco has arrived." Following a few seconds she smiled at Nick and sat at her desk. "Mr. Ridley is currently on the phone with another client. He'll be right with you. Would you care for anything to drink? Coffee? Water?"

"No thank you," said Nick.

Reaching for a pile of papers on the right side of her desk, she apologized, "Excuse me, but I've got some filing to do."

Nick was almost apologetic himself. "Go right ahead. Don't let me keep you from doing your work." Standing, he gestured toward the paintings. "Would it be alright if I had a gander at some of these paintings?"

"Go right ahead," said Gwen. "Khelen is very proud of his collection. He's got every Civil War painting Don Troiani has ever painted. There are a few that are actually autographed by Troiani himself."

As Nick looked at the paintings on the opposite side of the room where he had been seated, he inquired, "These picture frames appear to be custom made, not that I'm an expert or anything like that. They just don't look like normal frames."

Gwen removed the glasses from her eyes and spoke like she was an expert not only on the frames but the paintings as well. "Khelen is a big Civil War buff. All of the frames are custom made by him. Whenever there is a storm in the area he goes around and collects branches that have been knocked down from old oaks in town. He is quite the woodworker. He has a complete woodworking shop in the basement. He can tell you anything you want to know about each and every one of the paintings."

Khelen's voice on the intercom interrupted their conversation: "Gwen, would you please show Mr. Falco back to my office."

Motioning down a hallway, Gwen gave Nick directions, "Down that hall, second door on the right. Just go right in."

"Thank you," replied Nick as he started down the paneled hall, the walls adorned with more Civil War paintings. Stopping at the second door, he rapped on the solid oak and then entered. Ridley was standing in the corner of the room. Removing his suit coat, he hung it on an old coat rack. Taking his cuff links off, Ridley walked back to a large older wooden desk centered in the room, opened the top drawer, placed the links in and closed the drawer. Rolling up his sleeves, he sat and offered Nick a seat. "Please be seated. Lunch should be here in a few minutes. I hope sandwiches and soup will do?"

Sitting down, Nick responded, "That sounds fine."

While the lawyer loosened his necktie, Nick asked about the paintings in the outer office. "I couldn't help but notice all of your Civil War paintings. I'm a little familiar with some of them. I had a friend in college I roomed with my freshman year. He collected paintings of the war. Of course his collection wasn't as elaborate as yours."

Proudly, Ridley confirmed, "I find the Civil War simply fascinating. It's kind of a hobby with me. Do you have any hobbies, Nick?"

"No, I just don't seem to have the time. I'm always working."

"Your grandmother talked about you a lot. She told me you were an independent painting contractor in Cincinnati. How's business these days?"

"Well to be honest with you things are not going that good right now but I'm sure business will pick up."

The conversation was interrupted when Gwen knocked on the door and entered with two paper sacks and a cardboard drink tray which contained two plastic cups. "Lunch has arrived gentlemen. We have tuna fish sandwiches and broccoli cheese soup. We also have iced tea. You'll have to sweeten it yourselves if you like." Setting the lunches on the edge of the desk, she retreated back out of the office and asked, "Will there be anything else then?"

Ridley reached for one of the bags and answered, "No, that will be all, Gwen. Please see that we're not interrupted for the next hour. Thank you."

Unwrapping his sandwich, Ridley nodded at the second bag and suggested, "Dig in. Lunch is from a deli just down the street. I eat there a couple times a week. They have the best tuna fish in town bar none." Taking a large bite, he glanced out a window and commented, "I have been your grandparent's lawyer for a long time, even before you were born. When Edward died in that tragic automobile accident, Amelia really took it hard. She, as a general rule always confided in me if she any problems, but I felt there was something about that accident she wasn't telling me. She changed after Edward died. Here it is months later, and now she's gone."

Taking the lid from his cup of soup, Nick looked out the window. "I've been coming down here to Fripp ever since I was born." Biting down on his sandwich, he corrected himself, "Well that is except for an eight year period after my parents got divorced. My mother never got along that well with Amelia so she refused to let me come down. After I graduated high school I started to come down for a week each summer. This is the first time I've been back since Edward died. I wanted to drive down for his funeral but Amelia said it wasn't necessary. It was quite strange. It's like she didn't want me to come."

Pointing his sandwich at Nick, Ridley tried to explain, "I've got my own take on Edward's accident. He was found in the marsh just off the Sea Island Parkway on Harbor Island. They said he drown. The coroner said he had been drinking which probably caused him to veer off the road into the marsh. They figure it happened late at night and no one was around to see his car run off the road. He was either unconscious or passed out from too much alcohol. When the tide came in, he simply drown. Myself, I never knew Edward to drink all that much. The whole thing just seemed strange to me. The coroner said he had quite a bit of liquor in his system. There is just something odd about that accident and I think Amelia knew what it was, but she wouldn't say. The manner in which Big Ed died raised a lot of questions here in town and out on the island." Nodding at the window, Ridley took a drink of tea and shook his head. "Beaufort and the surrounding area has had a lot to think about the past two years. Aside from Edward Falco's death there is a serial killer on the loose down here in the lowcountry."

Wiping the side of his mouth with a napkin, Nick stopped chewing and looked at Ridley. "I haven't heard anything about that. You indicated that this has been going on for two years. Prior to last night, it's been about a year since I've been here. Neither Edward or Amelia said a word to me about any serial killer."

"Well, for one thing," said Ridley, "a year ago there had only been two killings. The police at that point were still trying to figure out the killer's motive, but this past year the killer has ramped up his reign of terror here in the lowcountry. The total number of victims now stands at eight. The last one was discovered this week out in the salt marsh on Fripp. From what the police have been able to uncover, apparently, the killer is abducting girls from Savannah, killing them over here and dumping them out on the islands."

Laying his sandwich down, Nick remarked, "The folks around here must be in a state of panic what with eight girls being killed in their own backyard."

"You'd think that to be the truth, but actually folks around these parts, even though concerned, are still going about their everyday lives. Now, the people in Savannah seem to be more concerned since all the victims are from their area. We seem to be just a dumping ground for the killer's victims."

Nick stared into his cup of tea and remained silent.

Ridley waved off their current conversation and interjected, "Enough of all the problems around here. Let's get down to why you're here in my office today."

Opening a desk drawer, he removed a white envelope which he placed on top of the desk. He closed the drawer, picked up the envelope and smiled. "This contains Amelia's last will and testament. She and Edward had it drawn up years ago, but after Edward died, she changed the will. She also decided at that time to be cremated and her ashes spread out at Ocean Point. The will was not to be read until she was at peace in the sea. Since that has been accomplished we can read the document. I already know what's in here, because I helped her draw it up. Now all that's left to be done is read it to you."

Reaching up on top of a file cabinet, Ridley flipped a switch on a small recorder and spoke. "Normally it is not required by the state to record the reading of a will but in this case it is. There is a stipulation here in the will that must be agreed to so our conversation from this point on has to be recorded and kept on file. I hope you don't have any objections to this?"

"Look, I don't even know why I'm here." said Nick. "What possible objection could I have to the reading of Amelia's will being recorded and filed?"

"Alright then," announced Ridley. "Then let's get started."

Opening the sealed envelope with a silver letter opener he unfolded the two page document, cleared his throat then began to read, "I Amelia J. Falco, being of sound mind and body..."

A minute later, Ridley finished up, "...signed Amelia J. Falco. The document is also signed by myself as the preparer of the will." Looking across the desk at Nick, Ridley commented, "I can only assume from the look of utter astonishment that there are a number of questions you have."

Nick stood and walked to the window and looked out at the river on the opposite side of the street. Turning back to Ridley, he shook his head in disbelief. "So, based upon what you have just read to me, Amelia left me everything she owned."

"That's correct, my dear friend. However, that being said, we have to place a value on what is mentioned in the will. Last week I took the liberty of calculating what she had left and what it is actually worth." Removing another envelope from the desk, he opened it, laid it in top of the desk and smoothed out a bent corner. "The house on Tarpon Boulevard is currently valued at just over 1.2 million. The furnishings in the home, which includes a great number of antiques comes in right at $47,000. Then there is the family car; a year old Lexus, a golf cart and an antique '49 Buick that Edward used to drive around the island. These three vehicles are estimated at around $120,000 and then there are stocks and bonds that at this time are worth $217,000. The last thing on the list is her savings account which as of now sets at $517,250. So, if you are in agreement with the terms of the will you stand to inherit a grand total of a little over two million in cash and assets."

Nick sat on the oversized window sill and placed his hand on his forehead. "I've never been much on hard liquor, but this is one of those moments in life that you wish you could have a good snort."

"Excellent idea!" stated Ridley. Getting up, he opened the top drawer of the filing cabinet. Removing a bottle and two glasses which clinked together, he suggested, "It just so happens I have in my possession a bottle of seventy-five year old scotch. It was a gift to me from a client after a very successful real estate deal last year. I've been waiting for a moment just like this to have a drink." Holding out the bottle and glasses toward Nick, the lawyer asked, "Thirsty?"

Nick walked to the desk and gave a thumbs up.

Ridley placed the two glasses on the desk, popped the cork and poured a full measure into both. Holding up his glass he remarked, "Here's to your new life of being a millionaire; that is if you accept the terms of the will."

Nick downed his drink in three swallows then wiped his mouth with the back of his hand. "Now let me get this straight. The will stated that in order to receive everything in the will I must reside in the house until my death or until I'm too old to live on my own. At that time I can sell the house to whomever I please. But, if I choose to sell the house now, I cannot. If I don't live in the house then it will be donated to the Fripp Island Home Owner's Association."

Ridley finished his drink and confirmed, "That's correct. On the other hand, you can sell off all of the furniture, including the antiques, the cars, withdraw all the money from the bank and cash in all the stocks and bonds, but by law you cannot sell the house. Either way, you make out. If you move into the house, you then have assets that amount to over two million dollars. In other words, you'll be a multi-millionaire. If you decide to liquidate everything but the house then you're simply a millionaire. It's your choice."

Nick placed the empty glass on the desk and asked, "When do you need my answer?"

"The will stipulates a decision must be made by you within six months, but if you want my opinion I say the sooner the better. Do you need some time to think things over?"

"Yes, I do," mumbled Nick. "I'm positive that I want to adhere to Amelia's wishes, but I just don't know what I want to do. This is so sudden. You always hear people say, 'If I only had a million dollars!'" Pointing at the will on the desk, he went on, "There it is in black and white. All I have to do is sign that document and I'm a millionaire, or according to you based on what I do, I guess a multi-millionaire. How about this? Can you give me until later this afternoon for an answer? I just need to get away and think this through."

"Of course," said Ridley. "It isn't everyday someone is faced with this sort of a decision. Most people would probably say this is a no-brainer, but I think you're doing the right thing by taking some time to sort this out. I'll be in my office all day, that is until six this evening when I have a dinner engagement. Can I expect you back before that time?"

"Yeah, that should give me enough time to hash things over."

Looking at his watch, Ridley remarked, "It's almost two o'clock now. I have to leave the office no later than five-thirty for dinner so if you're planning on coming back today, you might want to return here by four-thirty at the latest. If you decide to go with your grandmother's wishes, they'll be some papers we need to go over and sign."

"If I can't make my mind up by four-thirty, then I'll call your office and tell Gwen that I'll be in tomorrow. Think I'll head up town to the Common Ground. Do they still have the best coffee in Beaufort?"

Ridley stood and reached for his suit coat. "That's what some folks say."

Turning at the doorway to the hall, Nick repeated himself, "I'll try and get back here by four-thirty. See you then."

Walking through the reception area, Nick thanked Gwen for getting their lunch and told her he planned on returning later in the day. Outside in the parking lot, the heat was beating down on the pavement. Looking up at the ball of sun in the clear sky, Nick thought, *Another sweltering day in the lowcountry.*

Slipping into the last possible parking spot he could find at the Beaufort Waterfront Park, he purchased a ticket for two hours and walked up the brick paved walkway past a number of small shops until he came to the Common Ground, a local coffee shop located down a side street just off Bay. Entering the quaint shop, he stopped just inside the back porch door and took in a deep smell of the aroma of brewing coffee: another memory of his grandmother. When he had been a small boy whenever she brought him into Beaufort for shopping, they always stopped at the Common Ground. His grandmother would always order a large Coffee Mocha Grande and he would always opt for a peach smoothie. Sitting at a window table, where he and Amelia always sat, he looked around the tiny establishment. It looked the same: the old glass fronted counter crammed with baked goods and gift packages, the chalkboard behind and above the counter advertising a variety of coffee concoctions. Finally he stood and walked to the counter and ordered a peach smoothie in memory of his grandmother.

Back at the table, he looked out at the river and the enclosed low stone wall, grass covered area where a number of families were at play: small children playing kickball, a dog chasing a Frisbee, a young girl trying her best to better a hula hoop. Mothers sat on the wall and watched their children at play while young lovers sat on benches facing the river.

Sipping on his sweet drink, he thought about the average family in America. For the most part they were hard working people, many who lived from paycheck to paycheck, trying to save what little money they could from time to time. Just a few days ago he wasn't even at their level. He was nearly broke, had a van that wasn't running and soon he would have nowhere to live. But now, that was all different. He thought about what Amelia had often told him: *Things will always work out.* Life could sure be strange. All he had to do was get back on his bike, drive back to Ridley's office and sign some papers and he'd be a millionaire. But the thing was: was he prepared to live in his grandmother's home on Fripp for the rest of his life. Taking another swallow of his drink, he remembered what Ridley had said about the situation he was faced with being a no-brainer.

His pleasant thoughts about the possibility of becoming a millionaire were interrupted when Derek walked in the door, gave him a sarcastic look then went to the counter where he ordered two coffees to go. Looking out the window, Nick knew Charley Sparks had to be nearby. Sure enough, there he was sitting on the stone wall, sunglasses over his eyes, legs crossed, arms folded as he stared at the coffee shop. Derek left through the door, but not before nodding in Nick's direction. Nick got the intended message that he was still being watched. He watched as Derek crossed the walkway and handed Charley his coffee. They exchanged words, then walked down the walkway by the river and finally disappeared around a corner.

Nick pitched the remainder of his drink in a trashcan and walked out onto the porch. He had made his decision. Ridley was right. It was a no-brainer. The only thing that bothered him was the two men from New York. The past few days had unfolded like a giant puzzle. Everything seemed rather clear to Nick but there was a piece of the puzzle that was missing or at least didn't quite fall into place and that was the two men. Carson Pike had told him not to be overly concerned about them. He thought about the awkward conversation Carson had with them at the community center prior to the memorial service. It was obvious Carson knew these men and they didn't quite see eye to eye on something. Nick was positive that whatever the men wanted from him was somehow connected to his grandmother's death. Carson had commented that they worked for the same company Edward had worked for. This in itself was confusing since Nick never knew what his grandfather did for a living. *Screw it!* he thought. Standing there on the porch wasn't going to solve anything. Next stop: Khelen Ridley's office.

It was only a five minute drive back to the lawyer's office. This time, rather than knocking Nick simply walked in. Smiling at Gwen, he told her he had returned earlier than planned. Gwen nodded, and spoke professionally, "Just let me see if Khelen is available at the moment." Disappearing down the hallway, she returned within a few seconds and told him to go on back.

Khelen was busy watering a plant in the corner of the room when Nick entered. "Ah, Nicholas, I see you've made a decision. I didn't expect you back so soon."

"It wasn't that hard of a decision to make," said Nick. Sitting in a chair at the desk, Nick probed, "What did my grandmother tell you about me?"

Placing the small water can on top of a table in the corner of the room, Khelen wrung his hands and answered, "Not all that much. She told me you graduated from the University of Cincinnati with a business degree and that you had your own painting business. Other than that, she didn't say much. Why do you ask?"

"Because if you knew how screwed up my life is right now, you would be strongly advising me to just abide with Amelia's wishes."

Sitting behind his desk, Khelen placed his hands behind his head and remarked, "I don't think the nature of one's status in life is even in question here, that is unless you happen to be dirt poor."

Pointing at Khelen, Nick confirmed, "You're not too far off the mark. I'm not what you would call dirt poor but I am far from a successful man. It's true what my grandmother told you. I do have my own painting business; a business that recently this last year has taken a complete nosedive. Presently, I've got maybe about a grand in the bank, with no jobs lined up. My work van is out of commission and I really don't have the money to get it repaired. Besides that, I'm being evicted from my apartment. If I agree with the terms of the will, all my current problems will be solved. I'll have a place to live, two different cars that I assume are operable and money in the bank. Hell, if I play my cards right I might not have to work for years. I could become a beach bum of sorts, but a bum with plenty of money. So, get those papers out. I'm ready to sign on the dotted line."

Taking the envelope from the desk drawer, Ridley asked, "How soon do you want to take possession of the home?"

"As soon as possible. I'll need a couple of days to get things in order back in Cincinnati. I'll have to sell my van for whatever cash I can get, then I need to close out my pathetic back accounts. I guess I'll get a rental truck to haul my bike, furniture and painting tools and supplies back down here."

Ridley slid the document across the desk along with an ink pen. "Just sign there at the bottom designating that you agree with the terms of the will and then I'll sign below that. That will make things official."

Signing his name, Nick asked, "How is everything else handled: Amelia's bank account, the stocks and bonds?"

Scrawling his signature on the document, Ridley examined both signatures, folded the paper and placed it back in the envelope. "We can handle all that in one day. Give me a call when you'll be back here in Beaufort. We can meet here at my office. You can pick up the key to the house then or I can give it to you now. We'll have to go over to the bank your grandmother dealt with and have the money transferred to an account set up in your name. The same thing goes for the stocks and bonds. We'll also need to get the titles on both cars into your name. One other thing; don't worry about the condition of the property. Carson Pike has a key and has been taking care of the upkeep; inside and out. I'll contact him and make sure the house is standing tall when you get back. As far as I know all of the utilities are functioning. We'll have to get all that stuff over into your name as well. When you get back it'll simply be a matter of moving in."

Getting up, Nick walked over to the wall and looked at a number of framed professional looking documents of varied accomplishments by Ridley. Turning back he commented, "Despite the fact both of my grandparents are now gone, I still feel good about moving down here. Whenever I visited as a young boy I always dreamed of living out on Fripp. As I got older I realized I'd never have enough money to afford a place on the island. In just a matter of three days my life has taken a complete turn; a turn for the good."

Khelen got up and reached for Nick's hand. "When you finally get settled in out on Fripp, stay in touch. I've lived here in the Beaufort area all my life. I know a lot of people; influential people; people who knew your grandparents. Edward and Amelia were always willing to open their wallet when it came to local charities or to lend a helping hand. Who knows? You might get tired of being a wealthy beach bum and decide to start up your painting business down here. The difference being, you might not ever have to paint a house again in your life. With the financial position you'll be in, why you could get two or three vans, hire some workers, get yourself an office here in town. All in all, I'd say everything that's happened to you in the past three days has come in the *Nick* of time!" He hesitated on the work *Nick* for effect as they both laughed at his attempt at humor.

Nick turned and walked to the door, speaking back over his shoulder, "Thanks for everything Mr. Ridley. I'll see you in two to three days."

Chapter Six

STOPPING FOR GAS TEN MILES NORTH OF BEAUFORT, Nick munched on a candy bar and drank a chocolate milk. Just like he planned, it had taken him two days to get things straightened out in Cincinnati. After selling his van to a used car dealer known as a bit of a shyster and then closing out his bank accounts he had just over $3500.00 cash. *Not much to show,* he thought, *for a twenty-seven year old man with a college degree in business.* Looking at the rental truck parked next to the station he realized everything he presently owned was inside that truck: a couch, two chairs that didn't match, a kitchen table, an old bed, a lamp that didn't work, his limited selection of clothing, all his painting equipment, his Harley and some oddball knick-knacks.

He crumbled up the now empty candy wrapper and finished his drink, tossing the wrapper and the milk container into a trashcan. Looking at his watch he figured he'd be at Khelen Ridley's office no later than 1:30, a half hour before his scheduled meeting at 2:00 with the attorney.

Turning onto Rt. 21 he thought about what he was leaving behind and what was lying ahead of him. He hadn't said good bye to his mother. Maybe he was a bad son for not telling her he was moving to Fripp Island, but at the moment he didn't consider her a very good mother. After all, she didn't even pass on to him the information she had received about Amelia's death. His mother could have at least given him a call and maybe even said she was sorry. Hell, he hadn't seen or talked with her in months. A year down the road if he didn't call her and let her know he had moved she wouldn't even know the difference. For now, he had no remorse about leaving town without informing her, but he knew that after a few months living on Fripp that he'd probably give her a call and update her on his new life. He wasn't like her. His mother would hold a grudge forever. She never liked his grandmother and she definitely disliked her husband, Nick's father. No, in a couple of months he'd give her a call to make sure she was alright. How his mother could live day after day, month after month, year after year filled with hatred for someone else, especially a family member was beyond him.

Trying his best to get a clear station on the radio was a failed attempt. All he could get at the moment was annoying static. He turned off the radio and smiled and recalled when he was a youngster and his parents would bring him down to Fripp for a week. It was the only place they ever went on vacation and that was only because his grandparents paid for everything. He remembered how excited he always got when the bridge that spanned the Fripp Island Inlet came into view. Crossing that bridge, at least for him, was always the very beginning of a week of wonder and fun on the island. But then the week finally ended and when they left to head back home to Cincinnati, he would always look back and watch the bridge disappear and realize that vacation was over again for another year.

As a young boy, like most youngsters he had done a lot of daydreaming. There was many a time while walking the beach, he watched the morning sun come up over Ocean Point and compared a week at Fripp to what it must be like in heaven. He smiled again. It almost seemed like he was going on vacation again, but this time he would never have to leave or go back to Ohio.

Turning onto Bay Street, the downtown section of Beaufort was crammed with tourists: two couples stood just outside the ice cream parlor enjoying their summer treats. A woman was opening a shopping bag and displaying to her husband what she had purchased at one of the many quaint gift shops up and down the street. A group of people were climbing into one of the old buggies the town offered for a ride through historic Beaufort.

When he pulled into Ridley's office, he saw the lawyer, not in a suit but in a pair of jeans and a cut off sweat shirt going about trimming the hedges with a handheld trimmer. Parking the rental truck, Nick jumped out and joined Khelen at the side of the house and jokingly remarked, "Business must be bad if you can't even afford to have someone take care of your landscaping."

Placing the trimmers on top of the hedges, Khelen removed a white handkerchief from his pants pocket and wiped his sweating brow. "Business is always good." Looking up at the blazing sun, he stated, "Nick, I'm going to give you some advice, especially since you're about to become a man of wealth. Don't get lazy like a lot of folks do. Stay active and do everything you can yourself. It'll keep you healthy. No amount of money in the world can suffice for good health. That being said, let's go on in and have some iced tea, I'll change into more suitable business attire and then we can start to get you settled in."

Inside the front office, Nick noticed Gwen was not at her desk. "Where's Gwen?"

"It's her day off," said Khelen. "Other than the business you and I have to take care of, I have no clients scheduled for anything today. Listen, have a seat, relax and pour yourself a glass of tea. I'm just going to slip back to my office and change. Back in a few."

After pouring a glass of tea, Nick walked to the spacious front bay window and gazed out at the river. He watched when a Beaufort Police Cruiser passed by. He thought about what Khelen had revealed to him about the serial killer they had in the area and how the killer had been killing and dumping victims out on the islands.

His thoughts were interrupted by Khelen's voice when he entered the room, "All set to get this show on the road?"

The lawyer looked quite casual: perfectly pressed white pants, yellow polo shirt, dazzling white tennis shoes. "Rather casual for business," said Nick.

Waving off his comment, Khelen pointed at him and remarked comically, "Look who's talking! Shorts, deck shoes and a Cincinnati Red's shirt."

Defending his clothing, Nick explained, "I was prepared to change if need be."

"Not necessary. All we're doing is signing some papers. There is no negotiating, bantering or deal making. It's a done deal. About an hour or so from now you'll officially be a wealthy man and then I can get over to the country club for a rousing tennis match with a close friend of mine, followed by a steak dinner. Like I said before. I know a lot of important people here in Beaufort. I could probably get you a country club membership if you're interested."

Nick laughed. "You've got to be kidding me Khelen. Do I look anything like the country club type? Not that there's anything wrong with that lifestyle. My grandparents were members at the Beaufort Club. They took me to the club a few times for dinner. To be honest with you, I appreciate the offer but I doubt very seriously if I'd fit in. I don't play golf or tennis and I'm far too young to start taking up shuffleboard."

Ridley started toward the door. "I can assure you, there's much more to the country club than that. A lot of important deals are made at the club. The people with all the money in this town for the most part are members. It's more than playing tennis and golf.

It's about hobnobbing with the decision makers in this county.
Now, I'll be the first to admit that some of them are what I would
call assholes, but still, there are a lot of folks who are members
that you might want to get to know, especially if you plan on
starting a business of some sort here in the area."

Outside in the lot, Khelen motioned at his car, "Come on, we'll
take my car. It'll be easier since I probably know my way around
town better than you, at least for now."

Sitting in the vinyl seat of the black Bentley, Nick fastened his
seatbelt and asked, "So what's the first stop for the day?"

"The bank," said Khelen. "You have to sign off on papers that
transfer Amelia's bank accounts and all of the stocks and bonds
she and Edward accumulated. We'll be meeting with the bank
president, Albert Zellman. He's a very influential man here in
Beaufort *and he* is a member of the country club."

Starting to get the idea Ridley was strongly suggesting he join
the country club, Nick looked out the side window when Khelen
made a left hand turn onto Carteret Street. "You seem adamant
about me joining the club," said Nick. "To be honest with you I
don't think I'd feel comfortable around a lot of wealthy people."

"You might not have a choice," responded Khelen. "Let me put
it to you this way. You're about to set out on a journey few in life
get to experience. In short, you're going to be a rich man: two
million dollars rich. To the really wealthy people, having two
million is on the lower end of the totem pole of the rich. In
Beaufort County and out on Fripp there are a few what I call filthy
rich, those with more money than they could possibly ever spend.
Most of the folks on Fripp with any money fall into the same
category of wealth as you are about to enter into. They are a
different class of people than you are probably used to dealing
with. They have a different set of values and they look at money
differently than people who don't have much money. What I'm
saying is, it's hard to be a millionaire and to have great friendships
with people who don't have money *and power.*"

Khelen turned from the street into a bank parking lot, turned
off his car and faced Nick. "With a large amount of money comes
power, whether you desire to have it or not. Let me explain to you
how I see this. I grew up right here in Beaufort. My parents were
what we call lower middle class. We didn't have a lot of money but
just about enough to get by. In the neighborhood where I lived I
had three friends. We all grew up together as lower middle class
kids. When we were in high school we decided to all apply for jobs

at a new fast food place that opened up a few blocks from where we lived. We all got hired and worked on the second shift. My friends were not all that serious about success. They just wanted the money the positions offered, so they did about just what they had to, to get by, nothing more, nothing less. I, on the other hand busted my ass: came in early, stayed late, mopped floors, cleaned bathrooms, whatever it took. My efforts did not go unnoticed. I was promoted to shift manager and now in charge of my friends."

Khelen laughed to himself. "That was my first lesson on money and power. You see, my friends didn't respect me just because I was now their boss. They couldn't separate the two. Sometimes they'd do what I asked, other times, they just ignored me. At first, I was patient, but eventually I had to fire my best friend because he kept coming in late after repeated warnings from me. After that, my two other friends up and quit, saying they just couldn't understand my way of thinking. Here's the thing, Nick. Once I started to make more money than they did and had more power than they did, it became hard to communicate. I had something they didn't have and were not willing to work to get. After that, I was shunned by my three so called pals. I studied hard and got an academic scholarship and went to law school. Took me three tries to pass the bar exam, but I finally did and then I set up practice right here in Beaufort. My three friends still live here in town and to this day will not even acknowledge me when we pass on the street. And it's all because of money and power. You see, what it is, is that folks get jealous because someone gains a level of success they want but can never have. Mark my word, if your friends back up there in Ohio discover you now live in a million dollar home near the beach and have more money in the bank than they'll ever accumulate, their attitude about you will change. And, when that happens you'll be forced to change. You're about to step into a different socio-economic environment. It may take you some time to figure it out, but you'll get used to it. Come on, let's go on in the bank and meet Mr. Zellman."

Sitting in his car next to his office, Khelen turned the air-conditioner down a notch. Opening the console, he handed Nick an envelope. Here's the key to your grandmother's house. Carson called me this morning before you got in and told me he placed the key he had under the mat at the back door. He also told me the golf cart is plugged in and both cars have been gassed up. If you have any problems with the house whatsoever you are to give him a call."

Taking the key from the envelope, Nick tossed it into the air and caught it with his right hand. "What can you tell me about this Carson character?"

"Carson Pike," answered Ridley, "was a close and dear friend to both your grandmother and Edward. He did odd jobs for them over the years. I know, as their lawyer they trusted him impeccably. He knows more about what goes on over at Fripp than anyone. He's got his thumb on the pulse of the island. As a matter of fact, Carson is the person who found the most recent victim of our serial killer a few days ago out in the salt marsh over there. He's never come to me for any legal advice, but I can assure you, the way Edward talked about him, he's a good person to have on your team."

Khelen looked at the clock on the padded dash and commented, "Look I've got to run or I'm going to be late for my tennis match. Listen, after you get settled in; maybe in a couple of months we can get together here in town for lunch. Who knows: I might wind up being your lawyer in the future. Until then, if you have any questions or are in need of something, feel free to give me a jingle."

Stepping out of the Bentley, Nick watched the car exit the lot and disappear up the street. Climbing into the rental truck, he sat back and made his plans for the rest of the day. It had been quite a day so far and he and Ridley had accomplished a lot: his grandmother's accounts had been transferred over to his name, the bank also handled the deed transfer as far as the house was concerned. He and Khelen had driven over to the department of motor vehicles and had the titles to both of Amelia's cars transferred into his name. All that he had to do now was drive out to Fripp, unload the van, return the van back to Beaufort, then ride his bike back to Fripp. It was now four-thirty. With any luck, he'd have everything else he needed to do for the day done before darkness set in.

Within minutes, he was cruising down the Sea Island Parkway on Ladies Island when he saw Bill's Liquor Store on the right. Turning into the lot, he remembered when he and Amelia would stop by for her Bailey's and Cream and Edward's Jack Daniels. Once he got out to Fripp, if he wanted beer he was going to have to get it at the Spring Tide Store, which simply because it was convenient, everything in the small store was priced higher than closer to town.

It was late Thursday afternoon and between folks getting off work with the weekend ahead and the numerous tourists down for a week of vacation, the front of the lot was crammed with cars and

RV's. Parking the rental out in the center of the lot he walked to the store and held the door for three different customers who were leaving with their purchases. The interior was just the way he remembered it: beer, sodas and middle of the road drinks in a room on the right, along with a large display of cigars in a glass case, expensive wine in the middle of the store and on the left, whiskey, scotch, bourbon and every other imaginable type of liquor. The sales counter was manned by three sale associates, while a well-dressed woman stood at a whiskey barrel, passing out samples of a new alcoholic product. He went directly to the wall of glassed-in beer selections, grabbed a twelve-pack of his favorite brew and went to the counter where he stood in line for a minute and then paid for his purchase.

Waiting at the exit door for a customer to enter, Nick then stepped through and was no sooner outside when he came face to face with none other than Derek. Taking Nick by this arm, Derek nonchalantly guided him roughly down the front of the building and stopped next to the blue sedan where Sparks was waiting. Removing his sunglasses, Charley lit up a cigarette, then flipped his lighter closed. Looking out at the rental truck, Charley spoke calmly, "Looks like you're getting ready to move in?" Taking a drag on his smoke, Sparks asked firmly, "What have you been talking with Khelen Ridley about?"

Realizing the two men could do little harm to him in front of the store, Nick answered curtly, "None of your business!"

Squeezing his arm tightly, Derek leaned in toward his face, "You better start talking or..."

"Or what?" snapped Nick. "Carson Pike already warned you two about causing any trouble down here."

Looking around to make sure no one was really paying them any attention, Derek pushed him up against the side of the building and inches away from his face, stated vehemently, "You little shit. I should wring your neck!"

Sparks, seeing things were quickly getting out of hand, ordered Derek, "Ease off! We can't talk with him here. We know where he's going. There's plenty of time for this conversation later."

Derek released his arm and shoved him to the side. Nick, stepping on the edge of the curb, stumbled and fell into a pile of empty shipping cartons that had been set out for customers to take. Nick went down, rolled to his right and tried to prevent himself from getting injured. Sparks grabbed Derek by his arm. "We're leaving... now!"

It was then that Charley saw the Ladies Island Police patrol car pull to a stop next to their sedan. Getting out of the cruiser, the officer, placing his hat on his head approached the threesome and asked, "What seems to be the problem, gentlemen?"

Sparks responded immediately, "No problem officer. My friend here just bumped into this gentlemen... that's all."

Giving Derek and then Sparks a strange look, the officer spoke to Nick as he was getting to his feet. "That right son... is that what happened?"

Nick, not wanting any trouble and also recalling what Sparks had said about not going to the police, answered, "Yeah... that's what happened. This big fellah here bumped into me and knocked me down. No harm done."

The officer, skeptical, gave Derek and Sparks the once over, then remarked, "You boys don't look like you're from around here."

Sparks laughed. "Come on officer. Half the people going in the store aren't from around here."

"So you're telling me you're on vacation then?"

"Well, sort of. We're down from New York on some business and we decided to stay a few days. It's real nice down here. I can see why a lot of folks spend their vacation here."

The officer, still not convinced, ordered sternly, "I'll need to see some I.D." Turning to Nick, he nodded, "You too, son."

Laying his beer on the ground, Nick produced his wallet and then his driver's license. Sparks and Derek handed theirs over at the same time. Taking the three I.D.'s, the officer asked Nick, "I see you're from Ohio. You down here on vacation as well?"

"No sir," said Nick. "I was down here on Fripp Island earlier in the week for a memorial service for my grandmother. Turns out, I inherited her home on the island." Pointing at the rental truck, he went on to explain, "I had to go back to Ohio to get my belongings and I'm on my way right now to move in."

The officer scanned Nick's license, smiled and stated, "Nicholas Falco. Don't tell me your Amelia Falco's grandson?"

Holding out his hands to his side, Nick grinned, "The one and only."

Handing the license back to Nick, the officer smiled again and stated, "I have been heading up the Ladies Island Police Force Fund Raiser for the past six years. Your grandparents, Edward and Amelia were quite generous. They wrote us a substantial check every year. My brother is an officer on the Beaufort Police Department and I happen to know that the Falco's gave to his department as well." Nodding toward the rental truck he looked at Nick and nodded, "Have a safe drive out to Fripp. You can go."

Sparks and Derek started toward their vehicle but were stopped abruptly by the officer. "Hold on gentlemen. I didn't tell you, you could go just yet." Still somewhat skeptical of the men, he motioned toward their car. "Let's have a look in your trunk."

As Nick made his way back to the van he could hear Sparks who objected to being detained any further. Back in the confines of the truck, Nick started the engine and looked across the lot where the officer waited patiently while Sparks unlocked the trunk. Backing out of the parking spot, Nick thought about what Khelen Ridley had told him about money and power. At the time when Ridley had been giving him advice about the *new journey* he was about to start, Nick hadn't really paid him all that much attention, but after the incident at the liquor store, he realized Ridley had been right. He, indirectly had benefited from the generosity of Edward and Amelia in the past and the power it had generated. It was kind of amazing.

At the next light, he made a left and then a right into the Publix Grocery Store. Walking into the store, he looked up into the familiar tall trees that dotted the parking lot. The amount of times he and Amelia had come to the grocery, he couldn't remember. Inside, he grabbed a cart and started down the first aisle he came to. He hadn't been in the store for years but it looked the same: aisles crammed with a combination of locals and those on vacation, every register open, a bagger at the back of each, greeting folk's and bagging up their groceries.

It didn't even take ten minutes for Nick to get the limited things he would need for the next few days: coffee, eggs, sausage, bread, peanut butter and milk. Standing at the end of a short line at the last register, he looked over at the beer and liquor section in the far corner of the store where four young females were apparently having a disagreement with a man who was even larger than his current nemesis, Derek.

Placing his items on the moving conveyor belt he watched when one of the girls pointed her finger up into the towering man's face and in a loud voice, demanded, "Get the hell out of here and leave us alone!"

A blond headed girl forced her way to the front of the small group and tried her best, but to no avail, shove the man backwards and hollered, "Ike... we'll talk later. Right now... you need to go!"

The man she called Ike pushed her back and shouted, "The hell with you and your dumb ass friends!"

By this time a manager approached the group and placed his hand on Ike, who violently brushed his hand to the side. "Get your hands off me. Nobody's kickin' me out of this damn place! I'm walkin' out!" Turning and heading for the entrance, the big man yelled at the blond girl, "You're damn right we'll talk later!" Not paying attention to where he was going, he bumped into a display rack and knocked its contents to the floor, newspapers and magazines skidding every which way. Customers just stood and watched in amazement as the big man disappeared through the double doors out onto the lot.

The girl bagging Nick's groceries asked, "So, how are you today sir?"

Nick smiled and answered, "A damn site better than those folks are."

Outside in the parking lot, Nick looked for the violent man but he was nowhere to be seen. The four girls that had been involved in the in-store encounter were loading up a red Jeep Cherokee at the end of the lot. They pulled out just as he was leaving and turned down the Island Parkway in the same direction he was headed.

What a day, he thought as he passed the intersection in Frogmore that led to Lands End, another great fishing spot his grandmother used to take him to. It had been a long day. He had gotten up before the sun was even up in Cincinnati, loaded up the rental and made the long drive to Beaufort, spent the better part of the day with Khelen Ridley getting all the required paperwork signed and documented. Then there was the unpleasant run-in with Charley Sparks and his giant sidekick at the liquor store and finally the argument at Publix.

When he arrived at the Harbor Island Bridge there was a backup as a fishing trawler made its way beneath the bridge and then out to sea. The Jeep with the four girls was still directly in front of him. He looked closely at the tags on the vehicle: South Carolina - Beaufort County. *Locals,* he thought.

Surprisingly, he followed the Jeep all the way out the Parkway and across the Fripp Island Bridge. The vehicle stopped briefly at the guard shack and was signaled through. The air-conditioner in the rental truck wasn't in the best working order and Nick found himself sweating profusely despite the fact that he had ridden the entire way out to the island with both windows down. The Jeep moved off and he pulled up next to the guard shack.

Ironically, the same guard that had greeted him the day of his grandmother's funeral came out of the shack. At first she didn't recognize him, but on closer inspection gave him a sloppy salute. "Mr. Falco. We've been expecting you today. Carson Pike, a friend of your grandparents let us know you'd be coming in. He said you inherited her house down on Tarpon, past Bonito. Do you have a family?"

"No, just me," said Nick.

"I know exactly where that house is. It's one of my favorites. There must be at least four or five bedrooms." She looked at the rental and giggled. "Do you think you have enough furniture in there to fill the place up?"

Nick laughed, "Good Lord... no! The house is completely furnished. I'll probably give this stuff to Goodwill when I run the truck back to Beaufort tomorrow."

Reaching back inside the shack she pulled a pass from a bulletin board and handed it in the window to Nick. "Here's your residence pass. You'll have to keep this visible in your vehicle until all the guards get used to who you are. After that, they'll just wave you on through. Welcome to Fripp Island."

"Thank you," replied Nick. "One question. That Jeep that pulled in before I did. Are they residents?"

"One of those girls owns a property on Fiddlers Ridge. The other girls with her are guests."

Nodding at the guard, Nick pulled out and made his way slowly down Tarpon Boulevard, passing many of the homes he had always admired when he was here as a young boy. On the right he could see the salt marsh that disappeared in the distance and the wooden walkway that crossed the marsh leading over to Sawgrass: a development of houses tucked away in tall pines and oaks and completely surrounded by the marsh except for a two lane road that cut through the marsh.

He passed John Fripp condos on the left and the Tennis Club on the right, the marsh still running parallel to the road. He passed Bonito Road and within seconds his grandmother's house loomed up on the left. The two story gleaming white home framed with black shutters was fronted by an elaborate front porch with Savannah Style stairs and a stained glass front double door entryway. Getting out of the truck, he sat the beer on the hood of the truck, tore one out of the carton and decided to take the short walk down to the beach. The groceries would be alright for a few minutes inside the truck. He just wanted to see the ocean. It was the same thing he had done whenever he had come down as a young boy. Walking around the side of the spacious house, he passed the garage, crossed the backyard, then over a gravel road to a beach access, up some wooden steps over top of the dunes and there it was: *the Atlantic Ocean.*

Walking down the steps, he sat on the bottom and removed his shoes and socks and dug his toes into the warm sand. Taking a long swig of beer he leaned back and allowed the bright afternoon sun to caress his face. Despite the fact it was in the high nineties, the sun held a warm, cozy healing effect to it, as if it were penetrating his very bones. Standing, he started to make his way down a sand covered path, flanked on either side by Sea Oats that swayed gently in the ocean breeze. The path eventually ended as he passed more dunes just before stepping onto the actual beach. He decided to walk out to the water's edge which was a good seventy yards away since the tide was out.

It was late in the day and the all-day heat had driven most of the vacationers inside to their air-conditioned condos or homes. Looking to his left in the distance he could make out Ocean Point and to his right the low stone wall that signaled the beginning of the end of the beach. A man walking his dog nodded at him, a woman engrossed in a book didn't pay him any attention and a jogger took a drink of water from a plastic container she carried as she passed him by.

The soft warm, loose sand slowly changed to a hard packed surface and then a wet sand and finally a sinking muddy effect. He waited patiently until a wave broke and then the warm water washed over his toes. Finishing off his beer in four swallows, he toasted the vast water that spread out before him, *"I can't believe it. I'm living on Fripp Island!"*

Chapter Seven

THE BOOMING SOUND OF NEARBY THUNDER JERKED Nick out of a relaxing sleep. Sitting up in the recliner in the large, high vaulted living room, he rubbed his aching shoulders and the back of his neck. He knew he was going to be sorry for falling asleep in the chair rather than going upstairs to one of the bedrooms. A flash of lightning lit up the entire interior of the house and then the room returned to darkness. Turning on the shell-filled glass lamp on an antique end table, he looked over at the grandfather clock that stood next to the elaborate stone fireplace: 3:17 in the morning. Getting up, he walked to the wall of atrium, eight-foot windows and gazed out into the darkness, when a streak of lightning zigzagged across the sky. He was fully awake. Coffee sounded good.

Walking to the kitchen, he found the coffeemaker where his grandmother always kept it on the counter. If he remembered correctly, she always stored the coffee and the filters in the cabinet above the sink. Sure enough. *There they were.*

Dumping the coffee and a canister of cold water into the small appliance, Nick pushed in the small button at the bottom and a red light came on indicating the brewing process had started. Taking a mug down from the cabinets, the early morning silence of the house was pierced by the melodious chiming of the front doorbell. Rinsing out the cup, Nick looked toward the front door. *Who in the hell could that be,* he thought, *at three o'clock in the morning?*

Then, it hit him. *Charley Sparks and Derek. It could be them!* The last time he had seen the bothersome duo had been in front of the liquor store. They couldn't be pleased with the outcome of being confronted by the police. Opening the utensil drawer, he wrapped his hand around a heavy, eighteen inch rolling pin and slowly ventured down the dark hallway past the downstairs bath and into the spacious front sitting room. Approaching the oak front door, a flash of lightning revealed an opaque figure of someone standing by one of the sidelights. *I just can't open the door,* thought Nick. *At this time of the morning it couldn't be anything normal.*

Tip toeing across the cherry hardwood flooring, he gently pulled back the lace curtains at the corner of the high bay window and peered out. It was pitch black. He couldn't see a thing. Then, another flash of lightning revealed the visitor. It was Genevieve, his next door neighbor. Thinking that she had an emergency or some sort of problem, Nick turned on the side coach lights and unlatched the door.

There stood the octogenarian, holding a stainless steel pitcher in her wrinkled hands. Smiling broadly, she spoke, "Good morning neighbor!"

At a loss for words, Nick laid the rolling pin on top of a cast iron umbrella rack by the door and just stared at the woman. Forcing her way past him, she jokingly scolded him, "What the hell's wrong with you son. Why would you leave an old woman standing outside in this lightning?" Walking down the hallway, she continued to talk, "Coffee smells good!"

Closing the door, Nick trailed her into the kitchen and still somewhat confused, looked at the pitcher in her hands. "Do you need to borrow something or are you returning that?"

"Oh this," she said. 'This is some of my famous fresh squeezed orange juice. I remembered how much you loved it when you were a youngster whenever you came down."

Still, in a state of amazement, Nick probed, "What on earth are you doing up this time of night?"

Setting the pitcher on the counter, Genevieve nodded toward the windows at the back of the house. "I've always been a night owl. I was up watching an old movie and I just happened to see you standing at those windows. Thought you might want to have a glass of juice with me?" Before Nick could respond, she opened the refrigerator and rejoiced, "Good, you have eggs and sausage and I saw a loaf of bread on the counter." Turning, she placed her hands on her thin hips and asked, "Hungry? How about breakfast?"

Nick looked at the grandfather clock and threw his hands into the air in a friendly manner, "Why not! What else is there to do this early in the morning? What do you need me to do?"

Excited, Genevieve started to give orders, "Alright then, if you'll get two glasses down from that end cabinet and then grab me a skillet from beneath the sink, we'll get this meal underway."

Opening the cabinet, Nick watched the old woman slice open the package of sausage and remove two eggs from the carton. Reaching for the juice, he remarked, "The way you know where everything is in this kitchen, you'd think you lived here."

Breaking an egg on the side of the iron skillet, she explained, "I'll have you know that over the thirty-five years I lived next door to your grandparents I've cooked many a meal right here in this very kitchen with Amelia. How many eggs do you want? I'm only having one."

Checking to see if the coffee was ready, Nick answered, "Well, as long as you're doing the cooking I'll have three if it's okay."

Reaching for two more eggs, her answer came, "Three eggs it'll be. I think I'll just fry up this whole batch of sausage. If we don't finish it off you can always freeze it or eat it tomorrow."

Sitting at the kitchen table, Nick took a drink of juice. "You say you've lived next door for thirty-five years. I'm only twenty-seven. That means you were friends with Edward and Amelia before I was even born."

"Yep, me and Frank; that was my husband, moved down here to Fripp about two years before your grandparents moved in."

"It's amazing. In all the years I came down here for vacation as a young boy I never really got to talk to you that much. I mean, sure there were times when we'd pass on the beach and we'd swap our opinions about the weather or I'd show you the shells I found but other than that, I really don't know much about you."

Turning on the range, Genevieve turned and looked over the top of her glasses. "Are you sure you want to hear about my past. I was quite the pisser when I was in college."

Nick laughed and repeated what she said, "A pisser!"

"That's right," said Genevieve, pointing a spatula directly at him. "Growing up, I had what you might call *strict parents!*" Shaking the spatula up and down, she emphasized, "If you look the word *strict* up in the dictionary, my folk's pictures would be next to the word. I grew up for eighteen years being guided, according to my mother and father *down the right path.* Aside from the discipline my parents wielded I spent my school years in a private girls school; more discipline. Finally when I graduated high school, they shipped me off to a private all girl's college on the outskirts of New Orleans where I would be able to hone my skills as the perfect young woman. The one advantage the school offered was I was free in the evenings and on weekends.

I had never been on my own beforehand and was eager to venture out into the world and experience a less disciplined lifestyle. I got a job waiting tables at a greasy spoon just outside the French Quarter. I made pretty good tips, but the thing I enjoyed most was just getting out and rubbing shoulders with regular people, people who didn't always follow the rules of society."

Flipping the sausage, Genevieve continued, "After a couple of months this older man comes in for lunch. I got to talking with him and he told me he owned a club over in the Quarter and he was looking for some college girls who wanted to dance and make some serious money. He told me that I was cute and could do quite well there. When he told me I could make as much in one night as I made in a week at the diner, I asked for the address. The rest is history. I started dancing that week. The outfits were scanty to say the least and the clientele at times was sleazy."

Removing the eggs from the pan, she put three on one plate and the remaining on another, followed by two pieces of sausage each. "I was an instant hit." Patting her backside and tapping her sagging breasts with the spatula, she proudly announced, "Back then I was a looker: had a great butt and a nice set of Ta Ta's." Looking down over her aging body, she sadly said, "That was a long time ago. Anyways, before long my skimpy outfit was being stuffed nightly with money. I became the most popular dancer at the club. I was hauling in over two hundred dollars a night. The owner told me that it was up to me but if I wanted to make even more money I could take male customers into the back and for special services they would pay dearly... and they did! After being at the club for six months I was bringing in almost five-hundred a night. I quit school and got an apartment. My days of discipline had ended. My parents were livid to say the least but I was of age and capable of making my own decisions."

Popping two slices of bread into the toaster, she suggested, "I think the coffee might be ready. Why don't you pour us each a cup?"

Getting another cup down from the cabinet, Nick asked, "So you were saying that you were making quite a bit of money as a dancer."

Setting the two plates of food on the kitchen table, Genevieve went on to further explain, "Then one night a well-dressed gentleman, in his late thirties came into the club. He appeared to be wealthy. As the evening wore on I asked him if there was anything I could do for him aside from dancing. He asked me if I would have dinner with him when my shift was over. I agreed, thinking that after dinner, I would take care of his sexual desires and then I would be a couple of hundred dollars richer. That evening when I left the club he picked me up out front in a limo and we went to a very expensive eating establishment. After dinner, while we were eating dessert, I asked him what else he required of me. Smiling, he said he was looking for a wife and I fit the bill perfectly. Later that night he had us driven to a very expensive home he was renting. He was the perfect gentlemen and told me that if I married him I would have everything I desired for the rest of my life. I swear, looking back, I don't know what got into me, but I agreed. The next week we were married. I was nineteen and he was thirty-nine. The other girls at the club said it would never work out. He moved me to his elaborate home in upstate New York and we lived there for twenty-nine years when he retired at the age of sixty-eight, at which point we moved down here to Fripp and built the house next door."

Sitting at the table, she took a drink of coffee, then added, "Two years later, Edward and Amelia bought this lot and had this house built. Then, about a year later, Frank got a bad case of the flu and he just never recovered. He passed away from double pneumonia two months later and I became a widow at the age fifty-one. He was the only man I ever truly loved." Nodding out the window, she cut into her sausage and remarked, "That was thirty-five years ago and I've never even considered remarrying or even dating anyone. He was the love of my life."

Waving off her past life, she bit into a slice of toast, "Enough about me and my past." Pointing her fork at Nick, she gave him a disappointed look. "Why didn't you tell me when we met at the memorial service that you were going to live here at the house?"

"Because at the time," answered Nick, "I didn't know I was going to inherit the house. All I knew at the time was that Amelia's attorney wanted to discuss something in her will with me. How did you find out I got the house... and that I was moving in?"

"Carson told me yesterday when I was out getting my mail. He happened to be passing by and gave me the news. He said Amelia had left you everything: house, antiques, cars and plenty of cash."

Refilling his coffee, Nick gestured with his cup, displaying the house, "I'm still trying to get my hands around this whole situation. Don't get me wrong. I've always wanted to live on Fripp. It's a dream come true for me, but things just seem to be different than I recall. Like, for instance this serial killer I've just recently heard about. What's that about? They say there's been eight victims over the last two years."

Getting up and rinsing her plate off in the sink, Genevieve shook her head. "That's a subject I don't like to think about let alone talk about. Most of the folks out here on Fripp feel the same way." Opening the dishwasher she placed the partially clean plate in and closed the door. Pouring herself another cup of coffee, she walked into the living room. "Let's sit in here while we drink our coffee."

Leaving his plate on the table, Nick stood and walked to the living room where he planted himself in the recliner. Raising his cup in a toasting fashion, he stated, "Okay, let the conversation begin."

"Well, for one thing," said Genevieve, "you heard correctly. There has been eight victims. The last girl was found just about a week ago by none other than Carson Pike about a mile out from the marina in the salt marsh. I talked with Carson earlier in the week, a couple of days after he found the girl. He said the fingers on one of her hands had been ripped off and there was evidence she had been snake bitten a few times. Carson said when he found her it was horrible. It appears that it's the work of the RPS Killer as far as they can tell."

Curious, Nick asked, "As far as they can tell. What does that mean? It sounds like they're not absolutely sure."

"It's complicated. When the first girl was killed two years back, it was all over the news. By the time the third girl was discovered, the police and the newspaper started to hush up and not as much information was revealed to the public; things like conditions of the body, motive, any leads they had. I can tell you this. The manner in which this last victim died is not consistent with the way the other seven victims were killed. They're basing the way this girl died on evidence they collected from two girls that managed to escape the wrath of the killer."

Setting his cup on an end table, Nick asked, "So what you're saying is that two girls got away from this maniac?"

"No, that's not what I'm saying. The killer let them go free and according to both girls, it's part of a game he plays. He's referred to as the RPS Killer; RPS standing for Rock, paper, scissors. It's a simplistic game that children and adults as well play—"

Interrupting, Nick admitted, "I've seen the game played back in college. I've never had a reason to play it myself, but I understand how it works."

The girls that were freed, described the killer as very polite and brutally honest with the capability of losing his temper for short periods of time if things don't go his way. They said he was on the tall, slim side, very well spoken and a chain smoker. All of the victims, including the two that dodged the bullet were from the Savannah area. The police feel the killer apprehends them over in Georgia and then brings them across the state line to South Carolina, kills them and dumps them out here on the islands. The two he let go won the game: Rock, paper, scissors. But it's the way he frees them that's got everyone puzzled. The killer sets them free a good distance out in the salt marshes in the middle of the night and they have to walk or swim to safety. Myself, I've never been out in the marsh except to pass by in a boat. Carson told me, what with the gators, sharks, snakes and the tide a person's chance of survival is minimum, at best. He said the two girls who walked out and survived were what he considered quite lucky. Not so much for the latest victim."

"So, what about the girls who do not win the game? He just kills them?"

"Yes, and that's the part the police have not been overly open about, but you can't keep things like that hidden from the public very long. The word around here is the killings are very brutal. The girls that were killed supposedly had their faces smashed in with a rock and their elbows and kneecaps were also broken by the use of large rocks. The victims are always found with a pair of scissors stuck in their chests. It makes me sick to think about what those girls had to go through and how they must have suffered. I don't know what the world is coming to. To tell you the truth, I'm glad I've only got a few years left. I've had a good life, especially the years here on Fripp."

Changing the subject, Genevieve asked, "I know you're not married. Is there a girl up there in Ohio that will be visiting you from time to time?"

"No," said Nick. "There is no girl that will be coming down here to see me. I haven't dated for years. That's another story for another time." Now it was Nick who changed the subject. "You knew my grandparents quite well, right?"

"I guess one could say that. I lived next door to them for over three decades. I'd like to think I knew them well. They were not just great neighbors, but wonderful and loving friends. I recall, when Frank got sick and then eventually passed on how Edward and Amelia were there for me: cooking meals, watching over my house while I was at the hospital, spending time with me during the grieving process. So, yeah. I knew them quite well. Why do you ask?"

Sitting forward on the chair, Nick hesitated and then popped the question, "I was wondering about the fatal accident Edward had over on Harbor Island. Amelia's attorney said it went down as a DUI fatality. He told me they found my grandfather sitting in his car, drown to death from the high tide and that he had quite a bit of alcohol in his system. Ridley told me the whole thing didn't feel right to him. He said Edward never drank that much and that after the accident Amelia changed."

"Boy, you sure know how to pick subjects that piss me off," said Genevieve. "I agree wholeheartedly with Khelen Ridley when it comes to Edward's death. It was completely out of context for the man. I never saw the man in a state of drunkenness or even anything close to it. Sure, he had a drink now and then, like whenever he and Amelia would go out for a nice dinner, he'd have a glass of wine. He'd always have a drink on Christmas or at New Years. I really don't know what to think about the way they found him, but you can't argue with the police. There was a complete investigation into the accident. They found no traces of foul play, the car was in excellent working condition and Edward's blood alcohol level was off the chart. Personally, I think there was foul play involved. I'm not sure how or why; it's just the way I feel."

Not wanting to talk about the subject any longer, Genevieve got up and walked to the sink where she rinsed out her cup. "I have to head back on over to my place. You can keep the orange juice. I know how much you like it. You can return the pitcher later. The sun will be coming up in a couple of hours and I want to take a shower before I head out on my morning walk."

Getting up, Nick insisted, "At least let me walk you back to your place. It's dark out."

"Sonny! I've been walking back and forth in the dark from my house over here to your grandmother's for years. I think I'll be alright. Maybe I'll see you on the beach later in the week."

Nick watched until she disappeared inside her front door then turned to walk back up the stairs to his own home when he noticed a set of parking lights of an unseen vehicle, parked two houses up on the opposite side of the street. Suddenly, the lights were turned off. He stood and stared into the darkness up the street. Turning, he climbed the steps and thought, *Probably just a neighbor or some early morning tourist.*

Standing once again in the kitchen he thought about the things he and Genevieve had discussed, especially the RPS Killer and Edward's strange death. All in all, it had been a rather depressing morning considering the conversation he just had. Finishing off the remaining juice, he decided on a shower, then he would head into town around nine o'clock and return the rental and drive his bike back to the island. He had no idea what he was going to do the rest of the day. Maybe he'd take a long walk on the beach later on in the afternoon if it wasn't too hot.

His walk on the beach came sooner than he planned. His trip to and from Beaufort had been uneventful. He returned the rental truck back to a combination auto repair and rental location, then made the trip back out to the island on his Harley. As usual, the heat was relentless, the temperature hanging in the low nineties. Parking the bike at the side of the garage, Nick bounded up the rear steps and entered the screened-in Florida room, unlocked the door and went in the house. Ten minutes later, dressed in cut-off jeans, flip flops and one of his old painting tee-shirts, he crossed the gravel road behind the house and headed for the beach access.

It was just after twelve and the beach was bustling with activity: every shape and size of body imaginable sprawled out on blankets, their bodies smeared with sun tan lotion, people propped up in beach chairs beneath umbrellas as they read their novels, small children playing in the sand, people walking dogs. He decided to walk to the Skull Inlet end of the beach. It wasn't nearly as far as Ocean Point and normally not as packed with tourists. The tide was out, not a cloud in the sky and he was walking on the beach. *What a perfect day,* he thought.

Five minutes down the beach, he stopped to take a drink from a plastic water bottle he had brought along and watched a group of seagulls descend on a couple who were tossing peanuts into the air. On his way once again, he gazed up the beach. In the distance he could see only one person walking toward him. Based upon his past experience of walking on the beach, he knew the person would not be passing him for a good minute or so. Twenty seconds later, the person, who appeared to be a girl was practically on him. The reason being; she was speed walking.

The girl pumped her arms vigorously and moved toward him. She looked like the typical beach walker: straw hat, sunglasses, yellow tank top, grey, rolled up sweat pants, and dirty white sneakers. When they were side by side, she looked over at Nick, gave him a pleasant smile and spoke, "Excuse me. Do you happen to have the time?"

Reaching into his jeans pocket for his cell phone, he responded, "Sure, just let me look." Waiting, the girl took a swig of water from a sports bottle she clutched in her left hand.

Flipping open the top of his cell, he announced the time: "Twelve-twenty-seven."

The girl smiled back, displaying gleaming white teeth. "Thank you so much."

Turning to head up the beach, she was stopped from doing so when Nick blurted out awkwardly, "Go out with me to dinner?"

Stopping in her tracks, she looked at him as if she couldn't believe what she had heard. Nick couldn't believe what he had said himself. Following a few seconds of silence, the girl took a step back toward him and with a confusing look, asked, "Pardon me, but did you just ask me out to dinner?"

Nick, realizing what he had said being not only ridiculous, but far too forward, tried to think of a way to explain his strange request. The only thing he could think to say was, "Yes, I did!"

Placing one of her hands on her hip, she looked him over from head to toe. "What on earth motivated you to ask me out? Do we know each other? Have we met before? And, furthermore; why would I want to go to dinner with you?"

Trying to answer her questions in order, Nick fumbled with his words, "No... we... we don't know each other, and, and we've... never met... before and the reason I asked you... is because... I haven't been on a date... for five years."

The girl remained unresponsive and just stared at him.

Thinking the ball was still in his court, he added, "And why wouldn't you want to go to dinner with me?"

"Well, for one thing," pointed out the girl, "We've just met. I mean, you don't just meet someone and two seconds later ask them out to dinner."

"Why not?"

"Because that's not the way it's done. You say you haven't been on a date in five years. Well, it's no wonder if this is your standard approach."

Nick realized the girl was right in her opinion of him. "Look, I'm sorry. Aside from not having dated in five years I just moved to Fripp. I inherited my grandmother's house back up the beach there. I don't know anyone down here, so I thought I'd just ask you to dinner. Didn't mean to be so forward."

Despite the fact he had just apologized, she didn't accept the fact he was new to the area or that he hadn't dated in a long time.

Smartly, she responded, "If you want my advice, the next time you want to ask someone out, get to know them first. Might go a little smoother."

Her lack of compassion caused him to look her up and down. "I used to come down here every summer when I was a kid. I remember how everyone on the beach was so friendly. That was years ago. I guess things have changed down here."

Removing her sunglasses, the girl objected to his statement. "Now just hold a sec. Are you implying I'm unfriendly?"

Starting up the beach, Nick waved off her question. "If the shoe fits... wear it!"

In three quick steps she stopped in front of him. "I'll have you know, that in general, I'm known as a very friendly person. I have a lot of friends. As a matter of fact, I'll tell you what. I will go to dinner with you. If for no other reason than to prove that I am a friendly person! It's not a date... just dinner."

Nick apologized a second time, "I already apologized for my attitude and my actions. There doesn't seem to be much sense in making fun of me."

"I wasn't making fun of you. Are we on for dinner or not? Have you changed your mind?"

Now that the situation had been completely reversed, Nick wasn't sure how to answer.

The girl put her sunglasses back on and held her hands out to her side. "Look, it's not that difficult... yes or no!"

He answered meekly, "Yes."

Starting up the beach, she looked back at him. "If you're serious meet me tonight at The Dockside over in Port Royal... seven o'clock. If you don't show by seven-fifteen, I'm out of there." Tipping her hat, she winked and held out her hands, "Just sayin'!"

Nick stood and watched the girl walk up the beach until she was nothing more than a speck in the distance. Walking out into the low waves, he looked up into the intense sun and spoke aloud to himself, "This is insane! She can't be serious. If she is, I can't believe I'm actually going on a date of sorts with a woman. I don't even know her name. She doesn't know mine. Should I go? What if I go and she doesn't show up? Oh, what the hell! What else do I have to do tonight? I'll be there at seven and if she doesn't appear then I'll just have a nice dinner by myself."

***

The man lit a cigarette with the butt of his previous smoke and pitched the butt out the open window. Examining the wrinkled pack of smokes, he noted that he only had two left. He looked at his watch: 3:05 in the afternoon. He had been sitting in his pickup truck for the past three hours, watching the three girls on the beach at Tybee Island. The tallest girl, the one with blond hair was the one he had chosen. He had watched the girls for the past three days. They always left the beach around six o'clock. She was to be his next victim.

Chapter Eight

NICK STEPPED OUT OF THE GLASS ENCLOSED SHOWER, grabbed a towel from the eight-foot, marble covered custom built vanity in the master bath and walked out into the master bedroom. Sitting on the edge of the king size, walnut, four poster bed, he dried his legs and feet, then his back and shoulders. Throwing the towel on the quilted bedspread, he walked by the floor-length mirror, stopped, grinned and went into a body builder pose and thought to himself, *Not too bad!*

Opening one of the four cardboard boxes of clothes he had transported from Cincinnati, he slipped into a fresh pair of underwear and his favorite tan and black argyle socks. Next, he opened a small travel bag and removed a deodorant stick that he ran under his armpits. Splashing on some old cologne he hadn't used since he could remember, he searched for the most unwrinkled dress pants he had. Locating a beige pair that wasn't too bad, he slipped them on and added a light brown rope belt he never wore. Next, he needed a nice shirt. Searching the boxes he couldn't find anything suitable for his possible upcoming dinner engagement. Throwing on and older shirt, he realized he was going to have to purchase something at one of the gift shops on the island.

Putting on his cordovan penny loafers he hadn't wore since he bought them three years ago, he decided after driving over to the gift shop, he'd head over to the Bonito Boathouse and grab some lunch. The early morning breakfast he shared with Genevieve had worn off and he wasn't scheduled to eat dinner for another six hours. Maybe he'd just grab an appetizer and a beer at the marina. Running his fingers through his hair, he walked into the bedroom at the rear of the house where he had stayed whenever he had come down in the past.

The room looked just the way he remembered it: queen size, white bamboo fashioned bed with matching dresser and nightstand, his collection of jars of shells still lined up on top of the dresser. He noticed an envelope with his name penned on the front attached beneath the corner of the large mirror. Taking the envelope down, he sat on the bed and opened it. He unfolded the paper inside and read his grandmother's handwritten note:

> *Nicholas,*
>
> *If you're reading this note, then you have probably moved in. I am so happy that you have decided to live on the island. It is my hope that you will not only enjoy the house but everything mentioned in the will. Take care of Edward's old Buick. He loved that car. My husband associated with and worked for some very powerful and dangerous people. Some of these people may come to see you about the house. If you experience any problems with these people, go and see Carson. He'll know what to do. Enjoy Fripp!*
>
> *Love,*
> *Your grandmother, Amelia*

Reading the short letter a second time, Nick walked to the bedroom window and looked out. From where he was he could see the very edge of the beach and the vast ocean. He recalled as a youth how he would always look out the window and be amazed at the enormity of the sea.

Smiling, he thought about how intelligent his grandmother had been and also about how religious she always was. She had always influenced his life but for some reason he just never bought into being religious. Sure, he believed in God and he wasn't all that sure you had to attend a church to do so. He had mentioned that to his grandmother on one occasion when he had been visiting for the summer. She simply told him he had every right to make his own decision about God, but whenever he was down on Fripp and staying at her house, he'd sit and read the Bible with her in the morning and go to church in Beaufort every Sunday.

Turning, he saw her old Bible setting on the nightstand. She always kept the Bible in the master bedroom. Had she placed it in his old room for a reason? And what about the strange letter? What did she mean by mentioning powerful and dangerous men and that they may come to see him about the house? Folding the letter, he placed it in his front pants pocket and bounded down the carpeted stairs.

Reading the letter caused him to think about Edward's old Buick parked out in the two car garage. Khelen Ridley told him Carson had mentioned that both cars had been gassed up. Locking the house, he walked out to the garage and decided he'd take the old car for a spin around the island.

Unlocking the garage, he entered. The building was spotless: shiny grey concrete floor, the three walls covered with a few sparse tools and custom shelving, an old Sunoco Oil clock centered on the back wall. In the center of the two stall garage sat the two cars: the silver-grey Lexus, that wasn't even quite a year old and the tarp-covered '49 Buick.

Carefully removing the black tarp, Nick folded it and placed it on a long work bench. He had always admired Edward's old Buick: two tone maroon and cream custom paint job, rolled and tucked black leather interior, custom dash and original hub caps. He pushed the button on the garage opener and the double doors slowly opened. Climbing into the car, he sat back in the leather seat and placed the key into the ignition. He'd only ridden in the car three times he could remember and he always considered it a real treat. Now, he owned the antique automobile. Turning the key, the engine came to life, purring like a kitten. He pulled out onto the driveway and closed the doors then waited for a few minutes, allowing the engine to warm up.

Pulling out onto Tarpon Boulevard, he made a right. His first stop was the Ship's Store Gift shop located next to John Fripp condos. It was a short drive, not even two minutes. Pulling into a parking spot the area was quite busy, tourists going in and out of the various shops, a couple taking a photograph of some nearby deer who were grazing in the grass. Directly across the street he heard the sound of a riding mower as the grass was being professionally cut, another man trimming the bushes.

He no sooner entered the gift shop when he saw what he wanted. An assortment of polo shirts with Fripp Island embroidered just beneath the left shoulder caught his eye. Sorting through the shirts, he selected a light yellow, paid for his purchase at the tiny counter and exited the shop. Outside he found two different families admiring the Buick. A little boy from one of the families reached out to touch the car but was stopped by his father, who ordered him, "Don't touch! This is a special car."

An older man on the other side of the car asked Nick when he approached, "Did you purchase the car as is or did you restore it?"

Opening the driver's side door, Nick answered, "Neither. It was my grandfather's car. I'm pretty sure he restored it."

Placing his purchase on the passenger seat, he backed out, made a left on Tarpon and drove to Bonito Drive where he made a right, crossed the short concrete bridge that spanned the island canal and passed the Ocean Creek Golf Course on the left. He remembered the many times he had played golf there with Amelia. It was always an adventure whenever they went. Depending on the weather and the amount of players on the course, oftentimes he'd get to see smaller alligators basking in the sun, especially near the small lake. At first, he was afraid of the reptiles, but after his grandmother explained to him that they actually lived there and for the most part were harmless, if let be, his fear subsided.

Passing the long row of three-story pastel painted vacation homes on the left, he pulled into the marina and parked the Buick in front of the Bonito Boathouse where he had dined on occasion with his grandparents. He remembered how his grandfather always ordered crab cakes.

Walking up the steps at the front of the faded, clapboard structure, he looked to his right out toward the salt marsh that seemed to go on forever. *It was out there somewhere,* he thought, *where they had found the most recent victim of the RPS Killer.*

Inside, the combination restaurant-bar looked just the way he remembered: tables and chairs lined up against the window covered walls, various pictures of old fishing vessels scattered around the place, the long bar fronted by a number of old bar stools, the wall of assorted liquors lined up neatly behind the bar.

Sauntering up to one of the bar stools, he took a seat and waited patiently while the female bartender counted out some change and then closed the register. Sliding a circular cardboard Budweiser coaster and a napkin toward him, she asked, "What'll it be?"

Thinking for a moment, he answered, "I'll have a Bud Light please."

Turning, he looked out across the floor. There were only four couples at the moment who were in the process of eating their lunch. If he recalled, the Boathouse was the busiest at dinner time. He no sooner had his beer placed in front of him when he was joined by none other than Carson Pike, who flopped down on the stool next to him and spoke to the bartender, "Sally, give me my regular."

Looking Carson over, Nick remarked, "Well, you sure look different. The last time I saw you, you were... let's say, dressed quite well."

Carson looked down over his faded, yellow coveralls and mud-stained fishing boots. "Comes with the profession of being a fisherman. What brings you over here to the marina?"

Picking up his bottle of beer, Nick smiled and looked out the window. "It's hotter than hell out there. Thought I'd just grab me a brew and maybe a sandwich and sit here in the air-conditioning."

The bartender placed a shot of whiskey and a bottle of beer in front of Carson. He downed the shot and followed up with a long swig of beer, belched and commented, "Nothing like a bump and a beer for lunch."

Remembering the letter in his pocket, Nick snapped his fingers. "I've got something I want you to take a look at." Producing the letter, he unfolded it and slid it across the rough wooden counter. "I found this in an envelope attached to the dresser in the room where I always stayed when I came down here. It's written by Amelia and I think she or someone placed it there so I would find it. Read that, and tell me what you think."

Removing a set of reading glasses from his shirt pocket, Carson picked up the letter and read it slowly and then placed it back on the counter and remained quiet.

Nick, surprised that he had no reaction, asked, "Well, what do you think?"

Holding up the empty shot glass, Carson gestured at the bartender and ordered softly, "Hit me again!" He turned on the barstool and looked directly at Nick. "Before I can answer any questions you may have about this letter, it's important that you understand what your grandfather did for a living, which brings me to my first question for you. What kind of work do you think your grandfather, Edward did?"

Nick shrugged his shoulders, "I really don't know, I mean exactly. I remember when I was around seven or eight and I was down here on vacation, that I asked Amelia what grandpa's job was. She told him he was an entrepreneur of sorts, a businessman so to speak and his occupation required he travel a lot. That was almost twenty years ago. Being eight years old, her answer was good enough for me. I never questioned her any farther."

Slugging down his second shot of whiskey, Carson took another drink of his beer and spoke, "Your grandmother was right on all three counts. Edward was an entrepreneur and a businessman and he did indeed travel quite a bit. The truth is your grandfather, just like the letter says, worked for some very powerful and dangerous men."

"I think you're trying your best to tell me something," said Nick, "but I guess I'm just not comprehending what it is you're saying."

Finishing off his beer, Carson leaned forward and tapped the edge of the letter. "Your grandfather, for lack of a better way to put it was employed by an organized crime syndicate out of New York."

Nick, still in the dark, gave Carson an odd look and stated, "Are you saying my grandfather was in the mafia... the mob?"

"Well, that's not a term used much these days, but yes, I guess one could say that."

Upset, Nick, responded, "You guess? Either he was or he wasn't!"

"Look," said Carson, "your grandfather could never be classified as a gun-toting gangster. He worked on the clean side of the business."

Nick pushed his beer to the side. "I don't know much about the mafia, or as you call it, *an organized crime syndicate,* but how could there possibly be a clean side to anything they are involved with?"

Fortunately, the bartender had not overheard their conversation. Standing, Carson ordered that two beers be brought to a window table and guided Nick across the room. "We have to be careful that no one overhears us," said Carson.

Seated at the table, Carson picked up on their previous topic. "Your grandfather was never involved in any gunplay or all that crap you see on television, although he did have a gun; a 38 snub nose special. He always took it with him when he traveled. As far as I know, he never used it. When he was at home he kept the gun under the seat of the Buick, fully loaded with a box of shells. I see you drove the Buick over here today. Hell, that gun might still be under the driver's seat."

Nick's eyes grew wide as he repeated, "Still under the driver's seat! Do you mean to tell me I drove over here with a snub nosed whatever you called it gun right beneath my ass?"

"Calm down," said Carson. "We'll check when you're ready to leave. If it's still in the car then you need to take it into the house when you get back. You don't want to get pulled over by the police for some reason and wind up with them finding the gun under the seat. You'd be in deep shit since you probably don't have a license to carry a firearm. If you don't want it in the house, then you can just give it to me and I'll take care of it."

Now, even more confused, Nick asked, "How do you know all these things about my grandfather?"

Carson hesitated in his answer when the bartender delivered their drinks. After she left the table, Carson answered, "Because I worked for Edward. I was his right hand man. I never traveled with him but I looked after Amelia at times when he was away. I did a lot of odd jobs for him."

"Come to think of it," said Nick. "I do remember you being around the house quite a bit when Edward was off on business. So, explain to me this clean side of the business my grandfather was a part of."

"Edward was a genius when it came to money. Why he could take one hundred dollars and turn it into a thousand in a matter of days. He just had a knack for financing. He not only understood compound interest, but how money works. He was extremely shrewd when it came to investing, whether it was real estate or stocks and bonds or commodities. You see, an organized crime syndicate has a number of varied revenue flows generated from both legal and illegal activities. The illegal money comes from prostitution, gambling, drugs and any other number of things. Every penny the syndicate generated went through your grandfather. He knew where every dollar came from and where every dollar was invested. In other words, your grandfather took what is referred to as dirty money and turned it into clean money, generated from investments he made for the people he worked for. I can't even begin to tell you how many millions your grandfather made for these people. He was quite respected for his abilities and very well paid."

Nick looked out the window and then back at Carson. "So the way this whole situation pans out is the house I inherited and all the antiques and the money that came with it, are derived from illegal activities?"

Sipping his beer, Carson smiled, "I think that's stretching things a bit. The income your father received from those he worked for was just a part of his income. He made a lot of investments himself. Working for your grandfather, I'd say that overall he was an honest man. He took good care of Amelia and now some of his wise investing has filtered down to you. What's wrong with that?"

Nick shook his head. "Nothing... I guess, hell, I don't know what to think." Scratching his head, Nick went on, "Okay, so you've done a great job of explaining who the powerful and dangerous men are who my grandfather worked for, but why are they considered dangerous. You said they respected Edward and paid him well. How could they be considered dangerous and why would they want to come and see me about the house?"

"I was just getting to that. There's more to this story. What I am about to share with you no one on this island is aware of and that's the way it needs to stay... understand?"

Nick grabbed his beer and took a deep swallow, "Agreed."

Settling back in his chair, Carson began, "I guess it was about nine years back, when Edward confided in me and told me he wanted to retire from working for the people up in New York. He said he and Amelia had enough money to live on the rest of their lives, the house was paid for; they didn't own anything to anyone. They were completely financially free. He told me he was going to fly up to New York and talk things over with those he answered to. He was confident they would understand and free him from any further obligations to the syndicate, especially since he had made them so much money over the years, but as life can often go, things don't always work out the way we plan."

Pointing his bottle of beer at Nick, he continued, "When Edward got back from his New York trip, he had a meeting with Amelia and myself. He told us his request to retire from the syndicate had not been received well. He was informed in a friendly, but firm way that the *only way* to retire from their organization was by death... hopefully a natural death. He was told he knew too much about the organization, where their money came from and where it was invested. He knew names and things that went on. He was far too important to them and as long as they had him on a short leash, which everyone was on in the syndicate, they could keep an eye on him. That's just the way it was. He was informed he needed to just keep right on doing what he had done for years and they would keep paying him well. Needless to say Edward was not pleased with the end result of the meeting, but the way it had been put to him... he had no choice."

Nick couldn't believe what he was being told. Tearing the label off his beer with his thumbnail, he asked, "So, at that point my grandfather just kept right on working for these people?"

"Yes, he did," said Carson, "but with a twist. He was so infuriated with the outcome of the New York meeting he decided to start scamming money off the top of some of the investments he would make for them. Up until that point he had been above suspicion, and your grandfather was sharp as a tack. He would continue to play their game for years to come, but would put into play a system whereas he would make additional income aside from what they were paying him to invest their money. So for the next eight years he tucked away seven million dollars of their money and they never knew it. He was that good!"

Nick stood and placed his hand on his forehead. "The longer I sit here and listen to all this the more unbelievable and crazy it gets! I need another beer. How about you?"

Looking at his watch, Carson agreed, "Why not. It's too damn hot to go back out to the marsh anyway. Yeah, get me another."

Nick went to the bar and returned with their drinks. "You still haven't told me why the people my grandfather worked for might come to see me about the house. What's that all about?"

"I knew all along he was scamming the syndicate," explained Carson, "but he never told me what he did with the money, until just after Christmas last year. He told me he hid the money. He wasn't specific where, just that he had hid it on the property. He told me Amelia didn't even know where the money was hidden, just that it was on their property. He also told me the New York folks were on to him. He had gotten too greedy and slipped up in covering his tracks. Someone in the syndicate discovered or at least suspected him of embezzling money from them."

"Wait a minute!" said Nick "How can someone embezzle or I guess steal money from someone who essentially got it in the first place illegally?"

"Most people would tend to agree with you on that. But, that being said, try and convince the syndicate of that. It doesn't float. They wanted their money back. They were not sure how much your grandfather had taken, but they knew they were short a few million. Edward was called to New York for a meeting where they explained that if he did indeed take the money it must be returned. Edward lied and told them he didn't know what they were talking about. He came back home, but after that things changed. The syndicate no longer trusted your grandfather. A couple of months later Edward was found dead on the side of the road over on Harbor Island. The police, after investigating the accident, claimed Edward had an excessive blood alcohol level and he had apparently run off the road and drown when the tide came in. As far as I'm concerned that's a lot of crap! Your grandfather was killed by the very people he worked for. Did he deserve it? Well, I guess that depends on who you talk to. Both Amelia and I feel he got screwed but the syndicate feels differently. The thing is; they still don't have their seven million. It's still hidden somewhere in the house you live in or at least on the property. And that's the reason why the syndicate may send someone to see you about the house. They may want to search the property or maybe even purchase it. But here's the thing. Your grandmother was way ahead of the curve. As you are aware she set the will up so you couldn't sell the house, which the syndicate is probably not aware of."

Suddenly, it struck Nick. "Now things are starting to add up. Remember when Charley Sparks and that goon he runs with came to my grandmother's memorial service? I couldn't understand what your relationship was with them. It was apparent you didn't care for them and they didn't particularly appear to be all that fond of you either. You told me not to be overly concerned about them, that they were just some people my grandfather had worked with. So, now it turns out they might just be the people my grandmother was referring to; the men who might come and see me about the house."

Carson confirmed Nick's statement and nodded.

In amazement, Nick continued, "There's something about the two men I didn't tell you when you told me not to worry about them at the memorial service. Those two have been dogging me before I ever got down here. The day I received the call from my grandmother's attorney, they were watching me from across the street where I was painting a house. Then, later on that day, they approached me at a bank. The big one, I guess his name is Derek, started to rough me up but then Charley intervened and told him to back off. Then, this Sparks character proceeds to tell me as long as I don't go to the police I'm not in any danger and I may see them in a few days depending on the decisions I make. At the time, I had absolutely no idea what he was talking about. The morning of the memorial service, I discovered they had followed me down to Beaufort and had stayed the night at the same inn I did. You know what happened at the service, but then after I got back from Cincinnati after talking things over with Khelen Ridley, I had another run-in with them over at Bill's Liquor Store on Ladies Island. Do you think they are the ones who will come to see me about the house?"

"Maybe... maybe not," said Carson. "They might just be keeping an eye on things for now. Do you remember when we were leaving Ocean Point after you spread Amelia's ashes?"

"Yeah."

"You caught me staring off toward Hunting Island and asked me if there was something wrong. I told you it was nothing, but the truth is I spotted Charley and Derek watching our every move. Sooner or later, either they or someone they represent will pay you a visit."

"What should I do? Should I go to the police?"

"No, that would not be advisable. Besides, what would you tell them? There's seven million dollars of illegal money hidden on your property somewhere and that you don't know where it is. So far, these men haven't done anything other than be a pain in the ass. No, you just sit tight and we'll wait for them to make a move. Other than that, you just go on with your life as if nothing out of the ordinary has happened. Don't worry. If things start to get out of hand, I'll be around to bail you out. That's what your grandmother meant when she wrote that if you needed anything to contact me. Believe me. I can handle Charley Sparks and his sidekick."

Taking a drink, he changed the subject, "Moving on. How are things going at the house? Are you getting settled in?"

Nick, not quite ready to move on, answered as if he were not sure, "Yeah I guess things are go okay. I met a girl on the beach earlier today. I think I may have a dinner planned with her tonight over in Port Royal."

Carson gave him an odd look. "You think or you do have a dinner planned?"

"I know that sounds strange, but that's another story I really don't care to get into right now. I'm still reeling from everything I learned today about my grandfather. It's so hard to believe. I can't believe they killed him. It's so peaceful down here on the islands."

"Like I said, you just need to go on like nothing has happened. Don't dwell on the past. There's nothing you or I can do about that now."

Realizing Carson was serious about moving on and not worrying about the men who had been following him, Nick changed the topic again and looked out the window at the marsh. "I was talking with Genevieve Reign, my next door neighbor. She was telling me you were the one who discovered the latest victim in the RPS killings. That must have been horrible."

"It was horrible," said Carson. "I don't mean to seem rude, but if it's all the same I'd rather not discuss that. Every time someone mentions it to me, it does nothing but remind me of what that girl must have gone through. I don't like to think about it." Standing, he tossed a twenty on the table. "The beer is on me!" Leaning close to Nick so they would not be overheard, Carson whispered, "Before you go, let's check the Buick and see if the gun is still there."

Outside in the lot, Nick unlocked the car and stepped back while Carson leaned in and reached beneath the driver's side seat. Nick looked around to see if anyone was watching. There was a couple entering the Boathouse and a man driving by in a golf cart, but other than that, no one was paying them any attention. Nick's attention on the lot was interrupted when Carson spoke softly, "Got it! It's still here."

Nick was startled when someone from behind him commented, "That car belongs to Edward Falco... right?"

Nick turned and saw the approaching man who seemed quite interested in the Buick. Speaking in a voice that was loud enough to warn Carson, Nick answered, "Yes, it does, or at least it did. I own it now."

Carson, in an awkward position spoke up, fabricating his reason for looking beneath the seat, "Sure enough. You've got a loose connection under here. Won't take much to get it repaired."

The man, trying to look inside the car, asked, "Car troubles?"

Carson got up and waved the man's suggestion off as nothing. "Nope, just a loose wire. No big deal."

Looking Nick over, the man rubbed his chin and remarked, "Why you must be Edward's grandson? Heard you were inheriting his home. Edward was a good friend of mine. We played a lot of golf together. Shame about the way he died though. And now, Amelia as well is gone." Reaching for Nick's hand the man introduced himself, "Name's Parker Sims. I have a home down at the end of Wahoo. I see you've got ol' Carson Pike in there working on your car."

Carson stepped out of the car and shook the man's hand. "How goes it, Parker? You get that place of yours fixed up yet?"

"Pretty much. About all I have to do is give her a good painting. You don't happen to know of anybody that could get the job done reasonably, now do ya?"

Nick spoke up, "Tell ya what. I had a painting business in Cincinnati. After I get settled in, I could drop by in a few days and give you an estimate."

"Hey, now that sounds like a plan," bellowed Parker. "My house is next to the last one on Wahoo heading down toward the golf course clubhouse. You can't miss it. The yard is all dug up. Got me some new grass that's going to be planted later in the week. Drop by anytime. I'm usually working on the place. Thanks… gotta run."

Waiting until Parker was across the lot Carson reached under the seat and pulled out a black leather case, the polished wooden handle of the gun the only part that was exposed. Nick looked around to make sure no one else was close to the car. "It's clear!"

Making himself comfortable in the seat, Carson removed the gun from its case and flipped open the cylinder. Spinning it, he confirmed, "Yep… fully loaded and there's a full box of shells ender the seat." Replacing the gun back into the case, Carson looked up at Nick who was leaning in the car. "Do I keep this or do you want to take it back to the house?"

Nick thought for a moment, and then answered, "I think I'll just keep it. I can't believe I'm saying this, but maybe later on you could show me how to use it."

Placing the case back under the seat, Carson smiled. "Be glad to. I'll take you out fishing. We'll go deep out into the marsh and you can practice."

Climbing out of the car, Carson remarked, "Hope all the information you discovered in the last hour or so doesn't ruin your evening dinner plans."

Stepping into the Buick, Nick shook his head. "So far, this has been a very enlightening and confusing day." Backing out of the parking spot, he looked at Carson in wonder. "Hell, I don't even know the girl's name I'm supposed to have dinner with, but that seems rather insignificant when you consider everything else I've learned. See ya around, Carson."

Carson stood and watched the Buick make its way up the street and disappear around the corner. Turning, he started up the side of the building and thought, *I need to keep a close watch on this situation. I promised Amelia I'd look after the boy.*

Chapter Nine

SIX-THIRTY. *RIGHT ON SCHEDULE*, THOUGHT NICK AS HE made the left hand turn onto Rebaut Road in Beaufort. In a few minutes he'd be in Port Royal. He was starving. His lunch at the Boathouse turned out to be no more than three beers. If, whatever her name was didn't show up at the restaurant, he'd go ahead and eat dinner by himself. It might be just as well. He had a lot of things to sort out. His, what he always thought would be a ferry-tale life living on Fripp was running on the very edge of becoming a nightmare. Three people, Khelen Ridley, Genevieve Reign and now Carson Pike had expressed their opinions and there seemed to be no doubt whatsoever, at least in their minds that his grandfather, Edward, had been murdered. Carson knew why, while Khelen and Genevieve, not knowing the actual truth just thought it was strange. On top of that, he had learned his grandfather was a member of a New York crime syndicate and had duped them out of seven million dollars that was hidden somewhere on the property where he now lived. Then there was the loaded gun, which he had taken in the house as Carson suggested. For safe keeping, he hid it in a cookie jar above the kitchen cabinets. He also was faced with the possibility that Charley Sparks and the hulking Derek might pay him a visit at the house, in search of the money Edward had stolen from the organization they were employed by. Things hadn't exactly turned out the way he had planned after talking with Ridley.

Stopping for a red light in Port Royal, he reached over and opened the glove compartment if for no other reason than to see what he could find. Aside from a new owner's manual and some folded napkins the compartment was empty. He looked down at the odometer when the light changed and pulled out: 2717 miles. Smiling, he once again realized how fortunate he was. Just a week ago he was a twenty-seven year old business failure and now, at least according to Amelia's attorney, he was a multi-millionaire. But the more he thought about it the more he realized his new life of luxury living on Fripp had been overshadowed by a dark foreboding cloud that seemed to be getting darker by the day as he continued to discover things about his grandparents he would never have imagined. For some reason, he thought about the RPS Killer and the eight girls he had killed. Even though tragic, he was not directly involved in that situation, so at the moment, it was the farthest thing from his mind. He had enough potential problems of his own that he may or may not have to deal with. Pulling into the Dockside parking lot he thought, *Screw it! I'm going to enjoy a nice dinner with or without the girl from the beach.*

Parking the Lexus at the far edge of the gravel lot next to a grassy field, he hoped he was parked out far enough so the new car wouldn't get banged or scraped by some tourist opening their car door and hitting his. He looked at his watch: 6:45. He was going to be a little early. *A little early for what?* he thought. *A dinner date that was doomed from the very beginning... that's what!* If the girl showed up—it would be nothing short of a miracle.

He hadn't been to the Dockside in years but it looked the same: a white, one-story structure with a red roof and fronted by a welcoming porch lined with old benches and rocking chairs. To the right there were a number of fishing boats docked in Battery Creek. Just like always there were pelicans and seagulls perched high up on the masts as they flapped their wings and fluttered about.

Inside, he was greeted by a young hostess who asked him how many there were going to be for dinner.

"Two," responded Nick. "At least I think. I may be dining by myself. If the other individual doesn't show, then it'll just be me. Can we be seated between seven and seven-thirty?"

"Not a problem, sir. Would you care to wait outside or at the bar?"

"The bar will be fine. It's way too hot to sit outside for any length of time."

"Very well then, sir. We should have a table available around seven-fifteen. We'll announce your name."

Walking through a section of the dining room, he veered to the right and entered a dark, cozy sitting area attached to the rustic bar. Pulling out a bar stool, he ordered a beer and looked up at a television mounted on the wall. A female reporter was interviewing another woman. Nick didn't pay any attention until he heard the words: RPS Killer!

Focusing on the program, he watched intently when the reporter asked the woman, "Why do you think all of the victims have been abducted in the Savannah area?"

The other woman crossed her legs, smoothed her dress and answered, "I've been profiling killers for over twenty-five years. This case had been going on for just over two years now and we still don't seem to have a handle on any sort of motive. To answer your question, Alice, I believe the killer lives in the area."

"You mean over in Georgia?"

"Not necessarily. He could live over in the Savannah area or maybe even right here in Beaufort. It's still puzzling why he transports the girls across the state line over to the islands and then kills them here."

His interest in the program was interrupted by a pleasant voice, "Well, I'll be, I really didn't think you would show."

Nick turned on the stool and there she stood: bright yellow and white flowered summer dress, pearl necklace and fashionable sandals, her short blond hair neatly held in place with a white flower. Removing her sunglasses, she gave him a big smile.

Nick was taken by surprise and he didn't respond so she just sat on the stool next to him and tilted her head. "Cat got your tongue?"

"No... no," said Nick, "it's just that I wasn't expecting you."

"Then why are you here if you weren't expecting me?"

"Well, with the way everything went down on the beach earlier, I thought maybe you were just kidding. The reason I came is because if you did show up and I didn't... well, then I'd wind up looking like even more of an idiot than I must have seemed on the beach."

Signaling the barkeep, she spoke, "I'll have a Long Island Iced Tea please."

Nick spoke quickly, "And put that on my tab."

"No, I'll have my own tab, thank you."

The barkeep apologized, "I'm sorry. I thought you two were together."

Nick, seeing that things were getting confusing nodded at the girl and commented, "We are together, but we're not... sort of."

The barkeep raised his hands, "Let me just get that drink."

There was a brief moment of silence and Nick knew he had to say something. "Uh... are you from the area? I mean do you live on Fripp or are you on vacation?"

The girl answered all three questions at once. "Born and raised in Beaufort, currently live over in Savannah, and I am on vacation at Fripp, visiting three of my high school friends."

"Oh, I see. Do any of your friends live on the island?"

"Yes. My best friend lives there. She was raised on Fripp. A few years ago her parents moved to Florida and she bought their house."

Her drink was no sooner placed in front of her when she picked it up and held it in a toasting fashion, "My name is Shelby Lee Pickett."

Tapping his beer bottle on the side of her glass, Nick responded, "Nicholas Falco. My friends call me Nick."

"My friends call me Rebel, but I'm not quite sure that we are or will even become friends."

Nick was just about to take a drink, but hesitated and thought about what she said. Repeating her name, "Shelby Lee Pickett," he nodded his head as if he understood. "And your friends call you Rebel. Is there some sort of Civil War connection to your name? I'm far from an expert on the war, but I do know General Robert E. Lee, at one time, commanded the entire Confederate army and General George Pickett was at Gettysburg with Lee. Combine those two with the word Rebel which the confederates were referred to and, well it's obvious, someone in your family named you after southern generals, or I guess it could be a coincidence."

"No coincidence. My father is a distant relative of George Pickett. He also feels Robert E. Lee was the greatest American general ever and Jo Shelby was the most effective Calvary officer during the war. So, I guess it only made sense to my father that when I came into the world I'd be Shelby Lee Pickett. My father is a walking encyclopedia when it comes to the Civil War. He is a bit of a dinosaur when it comes to the way we live today. He is of the opinion Abraham Lincoln should have never freed the slaves and our economy and state of our country is the way it is because the south just gave up too easy. When I was growing up as a kid, I learned at an early age to never bring up anything around him about the Civil War. My mother always says, 'Dad is still fighting the war!' It wasn't until junior high that my friends started to call me Rebel and it just sort of stuck." Taking another drink, she asked, "How is it you know so much about the war?"

Nick laughed. "I don't know anything at all about the Civil War, except what they taught in school. I was always fond of history. Guess I just paid attention during class."

The conversation was interrupted by a pleasant voice from behind them, "Falco. Your table is ready."

Getting up, Nick gestured toward the dining area. "That's us!"

Seated at a window table, Shelby asked, "Have you ever eaten here before?"

Nick picked up a menu. "Yes I have. My grandparents always brought me here when I was down on vacation as a kid. That was a long time ago."

"I take it you're not from this area. I noticed you have a northern accent."

"I'm from Ohio, actually Cincinnati. I had a painting company up there but I just recently moved here to Fripp Island. Like I told you on the beach, I inherited my grandmother's home. I've only been here for about a week."

"Do you like Fripp?"

"I love Fripp! Moving here is something I would have never imagined happening to me."

A waitress waited patiently by their table until she could get a word in. Finally, she politely asked, "What can I get you guys to drink?"

Holding up her mixed drink, Shelby answered, "I'll have ice water and another Long Island Iced Tea."

Nick chimed in, "Another beer for me and water."

The waitress left the table and Shelby stood. "Will you excuse me? I have to use the ladies room."

Nick watched her walk across the room. Turning back to the table, he thought the evening, so far, was going okay. He was glad he had decided to show up. Considering this was the first time in five years he had spent an evening with a woman, he thought he was holding his own. Gazing casually around the large dining room, his eyes stopped at a table near the back wall where none other than Derek was staring directly at him. The next thing he knew Sparks sat next to Derek and removed his sunglasses. Nick wanted to look away but he just couldn't believe they were eating at the same place he was. *This can't be a coincidence,* he thought. *Those bastards followed me here!*

Pissed, Nick brazenly got up and approached their table. Derek just grinned while Sparks remained poker-faced. Leaning on their table, Nick spoke in a low voice, "Why can't you idiots leave me be? I don't want any trouble. For once I'd like to get through a complete day without you two on my ass!"

Derek was about to speak, but Sparks held up his hand for silence and then he responded, "Take it easy Falco. We're here having dinner just like you and your lady friend. Now, why don't you go back to your table and mind your own business."

"You're the ones who need to mind your own business. I was talking with Carson Pike earlier today and we talked about you two. He told me if you bothered me again that he'd take care of you."

Derek half stood, displaying his anger. "You can tell Pike whatever you want. He doesn't scare me one little bit!"

Looking around the restaurant, Sparks tugged on Derek's sleeve and whispered an order, "Derek... sit down... now!"

Smiling at Nick, Sparks continued, "Why don't you go back to your table. Your date is returning." With that, he picked up a menu and ignored the fact that Nick was still standing at the table. Derek sarcastically waved his hand in agreement with his partner.

Frustrated, Nick returned to his table at the same time as Shelby. Nodding at Sparks and Derek, she asked, "Friends of yours?"

Nick quickly changed his attitude since explaining who the men really were and why they were following him was just too complex. "No, not really. They just work for the same company my grandfather worked for. I really don't know them at all. We just met this week."

Looking over at the men, Shelby sat down and remarked, "That big man keeps staring over here at us. He really doesn't look all that friendly."

Lying, Nick thought quickly, "Don't pay him an attention. He's an oddball."

As she continued to stare back at Derek, Nick suddenly noticed something about her. "I've seen you before... I mean before we met on the beach. It just suddenly hit me where I saw you. You were at Publix a few days back... right?"

"Yes, I was there. I was there with my friends. I don't recall seeing you though."

"I was checking out when I noticed you and three other girls over by the liquor department. There was a rather large man that appeared to be having a disagreement with you. I couldn't hear everything that was said, but the exchange was loud and then you shoved the man, he yelled at you and then stormed out, knocking over a magazine display. That was you... right?" Not waiting for her answer, he went on, "I know it was you because the four of you pulled out in front of me in a Jeep and I followed you all the way out to Fripp."

The waitress returned with their drinks and asked if they were ready to order. Nick politely answered, "We're going to need a couple of minutes. We haven't even looked over the menu yet. Thank you."

"I already know what I want," said Shelby. "Seafood combo. I get it every time I come here."

Scanning the menu, Nick decided quickly and ordered, "I think I'm going to go with the crab cakes and maybe some clam chowder."

Finishing off his beer, Nick opened up a new topic. "You said you were raised in Beaufort. How did you wind up living in Savannah?"

Sitting back in her chair, she rolled her eyes. "Now that is a long and boring tale. I don't want to ruin your dinner with a doom and gloom story."

"I can handle doom and gloom. Since I've moved down here, in just the past week, I've had a dose of my own personal doom and gloom."

Laughing, she raised her glass and toasted Nick. "Well then, here's to our sad lives!" Wiping her mouth with a napkin, she started her explanation, "I was raised in Beaufort. I guess you could say I had an average, lowcountry, southern girl life growing up. My father is a plumber and my mother works part-time at a local florist. I was always a tom-boy sort of female, that is until I got to high school, when according to my mother I blossomed into an attractive young lady. My past tom-boy ways enabled me to land a position on the cheerleading squad and that's where I met my three best friends; the girls you saw me with at Publix. Anyway, my junior year, we decided to stay at my aunt's condo over on Foley Island, down by Charleston. We went to the beach daily: sun bathed, played Frisbee, took some beer down to the beach in our coolers. We were looking forward to a great summer before our senior year started."

She stopped talking when she saw the waitress approaching with their meals. "I think our food is up!"

The waitress placed the two plates of steaming seafood on the table, asked if there was anything else, then departed saying she'd be back to check on them.

Picking up a roll, Nick buttered it and took a bite. Shelby cleared her throat and asked, "You don't mind if we bless the food, do you?"

Embarrassed, Nick stopped chewing, his right cheek filled with the hot bread. Swallowing the bite, he apologized. "I'm so sorry. No, go right ahead. By all means. Bless the food."

Shelby bowed her head and after a short blessing looked across the table at him as if nothing had even happened. "Everything looks so good. Let's dig in!"

Nick, wanting desperately to get beyond his lack of Godliness stabbed a section of steamed broccoli. "So you were on Foley Beach having a great time with your cheerleader friends."

Cutting into her piece of fish, she answered, "Yes, we were having a great time, except for all the bothersome boys that were like a swarm of locusts. A real pain in the ass is what they were: immature, rude, impolite... you name it. Believe me, when you're a cheerleader you meet them all: the wannabe studs, the jocks, the nerds. Then, one Saturday up the beach struts these four boys: they looked like they were on a team. They all had very trim haircuts and appeared to be in great physical condition. They even had on the same identical swimsuits. They stopped to talk with us. They were so polite and courteous, quite different from the boys we were used to dealing with. Turns out they were senior cadets from a military school near Charleston."

Pointing his fork at Shelby, Nick confirmed, "Yeah, I've heard of military schools. They're quite prestigious. Didn't mean to interrupt. Please continue."

"We spent the rest of the day with them, just sitting around talking and enjoying one another's company. That evening, when the day came to an end, we agreed to meet them on the beach the next day for a picnic. Looking back, that was an incredible summer. Every weekend those boys would meet us on the beach. We'd played touch football, volley ball, built sand castles and swam in the ocean. As the weeks passed by, I fell in love with one of the cadets by the name of Harold. Then, one evening the stars and the ocean and my emotions got the best of me and I lost my virginity right there under the moonlight on Foley Beach." Taking a really long drink of alcohol, she smiled sadly, "Here's to being a seventeen-year-old, dumb ass, blond cheerleader!"

Nick could sense a tone of bitterness in her voice. Not quite sure what to say, he dunked a bite of crab cake into some tartar sauce and commented, "Hey, we all have to lose our virginity at some point in life." Realizing that what he had said might be out of line, he apologized, "I'm sorry, but I couldn't think of anything else to say. First of all, I didn't expect you to show up here tonight and then on top of that, I would have never imagined we would wind up talking about your virginity."

Surprisingly, Shelby laughed. "It's alright... no offense taken. It was just a stupid mistake I made as a young girl."

"Well then," said Nick. "That's just the way life is."

Popping a shrimp into the side of her mouth, she shook her head, "That's easy for a male to say. You don't have to worry about getting pregnant, which is exactly what happened to me because of my carelessness that night on the beach ten years ago."

Just about to take a bite, Nick stopped and put his fork back down. "So this Harold... what did he say when you told him? I mean... you did tell him... right?"

"Yes, I told him. It was the end of summer and I was getting ready to start my senior year. He became a different person, asking me things like was I sure it was his and how could I be so careless. He had a brilliant military career ahead of him. He told me he couldn't afford to be strapped down with a wife and baby. After that, he stopped taking my calls and wouldn't return my letters. I really didn't know where he lived. I was alone... and pregnant. Finally, I had no choice. I confronted my parents with the fact that I was with child. They were quite upset, but after a few days they were supportive. My mother seemed to be more compassionate but my father was pissed beyond belief. He contacted the military academy and explained the situation and managed to get Harold's home address. Turned out, he lived right there in Charleston. My father contacted Harold's parents. Can you believe it? They didn't even know their son was the father of my child. He never said a word to his folks. Seemingly, quite concerned Harold's father invited us to their home in Charleston to further discuss the dilemma."

Interested, Nick asked, "And how did that turn out?"

"Not well. Harold's parents were extremely wealthy and Harold was a fifth generation military cadet. His father is a retired admiral in the Navy and very influential in the community and at the school. The meeting was embarrassing: my father, the plumber and my mother, the part-time florist along with myself sat in the elaborate sitting room in their mansion across from Harold, his parents and their family lawyer."

Crossing her arms as if she were reliving the moment, Shelby went on to explain, "Harold said he didn't love me and therefore had no obligation to marry me, and besides that, stated the night on the beach had been consensual. He hadn't forced himself on me or raped me. It was at this point their lawyer did most of the talking on their behalf. He said the family was aware of Harold's responsibility as a father, and if I wanted to abort the child they would pay for everything. My mother and I had already decided I was going to keep the child. Abortion was not an option. Following some heated words between my father and their lawyer, we were offered a settlement of twenty thousand dollars. Needless to say we left their home that day realizing without a lawyer in our corner, Harold Theodore Benjamin V was going to skate for just twenty grand. Twenty thousand dollars was a lot of money to me back then, but it was nothing more than chump change to Harold's family."

Shelby hesitated in her story, which gave Nick an opportunity to ask, "So for a lousy twenty grand, this Harold character gets to walk away leaving you holding the bag?"

"I'm sure that's what the Benjamin's and their lawyer thought too, but my father just couldn't stomach the way they had blown us off, let alone their lack of concern for the baby I was carrying. He contacted a lawyer in Beaufort by the name of Khelen Ridley—"

At the name of Ridley, Nick instantly cut her off, "You said Khelen Ridley! What a coincidence. I just talked with him earlier this week. He was the one who handled my grandmother's will and who walked me through the inheritance. He handled my grandparents' affairs for years."

Pushing her plate to the side, she remarked, "Well, you know what they say about it being a small world!" Placing her silverware on the plate, she went on, "My father hired Ridley to see if something could be done. Khelen said he'd drive over to Charleston and speak with their lawyer. He guaranteed my father he'd come back with a better deal... a far better deal. A week later Ridley called us into his office where he presented me with a cashier's check for two hundred thousand dollars. The Benjamin's lawyer, at first, didn't want to cooperate, but after Ridley threatened to go to the newspaper in Charleston and to the academy, Mr. Benjamin wrote the check. On top of that, Harold T. Benjamin V was expelled from the school with disgrace, which pissed off his father to no end. Thus ends the doom and gloom tale of my past life."

"That can't be the end of the tale," said Nick. "What about the baby you were carrying?"

"That has nothing to do with the doom and gloom part of the story. If anything, my daughter, Kirby is the best part of the entire story. She just turned nine and she's cute as a button. I put the money from the settlement in the bank and after graduating I attended the University of South Carolina where I acquired a degree in business. Shortly after I graduated college, I got a great job over in Savannah working as a legal secretary for a prestigious law firm. I've been there five years now and I was just recently promoted to head secretary for the four lawyers who own the business. So, this tale does have a happy ending."

"And what about Harold, whatever his middle name was, Benjamin V?"

"I did see him again. Not by choice, but our paths did cross. I was in my freshmen year at college. It was right before Thanksgiving. I was walking across campus when out from behind a tree pops Harold. Apparently, he had been waiting for me. He had changed; he no longer held that sharp military look cadets seem to have about them. His hair had grown out and he had a light beard. He was dressed sloppily in jeans and a sweat shirt. The conversation, if you want to call it that was short and to the point, with him doing all the talking. In short, he told me his father had disowned him because he had dishonored the family tradition of men graduating from the academy. The illustrious military career his father had planned for him since the moment he had been born had been ripped away from him. He blamed me for ruining his life; a life of future prosperity and admiration. He stepped close to me and the look in his eyes frightened me. Inches from my face, he told me that he'd get even with me if it's the last thing he did. A group of students I knew approached and could tell I was uncomfortable. Harold turned and ran off into some nearby trees, and to this day I've never seen or heard from him again. That was ten years ago. It bothered me for a few months about what he said, but eventually I got over it and got on with my life."

Her silence indicated the story had come to an end. Nick patted his stomach, yawned and covered his mouth. "That was one good meal *and* quite a story. I don't know about you, but I'm thinking a slice of Key Lime pie sounds good right about now."

Holding up her hands Shelby bloated out her cheeks indicating she couldn't eat another bite. "Not for me… I'm stuffed."

Nick signaled for their waitress and ordered, "We'll have a slice of Key Lime and two forks please." After the waitress left the table, Nick winked at Shelby, "You might change your mind when that pie gets here."

Drumming his fingers on the table, he nodded at her hand and asked, "So I can only assume you've never had a ring on that hand?"

Holding up her left hand and wiggling her fingers, she responded, "Nope… never did marry. To be frank, after my incident with Harold I never wanted to put myself in a position where I could ever get hurt again. Actually, I've got your record beat by three years."

Not quite understanding, Nick repeated her statement in the form of a question, "My record?"

"Yeah... your record. Didn't you tell me when we met on the beach you hadn't dated in five years?"

"That's correct," said Nick, "and you're the one who managed to end my streak of dateless evenings."

Agreeing with him, Shelby held up three fingers and replied, "Like I said: beat your record by three years. Up until last year I didn't date for eight years."

The waitress appeared at the side of the table and announced, "One slice of Key Lime and two forks. Anyone care for coffee?"

Looking across the table, Nick asked, "How about you... coffee?"

Holding up her empty water glass, Shelby smiled, "Just a refill on my water will be fine."

Cutting into the pie, Nick added, "Second that." Placing the first bite of the wonderful dessert in his mouth, he began to chew, but then asked, "I take it from what you said you started up dating again last year?"

"That's correct. I met a fella over in Savannah and we started to see each other. Let's see, I think this coming week will be a year for us. You already met him. Let me rephrase that. You've already seen my boyfriend."

Almost choking on his pie, Nick swallowed the bite and took a swig of water and coughed. "Your boyfriend!"

"Yeah... my boyfriend. He was the man you saw arguing with me and my friends at Publix."

Laying down his fork, Nick emphasized, "That's your boyfriend! I'm missing something here. If you're dating another man why are you here with me?"

"Because this is not what I consider a date. We're just having a pleasant dinner together. Besides that, I'm about to put an end to my relationship with him."

Taking another drink, Nick remarked, "Well, the way you were acting in the grocery store it didn't appear you two were getting along that well, at least for the moment. He seemed... on the violent side."

"His name is Ike Miller and he's an ex-professional football player. He played for the New York Jets for three seasons and then retired after a series of injuries that prevented him from pursuing a professional football career." Shaking her head in disgust, Shelby continued, "For the first few months he was the perfect gentleman; opening doors for me, buying me flowers and taking me everywhere. Kirby, my daughter just loves him. But for the last two months he has changed for some reason. He has become very possessive and controlling. He demands to know where I'm going and what I'm doing. He can be every explosive, just like you witnessed at the grocery. Ike doesn't know it but I'm going to break things off with him. It'll be hard to explain to my daughter, but to be honest with you, the man scares me anymore."

Looking from side to side, Nick asked, "You don't think he'll show up here tonight, do you?"

"Oh... no. Whenever we have a tiff, he doesn't speak to me for a week."

"Thank God. The last thing I need today is to have some ex-football player bust in here and pummel me to a fine powder."

Just then, Charley leaned over and placed his hand on Shelby's shoulder. "Why, hello there. I don't believe we've met. My name is Charley. I just wanted to drop by and wish you two a nice evening. Nick here is a good egg. Dinner is on me." Dropping a fifty dollar bill on the table, he smiled at Nick and walked off. Derek just stood there for a moment, looking at the couple and then left.

Staring at the money, Shelby commented, "I thought you said you didn't know them all that well; that you just met them this week. Seems strange they would want to buy our dinner."

Nick, shocked that Charley had stopped by the table and put his hand on Shelby wasn't quite sure what to say. Blowing off the incident as insignificant, he picked up the fifty and stopped their waitress. "Could we please have our bill?"

Producing the bill from a clipboard she was carrying, she laid it on the table. Nick picked up the bill and waved the fifty at Shelby. "Looks like neither one of us has to pay our tab."

After the bill was paid, Shelby stood and commented, "Well, Mr. Nick Falco, I want you to know I had a nice evening. I've got to head back on over to Fripp, get packed and drive back to Savannah. It's back to the old grind for me come Monday."

Nick stood and gestured toward the door. "At least let me walk you to your car."

Out on the porch, Nick hesitated and looked around for Sparks and Derek, but they were nowhere to be seen. The lot was three-quarters full of cars and the porch was jammed with people waiting for their name to be called for seating. Turning, Shelby pointed at a red Jeep. "That's me... right over there. I think I can make it to my car by myself. Thank you for the evening and the pleasant conversation, Nick."

Realizing the evening was over, Nick smiled and answered, "It was a good evening." Laughing, he remarked. "I know this was not an actual date but I want to thank you for making my first encounter with a female in five years quite pleasant."

Shelby turned and walked off across the lot, then turned back and waved, "My pleasure. Just sayin'!"

Walking across the lot, Nick glanced at his watch: just after nine-thirty. Almost a two and a half hour dinner. They had talked a lot, mostly about her. She seemed like a nice girl. The sun had long since set in the west but the heat still lingered over the lowcountry. It felt like it was still in the mid-eighties. Digging his car keys out of his pocket he turned and watched as Shelby started to climb into her Jeep, when a man appeared from around the side of the vehicle and slammed his fist down on the hood and pointed his other fist at Shelby. From the enormous size of the man, Nick recognized him as the same man he had seen at Publix. It had to be Ike Miller!

Walking quickly across the lot, he wasn't sure what he was doing but he couldn't just leave Shelby to face his wrath on her own. Just when he got a few feet from the Jeep, he heard Ike speaking in a demanding tone. "What the hell do you think you're doin'? I can't trust you anymore! Who was that guy you had dinner with?"

Shelby tried to open the door, but Ike slammed it shut. "You're not goin' anywhere until you explain this to me!" shouted Ike.

Trying to push him away, Shelby raised her voice, "Back off. It was nothing more than a casual dinner. You don't own me. We're not engaged or married. I can go to dinner with whomever I want and it's none of your business!"

"Bullshit," exclaimed Ike. "You're my woman and you'll do what I say. If anyone's goin' to dinner with you... it's gonna be me!" Pushing her up against the side of the door, he got directly in her face. "Why do you do things like this to me? Who was that guy? I should kick his ass... and yours!"

Nick reluctantly stepped forward and tapped the huge man on his shoulder. "Right here I am Miller!"

Shelby pleaded with Nick, "Please, just go home Nick, I can handle this. You don't need to get involved."

"Yes... I do," explained Nick. "He threatened me ...and you. I can't walk away from something like this. It wouldn't be right."

Giving Shelby a slight push, Ike turned and faced Nick. Nick quickly sized up the man: He had to be at least six-foot-six, and weighed in at close to three hundred pounds which appeared to be pure muscle. He had piercing dark eyes set in a face of anger that, at the moment, Nick couldn't imagine anyone wanting to meet up with. Before Nick could even prepare himself for what he thought might come, Ike, who seemed quick as a cat, shoved him violently backward. Nick tried to keep his balance but was taken off-guard. Falling back he tried to reach out as he fell, his upper left arm that was bandaged bumping into the rearview side mirror of an adjacent car. Going down hard, his head hit the gravel lot. Ike stood over him, his fists clenched as he looked down at his helpless victim. "Whoever the hell you are, you just better git before I really get pissed. Nobody takes my woman from me... understand?"

Shelby tired her best to pull Ike away but he pushed her roughly back against the Jeep and yelled, "Get off me woman! I'll deal with you later!"

The slight interruption gave Nick just enough time to get to his feet. *Here goes,* thought Nick as he took two steps and threw a flying leg kick at the man's massive legs. The scissor like movement caused Ike's legs to buckle and surprisingly, he went down. Grabbing a handful of gravel Nick jammed it into his face as Ike rolled over, his arms and legs flailing. By this time three men who had witnessed the confrontation came to Nick's rescue, but even they had a difficult time keeping the big man on the ground.

Getting to his feet, Ike, with both fists clenched pushed his way through the three men with ease, advancing toward Nick who nervously stood his ground. Suddenly Ike was jerked from behind and punched in the stomach, then tossed to the ground by none other than Derek who proceeded to kick the ex-football played in his ribs with three swift hard kicks. Ike, trying his best to breathe, rolled over onto his side as Derek readied himself for another series of kicks. Sparks grabbed Derek by his arm and ordered, "I think that's enough." Bending down, Sparks grabbed Ike's collar and pulled his head up and ordered strongly, "You my dear friend need to get your sorry ass up and out of here if you know what's good for you. Nick here is a friend of ours and we don't appreciate you giving him a hard time. Understand?"

Ike shook his head in agreement and held his side. Sparks turned and addressed Shelby and Nick, "You two better scat before the police show up." With that the two men walked across the lot, got into their sedan and pulled out quickly, leaving a trail of flying gravel behind.

Ike sat up but remained silent. Nick walked to the Jeep and asked Shelby, "Will you be alright?"

Looking at his bleeding arm, Shelby ordered, "Get in the Jeep. I'm running you over to the immediate care center in Beaufort. You can't drive home like that."

Nick disagreed, "But—"

"There's no buts about it," demanded Shelby. "Get in the Jeep!"

A man standing nearby offered Nick a handkerchief and suggested, "I think the young lady is right. You should go have that arm looked at."

Nick looked at his bleeding arm and finally relented, "I guess you're right."

Wrapping the handkerchief around the reopened wound from Cincinnati, he walked around and climbed in the Jeep. Shelby pulled out of the lot, looked in her rearview mirror and commented, "For your first date in five years I'd say this has been quite an experience! Where did you learn to fight like that? I can't believe you took Ike down. That was incredible!"

Dabbing at the open wound with some paper towels Shelby had on the console, Nick answered, "I grew up in a rough part of town in Cincinnati. I had to learn as a young kid to defend myself by any means possible if I wanted to survive the streets."

Making a right hand turn, she reassured him, "We should be at the care center in less than ten minutes. Thanks for being there for me tonight."

Chapter Ten

SHELBY LOOKED UP FROM THE MAGAZINE SHE WAS reading and noted the time on the office clock: 12:15 in the a.m. Taking her cell phone from her purse, she pushed in the number and waited patiently. Her mother never turned in until one in the morning. She knew she would be up watching television. Finally, her mother's voice answered, "Hello."

"Mom... it's Rebel. I'm over here at the immediate care center. I had dinner with a friend tonight and there was a slight accident—"

Before Shelby could even explain, her mother interrupted, "Oh my, are you alright?"

"Yes, I'm fine. My friend just got a cut that needs some attention. Listen... is Kirby in bed?"

"Yes she is. We had pizza for supper and then we played some games. Your father is out at the moment on an emergency plumbing call. I guess somebody's water heater went out. Kirby watched TV with me until just after ten and then she went to bed. Are you still planning on picking her up tonight?"

"No. By the time I get back to Fripp and get packed it could be two in the morning. By the time I'd get Kirby and then drive to Savannah it'll be close to four. Tell her I'll see her sometime tomorrow. And... don't worry. Everything's fine. I'll see you tomorrow afternoon. Good night Mom."

Placing her cell back in her purse she looked up and saw Nick pushing his way through a set of swing doors as he held up his bandaged arm and smiled. "Got my arm re-stitched, some ointment and a prescription to prevent infection." Sitting next to her, he apologized, "Look, I'm really sorry you had to bring me over here. You still have to pack and drive to Savannah tonight."

"Change of plans," said Shelby. "I'll drive to Savannah tomorrow. It's not that big of a deal." Standing, she dangled her keys in the air and suggested, "I guess we better head back over to Port Royal so you can get your car."

Outside in the lot, Nick jumped in the Jeep, turned in the seat and faced Shelby. "Listen, I have an idea. It's up to you, but since you're not going to Savannah tonight, maybe when we get back to Fripp you'd like to join me on the front porch of my grandmother's house and share some wine with me."

Turning out of the lot onto the street, Shelby frowned. "I don't know. It's pretty late. I really should be getting back to my friend's house on the island."

Nick fidgeted with the new bandage on his arm and remarked, "Alright, here's what I'm going to do. When I get back to my house, I'm going to sit on the porch and have a drink... maybe a couple. After the confrontation with your boyfriend, Ike, I think I deserve some alcohol. I'll set out two glasses. If you show... great! If not, that's okay. I won't be offended."

Shelby, still undecided, stopped for a red light and looked across the seat at Nick. "Let's just say, and I'm not making any promises I'll show up, but if I do decide to stop by for a nightcap, which house is your grandmothers?"

Nick eagerly answered, "You can't miss it. It's that big white two-story just past Bonito Drive on Tarpon. I'm sure you've been by it a million times. It has the huge front porch with the Savannah style steps out front and a large, brightly lit fountain in the yard."

The light changed green and Shelby pulled out and held up her hand. "Tell you what. I'll think about it."

Reclining on one of the two expensive white wicker rockers on the porch after placing a bottle of chocolate wine in an ice filled bucket on a small matching wicker table, Nick lit a candle and placed it next to the bucket. *Perfect,* he thought. *If she's coming, it should be any minute now.* Pouring a glass of the light brown wine, a shot of pain raced up his arm. He had taken one of the pain pills when he got back to the house, but apparently the pain relieving benefits hadn't kicked in yet. He looked at the glowing face of his watch: 1:45 in the morning. Taking a sip of wine he thought about what a long day it had been, starting with breakfast with Genevieve, then his walk on the beach where he met Shelby Lee, followed by the revealing discussion with Carson over at the Boathouse, discovering the gun in his grandfather's car, his dinner with Shelby and finally a mismatched fight with Ike Miller which resulted in an unexpected trip to the immediate care center. Taking another long drink, he got up to check the temperature on a thermometer at the far end of the porch when he saw Shelby's red Jeep turn into the driveway. Smiling to himself, he thought, *The evening is not over.*

Climbing out of her Jeep, Shelby stood at the bottom of the steps and looked at the elevated porch. Starting up the steps, she remarked, "I thought this was the house you were talking about but I wasn't sure. And you're right. I have passed this place a million times. I always wondered who lived here. In all the years I've been coming to Fripp I never once saw anyone on the porch or mowing the grass. I figured it was someone's summer home." At the top of the steps, she ran her hand over the gleaming white railing and looked at the three giant hanging ferns suspended in brass urns. "These must have belonged to your grandmother. I say that because ever since I can remember there has always been a number of hanging plants displayed on the porch."

Standing and offering Shelby a seat, Nick responded and gestured with his wine glass, "Yes, they were my grandmother's, along with everything else around here."

Taking a seat, Shelby asked, "You said you just inherited the home. How did that come to be?"

Pouring her a glass of wine he was surprised she didn't know about his grandmother's death. He gave her a sideways look and answered, "She passed away about a week and a half ago. I'm surprised that being here on the island you didn't hear about her death. She was probably the most popular person living here on Fripp. Lived here for thirty-five years with her husband, my grandfather, Edward."

Looking at the wine and then taking a taste, she raised her eyebrows. "This is very good. It's almost like a spiked chocolate milk." Getting back to what they had been discussing, she emphasized, "Remember, I don't live here. I just visit my friend once a year. Maybe she knew your grandparents. I don't know."

Kicking off her sandals, she asked, "If you don't mind me asking... how did your grandmother die?"

Nick reached for the bottle and answered, "She passed away in her sleep."

"Is your grandfather still alive?"

"No, he died in an automobile accident about six months ago, so now the house and everything they owned has been passed on to me, including that new Lexus I drove tonight."

Shelby brushed a lock of hair away from her face and looked out into the darkness beyond the fountain. "I want you to know I just didn't drop by tonight for the wine. Remember, tonight at dinner when we both stated we had some doom and gloom in our lives?"

Not waiting for Nick to respond, she elaborated, "All we talked about was my past life and the problems I've faced. We never got into what doom and gloom you have faced recently. So, I'm here to listen to your story now."

Nick wanted desperately to share his recent problems with Charley Sparks and Derek with someone other than Carson Pike but the girl sitting across from him he had known less than twenty-four hours. Little did she know there was a lot more to the presence of the two men at the restaurant earlier in the evening. He certainly couldn't mention anything about his grandfather's involvement with a crime syndicate. Carson told him no one on the island was to know. He couldn't tell her about the gun they had found in the Buick or the massive amount of money hidden somewhere on the property. His doom and gloom story would have to be prior to coming to Fripp.

Waving his hand like it really wasn't all that important, Nick spoke, "My past life is not nearby as interesting as yours. In short, I grew up in a rough neighborhood in Cincinnati. About the only part of my childhood I really enjoyed is when I came here to Fripp for the summer as a youngster. My grandmother was always looking out for me. She paid for my college education and I graduated with a degree in business. I started a painting business that, after five years, turned out to be a flop. Just two weeks ago, I was a few months short of being flat broke, my van wasn't running and I got kicked out of the place where I was living because I was two months behind on the rent. On top of everything else, I received the call that my grandmother had passed away. I drove down for the service and found out I needed to talk with her attorney, which resulted in the inheritance of the house and all her belongings. So, I guess my doom and gloom story has a happy ending too... well, except for this." Nick held up his bandaged arm and laughed.

Shelby got up, walked to the railing and took a drink. "Look. I'm sorry for what happened with Ike. I should have known better than to meet someone with Ike being so upset about the way our relationship has been going. First of all, I really didn't think you would show up and I sure as hell didn't expect Ike to drop by. If it wouldn't have been for your two friends, your injuries could have been much worse." Placing her glass on the top rail, she pondered, "Speaking of those two men. They sure were an odd pair. If I recall you said you had just met them and you really didn't know them that well. It seems so strange they would buy our dinner and then come to your rescue out on the lot. And the way they took off out of there… that was strange. It almost seemed like they wanted to leave before the potential arrival of the police."

"Like I said before," lied Nick. "They're just some men who worked with my grandfather." Nick, wanting to get off the subject of the men, went in a different direction and asked, "How in the world did you ever get involved with Ike in the first place?"

Her glass now empty, Shelby walked back to the table and poured herself another glass and returned to her chair. "Ike Miler is a hometown hero in Savannah. He was a big football hero while in high school, leading one of the local schools to two state championships. After he graduated, he went to the University of Georgia where he continued to fascinate football fans with his gifted running abilities. They say he was considered as a candidate for the Heisman Trophy, but that didn't pan out. Even though, he still went high in the draft and entered the NFL. I already told you about how his career was cut short because of injuries. He came back to Savannah where he was treated like royalty. He presently owns one of the biggest car dealerships in town, a restaurant and more real estate properties than you can imagine. He does a lot of public speaking in the Savannah area and is involved in every fundraiser the community sponsors. When it comes to Ike Miller… he's Savannah's golden boy."

Yawning, she placed her hand over her mouth, then continued, "I met him at a fundraiser for the homeless where the legal firm I am employed by was a major sponsor. I'll never forget that day. I was struggling with a tent our company was putting up when Ike strolls by and gives me a hand. We started to talk and well, you know the rest of the story."

"Based upon what you've told me," said Nick, "I don't understand how he could be, as you say, Savannah's golden boy with the violent temper he has."

"He hasn't always been like that. Even now, when he's around people he does business with or at functions around town, he's quite the gentleman. His tough guy attitude has just erupted in the last few months and that's only when he's with me. It's not all the time, but it's enough that I'm beginning to see red flags… warning signs, if you will. I figure it this way. I've got to break things off with him now, before things get out of hand. I don't want to wind up like the women you always hear about. Ya know, the ones who know the man they are dating has a problem with violence, but they think they can change the man, so they marry up with them and then *bang!* They find themselves in an abusive marriage with no easy way out. That's not for me. I'm not going to go down that road. I'm getting out now while I can."

"Does anyone other than me know about Ike's temper?"

"My three friends and, of course, my mother... and then there's you."

"Well, for what it's worth. I think you're doing the right thing by breaking it off."

Sinking down further into the chair, Shelby took a drink and remarked in a relaxed tone, "It's really peaceful out here on the porch."

The sound of raindrops began to peck at the porch roof. Nick smiled and reached for the bottle. "I just love it out here on the porch when it rains. When I was a youngster and I'd come down here to visit my grandparents, sometimes late at night or in the early morning, especially if it started to rain, I'd sneak down the stairs, grab a glass of iced tea and a bowl of chips or pretzels and I'd come out here on the porch and sit and listen to the rain."

Shelby gulped down the last of the wine in her glass and stood. "It's late. What time is it? I better be getting back to my friend's house."

Nick looked at his watch and announced, "Two-forty-five."

"Listen," said Shelby, "I really did have a wonderful evening and I apologize again for your run-in with Ike. Maybe we could do this again sometime?"

Nick stood as Shelby made her way down the steps in the light rain when she stopped and raised her right hand. "Did you hear that?"

"Hear what?" said Nick

Cocking her head toward the street, she looked back at Nick. "I swear I heard someone calling out."

Nick made an odd face. "At this time of night?"

Shelby held a finger to her lips for silence and went down the stairs the rest of the way, walking toward the fountain. "There... there it is again. Someone called for help!"

Nick, now at her side, walked beyond the fountain and out toward the dark street. "You're right... I heard it to."

The rain started to pick up and then they both heard a woman's panicked voice, "Help... help me!"

A flash of lightning lit up the street for a second. Shelby pointed and exclaimed loudly, "There... on the side of the street. A person. Did you see them?"

Nick, who had been looking on the opposite side of the street answered, "No, I didn't see anyone."

"Wait here," said Shelby. "I have a flashlight in my Jeep."

Nick heard the voice again: "Please... someone help me!" Peering into the darkness, he wiped the rain from his face when Shelby returned with the light.

Crossing the grass, Shelby started up the side of the road, Nick at her side. A loud crack of lightning caused them to both wince when they came to the very edge of the property. The voice sounded again, "Help... help me!"

Shining the flashlight into some bushes, the beam revealed a girl in a two-piece bathing suit, down on her knees, her arms wrapped around her bare muddy shoulders. Shelby instantly knelt down next to the girl and shined the light into her face. The girl's face was smeared with mud and she had a bloody cut on her right cheek. Handing the light to Nick, Shelby placed her hand gently on the girl's right shoulder and asked softly, "Are you alright? What happened to you?"

The girl seemed traumatized and tried her best to communicate, "I... I... walked in... from... the marsh! He could... have killed... me but, he let... me go! Please... help me... Please!"

"Give me a hand," said Shelby. "We need to get her inside out of this rain."

Nick took the girl's left arm and Shelby the right and raised her to her feet. The girl, extremely weak, began to crumble back to the ground. Nick handed the light to Shelby and picked the girl up. "I'm going to carry her. The front door to the house is unlocked."

Shelby ran ahead of Nick and up the steps to the front door. Nick carefully made his way back up the road and crossed the grass. The girl looked up into his face and forced a weak smile, "Thank you... thank you... so much."

Trying his best to reassure the young girl, Nick spoke to her with compassion, "It's okay. You're safe now. Don't try to talk. I'll have you inside out of the rain in a few seconds."

A bolt of lightning hit nearby, causing Nick to wince and stumble on the very first porch step. Down he went, the girl falling onto the steps, Nick landing on his injured arm. The pain was excruciating, but he ignored it and apologized to the girl, "I'm sorry. Just hold on. All we have to do is get up these steps."

Shelby, who was standing by the front door, went to the edge of the steps and shouted, "Are you alright?"

On the third step, Nick yelled back, "I'm fine, just get the door open. When we get inside I'm taking her into the sitting room on the left. There's a couch against the wall that has an afghan thrown over the back. Lay that on the couch. We'll put her there."

Racing inside, Shelby located the afghan and spread it on the couch while Nick slowly traversed the steps. Once on the porch, he stopped for a breather then proceeded inside the house, closing the door behind him with his foot. It was only a matter of a few seconds before he laid the girl gently down onto the afghan. The girl, realizing she was now safe, reached up to Shelby and asked, "Can... I please... have a glass... of water?"

"I'll get the water," said Nick. "See if you can find out what happened to her."

Shelby pushed the girl's long matted blond hair from her mud-caked face and examined her mud-stained body to the best of her ability. "How did you get so muddy? Where did you come from?"

Nick, back with the water, handed the glass to Shelby, who lowered the glass to the girl's lips. The girl took three swallows then a deep breath and finally answered the questions, "I've been swimming... and walking... in the marsh for hours. I didn't think I was going to make it. I just kept moving toward the light."

Confused, Nick repeated, "The light, what light?"

The girl raised one of her muddy hands. "The light from the island. He told me to walk toward the light. He let me go. I won the... game!"

Shelby turned and whispered to Nick. "Oh my God! I think she's talking about the RPS Killer."

The girl, finally calming down, overheard what Shelby said and tried to sit up. "That's him, the RPS man! We played the game and I won. He let me go! I need to call my parents. I'm from Savannah."

"Okay," said Shelby, "but first things first. If you did encounter the RPS Killer then we need to call the police." Turning to Nick, she suggested, "Why don't you call the police and I'll see about getting her cleaned up some."

"I don't think that's a wise thing to do," interjected Nick. "I think we should notify the police but if we start cleaning her up we might be tampering with evidence of some sort."

Shelby realized he was right and turned back to the girl. "What's your name, honey?"

"Amanda Schrock, and like I said, I'm from Savannah. I was just leaving the beach when all of a sudden I blacked out and the next thing I knew I woke up in the woods..."

"Don't try and explain right now. We're going to contact the police."

"That's right," chimed in Nick. "I'm going to call island security and let them take care of calling over to Beaufort. They'll know what needs to be done."

Going into the kitchen, Nick looked at his grandmother's post-it note of handwritten important phone numbers stuck on the front of the refrigerator. Using his cell phone he punched in a number and waited. On the second ring, there was an answer, "Fripp Island Security. Connie speaking."

Nick really hadn't thought about what he was going to say, but suddenly a sense of nervousness seemed to overwhelm him. "Ah... my name is Nick Falco. I live at 942 Tarpon here on the island. I just had a young girl stumble onto my property. I'm not sure about the extent of her injuries but I think she may need some medical attention, so we might need an ambulance over here. I also think this may have something to do with the RPS Killer. How soon can someone be here?"

Connie, writing short notes on a pad of paper, responded, "I'll have someone there in less than five minutes. The ambulance will have to be called in either from Ladies Island or Beaufort. It could be a good twenty minutes or so before they roll in. I'm also going to contact the Beaufort Police. Is the girl conscious?"

"Yes. Aside from being covered in mud, she has some cuts and bruises. She is awake and responding to all the questions we asked her."

"Just keep her calm Mr. Falco and we'll be there directly."

Running back to the sitting room, Nick nodded at the girl and spoke to Shelby, "They said they'd be here in about five minutes. How's she doing?"

"Poor thing," said Shelby. "She looks exhausted. I told her to shut her eyes and try to rest. She seems to be breathing normally." Getting up, she sat in a nearby chair and looked out the bay window. "I guess I'm not going to get back to my friend's house as soon as I thought. This could wind up being a long night. I'm sure the police will have a lot of questions for us."

Picking the flashlight up from a small table, Nick started for the front door. "Keep an eye on her. I'm going out front and wait for security."

He stood at the edge of the steps and looked out at the rain. A gust of wind blew out the candle on the porch. Walking back to the window he looked through the lacy curtains and could see Shelby sitting quietly next to the girl. Shaking his head in wonder, he thought about everything that had happened to him since he had moved to Fripp. It was just one thing after another. Despite all the problems that seemed to be plaguing him, the one thing he hadn't been involved with was this RPS serial killer who was dropping girls off or near Fripp and had been for the past two years. But now that had even changed. If the girl lying on his couch had been one of the killer's potential victims, his involvement, as small as it might be, was just another unexpected situation that was being added to his portfolio of problems.

Problems! thought Nick. Everyone has problems of some sort: from the most simplistic thing like burning your morning toast to complex situations like losing your job or being involved in an automobile accident. It seemed that problems were a thinking, breathing entity, with no pity, whatsoever and had a way of screwing up your day. One problem didn't wait in line until a current problem was solved; they just kept piling up, making your life more frustrating.

Pulling his collar up around his neck, he walked across the yard to the edge of the street where he saw an approaching vehicle in the distance, its headlights piercing the darkness and the rain. It had to be island security. Who else would be out this time of night? When the vehicle was close enough for him to see it was the local authorities, he moved the flashlight up and down. The Fripp Island Security car turned left and parked in the driveway behind Shelby's Jeep.

An officer wearing a rain slicker and a hat stepped out of the car and instantly asked, "Are you Mr. Falco?"

Nick, shining the light on the officer, answered, "Yes sir, I'm the one who called."

Looking at the house, the officer introduced himself, "I'm officer Kemp. Where is the girl?"

Pointing the light at the house, Nick responded and started toward the steps. "She's inside in the front room. We've got her on the couch. She seems alright, but when we first found her she was scared out of her wits. I think she's calmed down quite a bit."

The officer followed and spoke, "The chief should be here in about a half hour. We called the Beaufort Police and we're getting an ambulance out here. How long has it been since you discovered her?"

Nick looked at his watch. "I guess about twenty minutes give or take."

Opening the front door, Nick gestured toward the couch. "She's right over there." As the officer approached, Nick made introductions, "Shelby Lee Pickett... Officer Kemp."

Kemp removed his hat and laid it on an end table and looked down at the girl whose eyes were wide open. Taking a pad from his shirt pocket, he clicked an ink pen and asked, "Are you up to answering some questions?"

"Yes... I am, but you need to notify my parents. They must be worried sick. I should have been home hours ago."

Nodding, Kemp smiled in agreement. "If you'll just give me their number, I'll call it into our office and they'll make the call."

"Thank you," said Amanda. "I'd rather not say too much until they get here, if that's alright."

Kemp gave Amanda a strange look and explained in a professional manner, "Young lady, let me explain something to you. I know from the looks of you that you've probably been through hell, but if you indeed had a run-in with the RPS Killer, it's important we get on this immediately. We've been trying to catch this killer for two years, so anything you can tell us will be of great help."

Wincing in pain, Amanda raised up on her bare elbows and took a deep breath. "It was officer Kemp, right?"

"That's correct."

"I don't mean you any disrespect, officer, but my parents didn't raise me up to be a fool. My father just so happens to be a lawyer over in Savannah. He always taught me to be careful what I say and who I say it to. I'd just as soon wait until my parents are present before I start answering all your questions."

Before Kemp could react, Shelby broke in on the conversation, "Schrock... Amanda Schrock! Your father's name wouldn't happen to be Franklin Schrock now would it."

Surprised, Amanda asked, "Yes it is. Do you know my father?"

"If he's the same Franklin Schrock of Wheller, James, Schrock and Levawitz Law Firm in Savannah. I not only know him, but I work for him."

Rather than being surprised that Shelby worked for her father, she tried to sit up and remarked sarcastically, "A lot of people work for my father."

Shelby looked at Nick and gave him a slight rolling of her eyes and then suggested to Amanda, "I think it would be best if you don't try to get up until medical help arrives."

Despite Shelby's advice, Amanda tried to stand but the severe pain in her feet caused her to sit back down as tears filled her eyes. Rolling up into a fetal position, Amanda groaned, "Why do my... feet... hurt so bad?"

Kemp leaned over and closely examined the bottoms of her muddy feet. "You have a number of broken shells in your feet. Where did you come from before you arrived here at the house?"

Wiping her face, Amanda, reiterated, "I don't want to talk about it until my parents are here."

Shelby stood and motioned silently for the officer to step back out into the foyer as she spoke softly to Nick. "Stay here with her. We'll be right back."

Standing by the front door, Shelby looked back at the girl who had closed her eyes once again. "When we first found her, she told us she had walked in from the marsh. That's probably where she picked up the shells. She told us she had been walking and swimming for hours. She said something about walking toward the light. I think she may have been referring to the lights over by the marina. She mumbled about winning the game and that *he* had let her go. Based on what she said we just assumed it was the RPS Killer and when we mentioned it, she agreed with us."

The chiming doorbell startled both Kemp and Shelby. Shelby, thinking it was the ambulance or additional police, opened the door and was confronted by an older woman. The woman, without waiting to be invited in pushed her way by Kemp and asked, "Is Nick at home?"

Nick looked toward the foyer and saw Genevieve walking into the sitting room. "Genevieve... what are you doing here?"

"What am I doing? I'm a concerned neighbor. Three in the morning, island security in your driveway. The question is: what the hell are you doing?"

Seeing the mud-covered girl lying on the couch, she put her hand to her mouth, "What the—"

Before she could finish speaking, Nick rose to his feet and intercepted her. "Genevieve! I'm so glad you dropped by. Let's go to the kitchen. The Beaufort Police and an ambulance are on the way. I think maybe we should get a pot of coffee on. Can you give me a hand?"

As Nick led her toward the kitchen, Genevieve looked back over her shoulder at the girl. "What happened to that girl?"

"We're not sure yet. She's not doing much talking until her parents are present. We think she walked in from the salt marsh.

Now don't panic, but this may have something to do with the RPS Killer."

Placing her hand over her chest, Genevieve reached for a kitchen chair. "Oh, my God! Right next door to where I live!"

The doorbell sounded again and Nick looked down the hall when Shelby opened the door. A pair of men dressed in suits were trailed by two paramedics, who were carrying a medical bag and a portable fold up gurney. Turning back to Genevieve, Nick spoke, "I have to get back in there in case they have any questions for me. I know you're upset, but do you think you can get the coffee going?"

Getting up from the chair she motioned with her right hand. "Go... go. I'll handle the coffee. You just go do what you need to."

When Nick entered the sitting room, a number of things were already taking place. Officer Kemp was talking with what appeared to be a detective out in the foyer, the other detective was kneeling next to a chair that Shelby had taken as they talked, the paramedics were now in control of Amanda.

Nick stood at the end of the couch and listened to the three different conversations going on at the same time:

"What is your name, Ma'am?"

"Shelby Lee Pickett."

"Do you live here?"

"No, I'm from Savannah."

Officer Kemp shook hands with the detective in the foyer. "Thanks for getting here so quickly, Paul."

Looking in the sitting room, the man he had called Paul, asked, "How long has she been here?"

"I guess maybe about a half hour or so."

"What have you found out so far?"

"She walked in from the marsh. She might be another one the RPS Killer let go. We're not sure just yet. She refuses to talk about what happened until her parents are present."

"Where is the girl from?"

"Savannah... just like the others."

Nick turned his attention back to the paramedics. The male member of the medical duo, opened the medical bag while the female member of the team looked the girl over, all the while asking Amanda questions, "What's your name, dear? How are you feeling? Where do you hurt?"

Amanda answered his questions instantly:

"Amanda Schrock. I'm feeling very tired. I hurt everywhere!"

Examining Amanda's eyes, the paramedic asked, "It appears you were in the marsh. If so, how long were you out there?"

Amanda looked at the other paramedic who was preparing a hypodermic needle. Skeptically, Amanda answered, "I was out in the marsh for hours."

The female paramedic patted her on the side of her face and explained, "Here's what we're going to do. You, at this point don't seem nauseous, but we can't take a chance. You may have been bitten by a poisonous snake... maybe not. But just to be on the side of caution, we're going to give you some snakebite antidote. You have a number of cuts and abrasions, the most serious are the shells that have been deeply imbedded into the bottoms of your feet. They will have to be surgically removed. We are also going to administer a shot to you to prevent lockjaw. Then, we're going to load you up and take you to the hospital in Beaufort. After you're examined for any physical evidence we'll get you cleaned up."

Kemp and Detective Graham now stood next to the couch. Graham turned to the other detective and ordered, "Dean, why don't you ride along with the paramedics to the hospital. When the girl's parents show up you can begin questioning her. Officer Kemp and myself will remain here at the house and see what we can find out from these folks."

Jeff Lysinger walked in the front door, removed his wet hat and hung it on a coat rack by the door. He no sooner stepped into the sitting room when the paramedics were making their way across the room with Amanda, who was strapped to the gurney. "The female paramedic smiled and requested softly, "Excuse us please."

Jeff watched while they carefully carried the girl down the steps to the ambulance. Turning to Kemp, he held up his hands. "What did I miss?"

Genevieve interrupted as she stood in the hallway and raised the pot, "No more than I did, Chief. Coffee is now being served in the kitchen."

Chapter Eleven

PLACING A NEW FILTER IN THE COFFEEMAKER, Genevieve filled the glass pot with cold water and looked at the collection of people seated around the kitchen table. Despite the fact that three of the five at the table were police, it reminded her of days past when Amelia would invite some of the neighbor ladies over for tea or coffee.

Detective Paul Graham fingered the edge of his cup and asked Shelby, "You mentioned out in the front room that you work for Amanda Schrock's father?"

"Yes, I do. I work for him and three other lawyers at a firm in Savannah. That being said, I'm afraid I can't tell you much about his daughter, Amanda. Until tonight, I never laid eyes on her. Let me rephrase that. I did run into her one time about four years ago when she was younger and dropped by the office with her mother. I just didn't recognize her tonight until she gave us her name... then it clicked. It's no surprise she won't say anything until her parents are with her. From listening to the typical office gossip that goes on, I do know she's her daddy's little girl. She gets about whatever she wants. Some of the office girls have made the remark she's high maintenance. Aside from that, meeting her tonight, she seems like a nice girl."

Taking notes, Graham asked his next question which he directed at both Shelby and Nick. "Where exactly did you find her and which direction did she come from?"

Shelby, taking a drink, didn't respond, so Nick answered, "We discovered her up the street at the edge of my property. She was hunkered down in the bushes next to the road. I can only assume she must have come from either Bonito Road or further up Tarpon by John Fripp Condos. I say this because she did tell us that *he,* and by *he,* I can only guess she was referring to the RPS Killer, told her to walk toward the light. When we asked her about the light, she said it's the light from the island. I suppose she could have come from any direction, but based on what she said the light could have been from the marina or the water tower."

"Strange," said Kemp. "Isn't that the same thing the other two girls the killer cut loose said... I mean about walking toward the light?"

Jeff jumped in on the conversation, "That's exactly what they said, and quite frankly, this whole thing scares the hell out of me. So far, the killer has killed eight girls, one who we discovered out in the marsh, which we assume he let go just over a week ago. Now, tonight, it looks like we've found another potential victim he set free. The other two girls we talked with said they won the game and that's why they were released—"

Shelby, remembering something, interrupted, "That's the same thing Amanda told Nick and I. She won the game!"

Jeff repeated himself, "Like I said, that's what scares the hell out of me. When those girls were set free, it was no more than two weeks when the killer grabbed another girl from Savannah and killed her... on both occasions. When he wins the game and kills the loser, he doesn't strike again for about three months. I guarantee you. He has failed to win the game two times in a row. We can expect him to strike again soon."

"Excuse me," said Nick. "I've only been a permanent resident here on Fripp for about a week. When I first arrived I heard about this RPS Killer, but didn't give it much thought, because at the time I didn't know I was going to inherit this house *and* wind up living here on the island. If it turns out this Amanda Schrock was to be his latest victim, but somehow got away and winds up in my front yard, that kind of puts me smack dab in the middle of a serial killer murder investigation. Up until tonight, I've only heard snippets about the killings or how the killer operates. There isn't much I can add to what has already happened, because I really don't know the ins and outs of what has gone on down here the past two years with this killer."

Officer Kemp held up his empty cup and silently signaled at Genevieve for a refill. Dumping a spoonful of sugar into his drink, he looked across the table at Nick. "The horrible and tragic actions of this killer are no secret. We have made everything we have on the previous killings public in hopes of someone seeing or hearing something that will help bring the person responsible to justice. We really haven't quite established why he, and I say he, because he has been described as a male by the previous two girls that were set free, is apprehending his victims from Savannah. We do know he targets girls in the age bracket between sixteen to eighteen years of age... high school girls. Aside from that there are no similarities in the eight girls he has killed. They all have varied colors of hair, different religious beliefs, they live in different sections of Savannah, one of the victims was black, the others white. The only common thread that ties the girls together is their age."

Nick thought how strange it was that yesterday morning right there in the kitchen he had a conversation with Genevieve about the killings and here it was not quite twenty-for hours later and he was having a similar discussion about the RPS Killer, once again in his kitchen. Cutting in on Kemp's rundown of the victims, Nick spoke up, "Genevieve was telling me about how brutal the killings have been: something about the girl's elbows and kneecaps being broken by means of a rock and also their faces being smashed in. I think, if I remember correctly, she said the victims are always left with a pair of scissors stuck in their chest."

"That's a pretty fair description of the way the girls were found," commented Graham. "There is no way to sugarcoat their deaths. Brutal is about the only way to describe the condition of the bodies we found. The medical examiner, still after all the killings, has not been able to pinpoint if the rock blows to their heads or the scissors in their chests is the actual cause of death. The time between when the blows to the head occur and the attack with the scissors is so close the M.E. has not been able to determine which causes the victim to die. At this point, we are of the opinion that it may be a combination of the two violent actions. We do know a bloody rock and the scissors are a direct result of losing the game of Rock, paper, scissors."

"Okay," said Nick, "I think I understand the significance of the rock and the scissors being left behind but where does the paper part come in. I'm confused."

Jeff pushed his empty cup to the side and raised his hands in confusion himself. "That's the one part of this puzzle we don't seem to have an answer for: the paper part. The only thing that could possibly represent paper is the fact the killer gives the girls he releases three one dollar bills and the ones he kills have a five dollar bill clutched in their right hand. This represents something about the way the killer feels about his victims but so far we haven't been able to figure it out. That reminds me. Did you by any chance happen to notice if Amanda had three one dollar bills with her?"

Shelby looked at Nick and shrugged, "I don't recall. She didn't have anything in her hands because I remember her asking for a glass of water. I think I would have remembered if she was holding any money."

Nick agreed, "That's right, and something else. She was wearing a two piece bathing suit. I didn't notice any dollar bills stuffed down into her bikini bottoms. But then again, she was pretty muddy. We may have just not seen the money."

Paul Graham stood. "Well, we can sit here until the sun comes up and speculate about which direction Miss Schrock came from or whether she had the bills on her or not and find hours from now we're no further ahead than when we started. I'm going to head back over to the hospital in Beaufort and see what, if anything, they were able to discover." Looking at Shelby, he requested, "If you'll just give your contact info to Chief Lysinger here, then if we need to ask you any more questions, we'll know how to get hold of you."

Shelby stood, walked to the sink, rinsed her cup out and answered Graham, "Sure thing. Listen, I hope the Schrock girl is okay. She must have been through a lot."

Jeff stood and yawned. "I have to be at work at eight. That's three hours from now. I might as well stay here on the island. There's no sense in going back to Ladies Island for a couple hours sleep and then driving back. Besides, I'm too keyed up." Gesturing at Officer Kemp, he went on, "If you'll get Miss Pickett's info, I'll see you back at the office. We need to make plans for what's going to happen later today. When word of this recent incident gets out, and it will, we need to be prepared for the onslaught of phone calls and questions we'll be plagued with around the island."

Genevieve started for the front door. "If you kids don't need me for anything else, I'm going to head on over to my place. Nick, if you need anything, give me a call."

Standing on the porch, Nick and Shelby watched as the three police vehicles pulled out and disappeared in the nearby trees by the road. Genevieve waved good bye and walked across the grass to her house. Turning to Nick, surprisingly, Shelby gave him a peck on his cheek and started down the steps. "I guess I better get packing."

Nick, not quite sure what to say touched his cheek and then commented, "Why the kiss? I thought this wasn't supposed to be a date."

Turning at the bottom of the steps, Shelby winked and remarked, "It certainly didn't start out that way, but you have to admit it was quite an interesting evening."

"I guess," said Nick. "Were you serious when you mentioned earlier tonight that maybe we could do this again... I mean, not what happened tonight, but ya know, maybe dinner or a movie?"

"Yes, I was serious. And something else! I think you've earned the right to call me Rebel. I wrote my phone number down and left it on the kitchen counter. Give me a call… maybe next week. Just sayin!"

Doctor Elijah Jacobs entered the waiting room in the emergency center at the Beaufort Hospital and looked over the various people seated on couches and chairs. Looking down at his clipboard, he announced, "Mr. and Mrs. Franklin Schrock." A well-dressed couple sitting by a large window stood and the man signaled the doctor. "We're the Schrocks!"

The doctor approached and motioned with the clipboard, "Please be seated." After they were seated the doctor introduced himself, "My name is Doctor Jacobs. I'll be the attending physician while your daughter, Amanda is with us."

Reaching out and touching the doctors wrist, the woman spoke with a tone of concern, "I'm Amanda's mother, Phyllis. Is she alright?"

Reassuring the parents, Doctor Jacobs smiled and patted her hand. "Your daughter is going to be fine. Right now she is resting. We had to give her a light sedative. She was quite upset when we arrived and you were not here yet."

The man spoke up, "I'm Franklin Schrock, Amanda's father. Is my daughter injured in any way?"

The doctor, looking at the clipboard smiled and stated, "First of all, she was covered in mud when they first brought her in. After we got her cleaned up we noticed she had quite a few cuts and bruises on her arms and legs. We've got those all medicated and bandaged. She did have one severe cut on her head that required four stitches. That has also been taken care of. She'll have a scar for a few months but then it will clear up. However, her feet are a matter of great concern. Apparently, she stepped on a number of sea shells that broke or were already broken. As she continued to walk, the pressure from her body forced and imbedded the broken pieces of shells deep into the bottoms of her feet. In order to remove them we have to perform minor surgery. It's nothing serious, but if we do not get the shell pieces removed she could get an infection. Considering she is not of age to make the decision on surgery I'm going to need you as her parents to sign off, giving us permission to proceed."

Reaching for the clipboard, Mrs. Schrock stated, "Of course we'll sign. Give me a pen!"

Handing her an ink pen the doctor stated, "It is not necessary for both of you to sign. As long as one of you approve, we'll be set to go."

Franklin, watched his wife sign and then asked, "Will the procedure be painful?"

"Not at all. Your daughter will be under. Even though the foot is not a vital organ, when you begin to cut or open the bottom of a person's feet it can be very painful. The bottom of the foot is one of the most sensitive parts of the human body. The procedure should only take about a half hour but that depends on what we find when we get in there. If you would like to see your daughter before we take her into the operating room, just follow me. You'll have about fifteen minutes to visit before they come for her."

After a short walk, the doctor opened the door of a room and pulled back a long green curtain. Dr. Jacobs looked at a chart hanging on the wall and asked the nurse, "How is our patient doing?"

"Still resting. She was just awake before you came back. She keeps asking for her parents."

Franklin stepped forward and spoke up, "I'm the girl's father and this is my wife. We were told we could visit with her for a few minutes prior to her going into surgery."

The nurse nodded and gently shook Amanda. "Let's see if we can get her awake." Gently, the nurse whispered, "Amanda... Amanda, your parents are here."

Amanda slowly opened her eyes and stared up into the white ceiling, then closed her eyes again. "Amanda," urged the nurse, "Amanda!"

Her eyes opened again and she looked at the nurse in confusion. Pointing across the bed the nurse spoke softly, "Your parents are here, Amanda."

When her eyes fell on her father, she burst into tears and sobbed, "Daddy... that man... he was going... to kill me! I want to go... home. Please... take me home... now!"

Amanda tried to sit up but the nurse prevented her from doing so while she ordered softly, "No, no... you mustn't get up. Just lay back and relax."

Mrs. Schrock gave the doctor a strange look and inquired, "What's all this about a man who was going to kill my daughter?"

Detective Potts, who had been seated in the far corner stood and approached the couple and introduced himself, "Excuse me. I'm Detective Potts of the Beaufort Police Department. I can explain what your daughter is talking about. We're not sure just yet, but we think Amanda had a run-in with the RPS Killer—"

Before he could finish speaking, Mr. Schrock broke in with a demanding voice, "Why were we not informed of this when we were contacted?"

Potts moved around Mrs. Schrock so he could speak directly to her husband. "Because at the time we were not sure if she was or was not apprehended by the RPS Killer. We were not able to question your daughter because she refused to talk with us until you folks showed up. That's why I'm here. We have a lot of unanswered questions your daughter can no doubt clear up for us."

Mrs. Schrock objected to Potts' explanation for not informing them about the RPS Killer. "I can't believe the local police department would not tell us exactly what happened to our daughter. Over in Savannah, where we're from... this would have never happened. Nothing would have been kept from us!"

Potts looked hopelessly at the doctor and tried to explain, "It was not our intention to hide or keep anything about your daughter from you. It's just that we don't know what happened because your daughter refused to allow us to question her. She requested you be contacted and that's what we did."

"I'm an attorney," snapped Franklin, "and I can assure you, Detective Potts. I'm going to look into this. You misinformed my wife and I and we don't appreciate it... one bit!"

Amanda covered her face with her hands and burst into tears, "Please... stop arguing!"

Doctor Jacobs spread his arms like he was shooing the Schrock's and Detective Potts out of the room as he moved them toward the door. "That's it! Everyone out of the room." Pulling the curtain shut, he closed the door. Pointing his clipboard at the Schrock's, and then at Potts, he explained in the most professional manner he could, "I realize you are her parents and you, Detective Potts represent the law, but until Amanda is out of surgery and completely recovered she is under *my care!* She is going into surgery and I don't need you three upsetting my patient. Now, if I was you I'd go have breakfast in the cafeteria or wait in the lounge. It's now six-thirty. She'll be out of surgery around seven-thirty and then we have to wait for her to recover which could be about an hour and a half. That means she will not be able to answer any questions until around nine o'clock... maybe ten. Until that time, she is completely in my hands. So, my advice is to try and chill out. We'll notify you when she is able to answer questions." Waving his hand down the hall, gesturing they should move on, he turned and walked back in the room.

Potts stared directly at Mr. Schrock, then turned, started down the hall and threw his hands in the air. "Lawyers!"

Mrs. Schrock took her husband by his arm as they followed Potts. "How good could the food be here at the hospital, Franklin? Maybe we should just have coffee and maybe a donut or something. Let's wait and see what Amanda says after she gets out of surgery. Maybe the detective was right. Maybe she wasn't attacked by this RPS Killer."

Doctor Jacobs looked at his watch and entered the waiting room. Scanning the large room, he saw Detective Potts who had recently been joined by Detective Graham sitting about as far as they could from where the Schrock's were seated. Walking to the center of the room resembling a referee at a boxing match, Jacobs signaled both couples to come to him. Mrs. Schrock, with a look of defiance gave Potts a dirty look, which the detective ignored. When both couples were standing on either side of Jacobs, he began, "I see Detective Graham has joined the group. How are you detective?"

"Fine," said Paul. "How is the girl doing? I understand she had some surgery?"

"She's fine. We found seven shards of shells in her right foot and five in the left." Addressing the Schrock's, he explained, "After the questioning, however long that may take we will be releasing your daughter. She must stay off her feet for at least a week." Handing them a handwritten prescription, he went on, "Here is a prescription for some pain medicine. You can get it filled right here at the hospital if you like. I'll need to see your daughter at my office, one week from today. At that time I will remove the bandages and if she has started to heal, then she may be able to start putting some pressure on her feet. At that time I will also be giving you some salve for her feet. Physically, she's fine. Mentally, she seems alright, but up until now she hasn't talked all that much about what happened to her. I'm going to take you back to her room, where the detectives can begin their questioning. That being said; I will not put up with any arguing between you folks. She appears to be stable but if she gets too upset, I'm going to have to put a stop to the process. Do we all understand?"

Everyone nodded and the doctor gestured toward the door. "Alright, then let's head back."

When they entered the room, Amanda, at the sight of her parents smiled as she sipped a glass of apple juice. Instantly,

Mrs. Schrock went to the bedside and placed her hand on her daughter's shoulder. "Are you alright? How do you feel?"

Setting the glass on a side table, Amanda held her free hand out to her father. "I'm fine. My feet are a little numb, but I feel fine."

The nurse on the opposite side of the bed, interjected, "That's from the pain medicine we administered to you. When the numbness begins to wear off, if you start to feel any pain please let me or one of the other nurses know."

Doctor Jacobs motioned to two chairs against the wall. Addressing the detectives, he explained, "If you gentlemen will be seated and let Amanda's parents have a few moments with her, then you can start the questioning." With that, he nodded for the nurse to follow him out of the room.

Outside of the partially closed door, he instructed the nurse. "There seems to be some sort of animosity between the parents and our local police. If things start to get out of control, I want you to get me immediately."

Mr. Schrock took a seat in a comfortable chair next to the window. He knew from past experience once his wife started talking it would be some time before he would be able to get a word in. Finally, after what seemed like five minutes, there was a break in the conversation at which point, he politely spoke up, "Amanda, excuse me, but the sooner we let these detectives ask you the questions they need to, the sooner we'll be able to get you home."

Mrs. Schrock, realizing her husband was growing impatient, turned to the detectives and motioned them forward. "Amanda dear, this is Detective Potts and Detective Graham. They need to ask you some questions about what happened to you."

Amanda nodded and responded, "I already know who they are. They were at the house of the nice couple who found me on the side of the road and took me into their home." Looking beyond her mother, she addressed her father, "Daddy, you need to do something nice for those people. If it wouldn't have been for them, well, I don't know what would have happened to me."

Crossing his legs, Franklin assured her, "I'll make sure they are rewarded in some fashion." Patting the chair next to him, he suggested, "Phyllis, please have a seat so these two gentlemen can do their job."

Moving the two wooden chairs next to the bed, Detective Graham removed a small tape recorder from his pocket and laid it at the bottom of the bed. "We'll be taping our conversation for the record. Any objections?"

Amanda looked at her father for approval. He nodded his approval and she answered, "That will be okay."

"Let me start out," said Graham, "by saying that the smallest bit of information may turn out to be the most important thing you remember. You must try and recall, to the best of your ability every detail, however small it may seem."

Detective Potts flipped open a pad and clicked an ink pen as he smiled at Mrs. Schrock who did not return his gesture of pleasantness.

Graham leaned forward and turned on the recorder. "Okay Amanda. Let's start from the very beginning. "What is the last thing you recall before you were apprehended?"

Making herself comfortable on the bed, Amanda held up an index finger. "I was with my three friends on the beach down on Tybee Island. The four of us have been going to the same beach, actually the same spot for years. Yesterday, we stayed longer than usual. We met some boys and they bought us dinner which we had right there on the beach. We played volleyball, threw a Frisbee around and swam some. Before we realized it, it was almost dark. I knew I had better be getting home or my folks would be worried. The other girls decided to stay and enjoy a small bonfire the boys had built. By the time I walked to my car which was parked on a side street, it was dark. The last thing I remember was bending over placing my beach chair and bag in the trunk of the car. It happened so quickly. I felt a burning sensation on my right side and then everything went blank."

"Before we go any further," said Potts, "did you notice anyone on the odd side hanging around the area? Did you notice what type of vehicles were parked nearby?"

"No, it was too dark out and the street where I was parked was not well lit."

Graham broke in with an observation, "We'll have to ask the doctor if there was a slight burn mark on your right side. All of the other girls that were set free or were found murdered had a burn mark on their right side, which is consistent with being hit with a stun gun."

Twisting slightly sideways, Amanda lifted her hospital gown exposing a small one-inch discolored section on her side. Making a note on his pad, Potts remarked and shook his head, "Yep, same as all the others. He used a stun gun."

Graham nodded in agreement and continued with his questioning. "When you finally came around, what is the first thing you noticed?"

"The first thing I noticed when my eyes opened was that I was blindfolded. I could feel the cloth wrapped around my head, covering my eyes. Another thing I noticed; I was moving. Not of my own accord, but I felt like I was in a moving vehicle. My hands and feet were bound and there was something over my mouth. I was lying on my side and I could smell rubber, like a new tire smells and I could smell oil or gasoline also. And, oh yeah. I could smell stale cigarette smoke."

"How long do you estimate you were in this vehicle?" asked Potts.

"After I woke up, well, it's hard to say because I was really scared. It seemed like it was maybe fifteen minutes or so before the car or whatever I was in stopped. Now, how long I was in there before I came around, I can't say."

Graham crossed his legs trying to get comfortable. "When the vehicle stopped, what happened next?"

"I heard a noise, like maybe a car trunk being opened and then I was lifted up, carried for a few seconds and laid on the ground."

Amanda hesitated and started to tear up. Mrs. Schrock started to get up to go to the bed, but Amanda motioned for her to sit as she composed herself. "It's alright mother, I'll be fine. It's just kind of hard to relive what happened, but I know we have to get through this." Wiping her eyes with a Kleenex, she continued, "I must have laid there on the ground for nearly ten minutes."

"Could you hear anything?" asked Potts.

"No, it was complete silence for the first minute or so and then I heard a clicking sound, which I discovered later on was a cigarette lighter. I can only assume the man was standing over me or nearby smoking. And another thing: he was constantly coughing. Later on, I heard a plane fly overhead. It didn't sound like a small plane but more like a commercial jetliner. Over in Savannah we live close to the airport so I am quite familiar with the noise the planes make when they take off and when they land. This was the sound of a plane in flight that was probably just passing over. Aside from that, there was silence."

Potts got up, stretched and walked to the window. Turning, he asked, "So you don't feel you were close to an actual airport; perhaps Savannah?"

"It could have been near the airport, but to be honest with you, it sounded like it was too far away for that."

"What happened next to the best of your recollection?" asked Graham.

"I wanted to shout out for help, but I figured the man was nearby watching me. I couldn't have made much noise anyway. My mouth was still taped shut. For some reason I decided to remain quiet. After a few minutes, I felt my head being raised at which point I did try to scream. That was the first time he spoke to me. In a very calm voice, he told me to settle down or he would hurt me."

Wiping her eyes once again, Amanda went on, "When the blindfold was removed I was in total darkness. After a few seconds, my eyes started to focus. The only thing I could see were a few stars in the sky. It was cloudy and I could only see the stars when the clouds would move off. Then I saw a tiny red glow which turned out to be the burning tip of his cigarette. The next thing I knew, he turned a flashlight on and shined it directly in my face. Between the occasional moonlight and the flashlight I could barely make out his silhouette. It was just a dark shape... nothing more."

"What happened next?" asked Graham.

He untied my hands and removed the tape from my mouth and explained that I was going to need them in order to play the game. I guess it was at that point that I knew he was the RPS Killer. I started to cry and I guess he could tell. He explained to me if I won the game I had nothing to worry about... I would be set free. He asked me if I knew how to play Rock, paper, scissors. I didn't want to answer but I thought it best if I did. I recall thinking, as I was pumping my fist and saying the words, this simplistic game was the most important thing I had ever done in my life and that I had a fifty-fifty chance of life or death and it would be determined in a few seconds. But as you can see, I'm still here. I won the game. I chose paper, he chose rock. Paper covers rock! I won. He didn't say a word at first. He just got up and lit a cigarette. I could tell from the glow of the cigarette that he was walking back and forth. I could hear him speaking to himself. He just kept saying he couldn't believe he had lost again... twice in a row."

"At what point did he release you?" asked Potts.

"I must have laid there for about a half hour. I remember he smoked three cigarettes in a row. Like I said, he coughed a lot... maybe from all the smoking, I don't know. Then, all of a sudden he walked over and without saying a word, he blindfolded me and taped my hands and mouth. He wasn't as gentle as he had previously been. He jerked me to my feet and then carried me, I assume back to the vehicle and literally threw me in the truck. I remember banging my head against a tire. He slammed the trunk shut and started to shout at me. Something about how lucky I was; that I had defied the odds of the game and he had half a mind to just go ahead and break the rules and kill me anyway. Then, it seemed like he calmed down. He said he had to keep the integrity of the game and he would follow the rules. The next thing I know the car is moving. I can't estimate how far we drove… maybe an hour I guess."

Writing on his pad, Potts asked, "Did you hear anything that sounded familiar or that could have been a clue to where he may have taken you?"

"No, nothing that stood out. I could hear the hum of the tires on the road and I could hear occasional cars or trucks passing by. I know we made a number of right and left hand turns. I tried to memorize how many, but after a while it just got too confusing. Just before the vehicle came to a stop, I remember we made a right onto what I thought was a gravel road. A short time later, maybe a few minutes, we stopped."

"And then?" asked Graham.

He popped the trunk and said we had to wait until one o'clock in the morning before our next trip which he said was going to be by boat. He took the blindfold off of me, but said I had to remain in the trunk until we shoved off."

"Can you recall what kind of vehicle you were in?"

"No, it was too dark for me to see much of anything."

"How long was it before you took this boat ride?"

"It felt like a couple of hours."

"Did he say anything to you during that time?"

"No, not much. He did mention that he was going to try and cut down on his smoking, maybe even try to quit."

Graham looked at Potts and remarked, "The other two girls mentioned that the killer seemed to smoke one cigarette after another."

Amanda agreed, "He did smoke a lot. His clothes and his breath smelled of cigarette smoke. When I was in the trunk of the car, I remember how it smelled like old cigarettes."

Moving on, Graham stood and stretched his legs. "Did the killer say anything else while you were waiting for the ride in the boat?"

"No, he just kept walking back and forth, smoking one cigarette after another. No, wait! Just before we left for the boat, he did mention it was almost one o'clock and we might as well head out."

"Did he get back in the car or did you walk to this boat?"

"He untied my feet and guided me. I think we may have walked for a minute or so. It seemed like a short distance. I know at one point I was crossing a dock because I could feel it moving beneath my feet. He positioned me in the boat and from the noise of the motor it didn't sound like a very large boat. He removed my blindfold and we headed out into a body of water. It didn't feel like the ocean because it was calm, no waves."

"During this boat ride, what if anything did he talk about?"

"At first, he didn't say a word. He just kept smoking... and coughing."

"During this time did you get a chance to see what he looked like?"

"Well, yes. There was a light behind him at the back of the boat. It was just enough so I could vaguely see him. I couldn't see his face because he was wearing a dark ski mask."

"What other type of clothes was he wearing?"

"It was just dark clothing, nothing I can actually describe."

Graham returned to his chair and Potts spoke up, "Where did he take you on the boat ride?"

"I have no idea. The entire boat ride was only about a half hour or so. He pulled over and we bumped into land. He told me to step out of the boat. I remember it was very muddy and my feet sank down into the ground. I was really scared, and wasn't quite sure if he was going to let me go like he said. He pointed out a distant light and told me to walk toward it. He told me I was in a salt marsh and I needed to get moving before the tide came in. In my mind I was already thinking about what would happen to me after he left. He said something about alligators and poisonous snakes but I really wasn't paying much attention. He lit up a cigarette, handed me some money and backed the boat out and within a minute or so disappeared in the darkness."

"How much money did he give you?"

"I don't know. It was too dark. It felt like a number of bills."

"What did you do with the money? The people who rescued you, said it didn't appear that you had any money with you."

"If I remember correctly, I tucked it into my bikini top and never gave it another thought. It must have come out when I was swimming. It's probably out in the marsh somewhere."

"And you never saw him again after that?"

"No, I just kept forcing my way through the deep mud until I came to water. I'd walk out until it was deep enough for me to swim. I kept repeating this process of land and water for what seemed like an hour. The light was getting closer but I was becoming exhausted and disorientated. I remember saying to myself out loud over and over, 'Go to the light... go to the light.' Somehow I made it to the edge of the marsh and eventually solid ground. I was confused and had no idea where I was. I could hardly walk from the pain in my feet. I thought I was walking on a paved road and then I saw a light, which I guess turned out to be the porch light where those two nice people live. They heard my cries for help and they rescued me. You know the rest from there on." Looking at the detectives, Amanda stated, "That's all there is. Did I do okay? Can I go home now?"

Graham reached for the recorder and turned the small machine off. Smiling at Amanda he nodded in approval. "You did a great job of answering our questions and relating to us what happened. I know that after what you've been through this must not have been easy, but you have given us a lot of information." Holding up the recorder he looked at Potts. "This combined with Detective Potts' notes will be compared with the information we got from the other two girls that survived." Turning to Mr. and Mrs. Schrock, Graham explained, "We'll need your home address and a number where you can be contacted in case we have any further questions for your daughter. On behalf of the Beaufort Police Department, I can assure you we will do everything in our power to bring this killer in."

As Potts and Graham started for the door, Mr. Schrock stopped the two men and spoke, "Amanda is the eleventh girl from Savannah this killer has abducted. Out of the four he let go, only one died, the girl last week. I guess I'm a little confused when it comes to this boat business. It seems to me the killer has this boat he uses hidden somewhere out there on the islands. What efforts have been made to locate it?"

Graham smiled and answered, "We have searched for the boat, but that task in itself, is a lot more complex than the average citizen can imagine. Between Ladies, St. Helena, Harbor, Hunting and Fripp Islands not to mention all of the other areas where a boat can be docked or hidden, it is an extremely large area. There are virtually hundreds if not thousands of inlets, creeks, docks and boathouses in the area that would have to be searched. We simply don't have the manpower to conduct that type of an operation. Now, I will say this. We have asked the public through the local media to be on the lookout for anything strange or unusual in the waterways down on the islands. Everyone is on the lookout for the killer. His time is coming. He'll slip up *and eventually* we'll bring him in. I don't like to utilize the term sooner or later in regard to capturing this man. As far as I'm concerned it needs to be sooner... not later, because the longer it takes us to nail this guy, the more girls could get killed." Shaking Mr. Schrock's hand, Graham with a look of relief, remarked, "I'm glad your daughter survived and I appreciate everything she shared with us. Here's one of my business cards, in case Amanda happens to remember something after she gets home. Thanks again for your cooperation."

Watching both detectives exit the room, Mr. Schrock turned to his wife. "Phyllis, let's get our daughter home."

The smoke-filled tavern was slow for nine-thirty at night. The bartender, with a bar towel draped over his shoulder sat and watched a ballgame on the overhead television behind the bar, two men were engaged in a game of pool in the back corner and one customer was seated at the bar. A man stood at the old-fashioned jukebox and plopped four quarters into the money slot and then went about making his selections. Just as he returned to his seat at the very end of the bar the first song filled the tavern with the sounds of The Kentucky Headhunters: *Let's go down... down to Dumas Walkers....*

The man downed the last of his draft and held up his empty glass for another. Lighting a fresh cigarette with the butt of his previous smoke, he lined the filtered end up next to nine other butts on the counter. The bartender, after delivering a cold glass of draft, changed the channel on the television to an early edition of the late night news, then went about wiping down the bar. He frowned as he watched the late breaking news: *Another girl from the Savannah area has been found on Fripp Island. The RPS Killer has stuck once again, however the girl, Amanda Schrock of Savannah has been treated for minor injuries, questioned and released from the Beaufort Hospital. Anyone having any information on this latest apprehension is asked to contact the local police. The two-year serial killer investigation continues as the police review the latest facts.*

The bartender flipped the channel back to the ballgame and walked to the end of the bar where the man was seated. Lighting a cigarette of his own, he commented to the man, "I wish they'd catch that son of a bitch! Two years, eight girls dead, three others traumatized, and it seems like we're no closer to catching this bastard, than when this whole mess started."

The man stubbed out his cigarette, coughed twice then corrected the bartender, "It's nine dead... not eight. You'd think with all the victims being apprehended here in Savannah that folks would keep their daughters off the streets. You watch! A week or so from now I bet they'll be saying the same thing: another girl found. But, what we don't know is... if she'll be dead or if she'll survive!"

The bartender agreed with the man. "You're right. If I had a daughter that was high school age I wouldn't let her out of my sight."

The man nodded and took a drag on his smoke, followed by a drink of beer. The bartender held up the cigarette he was smoking and commented, "They say these things will kill you. I've been smoking for forty years. My doctor keeps telling me I need to quit. I get a checkup every year. So far, no signs of cancer, but the doctor keeps informing me that I've been extremely lucky and I should quit while I'm ahead. I have cut down some. I'm down to a pack a day."

Tapping his pack of smokes laying on the bar, the man frowned, "I only wish I smoked a pack a day. I'm a four pack a day man." Throwing a twenty on the bar, the man picked up his cigarettes and commented, "I've got to get some sleep. I have to meet a crew of men tomorrow morning out in the suburbs. I haven't worked for a couple of weeks. It'll be good to be working again." Coughing hard a number of times, he stubbed out his cigarette in and ashtray and remarked, "Your doctor is right. These things will kill you."

Chapter Twelve

THE MID-DAY SUN WAS SHINING DIRECTLY IN THE bedroom window. The brightness caused Nick to sit up in bed and shield his eyes. He looked at the alarm clock on the nightstand: 2:10 in the afternoon. He couldn't remember sleeping in this late in his life. His mouth felt pasty and he was still wearing his clothes from the previous night. Getting up, he walked to the window and looked out at the ocean and then at the thermometer hanging on the deck: ninety-four degrees. It was the end of the week and the beach was not as crowded. He felt sweaty and nasty. A shower sounded good but at the moment a refreshing dip in the Atlantic was on his mind. Stripping off his clothes, he slipped into a pair of old jean shorts, flip flops and a tee-shirt. Down in the kitchen he stopped at the sink, splashed some cold water across his face and took a few swallows. Removing the small bandage on his arm, he checked the wound. The cut from the scuffle with Derek in Cincinnati had been reopened during his brief encounter with Ike Miller at the Dockside. The doctors at both locations told him that he could swim, but the cut had to remain bandaged. Opening the kitchen drawer he took out one of the extra bandages he had been supplied with and applied it to the wound.

Walking out onto the back, screened-in porch he bounded down the steps, across the dirt road and up the path that led to the beach. Stopping on the small wooden deck above the dunes, he looked out at the vast Atlantic Ocean. He kicked off his flip flops and hung his shirt on the deck railing, then down the three steps into the warm sand. Stretching his shoulders and neck, he was glad he decided to live in Amelia's house. Crossing the sand, he passed a number of people sitting on blankets reading or sun bathing. The tide was out and the waves were low. Approaching the water's edge, he stopped to pet a black lab returning from the water with a tattered tennis ball his owner had thrown for the dog.

Wading out into the water until his knees were covered he noticed eleven majestic brown Pelicans in their customary V-formation gliding by. Three young children frolicked in the waves while their mother stood nearby keeping watch. Looking east he could barely make out the distant rocks at Ocean Point and beyond that on the other side of the inlet, he knew Hunting Island was there. Hunting Island was where Amelia had taught him to swim. His recalled his grandmother being quite the swimmer. She taught him how to swim through the pain and how to float and relax in the water. Amelia always said it bordered on ridiculous for people not to know how to swim, especially when you lived in an area surrounded by water.

Venturing out until the water was up to his chest, he went under, came up and started to swim, taking strong, even strokes, diving beneath the waves just like Amelia had taught him. Following a few minutes, he rolled over onto his back and relaxed, the warm sun caressing his face.

He stood up and looked back at the beach. A girl who was speed walking reminded him of Shelby and the awkward conversation they had on the beach. Despite his seemingly inability to communicate with women, she had still agreed to go to dinner with him. When it was all said and done, the evening had turned out to be anything but boring; the fight with Ike Miller and the discovering of Amanda Schrock just down from his front yard. He couldn't believe Shelby had left her phone number on his kitchen counter and even kissed him. She told him to give her a call in the next week *and* that's exactly what he was going to do.

Crossing the beach, he sat on the bottom step of the deck. He knew it would only be a few minutes before he would be dry. It seemed ever since he had arrived on the island the things that had happened to him had been non-stop. What he needed was a day of relaxation: a day away from Charley Sparks and his goon partner, a day of not thinking about the RPS Killler, a day of not worrying about the gun hidden in the cookie jar in his kitchen. Then there was the seven million dollars hidden somewhere in the house or on the property. "Yep," he said out loud, "that's what I'm going to do. A day of relaxation." He had an idea: a day of riding around the island on the golf cart. He could visit all the places Amelia had taken him over the years. If he got hungry, and he knew he would, he could stop at the marina or over at the golf course for a quick bite. He'd take a couple of beers with him in a cooler and just enjoy the day.

Following a quick shower, he donned a frayed pair of jeans with holes in the knees, one of his old painting shirts and a Reds ball hat. Slipping into his flip flops he raced down the stairs, grabbed three beers out of the fridge and a cooler from the pantry, filled it with ice and walked out to the garage. Placing the cooler on the seat, he unplugged the cart and turned the key. The small square red indicator displayed a full charge. *Good to go!* he thought.

Making a right hand turn onto Tarpon, he only went a few feet when he had to stop for a young fawn who was trailing his mother across the street. It was strange to see deer at this time of the day in the summer. Amelia always said they laid up back in the trees where it was cooler and didn't venture out until the evening hours.

Glancing at the bushes near the edge of his property, he did a double-take. He couldn't believe what he was seeing: a folded one dollar bill. What was it the detectives had said last night about not understanding the paper part of the Rock, paper, scissors killings? The killer always gave the girls he released three one dollar bills and the ones he killed were found with a five clutched in their right hand. Picking up the bill carefully by its corner he placed it in the tiny indentation in the dash and cursed, "Damn it!" His day of relaxation had just started and here he was already thinking about the RPS Killer.

His first planned stop of the day had been Ocean Point where he spread his grandmother's ashes, but now things had changed. Heading down Tarpon, his next stop was the island security office. He couldn't be sure if the money he found was one of the three bills the killer had given Amanda Schrock or not. Anyone could have dropped the bill, maybe months ago and the wind just happened to blow it into his front yard.

It wasn't even four minutes when he pulled up in the parking lot of the security office. There were no vehicles parked in front and he wondered if anyone was in. Racing up the steps and across the porch he pushed open the door. The interior of the office was unlike any police station he had ever seen on television. In all the years he had come to Fripp he had never been inside the office. There had never been any reason.

He could have been walking into a doctor's office for all he knew. There was no glass wall or elevated desk with a uniformed sergeant seated behind it, no rows of cluttered desks where detectives sat and smoked and drank cups of coffee, the walls were not covered with wanted posters and maps. There was a single, very neat desk, two chairs, a potted plant and a water cooler in what he thought was their lobby. A woman seated behind the desk, looked up from a computer, raised her glasses and placed them on the bridge of her nose and spoke, "May I help you sir?"

Excited, Nick approached the desk and held up the dollar bill. "My name is Nick Falco. I live just up the street—"

Before he could elaborate on the reason for his visit, she cut him off. "Nick Falco! Yes, you're Amelia's grandson. I knew your grandparents quite well. I heard you were going to be living in their house."

"Yeah, well listen! I found this money at the scene of where we found that girl last night. This might have something to do with the RPS Killer. I need to give this to Chief Lysinger. I don't suppose he's in at the moment?"

The woman responded, "No, he isn't. He and Travis headed up to the marina. They're going out into the salt marsh for a few hours." Picking up the phone on her desk, she continued, "Let me see if I can get hold of him."

Turning in her swivel chair she looked out the window and waited for the Chief to pick up. Following a few seconds she hung up. "He's not picking up for some reason. If you hurry you might be able to catch them before they shove off."

Without even thanking the woman, Nick ran out the door and to the cart. Backing out, he headed back up Tarpon in the direction he had just come from. The posted speed limit for cars and golf carts was fifteen miles per hour but at the moment Nick could have cared less as he pushed the cart to its maximum speed of thirty. A woman who was sweeping off her porch gave him an odd look when he sped by. Amelia always told him most of the residents not only adhered to the rules of the island but enforced them as well. He considered the fact the woman might call security, but then again, who was going to arrest him? The Chief and probably the only other officer on duty were over at the marina.

Crossing Maxwell Bridge on Bonito Drive he pressed the accelerator to the floor and passed three golf carts, one of the drivers yelling at him, "Slow down... idiot!"

Pulling into the lot at the Bonito Boathouse, Nick jumped out and ran around the side of the building down the ramp that led to the water. Chief Lysinger and Travis were just pulling out when Nick yelled, "Chief Lysinger... wait... wait!"

Hearing the shouts, Jeff turned and saw Nick standing at the edge of the dock, the dollar bill raised high in the air. Tapping Travis on his shoulder, he ordered, "Turn back around."

The boat bumped up against the dock when Jeff asked, "What brings you out here today?"

Holding out the money, Nick explained, "I found this dollar bill no more than thirty minutes ago right where we found the Schrock girl last night. I thought it might be important."

Jeff signaled for him to get in the boat and took the dollar bill. "You're kidding me... right? You say you found it where the girl was discovered? How can that be? We walked over there last night and looked all around that area. How could we have missed this?"

"I don't know," said Nick. "Maybe it was the darkness or the rain. Hell, this might not even be one of the bills the killer gave the Schrock girl. It might have been blown there by the wind during the night. It might not even be one of the bills we're looking for."

Flipping the bill over carefully in his hand, Jeff reached into a briefcase he had laying on the floor of the boat. Removing a plastic bag, he placed the bill inside and commented, "I'll make sure the Beaufort boys get this."

"Speaking of the Beaufort police, how did they make out with Amanda last night after they got her to the hospital?"

Travis got a sullen look on his face and spoke up, "That's why we're going out today. Don't get me wrong. I think we should do everything in our power to bring this killer in, but not because some high powered lawyer from Savannah says so!"

Nick, somewhat confused, looked at the Chief. Jeff tried his best to explain, "It seems, during the questioning it was discovered the girl's parents were not informed up front that their daughter may have had a run-in with the RPS Killer. Then on top of that when Amanda started talking about the boat she took a ride in, the subject came up about how hard it was to locate this boat. Well, when Franklin Schrock, the girl's father gets back to Savannah, he decides to take matters in his own hands. Schrock has more money than you can imagine. He swings a lot of weight in Savannah and it's said he has political aspirations and is going to run for mayor over there next election. He knows anyone and everyone who's important. He's very tight with the current mayor in Savannah and he went to him with his concerns over the lack of effort in locating this boat. The mayor from Savannah calls the mayor in Beaufort and raises ten kinds of hell, and that's why we're going out today, and who knows how many more days to look for this mysterious boat."

Sitting down, Jeff opened a cooler and removed three bottles of cold water. Pitching a bottle to Travis and then one to Nick, he asked, "Got any plans for the rest of the day?"

Holding the cold bottle up to the side of his face, Nick answered, "Not really. I was just going to relax and drive around the island and maybe grab some dinner later on. Why do you ask?"

Taking a drink, Jeff looked out at the distant marsh. "I thought maybe you'd like to tag along... sort of like a volunteer. Three sets of eyes are better than two. This entire process is being coordinated from Beaufort. I guess the mayor, the city council and the police spent quite a few hours getting crews together all the way from Charleston down to Savannah. Aside from the police there are crews of volunteers all up and down the coast looking for this boat. The Charleston crews will be searching James and Kiawah Islands and the inlets around Edisto. The Beaufort folks will be looking around Coosaw, Morgan and Cat Islands. The Savannah people will be searching from Trenschards Inlet to Moon Creek."

"And that brings things to us," said Travis as he turned the boat out into the river. "We're heading for Pritchards Island on the other side of Skull Inlet... the backside of Fripp."

Nick, opening his water, asked, "The backside of Fripp. I don't think I've ever heard that before."

Jeff explained, "Part of the backside of Fripp is across Skull Inlet. When you get far enough out over there it's what we refer to as a harsh environment. Not much grows out there, well, except for cord grass. That stuff can get as high as five feet."

Nick looked out at the passing marsh on his right, then suddenly asked, "Aren't we heading the wrong direction to get to Skull Inlet?"

"That we are," said Jeff. "We have to run over to the crime scene of the girl that was found dead last week. Our investigation there is over. We're just going to drop by and gather up the caution tape, then we'll head Southwest over to Skull."

Travis turned to the right and cut the engine, the boat drifting toward the bank of the river. Nick saw the yellow tape draped from one stake to the next. Allowing the boat to run aground, Jeff put on a pair of black, high top waders and stepped out onto the muddy sand flat, sinking deeply into the mire.

Nick, looking around the surrounding area, asked Travis, "Out of the eleven girls the killer has apprehended, how many were found here on Fripp?"

Travis held up four fingers and answered, "Four. Counting the Schrock girl from last night and the girl that we found right here, there was another girl who was released by the killer. She came ashore somewhere over around Wardle's Landing. The other girl was found dead on this side of Fripp Inlet. If I remember correctly, she was the killer's first victim."

"Where were the other girls found? Were they all close to Fripp?"

"There were two girls found on the beach over on Hunting Island. As a matter of fact, they were his second and third victims. Another girl wondered out onto Highway 21 over near Hunting Island. One girl was found on St. Helena Island out in the marsh just north of the Gay Fish Company. There was a girl found over near Land's End by the Beaufort River, one near Battery Creek over in Port Royal, and one in an inlet over near Dataw Island."

"So this killer must know his way around these parts rather well."

Jeff who had been listening to their conversation climbed back in the boat and wrapped the tape around the stakes. "The way I see it, he'd have to be familiar with all the inlets in the area, especially if he's running around out here at night. If you don't know where you're going you can get turned around and get lost quite easily." Sitting down, he took a swig of water and nodded at Travis. "Take us over to Pritchards Island. I guess we'll start somewhere around there."

On the move again, Nick laid back in the boat and looked up at the blazing sun. "It was ninety-four when I got up at two o'clock. It feels hotter than that now."

Jeff, at the front of the boat reached down into the passing water and splashed his face. They say it's going to get up to ninety-nine, might even top one hundred degrees. When we get out there back in the marsh it's gonna seem even hotter."

Finishing up his water, Nick asked, "Did anything else besides a massive effort to find the killer's boat come out of questioning Amanda Schrock?"

"Same ol'… same ol'," said Jeff. "Her story pretty much lined up with what the other two surviving girls told us: dark ski mask, dark clothes, the killer was polite, he smoked and coughed a lot. She talked about her ride in the car and then the boat and about playing Rock, paper, scissors. We don't have any more now than we did before she was apprehended."

Pulling out into Skull Inlet, Nick saw the Atlantic on his left, Pritchards Island looming in the distance. "My grandmother used to bring me out here fishing but we never went over on the other side of Skull Inlet. Is the island anything like Fripp?"

Jeff frowned and answered, "No resemblance whatsoever. First off, the island is only accessible by boat. That in itself is a downer to most vacationers unless you just plain want to get away from everything. On Fripp if you want to go into town you simply jump in your car and twenty or so minutes later... you find yourself in Beaufort. Not so, on Pritchards Island. If you want to leave, you have to own a boat or know someone who does. Another thing; what if a medical emergency pops up? They can run an ambulance out to Fripp within a matter of minutes. Now, this is just my opinion but by the time they could get to Pritchards Island, depending on how sick a person is, it might be too late. What I'm saying is that it's not the most ideal place to spend a vacation. The island is actually owned by the University of South Carolina. The beaches there are uninhabited for the most part and a lot of the land is pristine maritime forest. What you will find there are a number of scientists who study the loggerhead turtles. It's the most remote barrier island there is down this way."

Stopping the boat twenty yards out from the island, Travis asked, "Which way, Chief?"

"We'll stay parallel with the shoreline until we break out into the marsh on the western side of the island. From there we can navigate up and down the smaller inlets." Looking at his watch, he then glanced up at the sun. "I figure we'll stay out until about eight o'clock then we'll call it a day. I'd like to get back across Skull Inlet before it gets too dark."

Nick was amazed at the number of Great Blue Heron and Snowy White Egrets he saw standing on the banks of the inlets while they waited patiently for their next meal. In one particular inlet he saw three snakes slither out of the water and disappear in the tall cord grass. Pointing at the green wall of vegetation he commented, "It's a different way of life out here, isn't it?"

"Yep," said Travis. "You're smack dab in the middle of South Carolina's coastal ecosystem. Why, I'll bet you a dime to a dollar there's land out here that humans haven't stepped on for years... maybe decades. I can't even imagine being dumped out here and having to make my way back like those girls. It's a wonder only one of the four died."

Swatting at a pesky mosquito Nick peered into the thick cord grass and agreed, "I can't even fathom how anyone could walk in there. I just saw three snakes. They're probably everywhere out here. I've noticed since we got into the marsh the insect activity has increased."

"That's why it's called an ecosystem," said Travis. "Areas like this are not fit for human existence, but for the creatures that live out here it's a veritable paradise. Every creature out here, except for the occasional gators is always on the search for food and are themselves food for other creatures. I will say this. It's great fishing out here. About two months ago, my uncle and I came over here. We caught us some nice sheephead and a few spottail bass. Not that many people like to fish over here. I guess it's just too far off the beaten path for some folks."

After an hour of sweeping back and forth across the marsh, they stopped for a rest in a small lagoon at the end of a long inlet. Two gators, lying on the bank sunning themselves could have cared less about the invaders. Nick pointed at the grayish-green reptiles and commented, "They seem larger over here than the ones I've seen near the golf course back on Fripp. They must be at least six-footers."

"I'm no expert on gators," said Travis. "I do know they prefer fresh water to salt. That's why they like to stay in or near the lagoons on the islands. The only reason they venture out here is if they experience a wound or if they want to clean themselves. They'll come out here for a couple of days, lay up in the salt water, then go back in. I guess we tend to forget they were here before we were. That's the one thing I like about Fripp being a natural animal preserve. We don't kill anything. If a gator gets too aggressive or the snake population starts to invade people's property, we've been known to capture a few now and then and haul them out here. The truth be known. They're probably better off."

At seven o'clock, Travis, in a state of hopelessness, wiped his forehead with a handkerchief and commented sarcastically, "Do the powers to be up there In Beaufort really think this guy... this killer is going to keep his boat out where it can easily be seen. That boat could be anywhere from Charleston to Savannah. If this guy is smart, and since we haven't caught him in two years, I think he is, I also think he's got this boat hidden where no one can find it... except him. He's not going to leave it out here in one of these inlets. If anything, I'd venture to say it's either in a boathouse or hidden back in the cord grass somewhere. Hell, for all we know this killer might live nearby. That boat might be tied up at a dock, right in front of our eyes at one of the homes back on Fripp or any one of the islands around here where people live. I personally think we're wasting our time, Chief."

"I agree," said Jeff, "but we're not giving the orders on what has to be done. This is a hard case. This killer has a killing ground that is virtually impossible to cover on a regular basis. I guess what I'm saying is we're not the ones with our asses on the line. We're just part of this whole picture. The mayor of Savannah not to mention the mayor of Beaufort and the police chiefs of those two cities are the ones who are catching all the crap from the public. I mean it's been two years since this killer first struck and we're still fumbling around in the dark. The only thing we can do at this point is what the bureaucrats in Beaufort instruct us to do. There's nothing else we can do. I do agree though. It seems like a waste of time. It's just too large an area."

Travis shook his head in agreement. "Think we should call it a day, Chief?"

"Yeah, I do. I think we should head back over to Fripp and grab some dinner at the Boathouse. Stuffed Flounder sounds mighty good right about now."

"Home we go," said Travis as he started the boat and guided it out of a long inlet. At the end of the inlet Travis hugged the left hand side of a large mud flat as they turned for Skull Inlet. Watching a group of small crabs run back and forth across the mud, Nick yelled, "Stop the boat... now!"

Travis and Jeff were startled at first and didn't react. Nick pointed back at the mud flat and spoke firmly. "Turn back, I think I saw something!"

Both Travis and Jeff looked back and Jeff asked, "What did you see?"

"I'm not sure. Just go back."

Travis circled around, cut the motor and allowed the boat to drift back into the mouth of the inlet. Searching the bank carefully, Nick scanned the muddy surface until he spotted what he had previously seen. "There... right there! A dollar bill stuck in the mud. It looks like it's caught in the corner of a broken shell."

Travis guided the boat up against the mud flat as he and Jeff looked in the direction he pointed."

Jeff was the first to see the bill. "Well, I'll be damned! It is a dollar bill."

Travis suddenly saw the money when the boat bumped into the muddy bank. "I can't believe it. Way the hell out here!"

Jeff started to pull his waders back on, when Nick kicked off his flip flops and climbed over the side of the boat. "I saw it... I'll get it!"

His bare feet sank deeply into the mud, all of the tiny crabs scurrying into small mud holes. Following three awkward and difficult steps through the deep mud, Nick bent down and gently picked up the shell and the bill. Instantly he dropped the shell and yelled, "Son of a bitch! It's not a shell... it's the remains of a human hand!"

Forgetting the waders, Jeff jumped out into the mud and struggled forward and then knelt down and examined the boney hand clutching the dollar bill. Carefully, he reached out and removed the bill from the bones. "Oh my God!" he exclaimed. "This isn't a one... it's a five!"

Travis, at the edge of the boat sat down and spoke sadly, "I think we just found the remains of Susan Dunn."

Nick looked at Travis, wondering what he was talking about, then asked, "Who is Susan Dunn?"

Jeff sat down in the mud and explained, "Susan Dunn was the second girl from Savannah who was reported missing. I'm going back two years now when the murders first started. There had only been one murder when the Dunn girl was reported as missing. At the time, it was far too early for us to connect the dots and we didn't know we had a serial killer on our hands. As time went on and the murders started to pile up, we, the authorities in both Savannah and Beaufort thought maybe the Dunn girl was killed by the RPS Killer, but the problem was, we never found her body. It was obvious at the time and still is today that the killer leaves the bodies of his victims in an area where they will be discovered. The Dunn girl's body never showed up and everyone figured her disappearance had nothing to do with the RPS Killer." Holding up the five, and flipping it over, Jeff let out a long sigh. "This five dollar bill in this hand is one of the RPS Killer's calling cards. He killed this girl. Now whether she is Susan Dunn, I can't say."

Looking down at the grotesque remains of the hand, Nick asked, "How long do you think she's been out here?"

"If it is the Dunn girl," verified Jeff, "then I'd say close to two years. I'm no medical examiner, but from the looks of the remains, it's been out here for some time. No flesh, sinews or muscle tissue... just bones, and the money."

Travis jumped in on the conversation, "With the tide changing twice a day and when you consider how long she's been out here that hand could have been washed in here from miles away over time." Looking around, he added, "She might not even have been killed here. She could have been killed miles from here."

Jeff turned and addressed Travis, "Get me an evidence bag. We need to bag this money and the remains."

Picking up the bones gently, Jeff examined them closely, "The flesh has been gone for a long time. The fish probably had a field day nibbling on the girl. If she was out here all this time, they probably stripped her to the bone."

Curious, Nick asked, "Why didn't the fish eat the money?"

Holding up the bill, Jeff pointed at the ragged edges. "They tried to. You can tell by the slightly torn edges that they had a go at it. I guess maybe it just didn't appeal to them." Placing the bill in the bag, Jeff stood and looked down over his mud soaked pants and then at Nick whose arms and legs were covered with the dark black mud. "Well there goes our supper at the boathouse! I don't think we'd be welcome, besides, we need to call this in to Beaufort. They'll probably send the M.E. and a crew out here immediately."

Travis looked at his watch. "It's almost seven thirty, Chief. By the time they'd get out here, it could be dark and then there's the tide coming in. This whole area will be underwater. I think we should stake this place out and head back in. We can come back tomorrow morning at first light when the tide is out."

"You're exactly right," said Jeff. "Nothing can really be done until tomorrow. We've got about an hour and a half of light left out here. Maybe we should poke around back in the grass a little farther and see if we can find any other remains. Grab that shovel and give it to Nick. You and I can look around back in the cord grass a few feet. Nick, you can dig in the mud and see if there are any more remains. We'll stay out here until eight-thirty then we'll head back in." Looking in the tall grass, Jeff remarked, "Well Nick, you're turning out to be quite the detective. First, you rescue the Schrock girl then find a dollar bill that could turn out to be evidence... and now this. You may have found Susan Dunn. Welcome to Fripp Island!"

Chapter Thirteen

TRAVIS DOCKED THE BOAT JUST AFTER NINE-THIRTY. Following Nick, Jeff stepped onto the dock with the briefcase containing the newest evidence. The side porch of the Bonito Boathouse was packed with people eating a late dinner or relaxing over evening drinks. Turning back to Jeff, Nick removed his mud-caked tee-shirt and remarked jokingly, "Well if we aren't a sight!"

Jeff, tying off the boat answered and looked at the restaurant. "Yeah I guess that stuffed flounder is out of the question now. Besides, Travis and I have to get back to the office and report what we found. If this turns out to be the Dunn girl, and to be honest, without dental records I don't see how they're going to identify her, it's still going to be big news. We don't know for sure who that girl was, and we may never know."

Nick agreed and turned to head up the dock. "If you don't need me for anything else, I'm going to head on home myself."

A familiar voice on the porch got his attention: "What the hell happened to you?"

Looking up, Nick saw Carson Pike dressed in casual slacks and a green polo shirt. "I need to talk to you about something," said Nick. "Meet me out front in the lot."

Jeff, overhearing the short conversation pulled Nick to the side and whispered, "I know it's been an exciting day, to say the least, but if I were you I wouldn't mention anything about the missing Dunn girl. We can't be sure it's her... just yet. You need to keep this to yourself until you hear from me. Depending on what happens tomorrow, when we go back out, the police might have some questions for you."

"Do you think they'll want me along?"

"Probably not, but you need to be close-mouthed about what we found until we see if there's any more body parts out there. I'll give you a ring sometime tomorrow after we get back from the marsh."

"Sure," said Nick. "I understand."

Walking out to his golf cart he found Carson waiting, who asked, "What was that all about?"

Nick looked back at the dock. "I can't talk here. Can you meet me at the house in, let's say, about an hour? I need to get cleaned up. The front door will be unlocked. Just come on in. I'll talk to you then."

"Sure," said Carson. "About an hour."

The hot, soapy water cut through the mud on his arms and hands and cascaded down over his body onto his filthy legs. Minutes later, he toweled off his hair and put on grey sweat pants, a clean tee shirt and a pair of white socks. Suddenly, he realized how hungry he was. He hadn't eaten anything since he had woke up earlier in the day. Down in the kitchen, his choices for dinner were quite limited; three leftover sausages, a loaf of bread, and some beer. Tossing the three patties in the microwave, he grabbed a beer from the fridge.

Thirty seconds later, the buzzer on the microwave sounded and his dinner was ready. Placing the sausage and a few squirts of ketchup between two slices of bread, he went into the living room and turned on a floor lamp next to the couch.

He was so sooner settled in a chair when the doorbell sounded, followed by Carson's voice, "Anyone home?"

"In here in the front room," shouted Nick. "Beer's in the fridge."

Seconds later, Carson entered the living room and plopped down on the couch and unscrewed the cap of a bottled beer. Looking around the room, he remarked, "Boy, I can't tell you how many times I sat right here in this room and talked with your grandparents." Raising his beer, he made a toast. "Here's to Big Ed and Amelia. Two nicer people I've never known."

Crossing his legs, he took a long drink and then commented, "Heard on the news about that girl, what was her name... Amanda Schrock, you and your honey rescued last night."

"News gets around fast," said Nick. "I guess you and I have more in common than my grandparents. You found that girl out in the marsh last week and I now I find the Schrock girl in my front yard."

"Yeah, but the one you found is still breathing." Winking at Nick, Carson went in a different direction. "So, I can only guess the date you had over at the Dockside turned out rather well. I mean, she's at your house at two-thirty in the morning. I can only assume things went okay, well, at least up until the point where the Schrock girl stumbled into your yard."

"Well, let's just say it was an interesting evening." Nick displayed the minor wound on his upper left arm. "Got into a fight following dinner over at Port Royal. Turns out, the girl I met there has a boyfriend that's somewhat controlling. When we were leaving the restaurant, this guy shows up and starts shoving the girl around. I already knew about him, because he was one of the many topics we discussed over dinner. She's on the verge of breaking up with him. He's an ex-professional football player and likes to throw his weight around. I guess from what she said, he owns a lot of businesses in Savannah."

Carson nodded in acknowledgement, "You're talking about none other than Ike Miller... right?"

"Yeah, how'd you know?"

"Everybody around these parts knows who Ike Miller is. Personally, I think he's an ass!" Giving Nick a look of doubt, Carson asked, "And you say you got into a fight with Miller?"

"That's right *and*, now get this: if it wouldn't have been for Charley Sparks and that Derek character jumping in the fray, I'd probably be in the hospital."

Sitting back on the couch, Carson was confused, "Okay, now you've really got me thinking. I don't understand what you're driving at. Do you mean to tell me they got involved in this fight?"

"That's exactly what I'm saying. Derek was on Miller like green on grass and Charley, he got right in Miller's face and told him to get his sorry ass out of there and that I was a friend of theirs. That's not all. Earlier inside the restaurant, I discover that Sparks and his cohort are having dinner. They even came over to the table and introduced themselves to the girl I was with. When they left they paid for our dinner. What the hell's up with those two? First they threaten me, then they buy us dinner and then save me from being annihilated by Ike Miller. Can you explain that?"

"You don't have to be a genius to figure it out, Nick. Think about it? You have something they want: seven million dollars, which oddly enough does actually belong to the people they work for. Now, we both know something they *don't know! You* know where the money is."

Nick disagreed, "But I don't know where the money is."

"Fair enough," said Carson, "You know the money is hidden somewhere here in the house or on the property, but you couldn't tell them where to look if you wanted to. They don't know what you know at this point, but they aim to find out. It's in their best interest to make sure nothing happens to you until they get their money. Let me tell you about Sparks and Simons. They are referred to as *muscle* for the syndicate. The people who run the organization don't get their hands dirty... ever! They have individuals like Charley Sparks and Derek Simons on the payroll to handle their dirty work. They'll do whatever it takes to get that money back. As long as they don't know exactly where it is, you're not in any danger."

Nick set his sandwich on an end table, stood and walked to the window and stared out into the night. "Look, Carson. I really don't want to talk about Sparks and what's his name... Simons. I don't know where their damn money is and when it comes down to it, that's what I'm going to tell them." Before Carson could react to Nick's frustration, Nick brought up another topic. "When we were over at the marina tonight, when Jeff Lysinger was talking to me you asked what that was all about. I'm going to tell you, but you have to promise me you won't say a word, because when this comes out, it's going to upset people not only here on the island but from Beaufort to Savannah."

"I don't have any idea what you're talking about, but yeah, I can keep my mouth shut, if that's what you're asking."

Walking back to his chair, Nick sat down and looked directly at Carson. "When I first came down here and heard about this RPS Killer business, I have to admit I thought it was horrible, but there wasn't anything I could do about it, so I didn't give it much thought one way or the other. But, a series of events over the last twenty four hours has landed me in the middle of these murders. Last night, finding the Schrock girl in my front yard was just the beginning. This morning, I was headed out for Ocean Point when I discovered a one dollar bill in the bushes where we found Amanda Schrock. The police didn't find it... I did! I took the money to Chief Lysinger and wound up going with him and one of his officers out to the marsh. Turns out, after the detectives questioned the Schrock girl last night, an organized push has been put in place to find the boat the killer has been using. Well, to make a long story short, we get out there over behind Pritchards Island somewhere and I found the remains of a severed hand with a five dollar bill still in it. Jeff Lysinger thinks it night be Susan Dunn, a girl who disappeared right after the first victim was discovered two years ago. They never found the Dunn girl and it's always been a mystery if she was one of the killer's victims. Whether it turns out to be her or not, we can be sure, because of the five in the hand, that's it's another murder we didn't know about. That puts the total number dead at nine instead of eight. Call it coincidence if you will. But the fact is, it seems in the last twenty-four hours I've discovered more about the RPS Killer and discovered more evidence than the police have in months. Does this make any sense to you?"

"You just hit the nail on the head when you mentioned it might be coincidence, because that's exactly what it is. There is nothing you or I can do about finding this killer. Hell, the authorities from Charleston down to Savannah have been looking for this killer for two years and they have had little to no success in bringing him in. What do you expect to come of these things you've discovered? Thinking you are going to, in some way, run this guy down is about as stupid as walking into the post office and seeing a wanted poster for someone, then going home and telling your wife you're quitting your job and you're going to track down this criminal. Bringing in the RPS Killer is the responsibility of the local police. Sure, they'll welcome any help or information they can get from the public, but still, they are the ones who, if it ever happens, will solve this case."

Walking to the refrigerator, Carson grabbed another beer and leaned on the counter and continued to address Nick. "You need to forget about this RPS Killer and start concentrating on what Sparks and Simons are planning. You have to prepare yourself for the moment when they will approach you with a deal, and they will."

Nick scratched his head. "I've thought about what you told me before about the money Edward hid around here someplace and it just doesn't make any sense. You told me, Edward informed you the money was hidden here, but not where it actually was, so that means after he was killed, my grandmother was the only person who knew the exact location. If this is true, how does the syndicate know the money is hidden here? Are they just assuming or guessing about its whereabouts?"

Walking back into the living room, Carson sat back down on the couch. "A few days after your grandfather's funeral, Sparks and Simons paid Amelia a visit here at the house. We talked about the fact that they would come to see her. She figured, and I agreed with her, the only way they would not kill her was if they thought she knew where the money was. If they killed her, then the money may not ever be located and they would still be out seven million. The syndicate only wants their money back and are willing to be patient, but only to a point. For months, Charley and Derek continued to contact her, each time increasing the pressure of what might happen to her if she didn't tell them where the money was. From the very beginning she stuck to her guns, telling them she knew the money was on the property, but didn't know where. They offered to purchase the house from her, but by that time she had restructured the family will so that everything, especially the house, went to you with a built-in clause that you had to live in the house... it could not be sold. They even suggested coming in as a remodeling crew to search the house, agreeing to pay for tearing out the walls or whatever else happened during the search. Amelia would not agree to this either."

"Why would they agree to pay for repairs to the house?"

"Mathematically, it makes sense. If you had an unending supply of money, would you invest a few thousand dollars in the hopes of gaining seven million?"

"When you put it that way... I guess so."

"Finally," said Carson, "after weeks of trying to negotiate with your grandmother with no luck, Sparks cornered Amelia in Beaufort one afternoon when she was shopping. He informed her, this was her last opportunity to agree with them on searching for the money. Your grandmother was one tough bird, I've got to give her that. She told Charley to stick it where the sun doesn't shine! That was a mistake on her part. The one thing you don't want to do is piss Charley Sparks off. Here's the thing. Between the two men, Sparks is the more intelligent... by far. Charley will negotiate until there is no other alternative *and* when that happens he becomes a different person. Don't let him fool you. His smooth manners and politeness can change in an instant. When it comes right down to it, he'd just as soon cut your throat as look at you. Now, Derek on the other hand is just a plain thug. He is controlled by Sparks and if he turns Derek loose, it can be very unpleasant. This is exactly what he told your grandmother in no uncertain terms. He told her he was done talking and the next time she saw either he or Derek, it would not be pleasant."

"So what you're saying is he threatened my grandmother?"

"That's exactly what he did. If he couldn't get the money, then he was going to take her life. How and when, she had no idea. We talked things over and she decided to disappear."

"Disappear... where?"

"You have no way of knowing this, but your grandparents owned a house up in Canada, right outside of Ontario on a large wooded lot. Amelia deeded the property over to me and told me she wanted to move up north. She felt she would be safe there."

"But what about the house here on Fripp?"

"As you are well aware, she left the home to you with the clause stating you could not sell it. If it turned out you were not interested in living here, she told me she was going to donate the house to the Fripp Island Home Owner's association. If, by some chance the money was never found, then, so be it. She had enough money of her own to live out the rest of her life."

"She never made it to Canada... did she?"

"No. I guess it was about two weeks before she was going to disappear, that she died in her sleep."

"Please don't tell me the syndicate killed her like Edward?"

"No, according to the coroner, your grandmother died of natural causes. So now, nobody knows exactly where the money is."

"And now that I own the house, it's back to the drawing board for the syndicate. Do you really think they'll approach me?"

"You can count on it. This is seven million we're talking about. They'll try and buy the house from you, but the will blocks that from ever happening. The only other recourse is if you agree to allow them to search the property."

"What should I do, Carson?"

"Nothing. You don't know where the money is. When they come to you just say you don't have any idea what they're talking about."

"I can do that, but what happens when their patience runs out. Will I be faced with the same situation as Amelia?"

"It won't get that far, believe me! Your grandmother told me if anything happened to her before or after the move to Canada, if you decided to live here at the house I should watch over you."

"I'm not sure what that means. You can't be with me every minute of the day."

"If it gets to the point where Charley makes it clear to you he's run out of patience, I'll step in and it'll be like he never saw you."

"I don't understand. How can you protect me?"

"You just let me worry about that. I'm not going to let anything happen to you. I have my ways, and that being said, this conversation is over. You don't have anything to worry about. You just go on living your new life here on Fripp like none of this ever happened. It'll all work out." Getting up, Carson walked to the fridge and grabbed another beer and held it up. "One for the road. And by the way, you need to get to the grocery store and stock up. Your grandmother would have a fit if she could see how empty this refrigerator is. I'm heading for the house."

Nick got up and followed Carson down the hall and out the front door. Standing on the porch, Carson put his beer on the porch railing and lit up a cigarette. Taking a short drag, he put his hand over his mouth and coughed three times. "Summer cold," asked Nick.

"No, it's these cigarettes. I've been smoking since I was fourteen years old. Guess it's catching up with me. I really should quit. Well, I'll see you around."

Nick stood at the edge of the steps and watched as Carson drove off. Looking at his watch, the time was 11:15. He wasn't the least bit tired seeing as how he had slept in until two in the afternoon. Snapping his fingers, he was going to take Carson's advice.

Ten minutes later, the Lexus passed the guard shack, the officer on duty, giving Nick a sloppy wave. Crossing the Fripp Island Bridge, he turned on the air, the temperature on the dash gauge reading eighty-three degrees. He couldn't believe how hot it was at midnight. Cruising past Hunting Island, he turned the air on high. At the moment, he'd give anything for one cold, snowy day in Cincinnati. Initially, he thought moving to Fripp would be a delightful and welcome change to his life. Smiling, he thought, *What have I gotten myself into?*

Crossing the Harbor River Bridge, he wondered if just maybe he should head up north to Cincinnati for a couple of weeks until things straightened themselves out. No, that would just be running away. Charley Sparks and Derek Simons would no doubt follow him. It seemed like they knew every move he made. If he knew where the money was hidden, he'd just as soon give it to them and let them be on their way so he could get on with his life. That seemed a lot easier than trying to con two men, who according to Carson could be very violent.

It was twelve-fifteen when he pulled into the Publix parking lot. Normally, during tourist season it was nearly impossible to get a spot close to the store, but the late hour and the lack of customers allowed him to park three spaces down from the main entrance.

Inside the huge store, he grabbed a cart and started his shopping. He wasn't much on cooking, so by the time he got to the checkout the cart was filled with assorted TV dinners, hotdogs and buns, cornflakes, milk, eggs, cheese and of course, his favorite beer. Waiting for the lady in front of him to pay for her purchases, he took a candy bar from the display next to the smut magazines, unwrapped it, and quickly devoured the chocolate treat.

While the clerk was bagging up his groceries, another clerk approached her and asked, "Is Mr. Kline in tonight?"

"I think so... why?"

Looking toward the exit door, the other clerk explained, "That old bum is still out in the lot trying to sell those puppies. You know Mr. Kline doesn't allow that sort of thing when he's the manager on duty."

The register girl frowned and inquired, "Has there been a complaint about the man out on the lot?"

"No, but..."

"The girl gave Nick his total. "That'll be $62.37, sir." Turning to her friend, she shrugged. "I wouldn't bother Mr. Kline tonight if I were you. He came in with a foul mood. He hasn't been out of his office for hours. Let's just keep it that way. If the man in the parking lot isn't bothering anyone, just let it be."

Nick, after paying for his goods walked out of the air-conditioned building into the late night heat. Just as he was about to cross the pavement in front of the store, he was startled by a gruff, low voice, "Care ta buy a puppy, sir?"

Huddled down next to a row of soda machines sat an older man, dressed in clothes that had seen their better day. His face was covered in a light beard, his head covered by an old fishing hat. Nick politely answered, "No," and turned to cross the lot when the man removed a small ball of black fur from a cardboard box and held it up. "Just got this one left. Only cost ten dollars."

Nick ignored the man, but then, after taking two steps stopped and returned to the man. "You say ten dollars?"

"That's right. This be my last one."

Pushing his cart up against the side of a vending machine, Nick reached out for the small puppy. "I have a friend who just lost her dog. He was a black Lab. What kind of dog is this? It looks like a Lab."

"Part Lab... part Shepherd."

Holding the dog up and looking it square in the eyes, Nick asked, "Where did you get the pups?"

Angling his thumb in the direction of the road, the old man answered, "Me an' my dog, Millie, a Shepherd, live up the road 'bout a mile in an abandoned trailer back in the woods. A few months back, she got out on me an' come home pregnant. There's a black Lab lives up the road a piece. From the looks of the pups I'd say they locked horns. They're three weeks old. I can't afford ta keep all of 'em, so I come up here ta the grocery to see if I could sell 'em. I need the money fer food fer me and Millie. Tried ta git twenty a piece, but folks were only willin' ta go ten. This be my last one. Ten bucks an' she's yours."

"Tell you what," said Nick. "I'll take your last pup but only if you sell me that box. I'll need something to carry her home in."

"Heck, I'll give ya the box if ya take the pup."

"No, the deal is I purchase the box... and the dog." Placing the pup back into the box, Nick opened his wallet and extracted six twenties. Holding them out toward the man, he said, "I'll take the pup for ten and the box for one hundred and ten. That's one hundred twenty dollars. Fair?"

The man was speechless for a few seconds but then stood and reached for the money. "Why would ya pay that much money fer a worthless box?"

Nick smiled. "Like I said, I need something to carry the pup in, and well, let's just say that right now, I have more money than I ever had before." Picking up the box and putting it in the cart, Nick nodded toward the store. "That should be enough money to keep you and Millie fed for a while."

"God bless ya, mister. I haven't had this much money since, well, I can't even remember."

Nick turned and started across the lot, the man still talking, "She ain't had no shots or nothin'. Take good care of her."

Back at the car, Nick placed the groceries in the back and the box containing the pup in the passenger seat. Pulling out of the lot, he felt good about what he had done and what he was going to do. He had given the old man enough money so he and his dog could live a little more comfortably, at least for a while. Looking at the clock on the dash, he noted the time at: 12:50 in the morning. Genevieve always took her morning walk just before the sun came up. That daily event wasn't going to happen for six hours. His plan was to meet her on the beach and present her with the pup. She had said she wasn't interested in having another dog because of her age and was afraid the dog would outlive her. Leaning over and looking down into the box he saw the pup curled up, apparently asleep. He hoped Genevieve would accept the pup.

Chapter Fourteen

TAKING THE LAST BITE OF A SWEEDISH MEATBALL TV
dinner, followed by a gulp of milk, Nick reclined into a black
wicker chair on the screened-in porch and looked out at the
pinkish hue the ocean had taken on. The sun was minutes away
from making its daily, early morning appearance in the eastern
sky somewhere beyond Ocean Point. He recalled how as a young
boy, he and his grandmother would often sit on the porch and wait
for the sun to cast its warmth over the island. Amelia always said,
The earlier you get up, the longer the day is!

Looking at his watch, he realized he had been up for close to
seventeen hours and the night before hadn't gone to bed until four
in the morning. He needed to get back to a normal pattern of sleep.
Yawning, he looked at the black pup curled up in a towel next to
the box. Surprisingly, it had been a peaceful night. He had
watched some television during the wee hours, the pup slept and
he had something a little more substantial to eat than his previous
sausage and ketchup sandwich.

Scooping up the pup, the towel and the box, he opened the
screen door. It was time to go down to the beach. Genevieve, just
like she had done for decades, would be walking up the stretch of
sand toward the rising sun. Walking out to the edge of the water,
he set the box down in the sand and looked up the beach. No sign
of Genevieve. Maybe he was too early.

Sitting down next to the box, he checked on the pup. She got
up, turned in a circle, curled up in the towel and went back to
sleep. The reddish-orange crescent shape of the sun was slowly
making its way above the ocean in the distance. Putting on his
sunglasses he stared directly into the slowly forming ball of heat
that would drive the temperature on the island into the high
nineties once again. He couldn't remember it ever being this hot
in the lowcountry for such an extended period of time. His
concentration on the rising sun was interrupted by a voice,
"Good morning Nick. Looks like it's going to be another blazer
today."

Genevieve walked toward him and continued to speak, "I might cut my walk short today. This heat has really got me down. Besides that, I don't like walking on the beach by myself."

Nick got to his feet, bent over, reached in the box and held up the pup. "Well there isn't anything I can do about the heat, but I can do something about you being alone on the beach. Found you a new walking partner."

A true dog lover, Genevieve's eyes lit up. She took the pup from Nick and held it up looking into the small black face. "He's so cute. Where did you get him?"

"First of all, it's a her, not a him and I got her from an old man outside of Publix. She's part Lab and I guess from what the man told me... part Shepherd."

Cuddling the pup next to her bosom, Genevieve gave Nick an odd look and questioned him. "I've never known you to have a pet. I mean, in all the years you came down, you never mentioned you had a dog."

"I never have had a dog... ever! It's not my intention to have one now either. I got her for you. She's probably too small to walk with you on the beach right now, but in a few weeks or maybe a couple of months, she can be your new companion. You've always had a dog. I can't see you living all alone."

Trying to hand the dog back to Nick, Genevieve objected, "No, I can't accept her. I already told you after Rex died I figured I was too old to own a dog, especially one this young. I'm in my mid-eighties, Nick. I have no doubt this dog will outlive me. Then, what would happen to her. Who would care for her when I'm gone?"

Holding his hands up, he refused to take the puppy. "Me... that's who. If she outlives you, I guarantee you she'll have a home with me for as long as she lives after you're gone."

Hugging the pup to the side of her face Genevieve got a tear in her eye. "You really bought her for me?"

"Hey," said Nick. "She needed a home and you needed a new companion. I know you'll take good care of her."

Smiling, Genevieve turned in a complete circle and held the dog up. "Okay then. This pup has a new home. I've got so much to do today. Ruby, a friend of mine lives up the street. Today is grocery day. She always drives us over to Ladies Island. I'll just call the vet and get an appointment for the little one here. She needs to get checked out. I don't suppose she's had any shots yet?"

"The owner... the man told me she needed her shots."

Genevieve pointed at the box. "I'll need that box too. She's probably used to it. She'll feel safe in the box."

Handing her the box, Nick laughed. "The box is yours. It's the most expensive box I've ever had."

Genevieve gave him a strange look as if she didn't understand.

Nick waved off his comment, "Just an inside joke. Listen, you better get her inside out of this heat."

Giving Nick a kiss on his cheek, Genevieve turned and started back up the beach toward her house. Nick looked back at the sun and noticed it was one of those rare moments when the sun appeared to be resting on the very edge of the distant ocean. Stretching his arms and back, he decided to take another shot at having a day of relaxation. Yesterday, he started out with good intentions, but he no sooner left the house when his plans changed. Walking across the sand to the wooden deck, he couldn't imagine another day like that.

Following a lawn maintenance truck down Tarpon, Nick made a right onto Deer Lake Road, then a left on Remora Drive. There were quite a few people out for seven-thirty in the morning: joggers, walkers, and people riding bikes. Nick figured they were out getting their exercise before the heat of the day settled in.

Driving past the Ocean Point Golf Course, he noticed a foursome standing around on the putting green near the rocks just up from the beach. Parking the cart in a small, sand covered cul-de-sac, he placed his sunglasses on the seat, jumped out, stripped off his shirt and grabbed his swimming goggles. Walking down a narrow path in between the large rocks on the Fripp side of the inlet, he stared across the quarter mile stretch of water over at Hunting Island. Taking a few deep knee bends in a small strip of sand next to the water, he looked up at the sun, the temperature climbing rapidly.

It was here, at this very spot where Amelia had, over the summer of his eighth birthday, taught him about endurance swimming. It had taken him all summer that year, swimming every day, until he could swim over to Hunting Island and back; a distance of a half mile. Amelia would swim out with him and when he got tired, she would urge him on, further than the previous day until he made it all the way across, and eventually back. The following summer when he returned to Fripp, he and Amelia twice a week would swim the inlet.

Stepping out into the warm water, he waded in until he was up to his waist. Slipping under, he came up, ran his fingers through his short hair, then dove in. The tide was out and the waves were not as choppy as when it was in. Cutting smoothly through the water, every fifth stroke he turned his head slightly to his right and took in a breath of sea air. It had been years since he had swam across the inlet, but it came back to him instantly and minutes later, he was wading through the ankle deep water that bordered Hunting Island.

Standing on the thin strip of sand he looked out across the Atlantic. It was right out there about a quarter mile beyond where the inlet merged with the ocean that he had spread his grandmother's ashes a little over a week ago. He smiled when he noticed the black fins of three dolphins about fifty yards off shore. Amelia always loved to come to the inlet from time to time and watch the dolphins at play.

He felt slightly winded. He needed to rest for a few minutes before swimming back to Fripp. Looking back at the trees that bordered the interior of the island, his thoughts drifted to one of the things he had learned yesterday while out with Jeff and Travis: one of the very first girls the RPS Killer had killed had been found on Hunting Island. Shaking the thought off, Nick started back toward the water. Talking to himself, he announced, "This is my day of relaxation. I'm not going to fill it with thoughts of the RPS Killer, Charley Sparks, Derek Simons, Ike Miller or anything else negative!"

The swim back to Fripp took considerably longer. He had to stop twice for a rest and float on top of the water, allowing his arm and leg muscles to relax. Finally, standing on the Fripp side of the inlet, Nick felt good about his swim. Aside from the heat, it was going to be a good day.

Back at the cart, he opened one of the beers in his cooler, holding the cold bottle to his forehead. Between the cold beer and the breeze that would be created from the speed of the cart, he knew he would be cooled off and dry within minutes.

Once on Tarpon, he decided on his next stop: Wardle's Landing; the opposite side of the island. He and Amelia had caught many a fish on the long wooden wharf that jutted out into Skull Inlet. Making a left on Wahoo Drive, a dirt road that bordered the left hand side of the Ocean Creek Golf Course, thoughts of the RPS Killer once again came to him. Wardle's Landing was one of the spots where one of the girls, who the killer had released, walked out from the marsh and then there was Skull Inlet and beyond that is where he found the remains of the hand with the tattered five; possibly the hand of Susan Dunn. Realizing he was allowing his relaxing day to be invaded by things he really didn't want to think about, he cursed, "Damn it, there I go again. Everywhere I go on the island, the killer seems to have left his mark. Why can't I get him off my mind?"

Pulling to the side of the road, he grabbed another beer from the cooler and took a long swig. If he had any chance of having a relaxing day he was going to have to get his mind off the killer. Looking to his left he saw a man on a ladder pounding nails into a fascia board just below the roof of a house. Then it hit him. It was Parker Sims, the man he and Carson had talked with in the parking lot at the marina; the man who was remodeling his house. The man had mentioned he was looking for someone who could do some painting. Nick remembered he told the man he would drop by and give him an estimate.

Pulling across the street, he stopped in the driveway, the lawn on both sides completely dug up. Sims looked down from his elevated position and acknowledged Nick as he waved a paintbrush, "Good morning!"

"Mornin'," yelled back Nick. "Remember, I said I'd drop by and give you an estimate on painting your house."

Snapping his fingers, Sims laughed and started down the ladder. "That's right, you did. You're Carson's friend." At the bottom of the ladder, he wiped his brow. "This heat in incessant." Looking at the beer Nick was holding, Sims asked, "I don't suppose you have another one of those handy?"

Holding up the bottle in a toasting fashion, Nick responded, "Got one more left. Here, let me get it for you. I've already had two this morning and it's not even nine o'clock yet. Actually, you'd be doing me a favor by drinking my last beer. The way I'm going I'll be crocked before lunch." Handing the beer to Sims, Nick looked at the faded and chipped old white paint on the two-story house. "Looks like she does need a good facelift."

"That she does. I live over on Blue Gill Road on the other side of Bonito. The people who owned this place were hardly ever here. It was strictly a rental, but as you can see, they didn't keep the place up. The husband died and the wife had no desire to spend the money to get the place updated so she put it on the market. I got it for a pretty good price. I've been working on it for almost a year now. The inside is done; new floors and cabinets, plus all the rooms have been repainted. All I have to do now is give her a good coat of paint on the outside and she'll be ready to rent." Taking a short drink, Sims went on, "If I recall, you said before you moved down here you had your own painting business."

"Yep. Worked my way through college painting houses and then after I graduated I opened my own business. I guess I've been painting houses for close to ten years." Walking up to the house, he ran his hand across the rough, peeling paint. "First thing you're going to have to do is to remove all this old paint. The new paint that's applied will only be as good as the surface it's covering. I would suggest a good power washing first, followed by scraping the really rough places. Do you have, or can you get your hands on a power washer?"

"No, but if we need one, I can rent one in Beaufort. If I get it cleaned up, do you think you can paint the house?"

"Sure, what color are you thinking?"

"I'm gonna go with a light yellow with the porch and the trim in black. I'm getting the paint at Lowes. I've got the color swatches already picked out."

Their conversation was interrupted when another golf cart pulled in the driveway. A man, dressed in bright red pants and a white polo shirt stepped out and approached, "What the hell, Sims. When are you going to stop working on this heap of crap and start hitting the greens again?"

Reaching for the man's hand, Sims made the introductions, "Pete Clark, this is Nick Falco. He just moved to the island. He's thinking about painting my latest investment here for me."

Shaking Nick's hand, Clark remarked, "Played some golf with your grandfather. He was quite the fellow. Sorry to hear about your grandmother."

Nick nodded but remained quiet.

Angling his thumb back in the direction of Bonito Drive, Clark asked, "You guys know what the hell's going on over at the marina? I just came from there. There's three television station and two radio station vans, the Beaufort Police and island security up there. I tried to ask ol' Jeff Lysinger what was going on and he told me not to worry about it. He told me to move on and said they didn't need to have a lot of people hanging around. Sounds fishy to me. Something's up for all those news people to be here on Fripp. If you ask me, I bet they found another girl."

Nick knew exactly, or had a pretty good idea what the media was doing on the island. "Listen, I've got to go. I'll come back later and do a walk around and get a price together for you." Jumping in the cart, he backed out and sped up Wahoo.

"Watching the cart disappear in a trail of dust, Pete remarked, "What's he in such a hurry for?"

Sims shrugged, "Beats me!"

Turning onto Bonito, Nick floored the cart, hoping he could make the marina before everything was over. When he arrived, he found he had to park all the way down where the boats were stored and repaired. In all his years of coming to Fripp he never saw the marina this crowded. People were milling around in small groups, walking in and out of the marina store with drinks and snacks. Cars and golf carts completely lined the paved area and there didn't seem to be a parking spot left.

Walking through the crowd, he finally arrived at the dock area. The porch of the restaurant was jammed with people staring out at the wharf. A number of media vans were parked on the side of the restaurant. News people were everywhere setting up cameras, and running long lengths of wiring across the lot.

Nick stopped a woman carrying a clipboard and asked, "What's going on?"

Looking at him as if he were not important, she answered, "We're not sure... just yet. Might be about a missing girl. You and everyone else will know soon enough."

Nick, on a mere hunch, pushed his luck. "This doesn't have anything to do with Susan Dunn... does it?"

The woman gave him a look of great interest. "Why, yes it does. How would you know that?"

Despite the fact Jeff had told him not to mention anything about the Dunn girl, based upon what the woman said, he figured the cat was already out of the bag. "I was the one who actually found the remains of the hand holding the money."

The woman, now quite excited, grabbed the sleeve of a man walking by, "Steve! That camera ready to roll?"

"Yeah but—"

"Yeah but hell. We're going to interview this man."

Making some quick adjustments to the camera, Steve spoke professionally, "We're live."

The woman moved next to Nick and held a mic to her lips. "Good morning. This is Cynthia Crane of WFWF TV 16 out of Beaufort. We are here on Fripp Island where yesterday the remains of a human hand was found clutching a tattered five dollar bill out in the salt marsh beyond Pritchards Island." Raising the mic toward Nick's face, the newswoman went on, "We have with us this morning a Mr..." Pushing the mic closer, she nodded for Nick to speak.

Nick, taken completely off guard, didn't know what to say, but realizing that he was on live television, stammered, "Ah... ah... my name... is Nick Falco."

The woman, being quite good at what she did for a living, intervened, "Mr. Falco. I understand that you are the individual who found the remains."

The mic once again in his face, Nick couldn't bring himself to what he considered a level of normalcy as far as talking was concerned. "Ah... that's right. I... I did find... the hand." Desiring not to become a bigger fool than what he probably already appeared, he excused himself, "Look, I have... to go. If you want any future information, you need to talk with the local police." Awkwardly he nodded at the camera and disappeared in the crowd.

Making good his escape, Nick pushed his way through a group of people until he was at the edge of the ramp leading down to the water. Looking around, he saw two vans lined up next to the curb: WSAV and WJCL, both out of Savannah. Beyond the vans there were two other vehicles advertising the Gazette newspaper from Savannah and the Tribune from Beaufort. A radio station, WLXP from Savannah was pulling into the lot.

Two Fripp Island officers stood watch next to the ramp, preventing the media from going down next to the water where he could see Chief Lysinger, Travis and Detective Graham talking with two other men dressed in suits. Approaching one of the officers, Nick tried to explain, "Excuse me. My name is Nick Falco. I need to speak with Chief Lysinger."

The officer gave Nick a look indicating that his request was out of the question. "The Chief can't be bothered right now. He's talking with the Savannah Police."

"But you don't understand. I need to talk with him now. Something just happened that he needs to know about."

"Look son," said one of the officers. "In less than five minutes we're going to be conducting a press conference. You can talk with the Chief after that."

"It'll be too late then," argued Nick.

Nick tried to brush by the officers but was held back as he struggled. "Let me be! I have to talk with the Chief."

Noticing the commotion, Jeff ran up the dock when he saw his officers struggling with Nick. "What the hell's the problem here? Let this young man go."

Stepping back from the officers, Nick looked at the curious crowd that was gathering, the news people closing in; three different cameras rolling. Turning to Jeff, he tried his best to explain, "Chief, I need to talk with you before the press conference."

Taking Nick off to the side, Jeff looked out at the crowd and asked, "What was that all about back there? Do you realize you're being filmed?"

"I don't care about that," said Nick. "I just wanted to give you a heads up that I accidentally mentioned to one of the women from the press I was the one who found the remains. I'm sorry. Things just kind of got out of hand."

Jeff smiled. "It's not a problem. The police in Beaufort decided to contact the news media. They already know about the hand and they also know there is a possibility it may be the Dunn girl. I was hoping to keep you out of this. The press doesn't know who found the hand, but since you told them, well, I guess now they do know. The press conference will be starting in a few minutes. Since they already started filming your confrontation with my officers, they'll want to talk with you. If you would rather not be interviewed, then just disappear. If you feel uncomfortable, I'll explain how you found the hand."

Looking back at the cameras, Nick agreed, "I think it would be best if I wasn't interviewed. I don't want to get any more involved in this RPS Killer business than I already am."

"Alright," said Jeff. "When the press conference starts, walk down to the boat and cut in behind the building. I don't think anyone will notice. If they do, they probably won't follow you because they'll be too interested in what we have to say."

"Thanks," said Nick. "I think I will just disappear."

On his way to the boat dock, he passed Detective Graham and the other two men in suits. Graham simply nodded while listening to something one of the other men was saying.

Stopping next to two boats, he spoke to Travis. "Are you getting ready to head out?"

Placing some bottles of water into a cooler, Travis answered, "Yep, that's the plan. Myself, I don't think we're going to find any other body parts out there. If it is the Dunn Girl, hell, it's been two years." Looking over at the ever growing number of media people, he commented, "The Beaufort Police should have never let on that it may be Susan Dunn. Now, look! We have a media circus here on the island."

Stepping up to a number of microphones that had been set up, Jeff spoke to the growing crowd. "Good morning. My name is Chief Lysinger, I'm the head of security here on the island. We also have a detective from Beaufort and two representatives from the Savannah Police Department with us this morning. I think you all know why we are here, so we're going to conduct a ten minute question and answer time and then we'll head out. First question, please."

A woman at the front of the crowd raised her hand. "Can we be sure that the remains found are from the Dunn girl?"

Jeff answered the question without hesitation, "No, we can't be sure and unless we find body parts that are more conclusive, like dental identification, we may never know the identity of the person."

Another reporter spoke up, "But we can be sure it is one if the RPS Killer's victims?"

"Most definitely," said Jeff. "The five dollar bill that was found in the remains of the hand is one of the killer's calling cards."

The questions and answers continued:

"Where were the remains found?"

"Over behind Pritchards Island."

"How long will the search take?"

"It's a large area, so the search could conceivably take days or maybe even weeks."

"This puts the number of dead at nine... right?"

"That's correct... nine dead."

Travis walked slowly toward where the other officers were standing. Realizing this was his opportunity, Nick casually walked up next to the building and down the ramp at the rear. Jeff had been right. Everyone was concentrating on the questions being asked. Just before he slipped behind the building, he shot a look out at the crowd. No one noticed his departure from the dock.

Walking across the dock at the rear of the building, he cut up the opposite side of the restaurant, stopped in the lot and looked at the back of the crowd twenty yards away. Turning to walk quickly across the lot, he accidentally bumped into someone. Before he could even apologize, the person spoke, "What are you doing here?"

Looking into the face of Shelby Lee, Nick was at a loss for words. Finally he joked, "I live here. The question is... why are you here? I thought you went back to Savannah."

"I did," explained Shelby, "but I had to come back. Kirby and I are living here temporarily with the friend I told you about."

Confused, Nick pulled her around to the side of the building. "I don't want any of those news people to see me."

"What are you talking about?"

Taking her by the arm, he started across the lot. "Come on, let's go into the marina store. We can grab a drink or something. You can explain to me why you're now living here on Fripp and I can tell you why I want to avoid the press."

At the bottom of the steps, Nick pointed at three concrete picnic tables under a protective roof. "Why don't you grab one of those tables and I'll get us a couple of iced teas."

Three minutes later, Nick returned with the drinks. Checking to see if anyone had seen them and satisfied they had gone unnoticed, he sat down and shoved one of the teas across the table. Shelby, thinking his actions were a bit dramatic, stated comically, "The last time we were together, it turned out to be quite the adventure. I'm getting the feeling the adventure is not over."

"I couldn't have put it better, myself," said Nick. "When you left my place the other evening, I figured our part in this whole mess was over. Not true! When I got up later on in the day, I decided to just have a day of relaxation. Didn't happen! When I was leaving my place what do I find in the bushes where we found Amanda Schrock? A one dollar bill!"

Shelby, about to take a drink, stopped and remarked in a surprised fashion, "You're kidding? We talked to those detectives about how Amanda didn't have any money with her when we found her."

"That's not the half of it. I decided Chief Lysinger should know about what I found. I finally ran him down just as he and one of his officers were headed out to the marsh. Apparently, ol' man Schrock, Amanda's father, got in a tiff about how no one has, to date, been able to locate the boat the killer has been using. So, this big push is being put on to find the boat. I went along with Jeff and Travis and spent the day out in the marsh. Just when we were ready to call it a day, I discover a severed hand holding an old five dollar bill. The hand was nothing but bones, but it was still holding the money. Jeff thinks it might be the remains of a girl by the name of Susan Dunn; a girl that disappeared from Savannah right after the first girl was killed two years ago. They never found the Dunn girl and up until I found that hand her disappearance has been a mystery. They can't be sure the hand I found is hers, but still, it's another one of the RPS Killer's victims. That's why all of the news people are over there at the boathouse. The police are going back out today to see if they can find any other body parts. All those people are out there because of what I found yesterday. The media might want to interview me. Hell, one of the TV stations has already filmed a short, and I must say, awkward interview with me. So, if you want a good laugh, watch the news tonight. I really made a fool of myself. That's why I wanted to get out of there. I don't want to be involved any more than what I already am. What I'm saying is, this so called adventure you referred to didn't end when you left the other night. It has continued for me *and* I don't want it to."

Shelby chuckled silently, then took a drink. "You're not the only one who wants what happened the other night to be over. Remember, finding Amanda Schrock was just part of what happened to us. We mustn't forget about my ex-boyfriend."

Surprised, Nick repeated, "Ex-boyfriend? So what you're saying is since we last saw each other, you broke up with Miller."

"I did, but it wasn't that easy. The night I left your place, I went back to my friend's house here on Fripp and packed for Savannah. I went directly to my apartment and who do I find waiting for me—"

Nick finished up the sentence. "Let me guess... Ike Miller!"

"Yep... big as life. There he was sitting on my sofa."

"How did he get in?"

Giving Nick a look as if he were stupid, she answered, "He has a key *and* I have a key to his place. Don't look so surprised. We've been dating for over a year. So, yes, if you're thinking we had sex during our relationship... you're right."

Holding up his hands, Nick acknowledged, "Okay, I get it. It's too much information for me... but I get it!" Wanting to move off the subject of sex, Nick rotated his hands and added, "Okay, so Ike Miller is sitting on your couch when you got home. Then, what happened?"

Shelby hesitated, then answered, "He was the perfect gentleman. He apologized for his actions at the Dockside and for the way he has been conducting himself for the past few months. The next thing I know he's down on his knee in front of me and he opens this small box that contains a diamond ring. He proceeds to ask me to marry him. He told me he purchased the ring weeks ago and had been working up the courage to ask me. I've got to tell you. It was one of the most awkward moments I think I've ever had in my life. After the incident at the Dockside, I pretty much decided to end it with Ike and here he was on his knee in front of me popping the question."

"What did you say?"

"I told him it was too little, too late. It's like he wasn't listening to what I was saying. He got up and went back to the couch and said I just needed some time to think things over. He said he knew I would come around. He was so confident, so sure of himself, almost arrogant. That really pissed me off. I told him there wasn't any more thinking to do. I was not only, not going to marry him, but I was breaking off our relationship... for good! He just sat there on the couch staring at me and then down at the ring. He looked so pathetic... like a rejected little boy or something. I told him I thought it best if he just left."

Shelby stopped talking and looked out toward the marsh as if she were about to start crying.

Nick sympathized with what she had been through. "Look, if you don't want to talk about it, it's alright."

"No, I need to tell you what happened." Composing herself, she continued, "Suggesting that he leave turned out to be the wrong thing to say. It was a Jekyll and Hyde moment. He seemed to explode. He got up from the couch, threw the ring across the room, picked up the coffee table and threw it into my china cabinet breaking the glass. He broke one of my lamps and then that's when I exploded! I pushed him and told him to stop. Before I knew it, he picked me up and tossed me to the side. At that point I knew I had to back off. I was so afraid of what he might do. He stood over me and yelled in my face that he was Ike Miller, that he had been a professional football player and had made millions of dollars. He had dated some of the most beautiful women in Savannah, but he had chosen me. No one broke up with him. He broke up with them. No one told him how it was going to be. He told others how things were going to go. He knew everyone in Savannah. He was important. He picked me up and got right in my face and told me he was going to make my life a living hell. Then, he stormed out, slamming the door."

Nick sat in silence, not believing what he had just heard. Finally, he spoke, "Of course, you went to the police... right?"

"No, I didn't contact the police. Are you kidding me! I was scared to death! If I were to go to the police all Ike Miller would get would be a slap on the wrist. I wasn't going to be able to prove anything. He didn't leave any marks on me. He'd talk his way right out of what happened. He knows most of the police. He's donated thousands of dollars not only to the police force but the city as well. They're not going to do anything to him, at least, that will make a difference."

"So, what are you going to do now?" asked Nick.

"I already did what I had to. I went to see Franklin Schrock, one of the lawyers I work for."

"You mean Amanda's father."

"That's right, Amanda's father. When I got to the office, he was surprised to see me. As soon as I walked into his office, he knew I was upset. I told him all about what happened with Ike. He told me that being a law abiding citizen, he probably should advise me to go to the police, but he agreed with me that Miller would get off easy. He went on to tell me Miller did a lot of good things for Savannah, but still, there had always been something about the man he couldn't put his finger on. Then, in the middle of our conversation, he changed the subject and told me he found out I was one of the two people who had rescued his daughter, Amanda. He explained to me that, while at the hospital, she had told him to make sure you and I were rewarded in some fashion. He went on to tell me he was giving me a five thousand dollar a year raise and he was going to spring for a two week cruise for you and I wherever we wanted to go. I didn't refuse what he was offering, but I did tell him if he really wanted to help me, I needed some advice on how to handle the Ike Miller situation."

Shelby leaned forward and spoke in a low tone as if someone were listening. "This is where it really got interesting. He told me not to bother with the police. He knew, and had represented some people there in Savannah who were not exactly what you would call upstanding citizens. He didn't go into any detail but did say these people owed him a favor. He would give them a call and see if they could pay Miller a visit. I told him I didn't understand what he meant by a visit. He told me not to worry. In a few days, Mr. Miller would never bother me again. He also suggested I go somewhere where it was safe for a few days. I told him I could go to Fripp because it was a gated and secure community. He gave me a week off with pay. So, that's why I'm living here on Fripp for the time being."

Nick looked back over at the crowd and then back to Shelby. "Boy, this tale just doesn't seem to have an ending to it... does it?"

"No, it doesn't. Look, I have a favor to ask."

"I'll do it... Rebel!"

"But you don't even know what I'm going to ask."

"It doesn't make a difference. When you think about it, I got you into all of this. What can I do for you?"

"I was wondering if you would drive me over to my apartment in Savannah. I need to pick up a few things. I left in such a hurry the other day. I wasn't thinking clearly. I don't want to go over there by myself."

Nick stood. "When do we leave?"

"In an hour. I have to go back to my friend's house and tell her to keep an eye on Kirby. Pick me up at the Island store. I'll drive my friend's golf cart and park it there."

"An hour it is," said Nick. "The adventure continues."

"This means a lot to me," said Shelby. "After we get over there and finish up at my place I'm going to buy you a good ol' southern Savannah dinner."

Chapter Fifteen

NICK BROUGHT THE SILVER LEXUS TO A COMPLETE STOP just short of the halfway point on the Talmadge Memorial Bridge. Tapping the glass enclosed clock on the padded dash, he remarked, "How can traffic be backed up this time of day? It's 1:10 in the afternoon."

Frowning, Shelby nodded at the forty-foot truck directly in front of them. "I can't see a thing with that truck blocking our view." Getting out of the car, she walked to the back of the truck and across in front of the Lexus and looked toward the Savannah side of the bridge. The flashing red and blue lights in the distance revealed the hold up. Back in the car, she spoke, "Looks like an accident up ahead. This happened to me twice before. We could be here for a while."

The driver in the inside lane gave Nick a look of amazement which Nick passed on to Shelby with a comment. "I can't believe you got out of the car in the middle of this bridge. Do you have any idea how high up we are?"

"Not exactly," said Shelby, "but I think it's somewhere around 186 feet."

Nick, still amazed, looked at the driver next to him and then back to Shelby. "And you know this how?"

Shelby laughed. "Remember, I grew up in Beaufort. My parents brought me to Savannah more times than I can count. I work and live here now. I go home on the weekends a lot to my parent's place. In short, I've crossed this bridge many times over the years. It's almost two miles long." Pointing to the left, she explained, "Down below us is the Savannah River which is one of the largest cargo container terminals on the Eastern Seaboard." Nodding at the buildings adjacent to the river bank and beyond, she spoke proudly, "And that's Savannah. I'm sure your grandmother brought you here."

The truck in front of them moved a few feet and then stopped. Nick, following closely answered, "Been here twice. Once when I was three years old. I can't recall much about that visit. The only other time I was here I was seven. Amelia and I drove over. I remember crossing this bridge. I was nervous. I'm not that fond of heights. What I'm saying is the last time I crossed this bridge, we sped right across the river, but this time we've stopped in the middle of the damn thing. So, if we could refrain from talking about how high up we are, I'd appreciate it."

Shelby sat back and laughed. "I thought you said you were a painter. Don't you have to get up on a ladder if you're painting a two-story house?"

"Yes, I do have to climb a ladder on occasion. Three stories is my limit. After that, I get dizzy."

Looking down over the side of the bridge, Shelby laughed again. "What are you worried about. You can swim... can't you?"

The truck in front of them was on the move again as Nick answered, "Yes, I can swim, but in the immortal words of Butch Cassidy when he said to The Sundance Kid just before they jumped off that cliff, 'Hell, the fall will probably kill ya!'"

Shelby agreed. "I remember that. I saw that movie years ago."

Moving slowly down the opposite side of the bridge, Shelby gestured to the right. "Take this first exit and go down under the bridge to Bay Street. We'll take that all the way to East Broad where we'll take a right. When we get to East Liberty, another right. My place is at 429 on the left. It's right between Colonial Park Cemetery and Lafayette Square. We should be there in ten minutes."

Parking on East Liberty, Nick looked at the surrounding houses. "Looks like a nice neighborhood. Is Kirby's school close by?"

"Up the street about ten blocks. Normally, I drop her off and my neighbor, who has a daughter Kirby's age, brings her home in the afternoon. She stays at their house until I get home."

Getting out of the car, Nick asked, "Is the office you work at nearby?"

"It's north of here on East Broughton Street. It's only a few blocks. When it's nice I walk to work." Pointing west, she took his hand and led him across the street. "My place is four houses up. Come on!"

Passing three, what looked like Brownstones, they stopped in front of four upscale red brick apartment units that were connected. Starting up the iron-railed steps, Shelby pointed out, "I live in the first unit, right here on the end."

Standing next to the door, Shelby removed a set of keys from her purse, but was prevented from entering when an older women came out onto the porch of the connecting unit. When she saw Shelby, she hollered, "Rebel Lee! You didn't come home last night. Is anything wrong?"

Rolling her eyes at Nick, she whispered, "That's Mrs. Lehman. She's a sweetheart but a bit of a busybody." Waving at the women, Shelby lied, "Everything's fine, Mrs. Lehman. I just had to run Kirby over to Beaufort last evening. It was late, so we stayed the night."

By this time, the woman was down her steps and standing at the bottom of Shelby's. "Well I was just concerned. That nice man you're dating... Mr. Miller. He was here early this morning. He said hello to me and told me he had to get something from your apartment. He seemed upset. Are you sure everything is alright?"

Giving Nick the once over from head to toe, Mrs. Lehman continued, "And who is this young man?"

Shelby placed her key in the lock and answered, "This is Nick. He's just a friend. He's helping me with something." Moving things along, she politely excused the woman. "I'd really like to talk but we're on a tight schedule." Opening the door, she motioned Nick inside and spoke to Mrs. Lehman one last time as she closed the door. "We'll talk later, Mrs. Lehman. Remember, Kirby and I still have to come over and bake cookies with you soon."

Leaning against the closed door, Shelby let out a long breath of frustration. "I swear, that woman is going to be the death of me."

Looking out one of the sidelight windows, Nick watched the woman going down the steps. "I thought she seemed nice. Sounds to me like she's just looking out for you and Kirby."

"Yes, I agree. She is nice, but she has a tendency to get involved in everyone's business. She can tell you the life story of every person who lives on this block."

"Does she know about your recent fallout with Ike?"

"No, not yet. But she did mention that he had been by this morning and how he seemed upset."

"Why do you think he came back?" asked Nick.

"I don't know. Mrs. Lehman said he mentioned he had to get something from the apartment." Standing in a small foyer, Shelby reached for the handle on the inside door, but was stopped from entering when Nick placed his hand over hers. "Wait a minute. Mrs. Lehman didn't say she saw Miller leave. She just saw him go in after she talked with him. He might be inside waiting for you just like the last time you came home. Maybe he had a change of heart and is still convinced he can salvage the relationship."

Putting her hands on her slim hips, Shelby pursed her lips as if she were thinking. "Maybe it wasn't such a great idea for you to come along with me. What if he is in there? You're not one of his favorite people right now. Besides getting the better of him at the Dockside the other evening, I'm sure he was quite embarrassed. Are you afraid to go in?"

Nick, not wanting to appear the coward, puffed out his chest. "Scared as hell, but here we go!" He shoved the door open quickly and jumped into the living room in a karate pose followed by what he thought was an appropriate yell. Once Shelby saw there was no one in the living room, she broke into hysterical laughter. "You remind me of Peter Sellers in one of those stupid Pink Panther movies."

Continuing the theatrics, Nick held his hands up and formed them into a make believe revolver. With his back to the wall, he made his way slowly to a bedroom door that he pushed open with his right foot. Jumping through the opening, he went down on one knee and pointed the fake gun in every direction. Satisfied, no one was in the room, he came back out holstering the unseen gun in an invisible holster hanging from his shoulder. "All clear! I don't think he's here."

Shelby was laughing so hard she had to sit on a nearby padded footstool. "Enough with the comedy already!"

Nick walked to the center of the room and stepped on a small piece of broken ceramic from the smashed lamp. Picking up the coffee table and placing it where he thought it may have been, he asked, "Does everything look the same as when you left?"

Shelby looked around the living room, got up and walked into the kitchen. "Yeah, it does. I still can't imagine what Ike came back for."

"Maybe he came back for some clothes or personal belongings."

"No, that can't be it. He didn't have anything like that here at the apartment." Leaning on the kitchen counter, she explained, "Ike spent many an evening here. We'd have dinner and maybe watch TV. He never stayed the night. I didn't want Kirby to ever wake up in the morning and see Ike here. I've tried my best to raise her with, at least, some moral values."

Nick picked up another section of the broken lamp and sat on the couch. "Okay, look. I don't want to get too personal, but you said you had sex with the man. In that case, maybe he did leave something here: a watch, maybe his wallet."

"No, no, no! That would have never happened. When I said we had sex I didn't mention it was here. When it came to that sort of stuff, it always occurred at his house which isn't even close to Liberty. He lives on the Northwest side of town in a swanky neighborhood. He lives in an old mansion that has to be worth millions. There is nothing here that could be considered personal to him. If anything, I probably have a few personal things at his house. No, there has to be another reason." Looking at the kitchen clock, she bent down and opened the cabinet below the sink. Tossing a small roll of trash liners at Nick, she held up a broom and dustpan. "It's not even three o'clock yet. What say we get this place cleaned up, then I'll take you for that dinner I promised?"

Removing one of the liners from the roll, Nick crossed the room, stopping in front of the china cabinet. Examining the contents of the four shelf, rounded piece of wooden furniture, he admired her collection. "It appears that you collect miniature cups and saucers."

At the couch, Shelby started to sweep up the broken lamp sections. "Yes, I've been collecting them ever since I was a little girl. I hope too many of them didn't get damaged."

Looking at the various lines of delicate collectables on the shelves, he stepped on some of the broken glass from the cabinet. Bending down, he picked up two saucers and a number of tiny cups and remarked, "Doesn't look that bad. From what I can tell only a few small pieces fell out. One of the saucers is broken in half but I think it can be glued back together. Everything else looks fine."

Shelby smiled. "Just put the pieces back in the cabinet. I'll have a look at them later." Removing the broken light bulb, she placed what was left of the lamp back on an end table, sat on the couch and gazed around the apartment. "What on earth could he have come back for?"

Nick picked up the last saucer from the floor and beneath it, he saw something. Holding up the engagement ring, he turned and held it out toward Shelby. "Maybe this is what he was after. Looks expensive."

Getting up, Shelby walked over and took the ring. "You know, you might be right. I remember him throwing the ring violently across the room. The fact that it's still here means he left without it." Holding the ring up for Nick's examination, she asked, "What do you think a ring like this is worth?"

"I have no idea," said Nick. "When it comes to jewelry, like most men, I'm an idiot. I bought one of these things when I was in college for that girl I told you about I was going to marry. Of course, that ring couldn't even compare with this one. The ring I purchased, if I remember correctly was only around five hundred dollars, give or take. This one, well, it might be worth thousands."

Tossing the ring in the air, she caught it in her hand and clenched her fist. "I'm only guessing here, but I think you're right. This ring does appear expensive. It only makes sense he'd come back for it."

The sound of the front door being unlocked and opened interrupted the conversation. Nick, in a low tone of voice, asked, "You did lock the door after we came in?"

Whispering back, Shelby answered, "Yes, of course."

Looking at the foyer door, Nick grimaced, "And the only other person with a key is—"

Shelby finished the sentence. "Ike!" Pointing the broom at a two door, walk-in closet, she spoke softly, "Come on, I don't want to face him again!"

"Me either!" said Nick.

Opening the closet, Shelby stepped in, but Nick ran back and grabbed the dust pan and the liners that were lying on the couch. He no sooner closed the plantation shuttered doors when the door to the living room opened. It was pitch black in the closet, but the afternoon sunshine from the windows pouring through the foyer allowed them to see through the slightly open shutters. Two men entered the apartment, the second man closing the door behind them. The first man, dressed in brown khaki's, black sweatshirt and sandals walked to the center of the living room, stopped and looked around.

The second man, wearing cargo shorts, a mesh tee-shirt and deck shoes followed and spoke, "So, tell me again why Ike sent us over here?"

Walking into the kitchen, the first man answered, "We're looking for a ring... an engagement ring. According to Ike, it's worth ten grand. I guess he had a fallout with that wench he was seeing. He told me he was so pissed when he ran out of here that he forgot he threw it across the room somewhere."

The second man, walking across the broken glass in front of the china cabinet replied, "It looks like that's not the only thing he threw. Why did he send us? Why didn't he come back here and get the ring himself?"

"He has something else on his calendar this afternoon. I think he said he was speaking at the Rotary Club."

"This is bullshit!" snapped the second man. "Why the hell do we care about his love affair, gone bad?"

The other man, obviously in charge, walked back into the living room and ordered, "Ike pays us well, so shut your trap and start looking for the damn ring!"

Shrugging, the second man asked, "And if we don't find this ring... then what?"

Flipping up the couch cushions, the first man held out his hands displaying the apartment. "If we don't find it that means the girl has it. If that turns out to be the case, he told me to trash the place."

Inside the closet Nick couldn't see Shelby, but he felt her hand wrap around his as she squeezed it, a silent signal that she was afraid. Reaching up, he found her face and eventually her lips. He placed his index finger over her lips, a sign for her to remain quiet.

They watched in silence while the first man walked into the bedroom and ordered the other man. "I'll go in the bedroom and have a look around. You check in this room. From the looks of the condition out here it appears this is where everything happened."

The second man walked to a roll top desk next to the front window. Opening the long drawer beneath the desk, he violently dumped the contents onto the wooden floor: papers, ink pens, a stapler and a box of paper clips going in every direction. Then, he systematically emptied the remaining side drawers flinging all of Shelby's important documents and personal papers across the floor. Pulling the desk away from the wall, the man checked the floor near the wall, then pushed the desk over onto its side. Next, he went to the china cabinet and stared at the contents and after not finding what he was looking for, tipped the cabinet forward, the delicate saucers and cups spilling onto the floor, the remainder of the glass in the antique piece of furniture breaking. Hearing the commotion from the bedroom, the first man entered the living room and spoke angrily at the other man. "Our orders were to trash the place only if we didn't locate the ring! You're jumping the gun a little bit... don't you think?"

The other man, walked across a number of cups and saucers, the intricate ceramic pieces crushing beneath his feet. "Come on, Lester. Do you really think the girl would leave a ring worth ten grand here?"

"Maybe not, but we still need to follow Ike's orders. I know the man. I've worked for him for three years now. You've only been on his payroll for a few months. Believe me. The one thing you don't want to do is piss Ike Miller off! Check that other bedroom. I'll have a look around in the kitchen. "

Shelby's hand was tightly wrapped around Nicks and he could just imagine how she felt with two strange men going through her personal belongings, dumping things on the floor with orders to trash her apartment. For the moment all they could do was wait things out. From their position inside the closet they couldn't see the kitchen or the second bedroom. All they could hear was an occasional drawer or cabinet being opened, pots and pans being rattled about and then her silverware being dumped on the kitchen table. Reaching up, Nick could feel the tears streaming down Shelby's face. He gave her hand a reassuring squeeze. It was all he could do at the moment.

Following another ten minutes, the man walked out from the bedroom and addressed the first. "There's nothing in there of any interest. Looks like a little girl's room. A lot of stupid posters on the wall and some stuffed animals. Find anything out here?"

"No," answered Lester. Walking back into the living room he suggested. "I think we need to concentrate on this room. Like I said, Ike told me he threw the ring across the living room. If the ring is here it's got to be in this room. Let's spend another fifteen to twenty minutes going over every inch of this area. If we don't find it, then that's it."

The two men flipped over the couch and matching stuffed chair, lifted up a circular throw rug and pitched it in the corner. Using their feet they pushed around the broken glass on the floor and looked in all the corners. Finally, Lester picked up a photograph of Shelby and Kirby. He looked at the picture then flung it against the wall, the glass shattering to the floor. "That's it! The ring is not here. The girl must have it in her possession. Let's go give Ike the bad news."

Starting for the front door, Lester stopped and looked over at the closet. "Did you check that closet?"

"No. You said Ike tossed the ring across the room. I didn't figure it would be inside a closet."

Walking back to the closet Lester spoke, "Yeah, that might be true but it could have rolled under the door. Nick pushed Shelby back into the clothes hanging on her left and then he slipped as far as he could back into the hanging clothes on the right when the doors opened. Lester ran his foot across the floor and bent down. From the light that was filtering in, Nick could see the top of the man's balding head. The tips of Nick's shoes were sticking out near the bottom of some long dresses and winter coats. Standing next to three other pair of shoes, Nick kept his feet together so his shoes appeared to be just another pair. The man looked at the shoes but then stood and grabbed a handful of coats and sweaters on hangers, backed out of the closet and threw them on the floor. "Nothing! Let's go see Ike."

Nick waited until he was sure the two men were gone. Opening the closet doors slowly, he took Shelby's hand and guided her out to the living room. Wiping the tears from her eyes, she asked, "Who were those two?"

"I don't have the slightest," said Nick. "I assume from what they said that they work for Miller." Looking down at the broken collection of cups and saucers, Nick sadly apologized, "I'm so sorry this happened. Maybe if I would have stayed out here and if we would have given them the ring, this wouldn't have happened."

Composing herself, Shelby patted his shoulder. "No, we did the right thing. They were not the most pleasant men a person would want to meet." Looking at the ring still clutched in her hand, she walked to the front window and looked out. "I had every intention of making sure Ike got this back, but when you consider all the damage he and his two friends did, I think I might just hock it and keep the cash."

Looking around at the mess, Nick suggested, "Maybe we ought to skip dinner and get this place back in order."

"No," said Shelby. "Right now I'm not in the right frame of mind to do anything like cleaning. I'm too pissed... and frustrated. Let's just go on to dinner. There are some great places to eat down near Tybee Island, which is south of the city. I'll deal with the apartment later."

Seated at a window table, Nick gazed out at the Atlantic Ocean. "I've never been over here to Tybee. I've always heard it was nice." Looking around the tiny restaurant, he asked, "Have you ever dined here before?"

Picking up one of the menus, Shelby smiled. "Many times. This is one of Kirby's favorite places. She loves their crab cakes... and their coleslaw. They also have great she crab soup and I usually get their catch of the day. Oh yeah, they have great yeast rolls here."

Looking at his own menu, Nick scanned the variety of seafood offered. "Just listening to you is making me hungry. I'm definitely going for some of that soup you mentioned. I think I'm going to get something with shrimp. All of a sudden, I've got a hankering for shrimp."

A young waitress dressed in shorts and a tank top stopped next to the table and asked, "What can I get you guys to drink?"

Shelby spoke up first. "I need some alcohol." Looking across the table at Nick, she suggested, "A pitcher of draft beer?"

Nick looked out the window at the beach and answered, "Considering what we've just been through, that sounds about right."

"The waitress gave them a thumbs up and replied, "Be right back with that pitcher and two ice cold mugs."

Taking on a more serious tone, Nick leaned forward and placed his elbows on the table. "Just before we left your place, you said you'd deal with the apartment later. Does later, mean later today or tomorrow... or what?"

"I'm not really sure," said Shelby. "One thing I want to do is pick up some clothes for Kirby and myself. As far as cleaning the place up, I'm not that keen on returning there anytime soon, like within the next few days. What if Ike is not satisfied with the results his two cronies report to him. Of course, one of the things I can do is go over to Ike's and just give him the ring back."

"That might solve things... it might not. You told me when he ran out of your place he said he was going to make your life a living hell. Maybe this is just the beginning. You may have to move... maybe back to Beaufort."

"I've thought of that. I really don't know what I want to do. I work in Savannah. I think I'll let things ride for a few days. Remember, Franklin Schrock promised me he would have someone speak to Ike and he all but guaranteed me that Ike would leave me be. I don't want to jump the gun and move if I don't have to. For now, as long as Kirby and I can stay at my friend's house on Fripp, Ike can't get to me. He might be important over here in Savannah, but unless he has a pass, he won't be allowed on the island."

"Well the way I see it, I don't think we should underestimate Mr. Miller. He could easily rent a place on Fripp for a week, and therefore have access to the island."

"Do you really think he would do that?"

"You know the man better than me. I don't know if he'd go that far or not, but I wouldn't put it past him. From what those two men said he definitely wants the ring back. If you sell it and he finds out, he's not going to be a happy camper. I agree with you. I think we should wait and see how he reacts to these people Schrock is sending to see him.

Their pitcher arrived and Nick filled the two mugs. Holding his cold mug up, he suggested, "Let's enjoy our dinner and worry about all this later."

Shelby clinked her glass against Nick's. "Sounds like a plan."

Patting his stomach, Nick stood on the restaurant porch and looked out at the long beach. "Now that was one great meal!" Pointing up the street at a large ice cream cone hanging from a sign, he suggested. "Since you bought dinner, how about if I spring for dessert?"

Shelby looked up the street at the sign and answered, "I don't think I can eat another bite, but there's always room for ice cream... especially chocolate."

Guiding her down the sidewalk, Nick suggested further, "If you're not in all that much of a hurry to get back to the apartment, what say we take a walk on the beach after our ice cream?"

"That sounds nice. To be honest, I'm still kind of keyed up over what happened back at my place."

Returning from the beach, Nick stood next to the Lexus and checked the time: 7:45. "It's getting close to eight o'clock. It'll be getting dark in less than two hours. We can head back to your place now, or wait until it's dark, if you'd rather."

Shelby reached for the door handle. "Let's go now. I don't want to go after it gets dark. If Ike drives by and sees lights on, that might be an invitation for him to come barging in."

Nick climbed in and turned the ignition key. "East Liberty Street... here we come!"

They weren't even a mile up the road when Shelby, drumming her fingers on the dash, blurted out, "Pull over to that tavern on the right! That beer we had didn't cut it for me. I'm still pissed! I need something stronger."

Turning into a sand covered lot, Nick looked at the tavern. It was nothing more than a one-story clapboard building with a number of beer signs in the six windows that lined the front of the structure. A sign on top of the building advertised the establishment: Chester's Grill and Tavern.

There was only one car parked and that was on the side of the building. Getting out, Nick commented, "Business looks slow. Only one car and that probably belongs to the bartender. Have you ever been in this place before?"

"No," said Shelby. "I've driven by it a number of times but never stopped in." Before Nick could say another word, she was headed for the door. Nick followed her inside and looked around at the interior: a number of mismatched tables and chairs scattered about, a pool table, dart board and juke box in an adjacent room, the wood planked walls adorned with old lobster traps and pictures of fishing trawlers. A well-used wooden bar ran across the back of the main room, the bar fronted with eight old barstools. Shelves of liquor and wine created a backdrop for the bar, a flickering beer sign hanging in the far corner.

Walking up to the bar, Nick and Shelby each sat on a stool. The bartender, a middle-aged man with a receding hairline, stubbed out a cigarette in a seashell ashtray and ran a wet towel across the bar top as he made his way down to where Nick and Shelby were seated. "What'll it be, folks?"

Shelby looked up at the large display of liquor bottles, rubbed her chin and then answered, "I think I'll go with a Seven and Seven and two shots of Wild Turkey; one for me and one for my friend here."

Nick, surprised, held up his hands, "Just a draft beer for me."

Shelby continued to speak with the bartender as he reached for a bottle of Wild Turkey and two shot glasses. "How long have you been tending bar?"

"More years that I care to admit. I guess, thirty some years. I bought this place about twenty years back."

Spinning around on the stool, Shelby commented, "Seems rather slow in here tonight."

Setting the two glasses in front of them, the bartender explained, "During the summer months it never gets busy until after ten o'clock. Come midnight, this place will be packed. You guys ever been in before?"

Shelby answered, "No."

Before Nick could respond, the man stared directly at him. "You look familiar to me. You sure you haven't been in?"

"Positive," stated Nick. "I just moved down from Cincinnati, well not here, but over in the Beaufort area about a week and a half ago. Unless, you've been over to Fripp Island lately, then we've never met."

"No, that's not it. I don't get over that way much. I've only been to Beaufort twice in my life and I've never been out on the islands over there. You must have a twin. I swear I saw either you or your double in the past couple of days." Turning to get the other drinks, he went on, "I know I've seen you before. Give me a minute and it'll come to me."

Mixing Seagrams with some Seven-up, he reached up and turned on the television above the bar just as a newswoman was speaking into the camera. *Tune in tonight on the eleven o'clock news for the latest on the search for Susan Dunn."*

Snapping his fingers, he sat Nick's beer and Shelby's mixed drink in front of them. "That's it! I saw you on the five o'clock news. They were interviewing you about the remains of a hand you found out in the marsh."

It was an awkward moment for Nick, the look that came across his face, a dead giveaway. "I knew it," said the bartender. "That was you... wasn't it?"

Nick downed his shot of Wild Turkey in one gulp and nodded, "Yeah, that was me. They really caught me off-guard. How did I look on TV?"

Lighting up another cigarette, the bartender laughed, "Do you want me to be honest?"

Nick took a swig of his beer. "Yes, I mean how did I come off?"

"If you ask me, you looked nervous, like you couldn't wait to get away from the camera."

"After my interview, did they say anything else?"

"No, not much. Just that they were going to camp out on Fripp Island at the marina until tonight when those searching for the rest of the Dunn girl's body would return and that there would be an update at that time." Holding up the Wild Turkey, he asked, "Another shot?"

Nick shook his head, "No, not for me!"

"How about you little lady?"

Taking a short sip, Shelby answered, "No, I'm still working on this one."

Putting the bottle back on a shelf the bartender introduced himself. "My name is Chester. Over the years I've had all kinds of folks in here, but this really takes the cake." Placing a wooden bowl of pretzels in front of Shelby, he spoke to Nick, "It's almost like you're some sort of celebrity."

Taking a pretzel, Shelby chimed in, "And that's just the tip of the iceberg! The other night, Nick and I were the ones who found the Schrock girl on Fripp Island."

"Oh, my God!" bellowed Chester. "This just keeps getting better. So, let me ask you. What was it like when you discovered that hand holding the five dollar bill? It must have been creepy."

Nick waved off his comment. "It really wasn't that big of a deal. Anyone could have found it. I just happened to be looking in the right direction at the right moment."

Stuffing a pretzel into the side of his mouth, Chester added, "That makes what... nine girls this RPS Killer has racked up over a two year period. People over here in the Savannah area are quite pissed. All this time and the police can't seem to nail this guy. Just like the other night. There was a guy sitting at the end of the bar. We get to talking about the RPS killings and I mentioned that there had been eight girls killed. He corrected me immediately and told me the number was nine... not eight. I mean... people are really upset over these murders."

Nick thought for a moment, then raised his hand for Chester to stop talking. "Wait, wait, wait! You said this customer... this man corrected you, telling you the number of dead was nine, not eight?"

"Yeah," said Chester, "That's what he said and he was really pissed off about it."

"When did this happen?"

Thinking back, Chester looked at the end of the bar where the man had sat. "I guess it was three, four nights back."

Nick looked at Shelby. "That doesn't make any sense! Up until yesterday when I discovered the remains of the hand there were only eight dead. How could this man know there were nine dead before the hand was found?"

Shelby gave him an odd look. "What are you driving at?"

"I'm not sure. It just doesn't add up. How could someone, or in this case, this man know there were nine dead before anyone else knew, before the hand was found?" Turning back to Chester, Nick stated, "I might be way out in left field here, but let me ask you this: what did this man look like?"

Chester shrugged. "Ah... he seemed rather normal looking. About six foot or so, kind of on the slender side. Come to think of it, he was kind of strange, but then again, I get a lot of different kinds of people in here."

Interested, Nick asked, "What do you mean by strange?"

"He was a chain smoker."

"What's so strange about that? A lot of people smoke."

"Yeah, but this guy lined up the filters when he was finished with each cigarette he smoked. And another thing. The way he held the cigarettes. He used his ring and little finger. Very weird. He was here about two hours, had four beers and probably smoked a half pack. The way he lined up the filters he seemed very organized. He didn't say much of anything. Just sat right there, drank and smoked one cigarette after another. Like I said we got into a conversation about the killings and he got upset when I mentioned there had been eight girls killed. He told me there had been nine."

"Did this man say anything else?"

"Come to think of it, he did. He had this really bad cough and he talked about how he needed to quit smoking and I told him that I had cut down myself."

"Anything else?"

"He mentioned something about how people in Savannah needed to start keeping their daughters off the street or something to that effect and then added that another girl would no doubt soon be found. What we didn't know is whether she would be dead or alive, and then just before he left he said he was glad that he was going back to work. He said he hadn't worked in a while and was glad he was working again. Said he was meeting a crew of men and they were going out to the suburbs."

"Does this man come here regularly?"

"No. I never saw him before that night and he hasn't been back since."

"And he didn't say what kind of work he did?"

"No, just that he was meeting a crew."

Laying a twenty on the bar, Nick got up and spoke to Shelby, "Come on, we have to go."

Shelby objected, "But I haven't finished my drink."

Pulling her to the side, Nick emphasized, "Look Rebel. Trust me. We have bigger fish to fry right now—"

Chester interrupted their conversation, "Excuse me folks, but what the hell is this all about? Are you saying you think the chain smoking man that was in here a few nights ago is the RPS Killer? That's insane!"

Nick tried to put Chester at ease. "Nobody said the man was the killer, but you have to admit he fits the bill: chain smoker, coughs a lot, and it's more than strange that he knew there were nine dead before anyone else did. All that being said, it's just a hunch... that's all."

Chester poured himself a shot of whiskey and drank it down. "Do you think we should notify the police?"

"No, not yet." said Nick. "We don't have enough information. We don't know where the guy lives, what his name is, where he works... nothing. Here's what I think we should do. I'm going to write down my cell number and give it to you. If the guy comes in again, see if you can get any more info from him and then give me a call. Before we go accusing anyone we have to be absolutely sure we're right."

"I don't know," muttered Chester. "It just doesn't seem right to keep any information about this killer from the police."

Grabbing a pen from the bar, Nick jotted down his cell number on a napkin and handed it to Chester. "Look, if the guy comes in again, maybe you could wait until he leaves and try to get the model and make of his vehicle, maybe the plate number, then give me a call... okay! Tell you what. Here's another twenty for your troubles."

"I wouldn't feel right taking money when it comes to something like this. I could get in trouble!"

"Trouble for what," said Nick. "Look at it this way. You said it was the only time you'd ever seen this man in your place. He'll probably never come back, you'll probably never see us again and you're twenty dollars to the good."

Taking the money, Chester agreed, "Okay... if the guy comes in again, I'll see what I can do."

Nick reached over the bar and shook Chester's hand. "Thanks. I really don't think this will go anywhere, but thanks anyways." Shuffling Shelby toward the door, he spoke back over his shoulder, "We gotta go!"

Shelby remained quiet until they were in the car and headed up the road. "You... Nick Falco, are really something. This is the second time we've been out socially. Our first night at the Dockside, what with your fight with Ike followed up with the discovery of Amanda Schrock in your front yard was definitely the most exciting evening out I think I've ever had, but today was over the top. First, we dodge the bullet at my place with those two goons who work for Ike and now, at least from what I can see, we might have a lead on the RPS Killer. You really have a knack for showing a girl, what I can only phrase as an unusual evening!"

Stopping at a four way stop, Nick looked across the seat at Shelby. "We have to go right through Savannah to get back to Fripp. What's the plan? Do we drop by your place or just head back to Fripp?"

Shelby didn't even hesitate. "Fripp it is. I really need to get home. I've been gone the entire day. Kirby, not to mention my friend are probably wondering where the hell I'm at."

On the move again, Shelby turned sideways in the seat. "Listen, I've been thinking about what Chester told us about that man. If by some remote chance, he is the RPS Killer, we know something about him no one else does. He works with a crew of men in the suburbs. Doesn't that sort of narrow things down?"

"Not really," said Nick. "He could be on a crew putting a new roof on a house or maybe a crew of men actually building a house. Then, there's crews who pave driveways and put up fences for people, not to mention countless other services that are offered by companies. Then you have to consider the suburbs of Savannah, if that's even the area the man was talking about."

"What do you think we should do, if anything?"

"I think that right now we both need to go home and get a good night's sleep. Let's meet tomorrow for breakfast at the marina. We can decide what to do not only about our suspicions about the man at Chester's, but also about when we want to go back to your apartment and get it cleaned up." Making a right turn, Nick started up the long ramp that led to the bridge over the Savannah River. "Promise me," said Nick, "you won't go back to your apartment by yourself."

Chapter Sixteen

THE IRRITATING BUZZ OF THE CELL PHONE SITTING ON the nightstand brought Nick up into a sitting position. Yawning, he picked up the phone, and still half asleep, answered, "Yeah!"

The voice of the caller was familiar: "Good morning... it's Rebel! You up yet?"

Half laughing, Nick answered, "I am now! What time is it?"

"Just after six," came the answer. "You said last night we were going to meet at the marina for breakfast this morning, but you forgot to mention a time."

Sitting on the side of the bed, Nick looked out the bedroom window. The sun wasn't even up yet. Standing, he stretched. "Give me about an hour and a half. I have to grab a shower, put on some duds and then I need to stop by a house on Wahoo Drive."

"Okay, but don't be late," said Shelby. "I'm starving! We have a lot of things to talk over today. See you there."

Following a long, cool shower, Nick threw on a pair of jeans, a sleeveless sweatshirt and sandals and walked out to the garage. The thermometer on the back porch read: eighty-one degrees. Looking at the rising ball of sun in the east, he knew it was going to be another day in what seemed like an endless string of days of relentless heat. Firing up his Harley, he backed out of the garage and headed up Tarpon to Bonito Drive.

Crossing the bridge over the canal, he made the first left onto Wahoo and sped up the dirt road leaving a trail of dust behind. Surprisingly, Parker Sims was once again perched on a ladder at the front of the house. Hearing the loud cycle pull into his driveway, he waved at Nick and climbed down.

Nick met him at the bottom of the ladder where they shook hands. Gesturing toward the house, Parker explained, "I took your advice and rented a power sprayer. It knocked off most of the peeling paint. I've just got a few rough spots to sand out, so if you can give me that estimate, maybe we can do some business."

"That's why I'm here," said Nick. "Looks like a pretty simple job to be honest with you. Let me walk around and have a gander at the exterior walls, the windows and the porch. Should only take me a few minutes."

Five minutes later, Nick approached Parker at the front of the house. Sims was seated on the porch drinking a can of soda. Holding up a second can, Sims smiled. "Remember, I owe you a drink from the other day."

"Thanks, but no thanks," said Nick. "I haven't even had breakfast yet. Okay, here's what we've got. I can paint the house in two, three days tops. I've got all the equipment I need over at my place: ladders, brushes, drop cloths, you name it. All you need to supply me with is the paint and some thinner to clean up with. If I recall, you told me yellow on the exterior walls and black for the trim and the porch. How soon do you want to paint the house again?"

Sims gave Nick and odd look. "What kind of a question is that? If I can get away with it, I'd like to avoid painting this place again for at least ten years or so. Why do you ask?"

"I'm just asking you in a polite way, how much money you want to spend on paint. For instance, if you go with their low-end paint, you'll be painting this house again in three years or less. If you go with a middle of the road brand, you'll get five, six, maybe seven years. If you want to use the top of the line, then you're looking at paint that'll last ten to twelve years."

Taking a drink, Sims thought, then answered, "How much is the top of the line?"

"Anywhere from twenty-five to thirty-two dollars a gallon," quoted Nick. "As close as I can figure you'll need about ten gallons of the yellow and four on the black. When you throw in a gallon of paint thinner, you're probably looking at somewhere in the vicinity of $375.00 to $450.00. I'll paint the house for $800.00."

"Sounds fair," said Sims. "How about this? You buy the paint up front and when you're finished up I'll write you a check for $1500.00."

Nick reached for Sims' hand. "Deal!"

Finishing up the soda, Sims asked, "When did you think you can get started?"

"Well let's see. When I leave here I'm meeting someone at the marina for breakfast. I may have to make a run over to Savannah. It just depends on what we decide. I'll get the paint either later today or early tomorrow. The earliest I can start will be tomorrow." Looking at the house, Nick shook Sims' hand and walked back to his bike. Climbing on, he saluted and started the cycle. Shouting over the noise, Nick pulled up next to Sims and spoke loudly, "Should have your house standing tall in about three days. Adios!" Sims waved at Nick as he pulled out onto Wahoo and headed up the road for Bonito.

Parking at the side of the marina store, Nick saw Shelby sitting on the bottom step sipping a coffee. Approaching the steps, Nick gestured at the coffee. "You already eat?"

"Nope. Just waiting on you. Had to have my morning coffee."

Shelby stood just as Chief Lysinger was coming down the steps. Stopping in front of Nick, Jeff patted his stomach and commented, "They've got some great fried egg sandwiches up there today. Had me two of 'em." Nodding toward the dock, he explained, "We're getting ready to head out to the marsh again."

"If you're going back out today," said Nick, "then I can only assume that yesterday was a bust. After I left yesterday, Shelby and I headed over to Savannah for the day. We didn't get back until late. So, I didn't get a chance to hear how things turned out." Looking toward the dock, he continued, "I see there are no media folks here today. Guess the novelty of finding the Dunn girl has worn off already."

"I guess one could say that. Media people always remind me of vultures. Wherever there is a carcass, and by carcass, I mean tragedy, they'll always flock to it. Like this morning. There was a warehouse explosion on Parris Island. There were some folks injured and two people that are serious. What I'm saying is what happened yesterday can and often is replaced with some new tragedy." Looking back at the dock area, Jeff went on, "They were here until late last night when we came back in. They were all expecting us to return with more body parts. We didn't find anything, just like I figured. Finding the remains of that hand was nothing but pure luck."

Shelby spoke up, "What about the Dunn girl's parents? As grotesque as it seems, they may have been hoping that it was their daughter."

"Yes, I suppose if it turned out that it is Susan Dunn, it would be a form of closure for them. Myself, I don't think we're going to find anything else. The only thing we did learn is the hand belonged to a girl that was killed by the RPS Killer. When we got back the media conducted a short Q and A interview with us, then they left... disappointed." Jeff gave Nick a funny look and went on, "Speaking of interviews, they had a short clip of their interview with you on the late night news, Nick. Lasted ten to fifteen seconds at best." Laughing, Jeff tipped his hat and started to walk across the lot. "Don't quit your day job, Falco. When it comes to being in front of the camera... you suck!"

Shelby started up the steps. "That's pretty much the same thing Chester said about your interview. At the time, I thought it was just his opinion, but according to Chief Lysinger... you do suck! Come on, let's get some of those egg sandwiches."

Seated at a window table overlooking the marina, Shelby washed down a bite of egg, bread and cheese with a swig of orange juice. "Another day just starting and we've already talked about the RPS Killer. When Chief Lysinger was talking about the Dunn girl, I got a queasy feeling in the pit of my stomach that when we talked with Chester yesterday we may have met someone who actually talked with the killer. That's just plain weird. The question is: what if anything can we do about it? If we go to the police based on what Chester told us, they still have no clue who the killer is. It's just speculation. And, if we try to locate this man ourselves; why it borders on impossible that we'd be able to find him. You said yourself, he could be on any number of different crews out there in the suburbs of Savannah... and that's even if the man was referring to Savannah."

Nick fiddled with a set of salt and paper shakers and changed the subject. "To answer your question of what can we do about the RPS Killer: there really isn't much we *can do!* I think what we need to concentrate on is your immediate problem with Ike Miller. Sooner or later, you and Kirby are going to have to go back to your apartment. And, before that can happen, you and I have to go back over there and get the place in order. I've never met your daughter, but I don't think a nine-year-old needs to be in the middle of this sort of thing. When she walks back in your apartment, it should be like nothing ever happened. Does she know you broke it off with Miller?"

"Yes, she does. I knew when I finally stopped seeing Ike, unless I prepared her for it, she would be confused. She has always thought the world of him. Right now, she's of the opinion things just didn't work out between us. Fortunately, it's summer which means she really doesn't have to go back to Savannah until September when school starts up. That gives me the entire summer to get my apartment back in order. My friend here on the island has already told me we could stay at her place indefinitely. If I have to, when I return to work next week, I can drive back and forth to Savannah. I don't really see this as a problem. If it turns out Kirby has to spend the summer here on Fripp, she'll be on cloud nine. She loves the beach."

"So I gather from what you said you don't want to go back over there just yet?"

"I think we should go back, but only for as long as it takes to grab some clothes for Kirby and I. We can be in and out in less than ten minutes."

"Hold on a minute," said Nick. "As long as we're going over there I think we should change the locks. Everything you own is no doubt in the apartment. What if Ike orders those two goons to clean out your place? You could lose everything Here's what I think we should do. I have to drop by Lowes in Beaufort and order some paint. While we're there we can pick up two locks and when we get over to your place I can change them. I'm not saying this will keep them from breaking in, but it might discourage them from doing so. What do you think?"

"I like the idea of changing the locks. That makes me feel better. I say we finish up our breakfast, then head over to Savannah. You can drop your bike off at your place. We'll take my Jeep."

Nick picked his egg sandwich up just as his cell phone buzzed. "Digging in his pocket, he grabbed the phone and answered, "Falco on this end."

The voice on the other end sounded confused at first. "Is this Nick Falco?"

"Yes it is. Who's calling?"

"It's Chester... from Tybee Island. Remember me? You told me to give you a call if I ever saw that man we talked about yesterday."

For Shelby's benefit, Nick raised his eyebrows and repeated what the caller said, "Chester from Tybee Island. Yeah, I do remember you. You say you saw the man again? He came back in your place?"

"No, he didn't come back to the bar. Right now I'm over here in Savannah. I had to run to town and get some bar supplies. I stopped for gas at the station where I always gas up and when I go inside to pay, who do I see getting a cup of coffee... our boy!"

"Are you sure? How can you be sure it's him?"

"The night he was in my bar, I was as close to him as I was to you and your lady friend when you were in. I had a face to face conversation with the man that lasted nearly five minutes. It was him alright... I guarantee you. I circled around to the back of the store so I could get close to him without being recognized. The whole time I stood there watching him, he was coughing like crazy. I got a coffee myself and followed him up to the checkout where he purchased a carton of cigarettes and paid for his coffee and gas. You told me if I had a chance to try and get the plate numbers on his vehicle. There was one customer between the two of us. When he walked back out to the lot, I sat my coffee on the counter and told the clerk I'd be right back, but just when I get to the door, a delivery man dumped a cartload of baked goods in the doorway. By the time I got outside, the man was gone, but then I saw him. I could only see the upper half of his body. He was standing next to a blue pickup truck and it was no surprise to me when he lit up a cigarette. I started across the lot thinking I could read his plate number when he pulled out, but a beer truck blocked my view for a few seconds. When I got around the truck the pickup was pulling out and I couldn't make out the tags."

"Did you try and follow him?"

"I couldn't. There wasn't enough time. I had to go back inside and pay for my gas."

"Okay, Chester. You did good. My friend and I just happen to be driving back to Savannah later today. We'll drop by the bar and talk this over. Do me a favor and don't discuss this with anyone else. There'll be a nice tip in it for you. See you later this afternoon."

Smiling, Nick put the phone in his pocket and stood, "Come on, Rebel. Now we have another reason to go to Savannah. You probably thought today was going to be boring. We're off on another adventure."

By the time they pulled into Lowes' parking lot, Nick had explained everything Chester told him. Shelby thumped her fist on the Jeep's steering wheel. "Wouldn't it be something if we could capture the RPS Killer?"

"There is no way that's going to happen." pointed out Nick. "We're not going to bite off more than we can chew. The closer we get to the killer the more dangerous this game we're playing could get. Don't forget, this man has killed nine times we know of... maybe more. If we can somehow find out where this man works or lives then we can go to the police. We have to be positive beyond any doubt that we are absolutely sure he's the killer. If they eventually pick our man up and it turns out he's not the killer, we're going to look like real idiots." Looking at the store, Nick suggested, "There's isn't any sense in hashing over what we think may or may not be when it comes to this killer. Later on, this afternoon, when we go back to Chester's, we can continue this conversation. Right now, we need to get those locks and head to Savannah." Getting out of the Jeep, he asked Shelby, "Know anything about locks?"

"What is there to know?" said Shelby. "They're metal objects imbedded in doorways that either allow or prevent you from entering or leaving."

Nick laughed, "I've never heard it put exactly that way, but from a mechanical viewpoint that's precisely what they do. I'm going to the paint counter and order what I need. You need to go to the hardware department, find a clerk and tell them you want two entry locks… keyed alike. Don't get the cheapest they have. The more expensive the lock the better protection you're going to have. It'll probably take the clerk ten minutes or so to key the locks. When you get the locks meet me at the paint desk."

After placing the fourteen gallons of paint and the gallon of thinner securely in the back of the Jeep, Nick sat in the passenger seat with the locks at his feet and announced, "East Liberty… here we come!"

At that very moment, Ike Miller closed and locked the huge oak door of his antebellum mansion. Pulling up the sleeve of his three-piece custom Italian suit, he glanced at his Rolex; 10:00 in the morning. He was right on schedule for his noon meeting with the sales staff at his dealership. Making his way down the semi-circular steps he admired his brand new, metallic blue Corvette parked in the paved driveway at the side of his palatial house. Bending down, he plucked a pink flower from the assorted floral arrangement that bordered the driveway. He no sooner placed the flower in the lapel of his suit coat when the blunt object slammed into the back of his head, causing him to black out.

Parking the Jeep one street over from Liberty, Shelby sat back and commented, "I thought it best if we don't park on Liberty. If Ike or his men see my vehicle, well, it might be looked upon as an unwelcome invite."

"Good idea," said Nick. "Let's get over there and get these locks changed. You can grab whatever clothes you want and we'll be out of there in no time."

It was no surprise to either Nick or Shelby when they walked in the apartment that the place looked like a disaster area. Shelby walked over to the china cabinet that was lying face down, many of her cups and saucers lay broken on the floor. Walking into the kitchen, she ran her fingers across the scattered silverware on the counter. Picking up the clothes the one man had thrown on the floor, she walked over and picked up the broken picture of herself and Kirby. "I guess when we left before I didn't realize the extent of the damage. There's no way Ike is going to get that ring back. If it is worth ten grand, I should at least be able to get a few thousand out of it." Composing herself, she took a deep breath and headed for Kirby's room. "Why don't you start on those locks and I'll gather up some stuff for Kirby and I."

Using a Phillips head screwdriver he brought along, Nick began to change out the lock on the front door when he noticed Mrs. Lehman climbing the steps. Not knowing Nick's name, she spoke enthusiastically, "Good morning, Shelby's friend." Nick quickly closed the foyer door so the woman could not see into the apartment.

"Good morning," answered Nick. Not giving the woman an opportunity to snoop, he held up the screwdriver and lied, "I guess you haven't heard about the break-ins up the street yet? Three apartments were broken into last night so we thought it best to change the locks. I hear quite a bit of damage was done. You might want to spread the word to the neighbors. Shelby can't talk right now. She's cleaning up some glass. Someone tried to break in her bathroom window. If I were you, I'd see about getting your locks changed."

Mrs. Lehman bought the story; hook, line and sinker. "Oh my! And you say this was last night? I've got to tell Mrs. Fairdale and the Reynolds family. Then, there is Mr. Charles and Mildred across the street. I've got to run. Tell Shelby I'll talk with her soon!"

Nick chuckled to himself. *What a busy body!*

Ten minutes later, finished with the front door, he walked back into the living room where he saw Shelby organizing some clothing on the couch. "One down, one to go," he announced.

Picking up the other lock he started for the rear door when he was stopped by Shelby, who mentioned, "Oh, by the way, I forgot to mention it on the way over but I saw one of your friends at Lowes."

Confused, Nick stopped. "Friends? Who are you talking about?"

"One of the men that I met when we were at the Dockside the other night. You remember... they bought our dinner. The men that work for the same company your grandfather did."

Nick, not thinking, asked nervously, "You saw Charley Sparks and Derek Simons?"

"No, I just saw Charley. He introduced himself to me just like when we were at the Dockside. The other man, Derek, the one who kicked the crap out of Ike was not with him. Anyway, Charley asked me what I was buying the locks for and where I was going. He asked me how you were doing and then he left."

Nick flopped down on the couch as if the air were let out of him. "And you told him what the locks were for and where you were going?"

"Sure, it seemed harmless enough." Sitting on the couch next to Nick, Shelby gave him a look of doubt and asked, "There's something about those two men you haven't told me... isn't there? I knew that night when they bought us dinner and then when they rescued us from Ike, something wasn't right. You told me you had just recently met them and you didn't know them all that well. It didn't make any sense, but at the time, I didn't know you that well, so I just let it slide. What's up, Nick?"

With a sigh, Nick looked toward the ceiling. "I wasn't supposed to say anything about this to anyone. I guess it's too late for that now." Shaking his head in wonder, he continued, "Remember this morning when you called me and you said we had a lot of things to talk about today? Well, you were right. There is something we need to add to the list of situations we find ourselves in. Are you sure you want to hear this, because once I tell you, you have to promise me you won't say a word to anyone. Can I trust you?"

"After everything we've been through the past few days how can you ask if you can trust me? I can't imagine what it is about those two men you can't tell anyone, or what you're about to tell me, but I can tell you this. I don't know what I would have done these past couple of days if you hadn't been with me. So yes... you can trust me!"

"Okay, but before I start explaining about these two men, let me emphasize to you that what we are presently involved in can only be described as a two dimensional situation. The first and most important dimension right now, up to this point is the situation with Miller. We both know how violent and ruthless he can be and once he finds out you're keeping the ring, things could get worse. He already informed you he was going to make your life a living hell. The second dimension is the RPS Killer and the more clues we uncover about this man the more intense it will become. Now, we add the third dimension to our adventure, as you have so aptly put it on a number of occasions."

Getting up, Nick walked to the front window and looked out. "This third situation that you are soon to learn of, could wind up being the most dangerous of all because it involves seven million dollars that doesn't belong to me. Those two men: Charley Sparks and Derek Simons want the money. I know where the money is, but not exactly. Sparks and Simons have been following me before I even knew of my grandmother's death. These men, or the organization they work for killed my grandfather because…"

Minutes later, Nick sat back down on the couch and finished up his story. "…and that's why Sparks and Simons will soon come pay me a visit. And depending on whether you are with me at that time, it could be dangerous for me *and you!*"

Standing, Shelby began to fold some blouses and tee shirts. "So let me get this straight. There is seven million dollars either hidden in your house or on your property and you're not sure where it is. This organization killed your grandfather because he wouldn't divulge the whereabouts of the money and according to you, would have probably killed your grandmother as well, but she died before they could get to her. This Carter Pike, a friend of your grandmother's is kind of keeping an eye out for you and has informed you these men will soon approach you with a deal in order to get their money. Oh yeah, and the will your grandmother left states, that you, in no way can sell the house. My question for you is: What are you going to do when they approach you?"

"I'm going to act like I don't know anything about it. And if they approach you, you need to do the same."

"And if they don't buy that, then what?"

"I don't know. I haven't thought that far ahead yet."

Folding a pair of pants, Shelby nodded at the back door. "We've probably been here longer than what we planned. You better get the other lock changed and then we can drive on down to Chester's and ask him a few more questions about this man who we may think is the killer."

When Ike opened his eyes, he was staring up into the clear blue sky. The pain in his head still lingered like a bad headache. He thought he was dreaming but then suddenly realized he was fully awake. Rolling his head to his right, he noticed rows of knee-high corn stalks. To the left, the same thing; more corn. Raising up on his elbows, he looked at his feet: rows of corn. His three-hundred dollar black wing tips were marred and dusty, his suit pants wrinkled and filthy. Trying to sit up, he was pushed roughly back to the ground by a muddy cowboy boot accompanied by a course voice, "Stay down, Miller! You're not going anywhere until we say."

Three rough looking characters stood over him, their bodies framed by the blue sky and the light brown corn. The man who had spoken was dressed in neatly pressed jeans, boots and a red shirt, a tan Stetson atop his head. The other two men, standing off to the side were both bearded, one with long hair tied in a ponytail, his muscular body encased in a tight fitting tee-shirt and black pants. The third man looked studious; tall, overweight, well dressed in a grey suit with a set of glasses perched on a nose that looked like it had been broken numerous times. The red shirt man bent down and turned Ike's head roughly so he was looking directly into the man's unfriendly face. "We have a message for you, Mr. Miller."

Ike, once again, tried to sit up, but was pushed back to the ground with the end of a baseball bat the third man was clutching in his right hand. Ike looked from one man to the next and then stated, "Do you have any idea who I am?"

Nodding at the muscular man, the first man answered, "Yeah, we know who you are and the information in your wallet verifies it."

The pony-tailed man stood directly over top of Ike, his legs straddling Ike's prone body. Systematically, he removed items from the wallet and threw them down on Ike: "Let's see: driver's license, Visa, Master Card, American Express, Diner's Club Member, Savannah Country Club, coffee card from a local gas station." The man tore the coffee card in half and went on, "What a shame! Two more punches and you're entitled to a free cup. Membership card to Gold's Gym, insurance card and quite a bit of money." Throwing the bills in the air, he counted, "One hundred, two hundred, three hundred, twenty, forty, sixty." Seconds later, he finished and dropped the empty wallet on Ike's chest. "A grand total of six hundred and ten dollars. Sales must be good over at the dealership."

Ike touched the back of his head which was still throbbing. "Who are you and where in the hell am I?"

The first man stood back up, removed his hat and wiped his brow with a handkerchief. Placing the hat back on his head, without any warning, he gave Ike a solid kick in his left side. Nick gritted his teeth and tried not to show any reaction to the pain racing up his side. During his football career he had received many a hard hit to his body.

"To answer your questions," said the man, "You're sixty-three miles north of Savannah in some farmer's cornfield."

The man wearing glasses pointed the bat down at him and with an evil smirk, spoke. "You're in rural Georgia, mister; the middle of nowhere."

The first man signaled the third man to back off and spoke again, "Like I said, we were sent to deliver a message to you. It's not important that you know who we are. Let's just say we work for a man who has a very good friend in Savannah who desires that you receive this message." Another swift kick in Ike's side caused him to wince.

"Here's the message." said the man. "There is a certain young woman by the name of Shelby Lee Pickett that you have been seeing for quite some time now. It is our understanding that recently, you roughed her up a bit and broke some items at her apartment. Our friend doesn't appreciate the manner in which you have treated Miss Pickett. From this moment on, you are not, in any way, to have contact with her."

Ike, who didn't like to be told what to do looked away from the man, who instantly kicked him a third time and ordered, "You need to pay attention to what I'm telling you, Mr. Miller. If you so much as look at Miss Pickett the wrong way, we'll come visit you again, but we won't be as pleasant as we are now." Looking at the bat wielding man, the first man nodded. In the next second the bat was jammed into Ike's stomach, followed by a kick from the pony-tailed man. Gesturing for the two men to back off, the first man placed his boot on Ike's chest and spoke calmly, "We can stay here all day and beat you until you confirm to us that you understand, or you can acknowledge me now and save yourself a lot of pain. Now, do you understand our message?"

Ike looked up at the man with defiance and answered slowly, "Yeah, I get your message!"

"And just to make sure," said the man. "What is the message?"

Ike didn't answer quickly enough. The man's right boot once again planted itself into Ike's side followed by his voice, "I didn't hear what you said, Miller!"

Ike took a deep breath and answered, "I'm not to have any contact with her."

The man smiled. "And the girl's name is..."

Ike realizing he wasn't in a position to argue, answered, "Shelby Lee Pickett."

"Very good!" said the man. "We'll be leaving you in a few minutes. There are two parts to this message. The first part has been delivered and the second is yet to come. The first part is sort of like placing the message in an envelope. The second part is to stamp the envelope. If there is no stamp placed on an envelope, its message will not be received." With that, the man backed away and gestured at the other two men.

Following a number of savage kicks to his side and his stomach being pummeled with the bat, Ike was dragged to his feet and held in place by the two men. The third man stood directly in front of him and grabbed him by his necktie and jerked his neck upward. "Mr. Ike Miller," announced the man. "Ex-professional football player, big man in Savannah, successful real estate baron, man about town. We're done with you, for now. If you don't want the pleasure of our company again, then we strongly suggest you refrain from seeing Miss Pickett... ever!" The man gave Ike a hard punch to his stomach followed by an upper cut that sent Ike crumbling to the ground.

The man bent down and seeing that Ike was barely conscious, spoke one last time. "You can find your own way back to Savannah." Holding one of the twenty dollar bills that had been removed from Ike's wallet in front of his face, the man stood and smirked. "Gas money back to Savannah. Have a nice day, Mr. Miller." The three men walked away, disappearing in the corn. Ike tried to rise up, but fell back to the ground unconscious.

Parking the Jeep at the far end of Chester's, Shelby looked across the lot. Seeing four cars parked near the front, she remarked, "Looks like Chester is busy this afternoon. We might not be able to talk with him right now."

Climbing out, Nick agreed, "Maybe so. We'll just have to go in and see how things shake out."

Inside, Nick and Shelby hesitated by the front door and looked around the establishment: Chester, with his back to them was busy at the bar, two men were seated at the bar at the far end, while two couples occupied two tables in the back room. Chester turned around and placed two drinks in front of the men at the bar when he noticed Nick and Shelby. Motioning at the opposite end of the bar, he smiled.

Nick and Shelby each took a stool as Chester approached. "I was wondering if you two were going to show up. What are you guys drinking?"

Nick shrugged and Shelby answered, "Give us a pitcher... draft."

"Coming right up."

Nick looked past Chester at the two men seated at the other end of the bar. "Are we going to be able to talk without being overheard?"

Reaching beneath the bar, Chester produced a small handful of quarters. "Pick out some songs on the jukebox. The music will drown out anything we have to say."

Shelby took the quarters and after looking over the selections, she dropped a number of the coins into the slot and pushed six different numbers. The first song: The Devil Went Down to Georgia filled the bar. When Shelby returned to her seat, Chester nodded his approval and asked, "Okay, so now that I've seen this man again, what do we do?"

"Well, that depends," said Nick. "Let's go over what we have so far: we know this man is a chain smoker and he works with a crew of men somewhere in the suburbs. We also know what he looks like. The newest information we now have is that he drives a blue pickup truck." Leaning close to Chester, he asked, "Did you happen to notice what type of truck is was: Ford, Chevy, Dodge?"

"No," said Chester. "I didn't get close enough to notice. It wasn't a brand new truck, but then again it wasn't that old either."

Shelby chimed in, "What shade of blue?"

"Sort of a dark blue... but not Navy."

Were there any distinguishing defects on the truck, like dents or missing parts?"

"Not that I could see."

Nick scooted closer to the bar, took a drink and asked, "Do you always get your gas at that particular station?"

Chester frowned, "Not always, but yeah... most of the time."

"Do you always get your gas at the same time of day... give or take."

"No," said Chester. "I've gotten gas there in the morning, the afternoon... sometimes at night after I close up. Why is that important?"

"It's simple," explained Nick. "Most people tend to get their gas at a station where they feel comfortable. A place where the clerks get to know you by name, a place where you can get your morning coffee and a donut. Human beings are creatures of habit. We don't like change. We like to shop at places where we feel welcome. That may be the case with our boy. The gas station where you stop on a regular basis, might be *his station*. Maybe he always gets his gas in the morning. It just might be you've never run into him before, or you may have not noticed him. Let's face it. Before we had any suspicions about this man, there wasn't any reason for you to pay him any attention."

"What's the plan?" asked Chester.

"I think we need to lay low for now. We still don't have enough on this man to go to the police... just yet. Let's give this a few days and see what turns up, if anything. Chester, you need to keep a watch out for him in case he comes back here. If you'll give us the location of the gas station, we can stake it out in the mornings and see if the man returns. Depending on how much he drives, it could be a few days before he gasses up again. You've got my number. If he shows up here again, give me a call."

An hour later, the pitcher was empty and they had discussed with Chester, in between customers, what they planned on doing for the next week. Outside, in the lot, Nick climbed in the Jeep and Shelby backed out of the lot. Heading toward Savannah, Nick commented, "If you want to you can stake out the station in the mornings. I can't help you out because I'm starting to paint a house tomorrow."

"This is so exciting; almost like a good movie," said Shelby. "I can't wait to start watching the station."

Nick gave her a sad look. "Yeah, and I get to go to work. If anything happens don't forget to call me. I can get away if I have to."

Stopping at a red light in Savannah, Shelby pointed at a large billboard that advertised: MILLER'S AUTO MART – SAVANNAH'S NUMBER ONE DEALERSHIP. Pulling out when the light changed, Shelby commented, "I wonder if those men paid Ike a visit yet?"

The now familiar blue sky hovered above Ike when he came to. Painfully, he sat up and looked in every direction. Nothing but corn. Searching his coat pocket for his cell phone, it was not to be found. He looked at his wrist to see the time. His Rolex was missing as well. Cursing, he got to his knees when he noticed both his cell phone and Rolex smashed to pieces on the ground next to him. Looking up at the blazing sun, he swore, "Those bastards!"

Getting slowly to his feet, he gathered up his wallet, cards and money. Aside from the pain in his stomach and his side from the numerous blows he had received, he didn't feel nearly as bad as he looked. His tailor-made custom suit was wrinkled and there were two rips in his jacket. His shoes were ruined. What was it the man had said? *Sixty-three miles north of Savannah.* He had no idea in which direction Savannah was, so he just started walking down a row of corn stalks. His first thoughts were to get out of the field. Walking along he thought, *Who could have sent those men? It couldn't have been Shelby. She didn't hang with those sort of people.* At the moment, he wasn't concerned about who the men were or who sent them. Somehow, he needed to get back to the city and think things out.

Thirty minutes later he emerged from the vast field which ran adjacent to a one-lane paved road. He started up the road not knowing if he was going toward Savannah or away from the city. Rounding a bend in the road, he heard what sounded like the chug, chug, chug of a tractor. Sure enough as the noise grew louder, a farmer seated on a huge John Deer tractor came into view. Flagging the green tractor down, Ike approached the old farmer. "How goes it?"

"I'm fine," said the farmer. "Question is... how 'bout you? Ya look like ya been run over by a herd o' stampedin' cattle. Ya ain't from 'round here... are ya?"

"No, I'm not. Can you tell me where the nearest community is located?"

"Pointing back over his shoulder with his thumb, the farmer answered, "That'd be Sligo. 'Bout three miles back down the road. That where yer headin' mister?"

Opening his wallet, Ike pulled out a hundred and handed it up to the man. "I'll pay you to run me over there."

The farmer just stared at the money. "Never seen a hundred dollar bill before. Got anythin' smaller?"

Amazed, Ike opened his wallet and removed ten twenties. "Will twenties do? I got two hundred right here for you if you'll turn this rig around and take me to... what'd you call it... Sligo."

Taking the money, the farmer counted it and stuck it in his dirty overalls. Opening a can of snuff he stuck a chaw in the side of his mouth and gestured at the wagon he was pulling. "Jump in. I'll git her turned 'round and you'll be in town fer ya know it!"

Sitting in some hay in the wagon, Ike asked, This Sligo... how big of a town is it?"

"Oh, 'bout forty ta fifty folk live there."

"Will there be a phone I can use to call Savannah?"

"Sure 'nough. They got one at the gas station. I'm sure Nellie 'ill let ya make a call."

Thirty-five minutes later, Ike downed a soda and dialed his dealership in Savannah. Following three rings, a pleasant voice answered, "Miller's Auto Mart. How can I help you?"

"Sue Anne! This is Ike. Put Peter on the line please."

Seconds passed when another voice sounded, "Peter Barnes."

"Pete, this is Ike. Listen, I don't have time to explain right now, but I need you to grab a car and a map. I'm stranded in some one-horse town called Sligo. It's about sixty some miles north of the city. I need you to come get me... now!"

Chapter Seventeen

TURNING ONTO WAHOO DRIVE, NICK GUIDED THE GOLF cart and attached trailer down the dirt road. He smiled to himself. He was back to doing what he was good at; painting houses. But this seemed different. He was a millionaire and really didn't need to paint this house in order to survive like he had always done in the past. He was painting this house because he wanted to. Pulling into Sims' driveway, he took the canvas covering from the cart and began to stack the cans of paint on the porch. Setting up two foldaway saw horses beneath two large trees that offered shade, he organized everything he was going to need: brushes, paint pans, rollers and handles, drop cloths, stir sticks and a can opener. He checked the time: 7:15 in the morning. The sun was already beating down on the island, the forecast for the day in the mid-nineties. Opening his cooler, he removed a bottle of cold water, took a swig and then wrapped a white bandana around his forehead. Stripping off his tee shirt, he hitched up his favorite pair of paint-stained, white painter's pants with a pair of wide suspenders and placed a pair of sunglasses over his eyes. He was ready.

Sims, like he promised, left his extension ladder leaning on the side of the house since Nick had no way of hauling his without the aid of a truck. Spreading a drop cloth along the west side of the house which, at least for the moment, would keep him out of the direct sun, he walked back to the makeshift table and opened his first gallon of yellow. He was glad Sims had elected to go with the better paint. Mixing the paint with a heavy duty stir stick, Nick surmised that the house, in its condition, would only require one coat. Adjusting the extension ladder to its full height, he was just about to start up the ladder when his cell buzzed.

He had a feeling the caller was Shelby. When she dropped him off the previous evening she said she'd give him a call from the gas station in Savannah. "Hello! Is this my little watch dog calling?"

Concerned, Shelby answered, "Do you think we should be saying things like that over the airways?"

Nick joked, "Boy, you're really taking this stake out business serious. You can relax. I can assure you no one has bugged your car or is listening in. So, how's it going over there?"

"At first, it was pretty exciting. I parked next to a dumpster out by the street. I have a great view of the station and the lot. I brought along a pair of old binoculars I bought at a flea market years ago. I've got a thermos of coffee, some Danish and plenty of water. I got here about six this morning. There have been quite a few pickup trucks that have pulled in, but so far, not one blue one. This could get old real quick. I think I'll stay put until around ten o'clock. If our man has a job out in the suburbs, he'd have to stop at the station early before going to work. When I leave here I thought I might start to cruise some of the suburb neighborhoods and see if I can locate any construction crews or men doing work. If anything important comes up I'll give you a call. How's the painting going?"

"Just getting started. Listen, I'll talk with you later."

Halfway up the ladder, Nick was stopped again when Carson Pike pulled a golf cart into the driveway. Carson, waving, cupped his hands around his mouth and yelled up at Nick, "Come on down a sec. I need to talk to you."

Back on solid ground Nick shook Carson's hand and remarked, "Haven't seen you for a while. What's up?"

"I could ask you the same thing," said Carson, "but I already know what's up with you. I saw you on the news the other night. Your interview was short and sweet as they say. Well, maybe not so sweet. You looked nervous as hell. I ran into Chief Lysinger at the marina yesterday and he filled me in on this Susan Dunn business."

"Yeah, well that turned out to be nothing but a shot in the dark. I hate to sound like I don't care but it's just another girl the RPS Killer dumped out there in the marsh."

Carson lit a cigarette and looked up at the side of the house. "I bumped into Parker Sims this morning and he told me you were getting started on his house today. He said it was going to take you two to three days. I was hoping I'd catch you here this morning. There's something I want to ask you about. Let's go sit on the porch."

Nick agreed, but then remarked, "Alright, but I really have to get started if I want to get this job done."

Sitting on the porch steps, Carson waved off the remark and stated, "This will only take a couple of minutes." Thumping the steps with his right hand, he suggested, "Take a load off."

Plopping down on the bottom step, Nick asked, "So what's so important this morning?"

Carson took on a serious tone. "I was just wondering if you'd seen our two friends, Sparks and Simons lately?"

Nick answered instantly, "No," but then remembered the incident at Lowes. "Yeah, come to think of it the girl I've been seeing saw Sparks yesterday when we were at Lowes buying paint."

"You say this girl saw Sparks, but you didn't?"

"Yes, I was at the paint desk. She was getting some locks and she said he approached her and introduced himself. They had a short conversation and then he went his way."

"What was the conversation about?"

"He just wanted to know why she was buying locks and where she was going."

"And I assume she told him what these locks were for and where she was going."

"Yeah, she did."

"If I can ask, what are the locks for? Are you changing the locks at your house?"

"No, these were for her apartment over in Savannah. She's been having some problems with Ike Miller."

"Look at me," said Carson. "I already told you Miller's an ass! You don't want to tangle with him. He can be quite nasty, so I've heard. You were lucky over at the Dockside when you got into it with him. If Sparks and Simons wouldn't have intervened, you might be in the hospital. I don't know where you're at with this girl, but take my advice and stay clear of Ike Miller. Now, let's get back to Sparks and Simons."

"Yeah, let's do that, because I have a question. You said that soon they would be approaching me about the house... offering me a deal. That's what's you said. This island is a gated community, surrounded by water. How can Sparks and Simons approach me while I'm on the island if they don't have a pass? We both know how strict security is about that sort of thing."

"I was wondering about that myself. I've been doing a little research. Turns out they're renting a place at John Fripp Condos. So, to answer your question... they do have a pass. And even if they didn't, they could still get on the island. There are any number of ways by boat that would give them access. Remember Nick. This is an organized crime syndicate. They have more money, resources and connections than you can imagine. You can't hide from these people. If they want to talk with you, they'll make it happen... believe me. Don't let your guard down. I guarantee you, they will come to you, sooner or later. You just have to stay cool and act like you don't know what they're talking about. If things get out of hand, I'll step in and protect you."

"Why can't you do something now, before they contact me about the house? I mean, can't we get them kicked off the island or something?"

"They haven't done anything wrong. What could we possibly tell Chief Lysinger without giving away the secret of your grandmother's house? The syndicate has to make the first move *and* until they do we need to just sit tight. Agreed?"

Nick agreed reluctantly, stood and shook Carson's hand. "I really need to get some paint on this house. I stepped on that ladder fifteen minutes ago and I still haven't got to the top yet. If anything happens with Sparks and his partner, you'll be the first to know... that is, after me."

Carson walked to his cart, but then stopped. "That reminds me. When Sims was telling me you were going to paint his house, he was with one of his neighbors who just happened to mention he's got a rental property that needs the interior painted. I gave him your name and number. Hope you don't mind."

Nick answered, jokingly, "If I ever get *this house* done, I might consider another job. Now get out of here so I can get to work."

Finishing off his water, he started up the ladder for the third time. On the third rung, his cell buzzed. "Jeez!" said Nick out loud. "Who in the hell is calling now?"

Frustrated, he answered, "Yeah!"

Shelby spoke in a defensive manner, "You need some serious work on phone manners."

"I'm sorry," said Nick, "It's just that I keep getting interrupted. What's going on now?"

"You'll never guess who called me?"

"I can't imagine who called you. I hope it wasn't Ike Miller."

"Close, but no cigar! It wasn't Ike, but it was about him."

Confused, Nick responded, "Go on."

"The call I received was from my boss, Franklin Schrock. He told me he had been informed some men paid Mr. Miller a visit and he was told in a very strong manner to stay away from me."

"And you think because someone talked with Ike, he'll steer clear of you?"

"That's the same thing I asked Franklin. He explained to me these people who talked with Ike could be very persuasive. He didn't tell me exactly what the men had said to Ike, but he did say they had been rather physical with him. He also told me if Ike Miller had half a brain, he'd leave me be. That's my good news for the day. Aside from that, nothing much is going on here at the station. Over and out!"

"Okay," said Nick. "I'll see you tonight."

Grabbing the can of yellow paint, he started up the ladder again, half expecting his phone to ring. Arriving at the top, he attached a can hook to one of the rungs and hung the can. Removing a two-inch trim brush from the deep pockets of his pants, he dipped it into the thick yellow paint and began the process of trimming out just beneath the fascia board. With any luck and providing he was not interrupted again, he should have the house trimmed out by noon.

Shelby adjusted the sun visor in the Jeep so the morning sun was not directly in her face. She checked the time: Just after nine o'clock. *An hour to go,* she thought. She never realized before how many people stopped for drinks at a gas station. It seemed that everyone who stopped for gas automatically went into the station for coffee or some other drink. Aside from drinks and gas, patrons were purchasing donuts, lottery tickets, hotdogs and cigarettes. Most of the customers appeared to be business people, and as the morning wore on the number of people stopping by seemed to drop off.

Taking a bite of Danish, she was taken by surprise when a blue pickup pulled up in front of the station. From where she was positioned her view of the driver, when he got out, was blocked by the truck itself. The man, dressed in old jeans, heavy boots, green and grey camouflage tee-shirt and tan ball hat stopped at the entrance and took a final drag on a cigarette then stubbed it out in a container of sand by the door. Quickly, she grabbed the binoculars, but the man was inside before she could bring them to her eyes. Putting the binoculars on the dash she picked up an ink pen and small notepad and reached for the door handle. She had to get close enough to get the plate number of the truck and maybe a better look at the man. Just as she was about to open the door, the passenger side door opened, followed by a voice, "I need to talk with you!" Shelby, in amazement, stared across the seat at Ike Miller.

Looking at the station and then back to Ike, she spoke nervously, "Now is not a good time Ike, and besides, you're not supposed to bother me anymore!"

"So, then it's true!" bellowed Ike. "You did send someone to talk with me."

Trying to keep her eyes on the station and Ike at the same time, she responded, "I *did not* send anyone to see you!"

Ike, noticed her attention was not totally focused on him. Looking in the direction of the station, he probed, "What the hell is so interesting over there?"

Shelby realized she needed to be careful of what she said and did. Ike was only two feet away from her and if he got in one of his moods, he could become dangerous. So many thoughts were running through her mind: *Should I jump out of the Jeep and run to the station? If I do that, will Ike follow me? I have to get those plate numbers! If I stay in the Jeep with Ike I won't be able to get the numbers.*

Ike interrupted her thoughts and looked toward the station. "Is that guy you've been seeing in there? You're meeting him here... right?"

Trying her best to remain calm, she answered, "I'm not seeing anyone. For your information the young man you saw me with at the Dockside is nothing more than a friend."

"Then why are you so focused on the gas station?"

"Look Ike... it's over between us. I don't have to explain anything to you. Now, if you don't mind I have to go into the store and get something."

Ike objected, "Wait... wait just a minute. Let me explain. Some men, for lack of a better phrase, knocked me over the head yesterday and kidnapped me. The next thing I know, I wake up in some Godforsaken cornfield in the middle of nowhere. They told me they worked for someone who knew you. They said they had a message for me. The message was, I was to not go near you or contact you in any way. Between kicking the hell out of me and working me over with a baseball bat, I eventually passed out. Look... we can still work things out. I've learned my lesson."

Shelby, keeping her eye on the truck, responded, "And what lesson is that Ike?"

"Well, for one thing I've learned there are more powerful people in Savannah than me. I've always bulled my way through everything I've ever done in my life. You're the best thing that ever happened to me, Shelby. I always felt you were with me because...

well, just because you liked me, not my money or because I was a football hero. It seems like I always wind up involved with people who are nothing but phonies. You were... you are, the real thing. I know, recently I haven't treated you the way you deserve. Like I said, I've learned my lesson. I assume you still have the ring. Tell you what. You just hold onto it and think over what I'm saying. I'm asking you for a second chance. Don't you think I deserve one?"

"I can't trust you Ike and I don't believe you'll change. The men who came to see you wasn't my idea. I simply told someone I know what happened to me and they decided those men should pay you a visit. I was afraid of you. I didn't know what else to do. But, you did the same thing to me when you sent two men who work for you to my apartment."

"What makes you think I sent any men to your place?"

"Because, I was there, Ike! I hid in the closet and watched with my own eyes while they went through all of my personal things. I listened to every word they said. They referred to me as a wench! One of the men said if they didn't find the ring they were told, by you, to trash the place... which they did! They talked about how the one thing they didn't want to do is piss you off! And yes, I still have your ring. I'm going to hock it and use the cash to replace everything your men damaged! Now, I have to go into the store. When I get back, if you're still here I'm going to call the person I talked with before about you and tell them you did not understand the message you were given. I have no idea what he'll do, but I wouldn't want to be in your shoes. Good bye, Ike!"

Before Ike could say a word, Shelby was out of the Jeep and started across the lot. The blue pickup was backing out. From where she was she could see the tags but couldn't make them out. Another driver, in a silver car, stopped and waited for the pickup to back out to the left, then pulled into the space. Shelby stopped running and continued on at a fast walk. She didn't want to appear suspicious to the pickup driver. She hesitated next to the end of the line of pumps and waited for the truck to pass by at which point she could write down the plate number, but then the driver did something odd. He backed into another space and then pulled out in the opposite direction. Cursing, Shelby ran across the lot, trying her best to see the numbers on the plate but she wasn't close enough. The driver had to stop at the station exit to wait for traffic. Shelby ran toward the truck thinking she would have enough time to jot down the numbers. With the pen in her right hand and the notepad in her left she ran between the pumps, her right foot catching the edge of the concrete abutment. Down she went, the pen and notepad falling to the pavement. She tried to get up but was prevented from doing so when a woman and two men came to her rescue:

"Are you alright young lady?"

"That was quite a fall?"

"Here, let me help you up."

By the time Shelby was on her feet, the truck had pulled out and was disappearing up the street. One of the men handed her a handkerchief and pointed out that her right knee was bleeding. The woman suggested she have the cut looked at. Shelby picked up her pen and pad and started back across the lot. "Thank you so much for your help and your concern. I'll be fine... thank you." Stopping at the end of the pumps she looked at her Jeep half expecting Ike to be waiting for her to return. He was nowhere in sight.

Back in the Jeep she dumped some water on the hanky and dabbed at the blood on her knee. On close inspection she discovered it was nothing but a minor abrasion that would require some cleaning up with some over the counter antibiotic and a couple of small adhesive bandages. Dialing Nick's number, she waited patiently.

Nick, on his way back from the marina was taking a bite out of a ham sandwich when his phone buzzed. Setting down the sandwich he reached for his phone on the dash and answered in an enthusiastic tone, "Falco's Painting Service... how may I help you?"

Shelby ignored his attempt at humor. "Nick! I'm calling it a day. I think I may have spotted our man at the gas station, but I didn't have an opportunity to get the plate numbers. That's not all! I ran into Ike Miller. We had quite the conversation. I fell and cut my knee—"

"Whoa, whoa, whoa... back up a minute. One thing at a time. What do you mean when you say you think you saw our man?"

"I don't have time to explain everything that happened over the phone. I'm going home to get cleaned up. Meet me tonight at Johnson's Creek for dinner. Let's say five. Is that good for you?"

"Sure, I can be there at five. I was thinking about quitting at four anyway."

Before Nick could utter another word, Shelby ended the call. "See you there."

Nick looked at the cell phone and answered, "Count me in!"

Pulling into Sims' driveway, Nick grabbed his cell and the sandwich and walked toward the house, when he heard the sound of another cart in the driveway. Turning, he saw Charley Sparks and Derek Simons step out of the cart. Charley, with his hands on his hips looked back up Wahoo and commented, "We followed you all the way from the marina. I was sure you'd notice us." Gesturing at the sandwich, he went on, "You have a nice lunch?"

Nick, wondering if this was what Carson had warned him about, remained calm and answered, "Sure did. What can I do for you gentlemen? Need a house painted?"

"That's right," said Sparks. "You are a painter. I remember the first time we saw you in Cincinnati. You were painting a house. Later that day, we ran into each other at the bank. Remember?"

Derek, holding a six-pack of beer stood at Charley's side but remained quiet.

"Yeah, I do recall that," answered Nick, "and you've been following me ever since."

Charley motioned at the porch. "Let's sit on the porch, drink a couple of beers and have a chat."

Nick laughed and stated, "I'm fine right here."

Charley looked at his feet, then back at Nick. "I would strongly suggest you have a seat on the porch. I'd hate to turn Derek here loose on you. You've already seen and experienced how upset he can get. Please, join us on the porch."

Nick, recalling when Derek had manhandled him in Cincinnati and the incidents at both Bill's Liquor Store and the Dockside, decided it best if he complied with Charley's request. Trying to act casual, Nick took the last bite of his sandwich and walked to the porch, sitting on the top step. Charley sat next to him while Derek sat on an old chair on the porch.

"That's better," said Charley. "Let's all have a beer while we talk." Derek ripped a can out of the plastic holder and handed it down to Charley, then handed one to Nick and opened a can himself." Charley popped the top of the can and held the beer up in a toasting fashion. "Here's to friends and good conversation."

Taking a long swig, he wiped his mouth with the back of his hand and smiled. "Nothing like a cold beer on a hot day!" Looking at the porch he asked, "How long do you think it'll take you to paint this place?"

Nick, trying to be congenial, opened his beer. "Two to three days... maybe four depending on how long you intend to sit here and keep me from doing my work."

Charley laughed. "Don't worry. What we have to discuss will only take, maybe ten to fifteen minutes. You'll be back to work before you know it." Pointing his can at Nick, he asked, "Do you remember what we talked about that day in the bank parking lot?"

"Not exactly," said Nick. "You mentioned that in the next few days I would have some decisions to make and you also said as long as I didn't go to the police I wouldn't be in any danger. I didn't understand what you were talking about, and I still don't."

Looking at Derek, Charley smiled and then explained, "Not to worry. In a few minutes, you'll understand what I meant about making some decisions. It is my understanding that your grandmother, Amelia Falco, after her unfortunate death left you a small fortune: her home, the furnishings within, a couple of cars and quite a tidy sum of money."

"That's right," said Nick. "It's no secret. I imagine she left me everything she had."

"That should make you a happy man," remarked Charley. "When we first met you in Cincinnati you were nothing but a young man with a failing business and no money to speak of. Now, here it is a couple of weeks later and here you are... a millionaire. Congratulations!"

"I'm sure you didn't follow me over here today to tell me that."

"You're right. We have a very specific reason for talking with you today."

Taking a drink, Nick looked Charley square in the eye. "I'm listening."

Charley stood and walked a few paces out into the yard. "I'm sure I don't have to tell you what fine people your grandparents were. That being said, there are some things about Edward and Amelia, that, most likely, you are unaware of. Your grandfather worked for the same company that Derek and I work for. The company has a number of business interests stretching from New York down to Florida. Edward was in the financial end of the business, handling the profits that came in and in general, making investments for the owners. Your grandfather was paid very well for his services and as you may well be aware of lived somewhat of a life of luxury."

Walking back to the porch, Charley leaned on the railing. "Your grandparents were not the most honest people in the world. Edward, after a number of years decided to start skimming money from the company. Your grandfather was very shrewd. He set up a little side business of stealing money from the company for years. If he would have stopped after the first million or so, we would have probably never caught him. But, Big Ed was greedy. We knew something was up, but we couldn't figure how he was stealing from us, so we decided to just simply confront him. Of course, he denied everything, saying he never stole a penny from the company. As close as we could estimate, he took the company for somewhere around six to seven million dollars."

Sitting down on the steps next to Nick, Charley asked, "Does any of this sound familiar to you?"

Nick laughed and answered, "You really can't be serious about any of this... can you?"

Charley looked up at Derek and then back to Nick and moved closer. *"Dead serious Nick!"* Crushing the empty beer can in his hand Charley looked deep into Nick's eyes. "I emphasize the word *dead*, because that's exactly what happened to your grandfather, when after a number of failed attempts he refused to tell us where the money was."

Nick, aware of the fact that the people Edward worked for had killed him, acted confused and stated, "My grandfather drown in an automobile accident over on Harbor Island."

Opening another can of beer, Charley went on to explain, "That may be what folks around here think and it may be what's in the police report in Beaufort, but the fact is: your grandfather is dead because he would not divulge the whereabouts of the money."

Nick had to act surprised if he was going to pull off the fact that he didn't know what they were talking about. "Are you saying my grandfather was murdered?"

Charley laughed, "You figure it out kid."

Nick, not sure how to react, remained silent.

Reaching down, Charley wiped a smudge of dirt from his shiny, black right shoe and continued talking, "Your grandfather and his *untimely death* is just the first part of what I wanted to discuss with you. The second part, and I must admit, the most important part... is your grandmother, Amelia. Since we didn't have much luck with Edward we contacted your grandmother at her home. I have to say, Amelia was more cooperative than her husband. She told us she knew about the money, but not where it had come from. Whether this is true or not, we didn't know... or care. We just wanted our money back. She told us the money was either hidden somewhere in the house or on the property, but she didn't know where. We gave her the benefit of the doubt and figured she was telling us the truth. We suggested she allow us to search the house and the property, but she refused, saying that in order to do that, the property would be ruined what with tearing up floors and knocking out walls, not to mention digging up the grass. Being understanding we suggested that if she allowed us to search the premises, we would pay for any repairs that needed to be done, provided we found the money. She didn't agree to our suggestion, so then we told her we would buy the house from her even if we didn't find the money. She wouldn't agree to this either. I gotta tell ya. She was one tough bird. We continued to negotiate with your grandmother, but she would not budge. Finally, the people we work for, the company, told us to give her one last chance, which we did. She still refused our offer. Unfortunately for us and fortunately for your grandmother, she died before our final unannounced meeting with her."

Nick, continuing his act, stood as if he were upset. "You, or someone from the company my grandfather worked for killed him because he wouldn't tell you where this money was and now you're suggesting that you would have killed Amelia because she didn't want to cooperate with you also."

"That about sums it up," said Charley. "Now, you own the house and we're offering you the same deal we gave your grandmother. We will buy the house at one hundred thousand dollars above the appraisal. You can keep all the antiques, cars and money she left you. We just want the house."

Continuing the act, Nick threw his beer can off into some nearby bushes. "So you just expect me to sell you my grandmother's house based on this cock and bull story about six or seven million dollars that's supposedly hidden on the property. This sounds like some kind of fairy tale."

"You can think whatever you please," snapped Charley. "That money is in your house somewhere and one way or the other we're going to get it back."

"I can't sell you the house even if I wanted to," stated Nick. "My grandmother's will has a clause in it stipulating that I have to live in the house. If I decide to not reside there then the house is donated to the Fripp Island Home Owner's Association."

"Well this is a new twist I didn't expect," said Charley. "Your ol' grandmother even from her grave is still giving us fits. I guess you're either going to allow us to search the property or move out. Our company will offer the home owners association more than it's worth."

Nick stepped toward Charley and spoke with respect, "Look, I don't know whether to believe you guys or not. Even if I did buy your story, you can't expect me to make a snap decision on something like this. I need some time to think."

Charley moved close to Nick and placed his hand on his shoulder. "You have one week, Falco! We'll be in touch."

Charley walked over and climbed in the cart. Derek threw his empty beer can on the porch, then walked over and tipped over the open gallon of yellow paint, the paint spilling across the porch and running down the steps. Derek smirked and spoke sarcastically, "Sorry, I'm so clumsy!"

Nick stood and watched as they disappeared in a cloud of dust. Looking at the spilled paint, he decided to clean up what he could. The rest would be covered when he painted the porch with the black.

It was just after one o'clock. At least the house was trimmed out. Pulling his cell out of his pants he had to contact Carson about the newest development with Sparks and Simons. Dialing Pike's number he waited: no answer.

He was done painting for the day. In four hours he was meeting Shelby for dinner at Johnson's Creek to discuss both Ike Miller and the RPS Killer. Little did she know they were also going to talk about Charley Sparks and Derek Simons. Cleaning up the excess paint, he wondered if he had done the right thing moving into Amelia's house. The previous problems he had faced in Cincinnati seemed petty compared to what he was now facing.

Chapter Eighteen

THERE WAS A TOTAL OF SEVEN CARS PARKED IN THE dirt lot at Johnson's Creek. It wasn't even five o'clock yet. In another hour or so the lot would be packed. Parking his bike beneath an old oak near the front of the lot, Nick remembered the last time he had dined at the popular island restaurant. It was his last year coming down to Fripp as a youngster. He was ten years old and Big Ed and Amelia had brought him to "The Creek," as the locals referred to the restaurant for his birthday. They sat by a window table, overlooking the marsh and nearby creek. He had a giant plate of Frogmore Stew and his grandmother even permitted him to have a sip of wine. He recalled how nasty it had tasted *and* to this day, he despised the taste of most wine.

The place looked the same, a casual deck area attached to the right side at the front of the one story building, where later in the evening couples and families would gather to listen to some local artist playing the piano or maybe a guitar. Stepping inside, he was met by a hostess who asked, "How many this evening sir?"

Nick politely answered, "There will be two of us. I didn't see her vehicle out on the lot, so I assume she hasn't arrived yet. Could we have a table by the window?"

"Of course, just follow me."

Seated at one of the rustic tables, Nick looked around the restaurant. It looked the way he remembered; the wood planked walls covered with autographed one dollar bills of those who dined at the restaurant over the years. He recalled that evening almost seventeen years ago when Edward gave him a dollar bill and using a black magic marker a waitress gave him, he scrawled his first name on the bill and then with a stapler, also supplied by the waitress, attached it with the help of his grandfather at the top of the door to the men's room.

A waiter approached and asked, "Would you care for something to drink, sir?"

"Yes, please. There will be two of us. Let's start with two glasses of water."

"Very good, sir," smiled the waiter.

Nick stopped the young man from walking away. "All of these autographed dollar bills. Do you ever take them down?"

"No. Once they are put on the wall, that's where they stay. I'll be right back with your water."

Out of curiosity, Nick got up and walked to the men's room door and there at the top right hand corner, the bill with his name on it was still there. Walking back to the table he thought, *Some things never change!* Seated again at the table he looked out the large window at the adjacent small marsh area bordered by Johnson Creek. Frowning, he thought about the fact that he would probably never look at a marsh again without thinking about the RPS Killer.

His thoughts were interrupted by a pleasant voice, "You got here early."

Turning, he saw Shelby standing next to the table. Dressed in white jeans, a brown weaved belt and teal blouse fronted by a thin strand of pearls, she curtsied, then sat. "Did you order drinks yet?"

"Just water," said Nick. "Wasn't sure what you'd be in the mood for this evening."

"Since you asked about my mood, I'm a bundle of nerves."

The waiter returned with two glasses of water. He no sooner set them on the table, when Nick spoke, "I've been informed that we're going to require something a tad bit stronger. I'll just have a draft beer."

He motioned at Shelby, who responded immediately, "Scotch... straight up!"

Nick waited for the waiter to walk away before he spoke to Shelby. Lowering his voice he leaned forward and asked, "So what's all this about you falling in Savannah?"

Keeping her voice equally low, Shelby responded, "I fell at the gas station. I was running across the lot trying to get close enough to get the tag numbers on the blue pickup when I went down."

"Are you alright?"

"Hurts like hell, but other than that, I'm fine. I was so close to getting the plate numbers. If it wouldn't have been for Ike's sudden appearance I would have not only got the numbers but I would have gotten a good look at the possible killer."

"I thought Miller wasn't supposed to bother you anymore?"

"That's what I was led to believe myself, but there he was sitting in the Jeep right next to me."

"How in hell did that happen?"

"I don't have any idea. I was just getting ready to get out and write down the numbers of the pickup when, all of a sudden, Ike opens the Jeep door and hops in."

"What did he say?"

"He told me some men had paid him a call. Apparently they kicked the hell out of him and went at him with a ball bat. He said he learned his lesson and wanted a second chance with me."

Nick sat back and gave Shelby a sideways look.

"Don't give me that look," said Shelby. "There's no way in hell I'd ever get back with that maniac."

"Did he say anything else?"

"He said I should keep the ring and think things over."

"Are you going to say something to Schrock about Miller approaching you after he was warned not to?"

"I don't know. I just want him to leave me alone. I don't want to see him wind up in the hospital... or worse. I feel like I'm in over my head with this Ike Miller business."

The waiter returned with their drinks and asked, "Will you need a few minutes to decide on your meals this evening?"

"Yes, I think so," said Nick. "Thank you."

Getting back to their conversation, Nick confessed, "I'm a little confused. Did all this happen before or after you saw the man in the pickup?"

Shelby downed her drink in four swallows and took a deep breath. "I think I need another." Answering Nick's question, she went on, "Ike showed up about the same time when the man came out of the station. It was difficult trying to keep an eye on the man and listening to what Ike was telling me."

"Did Ike notice you were watching the station?"

"Yes, but he didn't have any idea what I was looking for. He thought I was meeting you there. He was so focused on trying to convince me to give him a second chance he really wasn't paying attention to what I was looking at."

"At what point did he leave? Did he see you fall?"

"I have no idea. By the time I got back to the Jeep, he was gone."

Taking a drink of beer, Nick commented, "God, our lives are becoming one big soap opera!"

Sadly, Shelby looked out the window and sighed, "Are we the good guys or the bad?"

Nick nearly choked on his beer. Sputtering, he answered, "The good... guys... of course."

Reaching across the table, she placed her right hand over his. "In the movies the good guys always win."

"True... very true," agreed Nick. "But, this isn't the movies. This is life... our lives, and right now we seem to be surrounded by undesirables. Number one, we have Ike Miller, ex-football star, who I barely escape getting mangled by at the Dockside, not to mention that he roughs you up and has your apartment trashed right before our very eyes. Second, we have a serial killer who has killed nine girls and we, and *only we,* and Chester, may know who he is. Third, I have two thugs from New York, who may have killed my grandfather and would have killed my grandmother, dogging my every move because they want seven million dollars that's hidden in my house somewhere. Since I moved here to Fripp, it's been like a bad episode every day and things don't seem to be getting any better."

Signaling their waiter, Shelby held up her glass. "I believe I'll have another one of these." Looking at Nick, she smiled, "Well, at least for the time being, the Ike Miller situation is on the back burner. Let's talk about your second analogy; the killer; or I guess I should say, the man we think may be the killer. While I was at the station this morning I did see a blue pickup pull in. I didn't get a close look at the male driver but I did notice he was smoking. We're actually no further ahead than we were yesterday. If I could have gotten his plate number, we'd have more to go on. I guess I can return tomorrow for the next few days and hope he'll return. I really didn't get a chance today to drive through some of the suburbs to check out work crews. I've got a couple of days left before I have to return to work, so maybe I'll cruise some Savannah suburbs and see what I can discover."

"That's sounds like a good idea," said Nick, "but I won't be able to help you. I've got to get Parker Sims' house painted. I didn't get half as much accomplished today as I wanted to, which brings us to the third analogy I mentioned—"

"Excuse me," said their waiter. "Are you ready to order?"

Nick, who still hadn't looked at the menu, picked up the folded selection of food and beverages and remarked, "I already know what I want. Frogmore Stew. That's what I had the last time I was here. If I recall, it was delicious *and* a lot to eat."

Shelby scanned the menu and spoke to herself, "I'm not really very hungry—"

Nick jumped in and suggested, "Why don't you split the stew with me. I know I won't be able to eat it by myself."

"Alright," said Shelby. "That sounds good." Looking at the waiter, she asked, "Can we do that... I mean split a meal?"

"Of course," announced the waiter. "I'll bring two plates."

The waiter no sooner left the table when Shelby picked up where Nick had left off. "You were just about to explain your third analogy to me, which I can only assume is about Charley Sparks and Derek, whatever his last name is. Did you run into them today? You already told me you were expecting them to come to you with a deal about the house... and the money."

"I didn't exactly run into them," said Nick, "but yes, they did come to me with their deal. They followed me from the marina after I had lunch and cornered me at the house I'm painting. The long and short of it is they gave me a week to decide if I'll let them search the house."

"And if you don't?"

"Ya know, it's strange. They didn't, in so many words, say what was going to happen if I didn't allow the search. They did talk about my grandfather's unfortunate automobile accident and how my grandmother's death was fortunate because they never got to have their final meeting with her. They never actually said they killed my grandfather or that they would have killed my grandmother. They didn't have to. Just the way they talked about it, I knew they if fact, did kill Edward and would have killed Amelia."

Leaning toward Nick, Shelby whispered, "I can't believe I'm saying this, but do you think they have intentions of trying to kill you if you don't yield to their demands?"

"I can't believe I'm giving you this answer. Yes, I think they would kill me. I wouldn't put it past them. Carson told me how ruthless Sparks and Simons could be, not to mention the people *they work for!* This is seven million dollars we're talking about. If I had any idea where the money was, I'd give it to them and be done with this."

"The way I see this is you only have two choices that make any sense. You can contact the police or allow these men to search the property."

"I can't contact the police. It would be too difficult to explain. They'd want to know where the money came from in the first place, which could wind up with my grandfather being exposed as some sort of gangster and my grandmother as his accomplice because she didn't go to the police about the money. As far as allowing these people to search the property, why, depending on where the money is hidden, it could take days, weeks, maybe even months. There's no telling where Edward hid that money. I can't bring myself to permit these people to tear up the floors and knock down walls. The house itself is worth over a million dollars. And, besides that, I don't know for a fact that the money is even hidden there. I've just been told it's there. If I allow these people to search the house and the grounds and they do discover the money, what guarantee do I have, that they'll return the house to its previous condition? And another thing: If they don't find the money, they're not going to be happy. They could just pack up and leave me with a gigantic mess. Fripp Island isn't all that big. If something happens on the island it doesn't take long until everyone knows about it. How could I possibly explain that the men who are actually searching the house are really contractors who are remodeling every single room and completely re-landscaping the property? I don't know if I could pull that off. The thought that people here on the island would buy into the concept that I was completely revamping the entire property, inside and out, borders on ridiculous."

"Okay, I understand the way you feel about your grandparents, but they are no longer here... you are! Why should you suffer in any way because of what they did?"

"I shouldn't have to suffer and I have no desire to do so. I've just got to figure some way out of this mess and I only have a week."

"Ever since you told me about this hidden money, I've been thinking. There's something about this whole thing that doesn't add up. Why would your grandmother, who you have told me a number of times was close to you, leave her home to you, knowing full well there is seven million dollars hidden there that these people want. If it's true they killed your grandfather and would have killed your grandmother, why on earth would she want you to go through the same thing?"

"You're right... it doesn't make sense. Ever since Carson Pike told me about the money, I just couldn't believe it, but what possible reason would he have to fabricate his story?"

"Well, since both your grandparents are no longer here to verify this hidden money business, you have no other choice but to believe Pike."

The waiter returned with their dinner. Placing a steaming plate of the stew between them, he put an extra plate on the table and asked, "Will there be anything else?"

"I think we'll be fine for now," responded Nick. As the waiter turned and walked away, Nick handed the extra plate to Shelby and suggested, "Let's dig in!"

Shelby scooped a small portion on her plate and leaned over and smelled the seafood concoction. "Smells great!" Stabbing a chunk of potato, she pointed at Nick. "Okay, so we've already established that you can't go to the police and you don't want the house destroyed. There's a third option, but it would require a rather dramatic move."

Nick stuck a shrimp in his mouth and spoke at the same time, "I'm listening."

"Let's say you decide to take an extended vacation. You told me your grandmother left you quite a bit of money. You can finish up painting the house and then go somewhere for a few weeks or possibly months. Carson could keep an eye on your house... daily if need be. This way, during your absence, these people wouldn't have enough time to break in and search the house. And, if they did break in, they'd only have one day to search before island security would be alerted of the break-in, thus the house would become off-limits."

"I can see the logic behind your thinking, but, first of all where would I go? From what Carson has told me, these people are very powerful. Where could I go that they wouldn't follow? Since I left Cincinnati they've known my every move. We go to the Dockside... and they are there. I stop at Bill's Liquor store... and they are there. We go to Lowes... they are there." Looking around the restaurant, Nick gestured. "It wouldn't surprise me one bit if they are either here tonight, or close by. They know my every move... and yours too. If I did take a vacation, as you say, I'd have to keep on the move. I'd always be looking over my shoulder. It'd be like I was some sort of fugitive or something. I wouldn't feel right leaving you here alone. What if these men corner you and start asking you questions about where I went. No, I've got to come up with something else. I don't have a clue what, but the clock is ticking."

Nick's cell phone buzzed. Taking it from his pocket, he answered, "Hello."

"Nick, it's Carson."

"Where've you been? "I've called you five times since I stopped painting at four."

"It hasn't been my day," explained Carson. "The motor on my boat gave out. I had to call the marina and have them give me a tow back in. Then, to make things worse, I dropped my phone in the water at the marina dock. By the time I got it fished out, it was fried. Guess I should have got one of those waterproof models. Right now I'm on my way back from Beaufort. I drove over here and got myself a new phone. I had no idea you tried to call me. The reason I called is I thought maybe you'd like to go with me tonight over to John Fripp Condos. I found out what unit Sparks and Simons are staying at."

"It's strange you should mention those two. That's why I tried to call you earlier. It happened just like you said it would. They approached me and gave me their deal. I think we need to meet and discuss what they told me. I'm at dinner right now. What say we meet at my place around ten?"

"Are you with that girl you've been seeing?"

"Yeah, why?"

"Don't bring her along. She doesn't need to get involved in this. From here on out, it could get dangerous. See you at ten?"

Laying his phone on the table, Nick apologized, "Sorry for the interruption. That was Carson Pike. I'm meeting him tonight at ten to discuss Sparks and Simons. I'd like to invite you along but he still doesn't know I told you all about the money and the people who want it back. Depending on what we discuss tonight we might not be able to see each other for a few days."

"That's alright," said Shelby. "You've got a house to paint and I guess I'll spend the next couple of days in Savannah looking for a chain-smoking construction worker who drives a blue pickup."

A short musical jingle signaled Shelby that she had an incoming call on her cell. Reaching for her purse, she commented, "Well, aren't we the popular couple!" Rummaging through the purse, she located the phone and answered enthusiastically, "Shelby!"

Buttering a piece of bread, Nick nonchalantly listened to Shelby's end of the conversation in between whatever the caller was saying:

"I'm fine..."

"You're not serious..."

"What happened..."

"I see..."

"Okay, I'll see you Monday."

Shelby placed the phone back in her purse and stared out the window.

Waiting for her to say something, which she didn't, Nick inquired, "Should I ask who that was or what that was about, or isn't it any of my business?"

Shelby stopped the waiter who was walking by. "Excuse me! I'm going to need another scotch."

Folding her hands neatly on the table, she looked at Nick and sat back in her chair. "The soap opera continues. That was Franklin Schrock, my boss. He just informed me Ike Miller is in the hospital and probably won't get out for a week or so. Turns out, after those men gave Ike the message to leave me be, they put a tail on him to make sure he complied. They happened to be tailing him when he jumped in my Jeep at the gas station. From what Franklin said, they saw me run from my vehicle. Thinking I was running from him, at some point, later in the day, they grabbed Ike and drove him to some deserted beach south of Savannah where they beat the living tar out of him. Apparently, some joggers found him lying on the beach unconscious. From what Franklin was able to find out, the hospital reports that he has a broken right leg, broken left arm, broken nose and jaw, numerous cuts and abrasions and quite a few teeth missing. When he regained consciousness at the hospital the police questioned Ike. All Ike would tell them was that he had no idea who was responsible for his beating and when he was well enough to leave the hospital, he was moving down to Tampa. The police said he appeared to be scared to death. This has gotten out of hand. All I wanted was for Ike to leave me alone. I feel responsible for the condition he's in. If I wouldn't have gone to Schrock, Ike wouldn't be laid up in the hospital."

"Look, I don't want to come off like some kind of hard ass," remarked Nick, "but the guy asked for it. Think about the way he was ready to kick my ass at the Dockside. Your apartment is in the condition it is because of what he ordered done. He told you, if I'm not wrong, that he was going to make your life a living hell! The way I look at this, things just backfired on Ike and now his life has become a version of living hell. He finally ran into someone he couldn't push around. I have no idea who these people are who your boss contacted, but If I were you I'd be glad they're on your side."

"I guess you're right," muttered Shelby. "I just can't believe it's gone this far." Remembering something, she snapped her fingers. "I almost forgot. Schrock reminded me that you and I still have an all-expense paid cruise coming for saving his daughter."

The waiter returned with Shelby's drink and Nick asked, "I don't suppose you could bring me another draft?"

"Of course, sir. I'll be right back with that."

Nick sat back and folded his arms across his chest and looked at Shelby. "Something you said gives me an idea."

"That's rather vague," said Shelby. "I said quite a few things this evening."

"What you said about the cruise we have coming. That could very well be the answer to our problem. Talk about an extended vacation! We could wind up out in the middle of the ocean somewhere. We could go to another country... another continent. If nothing else, it would give me more than a week to sort things out. We leave the country and Carson could keep an eye on the house."

"I don't want to burst your bubble," said Shelby. "After all, this vacation thing was my idea in the first place, but when you think about it, it doesn't solve the problem, so to speak. We'd be doing nothing but putting a band aid over a wound. From what you've told me I don't think a few weeks is enough time to solve this problem, but it's something to consider. Why don't you discuss it with Carson when you meet him later tonight?"

"I think I will," said Nick. Stabbing a small piece of sausage, he smiled. "Let's finish up our dinner before it gets cold."

Nick parked his bike in the driveway and opened the garage door at his grandmother's home. Walking inside the two car garage, he looked at the walls. The lack of the standard tools that were normally on display hanging from hooks were not present, indicating that his grandfather was not much of a handyman. Nick figured that with the money Bid Ed made over the years, he could afford to pay those who were experts in their field to accomplish whatever he required around the house and property.

Lowering pull-down steps near the front of the garage, he climbed the steps and switched on a light near the top of the overhead storage area. Standing on three-quarter inch plywood he looked around the enclosed area. Aside from cobwebs and peanut shells and scraps left behind from small local wildlife, the overhead area was empty. Reaching up, he pushed on some plywood above his head. It gave a little, but seemed solid. For a moment he had a thought. *Maybe the money is hidden in the garage somewhere. It could be hidden in waterproof bags up in between the rafters or behind the plywood. No, that's too obvious.* He could spend hours walking around the garage, the house and the property and try to figure out where the money might be stashed away. He only had a week. He thought again about what Shelby said about the money; how things just didn't add up. Maybe there wasn't any money. If he could convince Sparks and Simons of that it would be great, but they seemed convinced that the money was currently in his possession.

It would be nearly two hours before his meeting with Carson. A walk on the beach sounded good. Climbing back down the steps, he turned off the light and then pulled his bike inside the garage and closed the door. The dust on the glass of the entrance door prevented most of the late evening sunlight from penetrating the dark interior of the garage. Reaching for the doorknob, he felt the heavy thud on the side of his head, followed by a sense of dizziness. The last thing he remembered seeing was the glowing clock on the wall that read: 8:17.

Chapter Nineteen

CARSON LOOKED DOWN AT HIS WATCH AND BROUGHT his Land Rover to a stop in Nick's driveway. It was 10:10; ten minutes late for their planned meeting. The large three-tier fountain in the front yard was running, the concrete angel centered on the top held a jug from which the recycled water emptied into the top tier and eventually cascaded down onto the second tier and then the bottom. The falling water sparkled like diamonds from the beam of light from a nearby spotlight. Bounding up the steps, he noticed that the house was completely dark. *Strange,* he thought. Knocking on the front door, he rang the doorbell, the melodious tune announcing his arrival. Following a few seconds of silence he repeated the process: no answer. After a third try, he walked down the steps and around the side of the house, thinking how odd it was that Nick didn't answer.

At the back of the house he opened the screen door to the Florida room and banged on the back door: no answer. Peering in the large picture window, he stared into complete darkness. There was not a light on in the house anywhere, upstairs or down. Something didn't seem right. Flipping up the circular throw rug in front of the door, Carson snatched up the spare key, unlocked the door and entered the dark house. Turning on the kitchen light, he walked down the hall toward the sitting room and yelled, "Nick... you home?" Walking back to the living room, he flipped on the upstairs hall light and climbed the stairs and yelled again, "Nick... where are you?"

Back down in the kitchen Carson looked at the key in his hand and smiled to himself. He opened the refrigerator and removed a beer. *It's that girl he's been running with,* he thought. *He's probably still with her.* Taking his new cell phone from his pocket, he punched in Nick's number. Following a number of rings and no answer, a message came up indicating that he leave a voice mail. Carson responded with a short message: "Nick, its Carson. Did you forget our meeting at ten? I'm at your house. Give me a call."

Walking out into the sun room, he sat on the steps at the back of the house. He had talked with Nick somewhere around six o'clock. That was four hours ago; more than enough time to eat dinner and then say good night. He was probably on his way home at the moment. Out of curiosity he walked out to the garage and found to his surprise that it was unlocked. Shoving open the door he switched on the light. The golf cart, Nick's motorcycle, the Lexus and the '49 Buick were all present. The presence of the four vehicles Nick owned brought up another question: had the girl Nick was seeing driven them to dinner?

Carson's thoughts were interrupted by a familiar voice, "Good evening Carson. What brings you by tonight?"

Turning, Carson saw his old friend, Genevieve standing by the back porch looking toward the garage door. Carson closed the door and answered, "Nothing much. I was supposed to meet Nick here at the house around ten, but he doesn't seem to be at home, which is strange because all his vehicles are parked in the garage. I don't suppose you saw him any time this evening... have you?"

"Come to think of it, I did see him. I think it was about eight o'clock. I was taking some garbage out when I saw him pull in on his bike. I was going to come over and talk with him, but he never came out of the garage, so I just went back in the house."

Rubbing her chin, thinking, she went on, "I guess it was about ten minutes or so later when I was out front watering some of my plants when I noticed a car pull in his driveway and two men got out. I recognized them from Amelia's memorial service. Ya know, those two men who work for the same company Edward did. Anyway, they went inside the garage."

"How long were the men here?"

"Not long, maybe five minutes."

"So you saw them when they left?"

"Yeah, I was at the side of my house filling up my watering can when they pulled out."

"Did you happen to notice if Nick was with them in the car?"

"No, I really didn't pay that much attention. Is there something wrong, Carson?"

"No, I don't think so. It's just not like Nick. He usually does what he says he's going to do. It's just odd. I was supposed to meet him here and he's not around."

"Maybe he took a quick walk on the beach," said Genevieve.

"You might be right," commented Carson. "I think I'll go to the beach and see if he's down there. If not, I'll just wait inside the house for him."

Carson was halfway across the dirt road that ran behind the house when he heard Genevieve's voice behind him, "Weatherman says it might rain later on tonight. We could use a good rain to cool things down some. They said it might not hit until around two this morning. Hell, with as hot as it's been why I might just run around in my back yard naked."

Walking backwards, Carson pointed his beer at Genevieve and joked, "Now, that's something I'd like to see!"

Placing her hands on her hips, Genevieve went into what she no doubt thought was a sexy pose and answered, "Well, tell you what. If it's raining around two o'clock and you're awake bring your naked self over and we'll run around in the rain together."

Waving his hand at her as if she were nuts, Carson remarked, "That'll be the day!"

Climbing the wooden steps that led up to the deck crossing the dunes he stared out at the black ocean, the surf from the waves occasionally shining from the moonlight in between the passing overhead clouds. In the distance, far out at sea, he could see the glow from lighting. There definitely was a storm brewing. He walked out across the sand to the water's edge and looked up and down the dark beach. If Nick was indeed out there walking somewhere he wouldn't be able to see him until he was almost on top of him. Finishing his beer, he decided to go back to the house.

Sitting in the darkness, Carson nursed another beer and stared out the window at the occasional distant lightning. The fact the two men, who had been identified as Charley Sparks and Derek Simons by Genevieve was cause to be concerned. According to what she said they were only at the house for a few minutes. Nick had told him they approached him earlier in the day and had given him a deal. That was the main reason why he and Nick were meeting. His absence was troubling. He wondered if Sparks and Simons had made their move already. But that didn't make any sense. When Nick told him they had approached him, he didn't indicate a sense of urgency. Getting up, he turned on the kitchen light and looked at the grandfather clock by the fireplace: just after eleven o'clock. He couldn't just sit around wondering what happened. He had to do something and he knew what it was.

Driving completely around John Fripp's parking area, the dark blue car Sparks drove was not to be seen. Parking at the front of the lot, Carson walked down to the end unit where Sparks and

Simons were staying. The front door was closed and the blinds were drawn shut. Looking up at the windows for the spare bedroom on the second floor, the blinds were also closed. He walked around the side of the unit through a maze of fencing that led to the grass covered area that was surrounded by a number of units. Peering through some bushes next to Sparks and Simons' unit, Carson could see that the drapes for the patio door were pulled back, a low light filtered out onto the patio. Stepping from the sidewalk onto the grass he crossed over to a dirt path that led to the beach. Walking toward the pool, he stopped in front of the unit and looked through a stand of trees into the open patio door. The low light coming from the unit was from a lamp next to the couch. It didn't appear anyone was at home.

Walking casually around the trees, Carson noticed a young couple on the patio of the adjoining unit. The woman was curled up in a chair, sipping at a drink while the man was busy flipping some burgers on a charcoal grill. Approaching the couple, Carson spoke, "Good evening. Kind of late to be grilling out."

The man turned and greeted Carson in a friendly manner. "Hey, when you're on vacation, anything goes!"

The woman held up her glass and added, "Besides that, we're celebrating our third year of marriage."

Stopping at the edge on their patio, Carson remarked, "Well, congratulations."

The man gestured with a spatula in his hand. "Perhaps I should explain. When we were married three years ago we spent our honeymoon right here in this unit. Our first night here, we grilled out about this time of night. This is our third year back and we always cook out on our wedding day." Pointing the spatula at the grill, he asked, "Care for a burger?"

Before Carson could answer, the woman held up a bottle. "How about some champagne?"

"No thank you," said Carson. "Actually, I'm here on business. I don't suppose the two fellows staying next door are home at the moment?"

The woman refilled her glass and answered, "If you're talking about Charley and Derek... they're never around. We met them one night earlier in the week when they were sitting out on their patio having some drinks. We struck up a conversation with them and they introduced themselves but that was about it. They said they were down here on business and then they went back inside. The big one, I think his name is Derek, is really on the strange side. What little talking they did was by Charley. Derek just sat there like some kind of Frankenstein character."

The man stuck out his hand and introduced himself, "My name's Greg and this is my wife, Ginny."

Shaking the man's hand, Carson responded, "My name's Carson." Lying, he went on, "I'm a professional fisherman here on the island and I was supposed to meet with Charley and Derek about a fishing excursion they wanted to take tomorrow. I figured they'd be in."

Ginny took a drink and spoke, "Doesn't surprise me. They're never here. And when they are here they never go down to the beach or to the pool. I've never seen them in bathing suits or casual clothes. Why on earth someone would rent one of these beautiful units and not even go down to the beach is beyond me."

"Well, like you said," muttered Carson, "when you're on vacation... anything goes!" Looking back at the end unit he shrugged. "I guess I'll just head on home and try to get in touch with them in the morning."

Placing one of the burgers on a bun, the man asked, "If they show up in the next couple of hours do you want us to mention you were by?"

"No, that's alright. It's getting too late. I'll try to see them tomorrow. Enjoy your burgers and congratulations again."

Walking back across the parking lot to his vehicle, he tried to call Nick again, but just like before: no answer. He left another message on Nick's voice mail. Pulling out of the lot, he headed back up Tarpon to Nick's house where he would wait. He looked at his watch. It was almost midnight. Nick was two hours late for their meeting. Something was amiss, and he hoped it wasn't what he was thinking.

Nick was brought out of his stupor as Derek grabbed his shirt collar, pulled him forward and slapped him savagely across his face. "Time to rise and shine... ass wipe!"

Before Nick could even respond he was dragged to his feet and shoved violently against a wall. Pinning Nick to the wall with his left hand, Derek pushed a button and spoke into a wall mounted intercom system, "Our boy's up. Do you want him topside?"

Nick recognized Charley's voice, who emphasized, "Yeah... and bring him up in one piece!"

During the short conversation between Sparks and Simons, Nick had a brief opportunity to take in his surroundings: expensive mahogany paneled walls, a barometer, framed map of the east coast, a liquor cabinet and the cot where he had been lying. Derek shoved him roughly and ordered, "Come on, get your ass up those steps!"

Halfway up the steps, Derek, not satisfied with Nick's progress shoved him down, grabbed him by his arm and ordered loudly, "Come on... come on... move it!"

Looking up at the top of the steps Nick could only see darkness, but then a few stars came into view. Stepping through an open hatch, he found himself standing on the deck of what appeared to be a large yacht. Two log strings of multi-colored Chinese lanterns ran from the bow, attached to the above deck cabin and then ran down to the opposite end of the luxurious watercraft. Making his way down two steps, Nick noticed a streak of lightning off to the south, zigzagging across the black sky. The stars he had seen were now covered with clouds. The wind was picking up as a nautical flag flapped wildly in the stiff ocean breeze.

Derek led him across the deck down another step where he found himself at the bow of the boat. Seated in front of him were four men. He recognized Charley but had never seen the other three. A man dressed in a white shirt, pants and deck shoes with no socks puffed on a large cigar as he motioned to Nick and spoke, "Ah, I see Mr. Falco has finally decided to join our little party. Very good." The man stood and ran his fingers through his long grey hair and offered his hand. "Good evening Nick. I hope Mr. Simons here hasn't roughed you up too much. Derek, at times, has a tendency to overreact to his assigned duties."

Nick refused to shake the man's hand and looked out at the dark ocean. The man shrugged, sat back down and continued to speak, "Not feeling all that congenial this evening? I guess I can understand the way you must feel." Motioning at a deck chair, the man ordered Derek, "Show Mr. Falco to a chair."

Derek, realizing he had been dressed down some by the man, guided Nick gently to the chair and ordered him, "Sit!"

Nick looked across the deck at the man dressed in white. He appeared to be in his mid-fifties and in excellent physical condition. The man picked up a mixed drink and motioned at a table that displayed a silver platter of peeled shrimp, grapes and assorted cheeses. "Care for a drink... maybe something to eat?"

Nick calmly refused the offer, "No thank you."

"Very well then," said the man. "Let's get down to business. My name is Joseph Carnahan. My brother, Emil and myself own the company your grandfather worked for. Emil could not be with us this evening. He had some business up in Albany to take care of." Gesturing at the other three men who were seated, he made introductions, "Of course you know Mr. Sparks. He along with Derek are employed by our company. These other two gentlemen are Hank and Carlton, also company employees. They travel with me wherever I go. It's a dangerous world out there, Nick. Hank and Carlton are always at my side to ensure my safety."

Nick looked over at the two men. They were dressed casually, both men wearing shoulder holsters, their hair cut to military standards. Neither man smiled at Nick. They appeared to be all business.

Joseph pointed his drink at two men dressed in tight fitting swimsuits, standing off to the side. Each man wore a knife attached to a slim belt around their suits. "These two fine specimens of manhood are Carlos and Hector. They are expert swimmers. I'll get back to them in a minute." Next, he pointed at a man standing high up in the cabin. "That's Mark, our captain for this evening."

Mark smiled and saluted sloppily and looked out to sea. "That storm will be here in less than a half hour."

Placing his cigar in a glass ashtray, Joseph addressed Mark again, "How far out are we?"

"Just over ten miles off the South Carolina coast. We should be alright, but if it gets too rough we'll have to head in."

"Okay, back to business," announced Joseph. Crossing his legs, he spoke to Nick. "As you are well aware of by now your grandfather worked for me. He was the best I've ever seen when it came to investing money. He was quite respected by not only myself but my brother, Emil as well. A few years ago, Big Ed decided to start a little side business of his own; a business where he steadily embezzled money from our company; money to the tune of approximately seven million dollars. He got away with it for a few years but then got greedy and became careless. At first, we couldn't believe he was behind the missing money. We investigated every other possible scenario in regard to the money, but everything just kept pointing to Edward."

Tapping his cigar ashes in the ashtray, Joseph stood, stretched and continued to speak, "We decided to approach Edward and give him an opportunity to come clean. He was cool as a cucumber, as they say. He said he didn't know what we were talking about. I happen to be a rather good judge of character, Nick. I looked into your grandfather's face and he almost had me convinced we were wrong... but we were not wrong. Over the years he left a paper trail that we stumbled on completely by accident. There was no doubt. Your grandfather stole our money. We contacted him two more times and informed him we wanted the money back, but he refused." Sitting back down in the chair, Joseph smiled sadly, "Unfortunately, your grandfather no longer walks the face of this earth because he was dishonest with me and my brother."

Nick couldn't believe how cold Carnahan was about Edward's death. "So what you're saying is that you killed my grandfather because of this so-called missing money."

Joseph raised his index finger and pointed out, "I did no such thing. I didn't kill the man."

"Maybe you didn't kill him, but I have no doubt that you ordered someone else to do the deed."

"That's beside the point," said Joseph. "Your grandfather was a fool. Before he started to embezzle money from me, he was already a millionaire many times over. Why on earth he wanted more money is beyond me, but there is a simple explanation for his actions. Are you a man of religion, Nick?"

Nick couldn't see where Carnahan was going so he answered honestly, "I guess as much as the next man."

"Joseph sat up straight and quoted, "The Bible tells us that the man who loves money will never have money enough."

Nick smiled and despite his lack of Biblical knowledge, quoted, "The Bible also states, Thou shalt not kill!"

Carnahan blew off Nick's timely comeback and spoke sternly, "Enough of Edward Falco. The man is gone and we still do not have what rightfully belongs to us. Our next course of action was to speak to your grandmother, Amelia. Now, there was a fine and I have to admit, a strong woman. We approached her about the money and to our surprise she told us she knew Edward had taken the money over a period of years. She even told us he had hidden the money somewhere in her house or on the property, but she didn't know where. At this point, we thought we were getting somewhere. We offered to purchase the house from Amelia for one hundred thousand above the appraised value, but she claimed that she had lived there for over three decades and was not interested in selling to us or anyone for that matter, regardless of the price offered. Next, we tried to convince her to allow us to search the property and the grounds by means of a construction-remodeling crew of our choice. If she agreed to this we would offer her one hundred thousand dollars in cash to offset any damage done to the property. In this way, we would recover our money and she could still live in her home. She turned this option down as well. We continued to negotiate with your grandmother for a couple of months, but sadly we could not come to an agreement. It was at that point that we had no other direction to go. We informed Amelia the next time we saw her we expected an answer that was agreeable to us...or else!"

Nick jumped in and added, "And I assume by, *or else*, you meant that you would take her life just like you took Edward's."

"She gave us no other choice, Nick. But, here's the thing. We never got to speak with your grandmother again. As you know, she passed away in her sleep before we had a final opportunity to come to terms with her."

Nick shook his head. "So you would have killed her, just like you killed Edward."

"Enough of who did what," said Joseph. "Now, the ball is in your court. You now own the house and the property where the money is hidden, but now we find that there is a new twist to this story. We have our ways of finding out the ins and outs of things. It would appear that Amelia changed her will and that she left the house and all her earthly belongings to you, her grandson. According to the will, you cannot sell the house if you choose not to live there. If that is the case, then the house is donated to the Fripp Island Home Owner's Association. This, in itself really doesn't change things, it just adds another step to the process." Motioning to Carlton, he ordered, "Bring me that briefcase."

Carlton picked up a briefcase and walked over to Joseph and placed it on a small table next to him. Opening the case, Joseph turned it and displayed stacks of money. In here we have one hundred thousand dollars; the same amount we offered your grandmother. You have three options to choose from." Closing the case, he went on to explain, "Number one, you go to Khelen Ridley, your attorney and tell him you've decided not to live in your grandmother's house. You can keep all the furniture, the cars and the money she left you, plus you get the hundred thousand from me. You can purchase another house on the island or live somewhere else. After you notify Ridley, at some point the house will fall to the home owner's association. We will have our attorney's contact the association and offer them two hundred thousand dollars more than the house is worth, or whatever it takes to convince them to sell the home to us. You walk away still a millionaire, with an additional one hundred thousand in your pocket and we finally get our money back. It's a win-win situation."

Stubbing out his cigar, Joseph held up two fingers and continued, "Number two; if you don't want to sell the house, you then allow us to conduct a search of the property. Another win-win situation. You can keep living on Fripp in your grandmother's home, plus you pick up one hundred grand. And once again; we get our money."

Joseph sat back in his chair and crossed his arms. "Those are your two options."

Confused, Nick spoke up, "You said I had three choices. You only mentioned two. What is the third choice?"

"Well, since you mentioned it, I'll clear that little matter up. The first two choices are what I call positive solutions to our problem. I was hoping that I didn't have to discuss the third option because it tends to lean toward the negative side of things. The plain truth is that if you do not accept option one or two, then the third option comes into play. Simply put; we kill you! That option doesn't bode well for you, but even if we do kill you, we still get the house and eventually our money."

Nodding at Carlos and Hector he continued to explain as Carlos held up a cinderblock attached to heavy duty rope. "It's now two-fifteen in the morning. That means that in less than four and a half hours the sun will be coming up. If you haven't opted to go with option one or two by then, we shackle you with eight cinderblocks and toss you over the side. You'll sink to the bottom, drown and never be heard from again. A few weeks or months will pass by after you have disappeared and eventually the house will go to the home owners association. We'll approach them with an attractive offer on the house, they'll sell it to us and we'll get our money. That's not what I call a win-win situation. You'll wind up dead... we'll wind up with our money and the house."

A bolt of lightning hit close by which caused everyone on board to wince. Joseph looked at Nick and remarked, "If you're thinking about any chance of escape put it out of your mind. It's a good ten mile swim to land. I swim five miles, three times a week. I consider myself a rather good swimmer, but to swim ten miles, especially with how rough the water is going to get when this storm finally hits, you'd never make it. Personally I don't think it would ever get that far. Remember, I said I'd get back to Carlos and Hector. Like I said; they are both expert swimmers. As a matter of fact, Hector there almost qualified for the Olympics a few years back. Isn't that right, Hector?"

Hector displayed a wide toothed smile and answered, "Si!"

"As you can plainly see, both Hector and Carlos are armed with knives. They have been previously instructed that if you jump overboard, they are to jump in after you, swim you down and kill you, hence you will become shark food. Our measures to prevent you from escaping go much farther than that. We have two fully gassed speedboats anchored on either side of the yacht manned with flood lights, not to mention the flood lamps we have on board. Hank and Carlos are crack shots. You'd never make it. The cards are stacked in our favor. Perhaps it would be best if you just retired to your cabin for a few hours to consider if you want to accept option one or two." Handing the briefcase to Nick, Joseph suggested, "Maybe you should take this money with you now. It's yours. You just need to make a decision before the sun comes up."

Another flash of lightning hit nearby, the rain started to come down. Nick took the case from Joseph and smiled. "I can give you an answer right now, if you want."

"I knew you were a smart fellow," said Joseph. "So, is it number one or number two?"

"Much to the surprise of Joseph and everyone else on deck, Nick answered, "Neither. I don't like option one or two, and I'm certainly not going to consider number three. I'm going with option four."

Joseph laughed as he looked at everyone else and held his hands up in confusion. "There is no option four!"

Nick smiled. "Yeah there is." In one single motion, Nick threw the briefcase in Joseph's face, yelled "Kiss my ass!" turned and dove over the side.

Chapter Twenty

AT THE SAME TIME NICK'S FEET HIT THE WATER, Carnahan was falling backward from the force of the thrown briefcase. Nick sank below the surface and immediately turned in the direction of the yacht. Joseph, quickly to his feet, began giving orders, "Hector, Carlos, over the side, now! Hank, Carlton; take Charley and Derek and get those speedboats in the water! Mark, turn on the floodlights!"

Nick swam underwater until he felt his right hand touch the side of the yacht. Slowly he surfaced, staying close to the boat, figuring the floodlights would shine farther out. Joseph leaned over the side and looked down into the water as Carlos and Hector surfaced and began to search the surrounding area. A floodlight lit up the water with a wide, directed beam of light. Just above him, Nick saw one of the speedboats being lowered and someone yelled, "Charley, you're with me!"

Nick made his way along the boat staying close to the hull. Hector, bathed in the floodlight looked in his direction, but between the rain and the shadow of darkness next to the yacht, Nick went unnoticed.

From up above, he could hear Joseph's voice, cursing and firing out orders, "Damn it! Hank, bring the other boat to this side. He'll be heading for the shoreline. He's not going to swim farther out. Mark, shine the lights out farther. We have to locate him before he gets too far!"

Once the speedboat was lowered, Carlton fired up the motor. He and Charley went out fifteen yards, circled around and aimed another light on the water. Within seconds, the second boat manned by Hank and Derek sped around the front of the yacht and joined the first.

Cupping his hands around his mouth, Carnahan shouted, "Spread out... find that bastard!"

A loud clap of thunder sounded, followed by a flash of nearby lightning, which sent Nick below the surface. When he resurfaced, he felt the driving rain pelting down on the ocean. From the floodlights he could see both Hector and Carlos, swimming in opposite directions, searching the ever-growing waves. Carlton and Charley were heading out farther from the yacht while Hank and Derek searched near the front. For the moment he was safe. They no doubt thought he would immediately swim toward the shore which was ten miles off. That was his plan when he had jumped ship, but now he knew he'd never make the distance, at least without them running him down. If the rain kept up, it would become difficult to distinguish which way land was. The last thing he wanted to do was swim farther out to sea.

Working his way down the side of the yacht, a flash of lightning revealed a chrome ladder leading up to the deck. Reaching up for the bottom rung, he found it was just out of his reach by a few inches. He tried to time the waves to elevate him upward, but he was still just short of grabbing the rung. Finally, on the fourth attempt his hand wrapped around the chrome bar and he pulled himself up. It was then that he got an idea. It would be risky, but it was better than drowning in the ocean in the middle of the night or being killed by one of Carnahan's employees.

A hard wave smashed into the side of the yacht, causing one of his hands to break free. Hanging on the side of the boat with one hand, Nick spit out a mouthful of salt water and twisted himself around where he could grab the rung with his other hand. He heard voices:

"See anything?"

"No, I can't see him anywhere!"

"I'm going to swim out farther."

"Carnahan, changing his mind, ordered, "Take one of the boats to the opposite side, just in case."

Hank swung his boat around and maneuvered the craft along the side of the yacht, the floodlight dancing on the side of the watercraft. Nick, realizing he didn't have time to climb the ladder had to let go or be exposed by the bright light. He slithered back into the water and held his breath for nearly a minute, then slowly resurfaced and saw the light from the rear of the speedboat disappear around the back of the yacht.

He once again began the difficult process of timing the waves so he could be lifted up and grab the bottom rung. On the fifth attempt his hand locked around the bar and he pulled himself up. The rain was coming down harder and he could only see a few feet out from the boat. If he couldn't see them, there was a better than average chance they couldn't see him. *It's now or never,* he thought. He pulled himself up to the next rung, took a deep breath then grabbed the third. Looking up into the rain he knew there were only a few more rungs until he reached the deck.

He heard more voices, but between the wind and the rain the words were muffled. A huge wave smashed into the side of the boat jamming his legs into the side. Hanging there, he mustered all his strength, and hand over hand continued up until his foot found one of the bottom rungs. Turning, he looked back out at the water. He couldn't see a thing, except the rain. A bright flash of lightning lit up the side of the yacht. Frozen, he remained still, praying no one was looking in his direction. The brightness of the lightning was soon replaced with the dark of night. He quickly climbed the remaining three rungs and carefully looked over the edge of the deck.

Carnahan was at the opposite end of the yacht, and Mark, the captain, he hoped, was still in the cabin operating the flood lamps. He was only guessing, but at the moment, they were the only other two people on board. At least, that was what he was hoping. He was going to need the element of surprise and deception if he had any chance at all of escape. Pulling himself up over the side of the deck he rolled in behind a large coil of rope.

Laying on his back, he tried to relax, the drops of rain dancing on his face with a stinging effect. The Chinese lanterns swung wildly in the stiff ocean wind, another flash of lightning lit up the boat for a second. Rolling over onto his stomach, he peered around the pile of rope toward the front of the boat. Looking up, he could see the image of Mark standing at the helm in the elevated cabin.

Staying close to the side wall of the cabin he crept toward the front of the yacht, constantly checking the men in the water searching for him. As long as no one saw him, his plan might just work.

At the edge of the cabin, he saw Carnahan leaning over the side as he continued to give direction, "Hector... go further out! Carlos... go wider!" Hank... go out about hundred yards so we can get in front of him. He must not escape! If he does, there's gonna be hell to pay!"

Crouching down against the side of the cabin, Nick went over his plan quickly. The longer he waited the more difficult it would become. Walking in front of the cabin, he looked up at Mark, who at the moment, had his back to him. If he turned and he was seen, he'd have no other choice but to jump overboard again. It was then that he noticed a revolver on the table next to where Carnahan had been seated. Taking a deep breath to steady himself, he quickly crossed the deck, came up behind Carnahan, grabbed him by his legs and flipped him over the side, Carnahan didn't even have an opportunity to yell out before he hit the rough water below.

Nick grabbed the revolver and went back to the cabin and hesitated at the open door. Cocking the weapon nervously, he started up the five steps that led to the upper cabin. Mark, focused on directing three different floodlights didn't notice Nick's presence in the cabin until he felt the barrel of the gun at the back of his head.

"Listen!" said Nick. "I don't know you from Adam, but since you and your partners have intentions of dropping me to the bottom of the ocean, you'll have to excuse my lack of compassion at the moment. You do what I tell you... you live. You refuse... well, this could be your last cruise."

"You must be crazy!" said Mark calmly. "Do you have any idea who the Carnahan's are? When Joseph get his hands on you, you're as good as dead!"

Pressing the revolver harder against the back of Mark's head, Nick emphasized, "At the present time, Joseph Carnahan is nothing more than a man floundering in the ocean. I just pushed his ass over the side. You need to get this barge moving... now! Take me over to the coastline, I jump off and you can be on your merry way."

"Joseph will kill me if I do that!"

Bluffing, Nick tapped Mark's right ear with the revolver and ordered sternly, "Carnahan is the least of your problems right now. If you don't get this tub underway... I'll kill you!"

"All right, all right! I'll run you over toward the shoreline, but when we start moving, Carnahan's going to realize something's up. He'll follow in the speedboats. Even if I open her up to full throttle, they'll be on us in minutes."

"Give her the gas and let me worry about that. Just get moving!"

Mark turned the ignition key and pushed the throttle all the way forward, the large yacht moving out slowly but picking up speed.

Joseph hit the water in an awkward sideways position that knocked the air out of him temporarily. Moving his arms sideways and kicking his feet he stayed afloat and tried to get his breath. He signaled by waving his arms wildly for one of the speedboats to come to his aid, but no one was looking toward the yacht. It was then he noticed the large craft slowing pulling away. He yelled up the side of the boat, "Mark! What the hell?"

Joseph, quickly realized that Nick had somehow got back on the yacht and tossed him overboard. Besides that, why would Mark be leaving the search area without being ordered to do so? Falco had to be on the boat. He had to get to one of the speedboats and catch up with the yacht. The closest speedboat was thirty yards out, the other boat, Hector and Carlos, he could not see. Cutting through the water smoothly, Joseph swam toward the boat that was moving slowly to his right. Just when he thought he was making progress, the boat turned in a circle and started back toward the left. He wanted to yell at Hank, but realized with the wind and the rain, he would be unheard until he got closer. Finally, following five minutes he pulled himself up on the side of the boat and ordered, "Hank! Help me in!"

Derek reached out and pulled Joseph into the boat with little effort as Hank, in amazement, asked, "What the hell are you doing out here?"

"Never mind that now," shouted Joseph. "Falco got back on the yacht. He's headed for shore. We've got to pick up Hector and Carlos and warn the other boat." Looking at the yacht in the distance, he ordered, "Move! We have to get to Falco before he gets ashore!"

Nick could barely make out the floodlights from the speedboats as Mark continued to put distance between the yacht and his pursuers. Tapping Mark on his shoulder with the revolver, Nick ordered, "Cut off all the floodlights and those lanterns. How soon will we be near the shoreline?"

"Depends on where you want to jump off," said Mark. "Out there to our left lays Pritchards Island, then a little farther on, Fripp Island and then Hunting Island."

"How far can we get before they catch up?"

"Fripp, and that's cutting it close. By the time we get to Hunting Island, they'll definitely be on us."

"Fripp Island it is then," said Nick. "How close in can you get me?"

"The tide is in right now which means I have to be careful how close in we go. We could get hung up on a sand bar. With any luck I might be able to drop you off two to three hundred yards out."

Pressing the gun into Mark's back, Nick spoke firmly, "Just keep on a course for Fripp until I tell you different."

It took nearly five minutes for Joseph to round up his entire crew before they were speeding after the yacht. Kneeling at the front of one of the speedboats, he ordered, "Come on... move it... move it! I want to be on that yacht in the next couple minutes."

So far, Nick's plan of deception was working, but he knew he was running out of time. The rain had slowed down considerably which was to Carnahan's advantage of visibility. Previously, the light from the cabin had been hidden from sight by the rain, but now the tiny light would be like a beacon in the middle of the black water. A flash of lightning revealed a quick view of land."

"How far are we out from land," asked Nick.

Mark answered, "A lot farther out than two to three hundred yards."

Pressing the gun into Mark's back, Nick asked again, "How far out are we?"

"About a mile and a half. It'll be a few minutes before we're out from Fripp."

Nick could not only see their lights, but could hear the two boats speeding across the water in their direction. He had to make his move now. Looking around the cabin he saw a long handled mop leaning up against the wall. Placing the end of the handle in Mark's back, he held it in place with a small statue on top of a file cabinet and then backed up two steps and spoke. "The gun is still in your back. Just keep on a course for Fripp. When you get about three hundred yards out, let me know."

He knew that he only a few seconds before Mark discovered he was no longer standing behind him in the cabin. Quietly he went down the steps to the rear of the yacht and looked out across the dark water. The speedboats were closing in fast. Tossing the revolver into the water, he lowered himself over the side and let go, splashing in the ocean. He watched as the yacht continued on, then turned and saw the approaching speedboats. Turning, he began the long swim to Pritchards Island.

Taking long, even strokes, he found that his shoes were slowing down his progress. Stopping momentarily, he brought his knees to his chest and removed his shoes and looked for the trailing speedboats. Twenty yards away they passed by him at top speed. He looked in the direction the yacht was travelling. Suddenly, the three floodlights and the lanterns came to life, the yacht standing out on the black ocean like a sore thumb. He had no doubt that Mark figured he either jumped overboard or was hiding on the yacht. Turning, he began swimming toward what he hoped was land.

A mile and a half, he thought. *Can I make it!* The longest distance he had ever swam was two miles, but that was under his grandmother's guidance. She had been right at his side, encouraging him on. He recalled all the things she had told him: *Relax, feel the water, breath normally.* And most important: *Don't wait until you're tired before you stop and rest.* At the moment he felt fine, strong, his breathing was not forced. *A few more strokes and then I'll rest.*

Stopping, he noticed the rain was now nothing but a fine mist. Turning, he looked for the yacht. The vessel had been turned sideways. He could no longer see or hear the speedboats. By this time they were probably near or at the yacht. Floating on his back, like Amelia taught him, he tried to guess what Carnahan's next move would be. Depending on where Mark estimated where he had jumped off again, Carnahan would send out the speedboats, but would they search in front of Fripp or come back to Pritchards Island?

Mark heard and saw the speedboats approaching. Hank guided his boat next to the ladder and within seconds Carnahan was back on his yacht. At the top of the ladder he turned and ordered his men, "Stay put! You'll be going back out as soon as I find out what happened." Mark met him at the edge of the deck and helped him up.

Joseph wiped his matted, wet hair from his face and with his hands on his hips, looked up at the cabin and asked, "What happened after Falco threw me over?"

Mark raised his hands in helplessness, "I'm sorry Mr. Carnahan. I had no idea he got back on board. He came up behind me and stuck a gun in my back. I had no idea you were not on board until Falco told me he tossed you over. He ordered me to take him as close to shore as possible. I really didn't have a choice. When we got about a mile and a half offshore which is where we're at right now, he must have jumped."

"What do you mean, 'he must have?' Didn't you see him jump?"

"No. Falco is a lot smarter than we've obviously given him credit for. He jammed a mop handle in my back and told me to stay on course for Fripp. It must have been a good thirty seconds before I realized it was a mop handle and not a gun in my back."

"So where do you think he jumped in at?"

"With the speed I was going, by the time I realized he had jumped, I'd say probably a quarter mile back."

"Where exactly are we right now?"

"We're just on the southern tip of Fripp Island."

"Then you think he's swimming for Pritchards Island?"

"It's hard to say. I think he'll just keep swimming until he hits land, wherever it is; Fripp or Pritchards."

Joseph thought for a moment then turned and ordered his men, "Hank; you, Derek and Carlos head on over to Pritchards Island and search that area. Carlton; you, Charley and Hector search the southern end of Fripp. Mark and I will cruise back and forth between both islands. If you spot him, I don't want him brought back to the boat alive. Kill him and then we'll dispose of the body like we planned. Now... move it! One other thing. I cannot express to you enough the importance that he must not escape!"

Nick stopped for another brief rest and tried to determine if he was indeed swimming toward land. Looking back out at the lights coming from the yacht and the movement of the swells of the water he was confident that eventually he'd reach shore. He heard the sound of the speedboats as they sped away from the yacht. He peered across the ocean to determine what direction they were going. He could barely see a set of lights going in what direction he thought was Fripp and then suddenly, another set heading in his general direction. He figured he'd only covered maybe a quarter mile which meant he had well over a mile stretch of ocean between himself and land. On the move again, he considered the fact that if one of the speedboats started to search the area he was in, he was going to have to be careful to stay out of the floodlight they had. As long as he stayed away from the boat he would be fine. If they spotted him, then it would be over.

The speedboat passed him fifty yards to his right and continued in the same general direction he was swimming. Stopping for a moment, he thought, *They're trying to cut me off.* Suddenly, the pale moonlight bathed the surface of the ocean, most of the rain clouds moving off. Looking off into the distance he got a brief glimpse of the shoreline which quickly disappeared as more clouds rolled in. Smiling to himself, at least he knew he was swimming in the right direction.

Joseph pointed toward the direction of Fripp Island and ordered, "Get as close to shore as we can. I'm going to change into some dry clothes."

Derek, who was operating the floodlight on the speedboat announced with great enthusiasm when the circular light revealed the shoreline, "Pritchards Island... straight in!"

Hank cut the motor and allowed the boat to drift toward what looked like a rough beach: rocks, vegetation; not much sand. A few feet out from the shore, Hank handed Derek a flashlight and a gun and ordered, "Derek, climb out. I want you on the beach. Go about a hundred yards in both directions and look for fresh footprints. For all we know Falco might still be out there swimming in this direction, but we can't leave anything to doubt. Carlos and I are going to cruise back and forth for about a quarter mile or so and see if we can locate him. If you see anything give us three flashes with the light. If you, by some chance run into Falco, kill him!"

Nick stopped swimming and watched the activity of the lights from the speedboat less than a mile away on Pritchards Island. He watched as the boat slowly made its way up the coastline toward Hilton Head. He then noticed the yacht, which was now closer to Pritchards than it was to Fripp. Swimming at an angle away from the speedboat, he stopped every thirty strokes and checked the surrounding water. For all he knew Hector and Carlos could be close by in the water. If he ran across either one of them, based upon what Carnahan had said about their swimming abilities, he knew he'd never be able to outswim them. He remembered the knives strapped to their sides. Aside from being expert swimmers, he considered the fact that they were both probably rather efficient with those knives. He was going to have to avoid them. If it came down to a hand to hand battle with one of the men while in the water, he realized he was no match.

Carlton entered Skull Inlet, then turned right and headed up the south end of Fripp, hugging the shore, the floodlight combing the beach. Charley pointed at the shoreline and suggested, "Why don't you let me out. I'll walk the beach and Hector can swim out and keep eye on this end of the island. You can cruise back and forth a little farther out. Remember what Carnahan said? Falco does not come back alive! When we find him... we end it!"

Nick halted his progress for another rest period. Floating on the water he stared up at the stars and the moon. He was still safe and he figured they were only guessing as to his whereabouts. Treading water he looked south. The speedboat was heading back in his direction. To the north, the yacht was getting much closer. Swimming again, he estimated that he only had about five minutes before they would be close to him. He couldn't worry about that now. He had to concentrate on getting to land. Every stroke brought him that much closer.

Derek made his way down the rough shoreline, stepping over large rocks and downed trees. There was not a footprint to be found in the occasional sand. Hank, after going a quarter mile, turned the speedboat around and started back the way he had just come, but a few yards farther out. Carlos manned the floodlight, constantly searching back and forth between the water's edge and out into the ocean.

The tide was in and the southern section of Fripp's beach was partially underwater. Charley shined a flashlight down at the sand along the water's edge. No footprints were evident. Looking toward Pritchards Island, he wondered if that's where Falco was heading.

For the next five minutes, Nick got into a rhythm of taking thirty strokes, then stopping to check for Carlos or Hector, then another thirty strokes. He figured he was still out a good half mile. He was getting tired, but if he paced himself he was confident he could make it. Treading water again, he noticed that the yacht, if it continued on its present course would cross between him and the island. He still had the advantage. He knew where they were but Carnahan and his men could only guess where he was.

Two more minutes went by while he continued to swim toward the island. The yacht was getting closer and it was hard for him to estimate if he could swim past it before it was in front of him. Looking at the yacht once again, he decided to let the vessel pass and then he would continue on. It was then, he heard the speedboat approaching from the south. Unknowingly, they were headed directly at him, the floodlight at the front of the boat illuminating the water. He had time for maybe twenty or so strokes and then he'd have to stop and let them pass.

The yacht came to a halt while the speedboat approached. Nick found himself sandwiched in between the two boats, the floodlights pointing north and south out into the vast ocean. There was no more than thirty feet separating the two watercraft. Quietly, Nick treaded water, ready to go under if need be. The speedboat stopped and circled around. Hank stood up in the boat and yelled up to Carnahan, "Nothing yet. Derek is on the island."

Carnahan looked at his watch and shouted back, "He hasn't had enough time to swim all the way to shore yet. He's still in the water, but if we don't find him soon, he'll make land. Keep up the search. If we don't locate him, at least we know where he'll go. Now, get back out there!"

The speedboat turned south and speed off. Nick looked up at Carnahan who was in the process of lighting a cigar. From what he had just overheard it was evident that if they were unsuccessful at locating him then they were going to go to his house and wait. That was another problem. Right now, he had to get out of the water and somehow contact Carson.

Silently, he sank beneath the surface and swam away from the boat. When he got far enough away then he could continue toward Pritchards Island. Resurfacing, he looked back at the yacht which was making a long turn to go back north. The speedboat was heading south. He was going to have to continue to tread water until the yacht was once again past where he was.

Minutes passed and he was growing tired of remaining in one place in the water. He was using a lot of energy and going nowhere. Finally, he made his move. He was determined to get to the island before any of the boats returned. The rain had completely stopped, the clouds had moved on and the moon was shining brightly. The waves were now nothing but gentle swells. He was no longer concerned about the boats. Now, Hector and Carlos were another thing. He had no idea where or if they had been dropped in the water. If he could just get to the island, then he could make his way over to Fripp.

Swimming into the darkness, he counted each stroke. Rather than resting every thirty strokes he was going to push himself to rest every ninety. So far he had been lucky. He was growing tired, but he knew he was getting close to land.

Derek made his way down the shoreline of Pritchards Island until he came to Skull Inlet. Finding no indications of footprints, he started back in the direction he had come.

Hank stopped the speedboat just off shore south of where Derek was walking and ordered Carlos, "Why don't you get out and walk the shoreline. We've been out here for quite some time. For all we know, Falco might be on land by now. Take a light with you. If you run into Derek, split up."

Charley walked down Fripp Island beach without detecting any fresh prints in the wet sand. Cutting across the sand, he walked across the deck over the dunes behind Nick's house. Crossing the dirt road, he saw a dim light filtering out from the back porch.

Drawing his revolver, he approached the porch and climbed the steps. On the porch, he looked through the picture window where he saw an opaque image of a person sitting in an easy chair. *This is too easy!* he thought. Falco had somehow made it back to the house and was reclining in his living room recouping from the long swim. He reached out and tried the back door. It was unlocked. Pushing the door open, he crossed the kitchen, his gun aimed at the figure seated in the easy chair in the adjoining room. Aiming the gun carefully, he thought about how proud and grateful Joseph was going to be with him for eliminating Falco. Suddenly, the person, thought to be Nick, sat upright in the chair and held up a cell phone. Punching in a number, Carson spoke to himself, "Damn kid! Where in the hell is he?"

Charley, realizing that the person in the chair was not Nick ducked in behind the kitchen wall when he recognized Carson's voice. Despite the fact that he and Carson were not on friendly terms, he had been given orders to kill Falco, not Carson Pike. Backing out of the kitchen, he stood on the porch and watched Pike as he threw down the phone and walked toward the kitchen. Retreating back across the road, Charley decided to keep watch on the house, but first he had to contact Carnahan.

Back out on the beach, he dialed Joseph's number which was answered immediately by Carnahan. "What have we got?"

"Joseph, this is Charley. I didn't find any indication that Falco has been on the beach recently. I went to the house and guess who I find waiting there... Carson Pike. From the way Pike acted I don't think he knows where Falco is at the moment. You need to pick up Hector and have him come on shore. That way one of us can watch the front of the house and the other the back. If Falco shows up we'll nail him before he knows what hit him."

Joseph agreed, "All right. I'll have Hector dropped on the beach. Should be about ten to fifteen minutes before he's with you."

Nick stopped again for what he hoped was his last rest period. The yacht had returned to Fripp and the only speedboat he could make out was a small speck of light to the south farther down Pritchards. A blanket of cloud cover returned and with it a light rain.

Determined to reach land, Nick swam for nearly five minutes, stopped and checked the position of the yacht and the speedboats once again. A wave broke behind him and sent a small two foot wall of water over his head. He knew he was close to shore.

Waves, as a general rule broke when they got close in to shore. The rain picked up as he turned and swam for another two minutes, then stopped again. He sank beneath the surface, trying to see if he could touch bottom. *Still too far out,* he thought and resurfaced.

Following two more attempts after swimming for a minute or so, his toes touched the sandy bottom of the ocean. A wave of relief swept over his tired body. He walked forward, realizing that the farther in he got the easier it would be to walk. He could continue swimming, but he was tuckered out.

Ten yards went by and the level of the water stayed the same, the waves continued to break over him. Suddenly, his right foot slipped off the edge on the bottom and down he went. Searching for the bottom, it was then he realized he had probably been on a sand bar. Taking a few deep breaths of air, he swam forward a few yards and sank below the surface in search of the ocean bottom. Finally, after three attempts, he found himself standing in waist deep water.

Hoping he was not on another sand bar he moved forward pushing his tired body through the water. He felt a great sense of relief when the water was only up to his knees and then his ankles. *Just a few more feet,* he guessed and then he'd be completely out of the water. Seconds later, he found himself standing on wet sand staring into an outline of trees that was exposed by a break in the clouds, the moon casting an eerie pale glow on the rock strewn beach. Collapsing in the sand he laid on his back and breathed in the ocean breeze while the water from the tail end of a wave washed up around his body.

Realizing he couldn't stay there for long he sat up, looking up and down the shoreline. He recalled the conversation between Hank and Carnahan; about how Derek had been put on Pritchards Island. He was somewhere on the island, no doubt near the shoreline. Checking north and south for any sign of light, he saw nothing but endless darkness. Then he heard it; the sound of the speedboat. He couldn't see it because of the rain, but he could tell from the sound of the motor they were getting closer to shore. Getting to his feet, he stepped out into the water and started walking north, toward what he thought would be Fripp.

The beach, if that's what one wanted to call it was much more difficult to walk on than Fripp. Fripp Island was a natural beach, but the area next to the water on Pritchards was rough going to say the least. Logs, rocks and vegetation made for tough going, so he remained out in the water. Following ten minutes of walking in the low surf, a welcome sight popped into view in between the clouds; a red light in the distance, no doubt the light on the Fripp Island tower. If he could just get close to that light, he'd be home.

Walking in the ankle deep surf was normally something he had always enjoyed, but his legs ached from the long swim in the Atlantic. The muscles in his upper arms were throbbing from battling the rough ocean. Aside from the fact that he was dog-tired, he had to keep a constant vigil out for his pursuers. He knew he was only about three miles from the house, but he still had to get across Skull Inlet which meant another quarter mile swim, then he was going to have to either walk down Tarpon in the darkness or venture out onto the beach. Either way, he was going to have to be careful. For all he knew they might already have someone watching the house.

The sound of the speedboat had disappeared and he turned to look out across the water in search of the small vessel. The yacht appeared to be anchored out from Fripp but the other two boats were not in sight. Turning to start back up the shoreline, the breath was knocked out of him as he was slammed down hard to the sand. Before he realized what happened he felt a large arm wrap around his throat and he was being dragged out to sea. Then, the familiar voice of Derek pierced the darkness. "Hello... asshole! We meet again! Carnahan wants you dead. So be it! I should have killed you back when we first met in Cincinnati, but Charley wouldn't allow it. Now, I have orders to take you out. I'm really gonna enjoy drowning your little ass. I enjoyed it when Charley and I killed your grandfather and I'm going to enjoy killing you!"

Between trying to get his breath back and struggling to escape the deathlike lock around his neck, Nick tried to drive his elbows into Derek's side, digging his feet into the soft sand for leverage. The very life was being squeezed out of his lungs while he was dragged effortlessly father out into deeper water. His tired muscles were no match for the hulking Derek who he could hear laughing. The water was now up to his neck and Nick knew it was only a matter of seconds before the sea water would be filling his eyes, ears, nose and mouth. He continued to struggle, but his efforts only made him weaker. Then, it happened. His head was pulled down beneath the surface. His instinct to survive kicked in and he took a deep breath. He could feel his body sinking down, but then Derek's arm was released from his neck. Kicking hard he rose to the surface and swam toward shore without looking back.

Reaching a point where he could no longer swim because of the depth, Nick stood and ran to the shoreline, turned and looked back. The dark outline of Derek's shadow appeared as he struggled to get to his feet. Nick could not understand what happened and why he hadn't drown, but at the moment the only thought on his mind was... *run!*

Running in the low surf, he only made it a few yards when he tripped on a rock just below the surface. Getting up, he looked back. Derek was just stepping out of the water. Despite the fact that he was tired he knew he could outrun the big man. Derek looked in his direction and from the moonlight Nick watched as he walked a few paces in land, bent over and picked something up. He heard the sound of the revolver fire three times. Looking to his right, he decided to go into the trees a few yards away. Three more shots sounded, the third ricocheting off the side of a nearby tree trunk.

Stumbling through the dense overgrowth, Nick forged deeper into the trees. Ten minutes passed and he stopped for a breather. Sitting on a downed tree, he took deep breaths trying to compose himself. The moonlight filtered down through the trees giving him just enough light to vaguely see his surroundings for a few feet in every direction. He listened intently for Derek who might be close behind, but the only sound he could hear was the rain beating down on the leaves.

Derek, in his excitement at the prospect of killing Falco had forgotten to remove his cell phone from his pocket before dragging his prey into the ocean. Taking the soaked instrument from his pants pocket, he dialed Carnahan's number, but the phone had been destroyed by the water. Cursing, Derek walked to the edge of the water and flashed his flashlight three times, waited and then repeated the process. He had to get a massage to Carnahan.

Nick's progress through the thick forest of trees and vegetation was slow going. At times, when the clouds covered the moon, it was nearly impossible to continue on. In between the cloud cover, he continued on a course he thought was north, hoping to come out somewhere along the banks of Skull Inlet.

Mark tapped Joseph on his shoulder and pointed in the direction of Pritchards Island when he noticed the blinking light. "Joseph, over there... a signal."

Joseph tried to call Derek, but there was no answer. Next, he called Hank, ordering him to pick up Derek and Carlos and find out what was going on. Hopefully, based on the numerous shots they had heard, Falco was dead.

Hector joined Charley on the beach just down from Nick's house. After giving Hector instructions, Charley remained at the rear of the house while Hector walked around to the front and hid in the trees on the side of the property.

Finally, after what seemed like an hour, Nick emerged from the trees, the light from Fripp still in the distance but now on his right rather than the left. The moonlight reflected off Skull Inlet. The rain had stopped and the water was now calm. He had no idea what time it was but he figured it had to be four or five in the morning. He had to get back to the house before the sun came up, which meant he had somewhere in the area of two to three hours to swim across the inlet and then walk to the house.

Stepping into the water, he knew the swim was going to be the most difficult part of the journey. It was only a quarter mile across the inlet, but with everything he'd been through, he was about at the end of any strength he had left. He knew there were a lot of sandbars in the inlet. On many of his walks on the beach he had seen people walking out into the low water. The tide was still in so walking on any sandbars was ruled out. He was going to have to swim the entire distance.

Chapter Twenty-One

NICK COLLAPSED IN THE ANKLE DEEP WATER ON THE Fripp side of Skull Inlet. Totally exhausted, he rolled over on his back and watched the clouds pass in front of the bright moon. Looking to his left he saw the yacht anchored just out from the inlet, its lights shining brightly in the night. Sitting up, he wondered if they could make it up the inlet. With all the sandbars, most likely they wouldn't chance it. Then he heard the sound of both speedboats, their lights penetrating the darkness. He wanted to lay there for a few minutes and catch his breath, but he knew he had to move. Getting up, he staggered toward the shoreline and soon found himself stepping onto a mud flat, his feet sinking deeply into the black oozing surface. On his right, a quarter mile off, he saw a porch light from a house located at the southern end of the beach on Fripp. He knew there was a salt marsh area just off Tarpon. He was pretty sure that's where he was.

Twenty yards into the marsh he turned and watched the two speedboats split up; one of the boats hugging the Pritchards Island side of the inlet, its floodlight scanning the rough shoreline, the other watercraft cruising slowly next to the Fripp side of Skull. Crouching down, he watched the boat drift by and ducked down when the floodlight passed over his head. The boat moved off and Nick continued to watch when the floodlight suddenly illuminated a long wharf that jutted out into the inlet. A sense of relief came over his body and he realized exactly where he was; just down from Wardle's Landing. If he kept moving to his right he'd soon come to Tarpon.

Each and every step he took in the thick mud just below the surface of the water seemed to drain any energy left in his body. For some unexpected reason he thought about the girls the RPS Killer had released in the marsh and how difficult it must have been for them; how afraid they must have been, not knowing where they were or if they were going to survive. Erasing thoughts of the killer from his mind, he concentrated on getting to Tarpon.

Carnahan, puffing on his cigar, gulped down a shot of whiskey and stared out at the water on Skull Inlet. Gesturing toward Pritchards Island, he sarcastically asked Mark, "How in the hell did Falco manage to get way from Derek? That baffles me to no end. This kid has more luck than the Irish. He jumps out of the yacht, then climbs back on board, dumps me over the side, swims ashore, tangles with Derek, who is twice his size and still gets away. Tell me again... what was it Derek said about his escape?"

Mark shrugged and answered, "When Hank picked him up the way Derek explained it was that he had Falco underwater just offshore when he suddenly fell into deep water. The only thing I can guess is that he stepped off a sand bar or something. Derek isn't that fond of water. He can't swim all that well. I don't know why he just didn't go ahead and shoot him."

"Well, that doesn't make any difference now. Falco has to go back to his house sometime... and when he does, he's ours! Call Charley and tell him again to be on the alert. Falco could be getting close to the house as we speak."

Pushing himself, Nick continued, step by step to maneuver his way through the marsh, all the while the light from the house on what he thought was Tarpon getting closer. Stopping for a breather, he looked north and saw the light at the top of the water tower on the island. He checked the inlet again; the yacht had not moved and the speedboats were farther up the inlet.

Ten minutes passed when Nick found himself on solid ground. Walking blindly through a maze of low grass, he came to a slight incline. Checking the inlet one last time, he climbed up the side of the wet sand, using protruding rocks for support and after a few seconds, found himself standing at the large dirt turnaround at the end of Tarpon.

Standing at the edge of the road that overlooked the inlet he saw the yacht to the Southwest and the two speedboats toward the Northwest. A total of eight men were searching for him, and up until this point he had managed to avoid being killed. Staring down Tarpon Boulevard in the pitch black, he looked up at the dark sky: the rain had returned, the wind picked up. His soggy clothes weighed him down like an anchor. He tried his best to remain on the pavement since walking along the side of the road in his bare feet would slow him down, what with numerous pinecones, tiny rocks and the occasional small pointed thistles that blew in from the beach vegetation.

It wasn't surprising to him that there was not a car or golf cart on the road. He estimated the time at somewhere around five in the morning. A little over two miles up the road sat his house. Barring any unforeseen problems he had plenty of time to get there before the sun came up.

Not even down the road a hundred yards, a set of lights shone brightly up the road a mile where it made a slight turn to the left. Walking up the driveway of a house, he hid behind a large Palmetto tree and waited. A minute later a golf cart sped by at top speed. He tried to make out the driver but between the darkness and the speed of the small vehicle he couldn't tell if it was one of Carnahan's men. After the cart passed, he stepped back on the road and continued north, ready to disappear if the cart returned.

Every few steps he turned to see where the cart was going. He watched when it stopped momentarily, then turned and headed back up Tarpon, its lights shining in his direction once again. Another minute passed when the cart sped by and finally disappeared at the bend on Tarpon. Stepping out from behind a vehicle parked in front of a house, he continued his journey. The fact that the cart had sped down Tarpon, turned around at the end and came back at five in the morning didn't make much sense. The main reason why people drove down Tarpon was they were going to a rental property or a house they lived in. The other reason was to view the sunset from the dirt parking lot at the turnaround. There had been many an evening when he and his grandmother had hopped in their golf cart and drove down Tarpon at the end of the day to watch the sun set over the distant marsh beyond Pritchards Island. Whoever was driving the mysterious cart hadn't stopped at a house and besides that it was raining. It could have been one of Carnahan's men. The closer he got to the house the more alert he was going to have to be.

Arriving at the bend in the road, he knew from where he was it was only a ten minute walk to the house. A doe, two small fawns, a buck and then two more female deer crossed the road in front of him, stopped in the yard and began to munch on the tender grass. Stopping for a moment, he took in the peaceful sight. Looking up into the falling rain he thought about how strange life could be. There were probably men back at the house, there were men anchored just off shore and there were men searching the banks of Skull Inlet; all who had orders to kill him on sight, and yet, here he sat, just ten feet away from a peaceful group of deer in the middle of the night. He listened to the music of the rain on the nearby trees, finally deciding to continue the journey to his house.

Hiding in the bushes that ran along the north side of Genevieve's house, he looked across at his front yard. The spotlight lit up the fountain which, at the moment, was overflowing due to the rain. A dim light filtered through the lacy curtains in the front room. That was odd because he couldn't recall leaving any lights on in the house. Could Carnahan already have someone inside waiting for him? No, that didn't make sense. They wouldn't turn on a light. They would wait in the dark.

Then, he noticed Carson's Land Rover parked in front of the garage and he remembered he was supposed to meet him at the house around ten. Ten o'clock had come and gone quite some time ago. The fact that Carson's vehicle was parked in the driveway probably meant he was inside waiting for him to come home. If Carson would have tried to call him, the call would have gone unanswered since Carnahan had taken his cell phone.

Squinting through the rain, he searched the bushes on the other end of his property. The spotlight on the fountain wasn't shining far enough for him to see the bushes clearly. He couldn't chance going up onto the front porch. Anyone hiding in the front yard area would see him before he even got up the steps. He considered going around the garage to the back of the house, but he was sure they would have a man watching the rear entrance as well. Looking at Carson's Land Rover, he pondered the possibility of using the vehicle as a shield, climbing inside, that is if it was unlocked, and wait in the backseat for Carson to leave. Then he thought, *That won't work!* When he opened the door of the Rover the interior light would probably come on—a dead giveaway of his intentions.

Whatever he was going to do he had to accomplish it before the sun was up. As long as it was dark it was to his advantage. Sitting on the ground he buried his face in his hands, then looked up at Genevieve's house. Her kitchen light was on. *Maybe she was up!*

Creeping along the bushes at the side of her house, Nick stayed in the shadows and made his way across her small backyard. Moving quickly up the back steps to her porch, he opened the screen door and knocked a number of times, waited, then repeated the process. He could see into the kitchen but she was nowhere in sight.

Suddenly, she appeared out of the darkness of the living room, a coffee cup clutched in her hand. Approaching the back door she shook her head in frustration. Nick was just about to wave at her through the round circular glass centered in the door, when the back porch light came on. The entire porch was instantly blanketed with bright light; the last thing Nick needed at the moment. Diving down on the floor behind an old glider, Nick whispered to himself, "Come on Genevieve... you're gonna kill me!"

Opening the door, Genevieve walked out onto the enclosed porch and looked out into the rain and remarked to herself, "I swear I heard someone at the door." Turning to go back inside, she continued, "Oh well, must have been the wind."

From behind the glider she heard a voice, "Genevieve... it's me... Nick! I need your help and *I need it now!* Don't ask me any questions. There isn't any time for that right now. Just go back inside, leave the door slightly open and turn off the porch light. I'm going to crawl through once you're inside."

Genevieve stared down at Nick who was squeezed in between the back wall and the glider. Not completely understanding, she twisted her face in confusion and asked, "What the hell are you talking about?"

Nick, growing impatient, spoke firmly, "I'll explain later. Just do what I tell you... now! Please, I need your help!"

Looking out into the rain, Genevieve hesitated and was about to speak again when Nick demanded, "Genevieve... for God's sake, do what I say!"

The old woman shrugged, opened the door, went inside and turned off the porch light. Within seconds, Nick shoved the door open enough to allow him to crawl through and then shut the door with his foot. Laying on the floor he looked up at his neighbor and smiled weakly. "Good morning!"

Genevieve, not finding his statement amusing, responded, "Do you mind telling me what the hell is wrong with you?"

Getting up, Nick looked out the back window and answered, "There may be some men watching my house. I don't have time to answer a lot of questions right now, but they mean to kill me. I know that must sound odd coming from me, but it happens to be true. I was kidnapped earlier tonight but I managed to escape. I was supposed to meet Carson at my house last night. His Land Rover is parked in front of my garage so I think he's still in there waiting for me. He doesn't have any idea what happened to me and he needs to know."

Facing Genevieve, he calmly gave her instructions, "I need you to call my house. If anyone other than Carson answers, hang up immediately. If Carson answers tell him to leave the house and pick me up in his Rover about three houses down on Tarpon going south. Don't get into a long conversation. Just tell him to pick me up. Tell him it's urgent!"

Carson sat in the darkness of the house and looked at the glowing face of his watch: 5:45 in the morning. Something was definitely wrong for Nick not to show up. It had been nearly eight hours since they were supposed to have met. Nick had told him he'd been approached by Sparks and Simons. If anything happened to that boy, he'd never forgive himself. He had promised Amelia he would look after her grandson and as the hours ticked by, he was starting to think he may have failed. He hoped not.

The phone on an end table next to the couch startled Carson when it rang. Thinking it was Nick, he picked up on the second ring and spoke, "Nick, where in the hell have you been—?"

Not allowing him to finish, Genevieve explained, "This isn't Nick... it's Genevieve! Nick is next door with me. Don't say anything... just listen. Pick him up in your vehicle three houses down from mine. He'll be waiting. He said it's urgent! Do you understand?"

"Yes, but—"

"Yes but, my ass! Get moving!"

Carson, in one motion spoke into the phone and hung up. "Tell Nick I'll be there in a few minutes."

Turning off the living room light, Carson walked out the back door, locked the house and walked around the side of the garage to where the Land Rover was parked.

Sparks saw Carson exit the back of the house and notified Hector that he was walking around to the front. By the time Hector received the call Carson was backing out of the driveway. Sparks ran around the side of the house and called Carnahan.

Joseph, growing impatient with the way things were progressing, answered immediately, "What's going on?"

Charley watched the Land Rover go south on Tarpon and explained, "Carson Pike just left the house. We have no way of following him right now. The only thing I can do is walk down to where Derek and I are staying and drive the golf cart over to where Pike lives here on the island. Falco might be headed over there. Hector can remain here and keep an eye on the house."

"That sounds like the logical thing to do at this point," said Joseph. "Get moving. I'll be in touch soon."

Staring up Skull Inlet, Joseph ordered Mark, "Notify Hank and Carlton. Have them return here to the yacht. Plan A is off the table. Falco has had enough time to make land by now. We now need to go with plan B."

Carson drove slowly down Tarpon, squinting through the front windshield out into the rain. Looking to his left he was surprised when Nick opened the passenger door, hopped in and commented sarcastically, "I know I'm a tad bit late for our planned meeting but we still have a lot to discuss. For right now, we need to get off the island. It's not safe for me to stay here. Is there somewhere we can go?"

Carson turned the vehicle around and answered, "Yeah, I've got a charter boat that I keep anchored up in Beaufort. It can sleep four, it has a small refrigerator. It'll be a little cramped, but you could actually stay on it for weeks right there in the marina in Beaufort or we can shove off and go down river to Land's End. I've got a cabin over there Sparks and Simons probably don't know about." Looking Nick over, Carson asked, "Are you alright?"

"I'm okay now, but earlier this morning I wasn't so sure. I met Joseph Carnahan. Do you know who he is?"

"Yes. He's a dangerous man and if you've crossed paths with him that means they've run out of patience. This whole situation with the hidden money in the house is about to come to a head. What happened?"

Nodding up the dark road, Nick answered, "Just get me to Beaufort. I'll explain on the way."

Joseph stood at the rear of the yacht and addressed his men. "I have no doubt based upon what Derek has shared with us that Falco may be on Fripp. This is nothing more than a minor setback. We can, *and we will,* still get to him. It's just going to take a little longer than I anticipated. Mark is going to drop all of you off on Fripp where you'll meet up with Charley at John Fripp condos. Charley, by means of the golf cart will transport Hector and Carlos over to keep an eye on the house where Falco's girlfriend is staying and Pike's place, then Charley and Derek will watch Falco's house. Hank and Carlton will drive the car over to Savannah to keep an eye on the girl's apartment. Falco is tired and on the run. He'll have to hold up somewhere. I was planning on resolving out little problem tonight, but depending on what Falco does and where he goes next, it may take a few more days. I want to be contacted every hour on the hour in regard to what's happening. Now... get cracking!"

The sun was just coming up over the Beaufort River. Carson guided the Land Rover across the Woods Memorial Bridge in downtown Beaufort and turned onto Bay Street, while Nick finished up his story of the previous horrifying night: "I walked up Tarpon, contacted Genevieve and had her call you. You know the rest from there."

Parking at the marina, Carson got out and looked back toward Bay Street. Nick, now out of the vehicle as well, asked, "Something wrong?"

Carson scanned the street and answered, "After what you just told me, I can't help feeling that they may have followed us."

"I don't think so," said Nick. "The only way that could happen is if they had extra men on the island with a car. I might be wrong, but I think everyone involved was on that yacht tonight. There was no reason for them to have any men on Fripp. I'm sure that Carnahan figured he'd wrap everything up one way or the other out there on the ocean. When I jumped over the side, I think I really screwed up their initial plans. Personally, I believe we got off the island before they could get organized."

Pointing toward a wharf leading out into the river, Carson commented, "Come on, my boat is the forth on the left. It's not all that much but it's a place you can stay until we figure out what to do. There's some beer and juice and I think a few snacks in the fridge. I can run to the store and pick you up a few things later today."

Stepping from the wharf onto Carson's boat, Nick snapped his fingers. "Carson. After what happened last night, especially with me screwing up their plans, Carnahan might go after Shelby Lee. We have to contact her and let her know she may be in danger."

Standing on the deck of the boat, Carson pulled out his new phone and offered it to Nick. "Seeing as how she knows about the money, I'd say that's a good idea. Here, give her a call."

Nick looked out across the river. "Calling is not going to work. I don't know her number. I had it programmed into my phone, but at the moment it's in the possession of Carnahan."

"Well, if we can't call her," suggested, Carson, "then we'll just have to go see her. Tell me where she's staying on Fripp and I'll get a message to her."

"That's not going to work either. I've only known here for a few days. I've never been to her friend's house. I'm not sure where it is on the island. Her parents live here in Beaufort somewhere. I suppose we could try and contact them, but what could we say that wouldn't raise any suspicion? She has an apartment over in Savannah, but I don't think she's planning on going there in a while." Pointing his finger at Carson, Nick remembered, "I know where she's supposed to be this morning. Right about now she should be sitting at a gas station in Savannah looking for a man we think may be the RPS Killer."

Carson gave Nick an odd look to which Nick responded, "That's another story altogether which at the moment is not on the top of my priority list."

"Alright, here's what I think we should do," said Carson. "You need to go down below and get cleaned up. I've got a sweat suit and some old deck shoes you can borrow for now." Looking at his watch, he went on, "We leave for Savannah in ten minutes. We'll grab something to eat on the way over. Chop... chop!"

Shelby Lee was parked at the far end of the convenient store at the gas station. She had arrived at six o'clock in the morning; right on the nose. Looking at the large clock on the bank across the street, she noted the exact time: 7:45. She had been sitting there for almost two hours. She decided on a coffee and a breakfast sandwich.

The small store was packed with customers carrying cups of coffee and bags of donuts. Shelby walked to the far corner and opened a sliding glass door where there was a selection of breakfast sandwiches. Grabbing a sausage and cheese, she then proceeded to the line of elevated stainless steel coffee urns situated along the front windows and waited her turn for a cup of decaf. Someone bumped into her and excused themselves. Without turning around, she frowned and stepped forward.

Paying for her purchase, she exited the store and walked down to the end where she was parked. On the other side of a bread delivery truck a blue pickup sat next to her Jeep. Stopping dead in her tracks she looked around the lot for the driver. There were a number of people at the pumps and two females entering the store. Retracing her steps, she casually looked in the front window of the store. There were at least twenty people she could see inside the building. Most of those she could see were men. She wasn't exactly sure what the man she was looking for looked like, but she was sure, he was, at that moment, inside the store.

Walking quickly to her Jeep, she memorized the plate number on the blue truck, laid her coffee and sandwich on the passenger seat and jotted down the license number. She was just about to get out of the Jeep and have a quick look in the front seat of the truck when a man came out of the store and started down the walk in her direction. Getting back in the Jeep she tried to act normal as she unwrapped the sandwich, all the while keeping an eye on the man. He walked right past her and crossed the lot to a motorcycle.

When she looked back at the front of the store, there stood another man on the sidewalk: tall, slender, blue coveralls, a camouflaged ball hat pulled down to just above his eyes. He was staring right at her. Lighting up a cigarette, he coughed twice, looked up at the sky, blew out a long stream of smoke, walked around and climbed in the pickup.

She needed to call Nick and let him know what had happened, but that was going to have to wait. Turning right onto the street, she followed the pickup. Quickly, she double checked to make sure she had written down the plate number correctly. Two streets up, she made another right, still right behind the pickup. Stopping at a stop sign the driver appeared to look in the rearview mirror, then continued on. Thinking she was a little too obvious, she hung back a little and continued to trail the blue pickup.

At the next intersection, she followed the truck just as the light turned red. At the following intersection she had to run the light to keep from losing the truck. Following two more right hand turns, the truck headed out into the suburbs. On a long straight stretch of road, a car passed her, but then cut in between her and the truck. It was just as well. This way she could continue to follow without being conspicuous.

Suddenly, the truck sped up and was pulling away. "I can't lose him!" she yelled. Punching the gas, she moved around the car in front of her. Up ahead she saw the pickup stop, then make a right hand turn into a large sub-division. Making the right turn herself, she watched the truck disappear in the maze of houses. Cursing, she ran the stop sign and was no more than three houses into the development when she heard the loud siren behind her, followed by a magnified deep voice, "Please pull your vehicle to the curb!"

Looking in the rearview mirror she saw the red and blue flashing lights. Cursing, she pulled to the side. The officer stepped out of his cruiser and placed his hat on his head. Shelby couldn't recall the last time she had received a ticket but she knew the drill. Rolling down her window, she waited while the officer approached. Stopping at the window, the officer smiled and commented, "Good morning. Could I please see your driver's license and registration?"

Shelby looked up at the officer. "Did I do something wrong, sir?"

"I'm afraid so. You ran a stop sign back there at the front of the sub-division."

Shelby, looking out the passenger side window for any sign of the truck, answered, "Well, if you say so."

The officer, somewhat irritated because of her lack of attention, mentioned, "Yeah, I do say so! You didn't even come to a rolling stop, let alone stop. You just plain ran the sign." Glancing at the sub-division, he questioned her, "You seem to be in a rush to get to those houses. You live there?"

Shelby, realizing she was pissing the man off, lied, "No, my sister lives there. I just wasn't paying any attention."

"That doesn't make much sense, young lady. Have you ever been here before?"

"Sure, plenty of times."

"Well if you've been here on a number of occasions then you're aware of that stop sign."

Shelby was becoming impatient. The longer she was prevented from entering the sub-division, the longer it would take to relocate the truck. She felt like yelling, *Look, I'm in the process of following the RPS Killer,* but she calmly looked at the officer, handed him the articles he had requested and apologized, "I'm sorry officer, I guess I'm just a little tired this morning."

The officer scanned the two documents, then ordered, "Stay in your vehicle. I'll be right back."

She watched the officer walk back and get in the cruiser. There was nothing at the moment she could do to speed up the process. She looked at the sub-division. It was enormous: row after row of identical looking homes that seemed to go on forever.

Nearly five minutes passed when the officer returned and handed her license and registration back along with a ticket. Smiling pleasantly, he explained, "You have thirty days to pay that fine or you can appear in traffic court and dispute the ticket."

Anxious to get moving again, she answered politely, "I'll just pay the fine if it's all the same."

Tipping his hat, the officer replied, "Drive safe and have a nice day, Miss Pickett."

The officer made a U-turn in front of the development and headed back onto the highway. Looking at a large sign indicating all of the streets in the sub-division, Shelby slumped in the seat and spoke to herself, "That's just great! That truck could have gone anywhere in there. I was so close to finding out where he was going."

Pulling out into the street, although discouraged, she decided to use the process of elimination. The man was dressed in what appeared to be work clothes. If she remembered correctly, the man told the bartender that he was glad because he was returning to work and that he was meeting a group of men in the suburbs. Maybe this was the sub-division he was referring to. Maybe he was reporting to work. But, then again, maybe he lived here. If that was the case, he might pull his truck into a garage and she might drive by his house without even knowing it. *First things first,* she thought. She would drive up and down every single street and look for a crew of men working in the area.

Cruising up and down the first four streets the only people she saw were two women walking dogs and a man weeding at the side of his house. Thirty minutes passed as she drove up one street after another. Finally, she came to three men who were installing white fencing at a house. She slowed the Jeep down and passed, but none of the men fit the description of the man she was searching for. On the next street over, there was a crew of men replacing a roof on a house. Each man she saw was Hispanic except for a man who appeared to be the foreman. He was overweight and wore brown pants and a white shirt. Besides that, the blue pickup was not parked near the workers' vehicles down the street.

Two more streets to the west she passed a man who was painting a house. The man was high up on a ladder. He had long blond hair and his painting van was parked next to the house. The painter reminded her of Nick and how they had joked about his fear of heights. Since she wasn't having any luck in locating the blue truck or its driver, she decided to give Nick a call and update him on her progress. Punching in his cell number, there was no familiar ring tone; only dead silence. Putting her phone on the console, she checked the time: almost eight-thirty. Maybe he was sleeping in and had turned his phone off. She'd wait and call later.

An hour later, driving down the last street of the sub-division she came to an area where seven houses were being constructed. Unlike the other streets that were paved and lined with streetlights and Bradford Pear trees, the street was caked with mud and dirt. Pulling over to the curb, she took in the seven house area which was a mass of activity: carpenters nailing sheets of plywood onto a roof, another group of men pushing a frame wall into position, plumbers digging a hole next to the house on the end, a cement truck, emptying its grey, slimy cargo down a long metal chute into a framed in slab; workers of every size and shape going in every direction, each with their own assigned duties. Smiling to herself, she was confident this was where the man had gone.

Driving up the street slowly, she surveyed each property for the man she was looking for. There were just too many workers and took much activity to take in at one time. She looked for the blue pickup. Wherever it was parked was probably near to where the man was working. To her surprise there were no personal vehicles on the street near the houses, only plumbing and electrical vans and the cement truck. At the end of the street she came to a cul-de-sac that was backed up by a large field where lines of cars and pickup trucks were parked. The field was rough and lined with deep ruts. Parking the Jeep in the driveway of a house that was not being worked on, she got out and decided to walk the field in search of the blue pickup.

Sure enough, near the end of the lot next to some trees she spotted the truck. No one seemed to be around at the moment; she decided to give the truck a good going over. The first thing she checked was the plate number. The numbers matched what she had written down. There was no doubt. It was the same truck from the gas station. Then, she noticed something odd. The license plate was encased in a plastic holder with embossed writing at the bottom which read: *Miller's Auto Mart.* Frowning, she shook her head. This was the first day in quite some time that she hadn't thought about Ike Miller. She looked in every direction almost expecting the large man to jump out from behind one of the vehicles and screw up her plans. It was nothing but her imagination. According to her boss, Franklin Schrock, Ike was laid up in the hospital and had intentions of blowing town when he was released.

Moving to the side of the truck, she looked in the back. The rusted metal bed was empty except for an old spare tire that was rotted out, a broken handled shovel and a pair of mud-caked work boots. Checking to see if anyone was watching, she walked to the driver's side door and looked inside the cab. The interior was filthy: a layer of thick dust on the dashboard, an open carton of cigarettes on the passenger seat and the ashtray overflowing with cigarette ashes and butts. On the floorboard sat a thermos and a small cooler. *Probably, his lunch,* she surmised. She tried the door but it was locked. Walking around to the other side of the truck she tried the passenger door; same thing, locked.

She looked at her watch: just after ten o'clock. She saw an empty parking spot at the edge of the field, three cars down on the opposite side of where the truck was parked. She decided to move the Jeep to the spot, give Nick a call and then wait for the man to return to his truck. On the way back to the Jeep, she punched in Nick's number: There was no ring, just silence.

Carson made a left on Liberty Street while Nick looked for Shelby's Jeep and spoke at the same time. "Since she wasn't at the station she might have decided to drop by her place." Halfway up the street, Nick tapped Carson on his shoulder and ducked down, suggesting strongly, "Speed up!"

Turning left at the end of the block, Carson asked, "What's wrong? Why the quick exit?"

Looking over the top of the seat, Nick answered, "I think we're being followed. I saw a blue sedan parked back there across from Shelby's place when we drove down the street. It had New York tags. It's the same car Sparks and Simons were driving when I first ran into them in Cincinnati, the same car they drove down to Beaufort. Someone is watching Shelby Lee's apartment. The car pulled out when we passed. They probably know your vehicle."

Looking in the side view mirror, Carson swore, "Son of a bitch! Hold on, I'm going to try and lose them."

Nick no sooner fastened his seatbelt when Carson, at the last second made a hard right turn and hit the accelerator causing Nick to bang his head against the passenger side window. At the next street, Carson made a right and then a quick left into an alley. Stopping the Land Rover, he hopped out and moved four garbage cans to the middle of the small alley, jumped back in and sped off, making a right at the next street.

Looking in the rear view mirror, Carson smiled. "That should slow them down some." Pulling into a shopping center parking lot, he pulled in behind a delivery truck and stopped. A minute later, the blue sedan sped by them and moved off up the street. Backing out, Carson stated, "It's back to Beaufort for us. You need to disappear until I can figure out what to do."

The late morning sun was beating down on the open field and sitting in the Jeep for any length of time was uncomfortable. Shelby Lee got out and walked into the shade the trees offered.

She tried to call Nick again, but his phone was still dead. She checked the time: a few minutes after eleven. Looking back across the field she saw three different groups of men walking to vehicles. She thought to herself, *It must be lunchtime.* Most of the men climbed into vehicles and drove off, while others sat in their cars and went about eating their lunch. Then, she noticed the man she had been tailing. He was walking by himself, smoking a cigarette. Slipping back farther into the tree line, she watched while the man unlocked his truck, removed his thermos and cooler, lowered the tailgate of the pickup and sat on the back.

Ten minutes passed when the man closed the cooler and laid down in the truck bed for a late morning nap. Forty-five minutes later, he sat up, stretched, got out of the back, placed the cooler and thermos back in the cab, locked the truck and walked back across the field.

The trees did little to stifle the heat. Shelby walked back to the Jeep, climbed in and turned on the air. As the coolness blew across her sweaty face, she tried once again to contact Nick; no ring, no answer.

At three o'clock, a large number of workers walked into the field, climbed in cars and trucks and pulled out, their work day at an end. Shelby looked for the man, but he was not to be seen. Finally, he appeared when he approached his truck. He was smoking again and he bent down and coughed four times next to the truck.

Peering through the front windshield of the Jeep, Shelby thought, *He has to be the RPS Killer. The girls who had escaped his wrath agreed that he was tall, slim, smoked and coughed a lot.* The man she was now staring at fit the description to a tee. Standing, the man looked in her direction. Shelby slumped down in the seat, praying he hadn't noticed her.

Chancing another look over the dashboard she watched while he backed the truck out and drove across the field. She followed at a safe distance as the man drove through the sub-division and then back the way he had come earlier in the day.

A few miles down the highway, he pulled over at a truck stop, got out and entered a restaurant. When he didn't return Shelby ventured inside and saw him seated at a window table eating a meal and smoking. She went back outside to wait. She had come this far. She was going to follow him until he returned to his home, wherever that was.

Just after four o'clock, the man walked out of the restaurant, got back in his truck and drove toward Savannah. Shelby followed him all the way through the city until he pulled over, surprisingly at Chester's Grill and Tavern on the outskirts of Tybee Island. Parking at the end of the lot, she watched the man get out and enter the bar. *Perfect,* she thought. If she could go in and talk with Chester, he could then verify if the man she was following was the same man he had described to she and Nick.

There were a lot of cars in the lot and she was glad the bar was busy when she walked in. Stepping inside the doorway, she looked for the man. The place was packed with customers standing at the bar or sitting at tables. Two couples were playing pool in the adjacent room. Scanning the customers, she saw the man seated at the very end of the bar. Taking a drink, he lit a cigarette with the butt of another. She spotted Chester standing at the opposite end of the bar. Sitting at a table near the front door, Shelby grabbed a passing waitress by her arm and asked pleasantly, "I was wondering if I could speak with Chester for a moment?"

The waitress, who seemed to care less, answered, "Yeah, sure."

Shelby watched the young girl approach Chester and gesture toward her table. Chester, recognizing Shelby, glanced at the man at the end of the bar and casually walked across the room. He no sooner got to her table, when Shelby suggested, "I think we should step outside."

Following Shelby around the side of the building, Chester asked nervously, "Did you see him? He's here... at the end of the Bar! That's the man I told you about before. He's the one!"

"I know," said Shelby. "I've been following him all day. I'm not going back in. I'm going to wait out here until he leaves. Maybe I can find out where he lives."

Chester looked at his watch. "You could be in for a long wait. It's only five o'clock. Hell, he could stay in there until closing time which is nine hours from now."

"Look, I've come this far. I'm so close to finding out where he lives. I'm not going to back off now."

Looking around, Chester asked, "Where's Nick?"

"I don't know. I've been trying to call him all day. I'm sure I'll get hold of him later. Now, go back inside and try to act normal. We don't want to tip our man off. I'll be fine out here. I'll just wait in my Jeep until he leaves."

"Okay, but be careful... promise?"

"Like I said, I'll be fine. What could happen? He's in there... I'm out here."

Three hours passed and she tried to call Nick again. The results were the same: his phone was dead. Shelby looked at her watch: just after eight o'clock. Six more hours until the bar closed for the night.

Two more hours passed and darkness was setting in. She checked the time again: ten-fifteen. The lot was packed with cars. She was stiff from her prolonged sitting position in the Jeep. Opening the door, she stepped out and walked to the back of the Jeep. She stretched her shoulders, thinking about what a long day it had been and at the same time wondered what the hell was going on with Nick. She bent over and touched her toes, then went into a deep knee bend. The intense pain in her side caused her to cry out softly, then she fell unconscious to the ground.

Chapter Twenty-Two

CARSON LEANED ON THE RAILING OF HIS BOAT AND looked out across the Beaufort River. Nick, sitting in a deck chair finished up a water, wiped his mouth and spoke, "I've got three questions: First; do you think I'll be safe here on the river? Second; do you think Shelby Lee is safe and third; what do we do now?"

Carson walked to another deck chair, sat and looked at his watch. "It's almost midnight. There's not much Carnahan can do until tomorrow. All they can do for now, is keep an eye on the places they figure you may try going: We lost those bozos who were at Shelby's apartment. Since we showed up there, Carnahan will probably have them stay near her place. So, to answer your first question, I'd say, for the moment you're safe here on the river. I can't answer your second question with complete honesty. They may let Shelby be, but if they can't locate you within a couple of days, then they may consider questioning her about your whereabouts. Third: we're not going to wait for a couple of days to decide what we're going to do. I have a plan, but I have to meet with someone first."

Getting up, Carson started for the back of the boat. "Stay put. Don't leave the boat. I'll be back later in the morning. If everything goes the way I think it will, well, let's just say we'll be going on the offensive. Don't try to figure any of this out. Just relax and let me handle things. See ya in a few hours."

Watching Carson walk down the wharf, Nick suddenly realized how tired he was. Easing back in the chair he opened another water and yawned and thought about what Carson said about meeting someone and that he had a plan. He closed his eyes. He was so tired he couldn't reason anything out. What he needed was a good night's rest.

Shelby Lee opened her eyes and looked out a dusty window. She could barely make out what she thought were trees illuminated by a dim porch light. Next to the window there was an eight foot set of poorly stained kitchen cabinets topped with a dated white speckled counter top. The kitchen sink was piled full with dirty dishes and utensils. The curtain on either side of the single window was filthy and ripped in three areas. There was an old frayed circular throw rug beneath a round rickety kitchen table with three unmatched chairs scattered about. The walls were planked wood and bare of any pictures. The room reeked with the offensive odor of stale cigarettes.

It was then she discovered her hands and feet were bound with electrical tape. Her right side hurt; like a burning sensation. Her attention was drawn to the other side of the room by a voice. "I see you're finally awake."

Framed in what appeared to be a bedroom door, stood a tall, slim man, his hair in complete disarray. He stubbed out a cigarette on the nicotine stained wall casing and placed the butt in an overflowing glass ashtray on a nearby hutch. Shelby, taken off-guard, tried to struggle with her bindings.

The man lit up another cigarette and spoke gently, "There's no need to be afraid. You certainly weren't afraid of me that night on Foley Beach ten years ago."

Shelby stared at the face covered by a light unkempt beard and then at the man's eyes. Gasping, she remained silent, but then spoke as if she couldn't believe who she was looking at. "Harold, is that you?" Taking a closer look, she emphasized, "Oh my God... it is you!"

Harold walked across the room and looked out the kitchen window, then turned off the porch light. Turning, he leaned on the kitchen counter and took a long drag on his smoke. Displaying himself in a cocky fashion, he answered, "That's right... the one and only; Harold T. Benjamin V. The young man, who ten years back was on the verge of a brilliant military career, not to mention a future of great wealth and prosperity." Pointing a finger at Shelby, he continued, "But you put an end to all that. Thanks to you and that lawyer, Khelen Ridley, I not only got expelled from the academy, but my father disowned me. According to him, I'm a disgrace to the family. I was to be the fifth generation of Benjamin men to graduate from the academy. Now, look at me! A thirty one year old man who can't hold a good job, who lives on an old run down farm, a man who can't even have an affair with a woman. Thanks to you, all the things most people consider normal were taken from me."

Looking down at her hands and feet, Shelby asked, "Harold, why am I bound with this tape?"

Harold half laughed. "You're asking *me* that question. You seem to forget darlin'. You're the one who's been following me. What did you expect to accomplish when you discovered who the RPS Killer was? Did you expect the killer to just simply turn himself in because *you* were smart enough to figure out who he is? I knew you and that boy you've been seeing from Fripp were following me. Even before you met him, I was aware of what was going on in your life. I know for the past year or so that you've been seeing that stupid ass Ike Miller. I know where your apartment in Savannah is, where you work, where Kirby goes to school. You've only been following me for a few days. I've been following you for ten years. Remember that day I confronted you when you were at college? I told you that day, if it was the last thing I'd do, I'd get even with you for ruining my life; a life my parents planned for me from the moment I was born. I was strictly trained from a very young age to follow in the footsteps of my family predecessors. My father is a retired admiral in the United States Navy, my grandfather as well is a retired admiral, not to mention a congressman who has served the people of South Carolina for over twenty years. My great grandfather was wounded in combat and received the Purple Heart and retired from the army a two-star general. My great-great grandfather served his country for over thirty years in the United States Marine Corps. And after he retired, he became a successful businessman owning a number of businesses. I come from a long line of Benjamin men who, after graduating from the academy, went on to astounding military and eventually civilian careers. Well, the legacy I was destined for was ruined that night on the beach—"

Cutting Harold off, Shelby interjected, "Harold, it's all well and fine to sit here and listen to how successful the male relatives in your family have been, but that still does not answer the question of why I am bound hand and foot."

"It has everything to do with it," snapped Harold. "I wasn't planning on getting to you until the tenth anniversary of our fallout. Simply put, you're following me just speeded up the process. I can still accomplish what I want... it's just going to happen quicker than I planned. So, to answer your question why you're bound... well, it would have eventually happened anyway. You didn't leave me a choice."

"I don't understand any of this, Harold," said Shelby. "I was in love with you. I sat in front of your parents and your lawyer ten years ago in your own home and told them I loved you. You just sat there like a little puppet and remained quiet. I recall the words of your father: things like how could we, and by we, I mean not only myself but my parents expect you, his son to accept me as his wife if you were not in love with me. And another thing your father was very adamant about. Saying that *his son*, at this point in his life could not afford to be burdened with a wife and baby. Your parents even had the gall to suggest that I should have an abortion and that they would be more than glad to pay for the entire process. My parents and I were treated like second class citizens. The baby I was carrying... your daughter, meant nothing to them... and you. I was nothing more than a small hurdle that had to be jumped. And then, to top things off, they thought they could buy me off for a measly twenty thousand dollars. I had nothing to do with screwing your precious life up. You've managed to do that all by yourself."

Surprisingly, Harold remained calm and sat next to Shelby on the faded green couch, the burning cigarette hanging from his lips. Patting her gently on the cheek, he explained, "I'm well beyond getting upset with our situation. For the past ten years I've been waiting for the day when I could get my revenge for a life ruined... mine!" With a look of great sadness on his face, Harold hesitated and then stated, "Over the past two years I've killed nine girls—"

Once again, Shelby cut him off, "So, you are the RPS Killer?"

"It would seem that's the name society has chosen to give me, so yes, I guess I am."

"But why... why all those young girls?"

"Because of you. Does that surprise you?"

"I don't understand. What do any of the girls you murdered have to do with me?"

"Think about it," emphasized Harold. "All the girls I killed were between seventeen to nineteen years of age. Just about the same age you were when we met that summer over at Foley. They were all cute as a button. Just like you were when we first met. All those girls I killed ran around on the beach or around town in their tiny bikinis and shorts. Well, the truth of the matter is, those nine girls won't be ruining any young men's lives. I figure I saved nine young men from a life of grief."

"That's insane, Harold. What makes you think those young men, who you've never even met, will not meet another girl down the line somewhere in their life?"

Getting up from the couch, Harold sucked on his cigarette and responded, "You're right, Rebel. It does seem insane to think that I can save every young boy from what I experienced with you, but I only have one more girl to kill and then it's over."

Looking at Harold, Shelby spoke softly, "Harold, you're not making any sense."

"It makes perfect sense to me. In case you haven't quite figured this out yet... you're going to be the tenth girl that's killed; one girl for every year that my life has been screwed up. Actually, I wasn't going to kill you until next month on the tenth anniversary of when we met, but since you have elected to follow me, I have to move my plans up."

Pacing back and forth across the room, Harold continued to smoke and went on, "It will take a few months after your death, maybe longer, for everything to pan out. One can only assume Kirby will live with your parents after your untimely demise, but here's the thing. I'm still her father whether you like it or not. The fact that my father wrote you a check for two hundred thousand dollars and you signed off that you would never approach me or my family again for money does not erase the fact that I'm her blood father."

Amazed, Shelby shook her head in disbelief. "I don't know exactly where you're going with this, but you can't possibly believe that after my death my parents would even consider allowing you into Kirby's life."

"Oh ye of little faith," stated Harold boldly. "You have no idea of the power my father can wield. Despite the fact that he disowned me, my mother still supports me as her son. After my father kicked me out of their home my mother arranged to give me the same amount of money that my father gave you. I kicked around for a couple of years and tried to find employment but I had no training in anything other than military procedures. I tried some fast food jobs, but they seemed so beneath me. Then I tried my hand at being a security guard. That didn't work out so well either. I realized the two hundred thousand my mother gave me wasn't going to last long, so I bought this old farm here on St. Helena Island. I work odd jobs from time to time, mostly through temp agencies." Holding up his index finger to make a point, he stated, "Not the life my parents had raised me to live, but I think there's a very good chance that the cards of life, as they say are going to fall in my favor once again."

Going to the sink, Harold turned on the spigot and splashed cold water on his face, turned and continued to speak, "My mother is controlled by my father and despite the fact that they are incredibly wealthy, she comes from money herself. A little over two years ago, before I set out on my killing spree, I went to visit her and asked her that if by some unfortunate means you passed away and I became the sole parent of Kirby, would she then support me? A few months went by and she contacted me, telling me she had discussed the possibility with my father. My father said that the chances of your dying and leaving Kirby without a parent was a stretch, but if that ever happened, he then would consider allowing me back into the family fold. So, you see my plan makes perfect sense!"

"There's something you're overlooking, Harold. My parents would never allow you sole custody of Kirby."

Harold stubbed out his cigarette in the sink and laughed, "Shelby, Shelby, Shelby, you poor little thing. I guess it's just as well we never married. You just don't understand how money and power work. I was raised in the midst of power. You say your parents would never allow Kirby to be raised by me or my parents. There isn't any allowing on their part to even be considered. When my parents turn loose their high priced lawyers and wave their checkbook at your folks they'll fold like a cheap suit. People will do anything for the right amount of money. *You did!* You left me off the hook for a paltry two hundred thousand."

Shelby looked at Harold, frowned and remarked, "You're crazy! There is no way possible you can kill ten people, then suddenly turn your life around, start raising a daughter and live what you may think is a normal life."

Harold was getting upset at how calm Shelby had remained despite the fact he told her she was to be his tenth and last victim. Picking up a dish from the sink, he violently threw it across the room, the plate smashing into the wall above her head, shards and slivers of broken ceramic raining down around her. Getting directly in her face, he pointed a finger at her and raised his voice, "Think what you will, Shelby! I happen to be a lot smarter than you can possibly imagine. If I was a stupid man, don't you think the local authorities would have caught me by now? They don't have a clue who the RPS Killer is. That makes me more intelligent than all of them! You and that fellow you've recently hooked up with are fools. Once I discovered you were on to me, I devised a plan to suck you in and you bought it hook, line and sinker. I saw you at the gas station that morning when you tried to write down my plate number. I was the one who bumped into you while you were waiting to get coffee. I knew you were following me this morning to the work site and then to the bar. Hell, I even knew you were watching me while I ate my lunch in the back of my truck. I waited for the right moment and *bam,* here you are."

Holding up his wrist, he checked his watch and commented, "It's twelve fifteen. We could sit here all night and reminisce, but that isn't going to accomplish anything. It's time for a little car ride and then after we arrive at our destination, you'll have a choice to make. Just sit tight. I'll be right back."

Harold walked to the hutch, opened a drawer and removed a roll of electrical tape, a pair of scissors and a white bandana. His back was turned to Shelby when she noticed a small two inch section of broken ceramic lying next to her left side. Quickly bending over she managed to reach around and clutch the broken piece in her hand.

Going around the back of the couch, Harold explained, "I'm going to blindfold you and tape your mouth. Then, we'll take our ride. Our destination is only about fifteen minutes from here." Placing the bandana around her head and over her eyes, he continued to talk, "In a strange sort of way, I'm really sorry that things had to come to this. I remember when I was growing up as a young boy how my father would punish me for not adhering to his strict military lifestyle. If my room wasn't perfectly clean or my shoes were not shined, he'd make me do pushups or run laps until I was exhausted. He always told me it wasn't personal, it was business; the business of raising me up to be a Benjamin. So, I say to you. Don't take the fact that you have to die personal. It's just business; the business of me getting my life back. Don't worry. It's for the best. After you're gone and Kirby comes to live with the Benjamin's she'll have the best of everything; the best schools and education, the best clothing, the best food. She'll want for nothing. Who knows! Maybe later on in her life, she'll go to the academy and then my father can be proud of me once again."

Shelby could feel the tape cover her mouth and then she was helped to her feet, then picked up and carried across the room. She concealed the broken section of plate in her right hand when she heard a door open and could feel a slight breeze blow across her face as she was carried across the porch and down some steps.

A short time passed when she was stood on her feet and leaned up against the side of what she thought was some sort of vehicle. Harold remained silent and the next sound she heard was the trunk being opened. She was picked up again and laid in the trunk, then heard the trunk door slam shut. She laid perfectly still and seconds later she heard the motor come to life when the vehicle pulled out.

Laying in the darkness, Shelby could feel every bump and rut in the road they were passing over. The stale odor from cigarettes almost caused her to gag. So far she had remained relatively calm, but that was only because she was only facing the possibility that she would be killed by Harold. She realized she had to start to put a plan together if she was going to survive, because it was now more than a possibility; it was reality.

Based on what Harold talked about, she figured he was either crazy or a cold blooded killer. *Maybe he's both,* she thought. *Stay calm... relax. There has to be a way out of this. Somehow I've got to outsmart Harold.*

Harold had mentioned that their destination was only about fifteen minutes from the farm. When they arrived and he popped the trunk she had no idea what he had in mind as far as a time line for her upcoming death. She had less than fifteen minutes to think of something. Awkwardly twisting herself, she worked the small section of broken plate in between her right hand thumb and index finger and located the rough edge. Slowly, she concentrated and began to run the edge over the electrical tape wrapped tightly around her wrists. If she could get her hands free, then she could remove the blindfold, the tape from her mouth and feet and when Harold opened the trunk she would attack. If she was lucky he wouldn't be expecting her to free herself and the element of surprise would be in her corner. Maybe she could knock him down long enough for her to run off into the darkness.

The vehicle suddenly stopped and made a right hand turn, then continued down another rough section of road. She had no idea how much time had passed as she continued to work at cutting the tape. She was sweating profusely and the beads of perspiration ran behind the blindfold down into her eyes.

Another minute passed. She stopped for a rest and strained her wrists, trying to break the tape. The tips of her fingers on her left hand brushed against a small section of tape that had loosened. It was then she realized Harold had wrapped her wrists a number of times with the tape. She had only cut through the first layer. Pressing down hard on the tape with the edge of the ceramic piece, she gritted her teeth and thought, *At this rate I'll never make it!*

Suddenly, she was jolted to the side when the vehicle went through a deep rut, causing her to drop the piece of broken plate as she banged her head against a spare tire. Rolling back onto her side, she searched desperately for the crude cutting tool. Her fingers ran over small pebbles and dirt. The salt from the sweat was stinging her eyes and her clothes were soaked with perspiration. Every second she wasn't working at cutting the tape brought her closer to being at Harold's mercy. She recalled what she had been told about how those girls had been killed: their heads bashed in and their elbows and knees beaten to a pulp by means of large rocks, not to mention how they were found with a pair of scissors stuck in the chests. She stopped for a moment, realizing she was allowing herself to panic. Taking a deep breath to calm herself, she thought, *Don't panic. Focus. Find the broken piece and get to work on the tape.*

Sliding her fingers across the rough, dirty carpet in the trunk she moved slightly to the right and then all of a sudden her fingers found the wonderful broken piece. Grasping it in her right hand, she positioned it in her fingers and went to work, forcing the edge across the face of the tape. She felt a stab of pain when she missed the tape and ran the sharp edge across her left hand. She could feel the warm blood running down her wrist over the tape.

After what seemed like an eternity a second strand of the tape broke loose. Now, confident, Shelby tried to separate her hands and break free, but the remaining tape held. The trickling blood from the cut on her hand ran down onto her fingers making it difficult to hold the broken piece. Then, the vehicle stopped!

She prayed that they had stopped to make another turn and would then continue on, giving her more time to escape the tape, but the vehicle did not move. The sound of the motor came to a frightening end as it was shut off. It would only be a matter of seconds before the trunk was opened. Feverishly she worked at the tape, but she was running out of time.

The sound of the trunk being opened caused her to hide her hands and the cutting tool behind her back as she curled up into a ball. She heard Harold's voice, "I hope your ride wasn't too uncomfortable. Here, let me get that blindfold off so we can continue."

She could feel the bandana being removed from her head and then her eyes. A flashlight laying in the corner of the trunk lit up the confines enough for her to see Harold's outline against the black backdrop of the dark sky. Surprisingly, he removed the tape from her mouth and warned her, "If you scream, I'll kill you within seconds."

Shelby, still trying to cut the tape knew she had to buy some time. If she could just keep Harold talking for a few minutes then maybe she could break free. "Harold, explain something to me, because if you're going to kill me then at least I deserve to know."

Harold smiled, but the slant of his lips indicated his evil intent. "Ask me anything you'd like. Neither one of us has anything to lose at this point."

"But that's where you're wrong. I'm going to lose my life and you will continue on, according to you, back in your father's graces. I deserve to know why you killed all those girls in such a brutal fashion, especially because you said you killed them because of me."

"All right, I'll tell you the whole truth. You were not the only one to ruin my life. My uncle played a major part in ruining me." Lighting up a cigarette, he leaned against the back of the trunk and looked up at the sky while Shelby continued to work at the tape.

"My uncle on my mother's side, her brother, served in the Persian Gulf War. His name is Dennis. He was sent home before the war ended with a severe concussion to his head from a massive explosion at a building he was near. He had nowhere to go and my father, who is military to the bitter end had great respect for Dennis as a soldier who had served, so he came to live at our home."

Shaking his head, he took a drag on his smoke and continued with the story, "I remember the year he came to live with us. It was 1991; twenty-three years ago. I was only seven years old at the time. When he first came to live with us I thought he was a strange sort of character. I asked my father what was wrong with Dennis and he explained to me that he was just a little bit off, meaning that he had suffered from the explosion he had experienced. He could reason things out, he could work, he could communicate with people; he just wasn't sure of himself at times. He lived in an apartment over top of our four car garage. To keep busy he worked in a large garden we had and kept the landscaping on the property in good order. He did a lot of odd jobs around the property. He was like a member of the family. I found him to be a very interesting person to talk with. He knew everything about gardening and could fix most anything, but the most interesting stories he shared with me were about his experience in the war. Being raised as a future military academy cadet, I was quite interested in what Dennis always had to say. My father told me that I needed to show respect for Dennis because of how he had served in our military. I trusted Dennis. He became like an older brother to me."

The broken piece slid from Shelby's hand as she swore beneath her breath. Searching the dirty floor of the trunk for the piece, she urged Harold to keep talking, "That must have been a good feeling for you to have an older brother you could talk to."

Harold frowned. "That's what I thought too. But then things changed. When I was eight years old he introduced me to the game of Rock, paper, scissors. At first, it was fun. If I won, he'd shine my shoes for me and if I lost then I would have to weed the garden for him; simple things like that. Then, one night when my parents were out for an evening, Dennis suggested that we add a dimension to the game that would make it even more interesting. That was the beginning of my five years of being sexually molested. If I won he'd reward me with three one dollar bills and I was free to go, but if he won then he got to do to me what he wanted, but still rewarded me with a five dollar bill."

Reaching up, Harold wiped a tear from his eye, then pitched his unfinished cigarette to the ground and composed himself. "Just after my twelfth birthday, he just up and left. My family never heard from him again."

Shelby could feel the tape loosening as she asked, "And you never said anything to your parents about how Dennis molested you?"

"Harold chuckled, indicating that what Shelby asked was absurd. "Are you kidding me? You don't know my parents, especially my father. This was my mother's brother we're talking about. My father would have blamed her for Dennis's horrible actions. And my father; I could have never gone to him. He would have punished me for letting the situation go on for five years. So, I just kept what happened to myself. No one ever knew how I had been molested. In high school, when all my friends began to show interest in girls, I remained distant to the female population. Those five years of molestation ruined me. I had no desire to be involved in any activity that could eventually lead to sexual contact of any kind. My mother was quick to notice my lack of interest in the opposite sex, but I explained my way out of telling her the truth by saying that I had time later on in life for those type of things and that I was going to focus all my efforts on preparing myself for the academy and my future military career. So, my parents never knew, and still to this day, do not know the truth."

Harold's sad tale caused Shelby for a brief moment to feel compassion for him and she asked in wonder, "But what about when we met on the beach that summer and then, weeks later we had sexual relations on the beach. You didn't seem to have a problem then, so I can only assume that you were healed of the pain of molestation and did have interest in girls."

Harold smiled genuinely, and replied, "That night on the beach was my first sexual encounter with a woman. I was a virgin... as you were. I guess most people would say that's a beautiful thing. For me, it was like being released from prison. You, at that time were the best thing that could have happened to me. I felt like a normal boy, a normal man for the first time in my life. But then, you got pregnant and it dawned on me that just when my life was turning around I was going to be faced with a future wife and baby. I was right back where I started; trapped once again from being free. The truth is, I never loved you. At least, I don't think I did. To tell you the truth, I don't know how to feel love."

Another strand of tape broke loose and Shelby could begin to feel her wrists twist out of the remaining binding. She had to keep Harold talking for just another minute or so. "So, that's why you used the game while killing those girls: three dollars if they won and five dollars if they lost. But why did you have to bash their heads in and beat the arms and legs with rocks and then end it all by stabbing them with scissors?"

"That's a difficult question to answer. I killed the girls because they were all your age. I suppose the brutality came from my anger of being molested. It became my calling card, hence the name RPS Killer." Harold took a deep breath and wiped tears from his eyes and stated through a choked voice, "But's that's just about to end. After you and I play the game and you're dead and gone, everything will return to normal. Kirby will come and live with me and my parents and I'll go back to the lifestyle I'm accustomed to living."

"The game," said Shelby. "According to you the way the game is played is that if I win I get three dollars and am set free. If that happens, then I live and your chances of getting Kirby to live with you and your parents will not happen."

"That only pertained to the other girls. The rules when we play the game are going to be altered. If you'll recall, back at the house I told you that you were going to have to make a choice. The choice you're going to have to make is how you die, not if you're going to die! It's really quite simple. If I win, then you die just like all the others… brutal! If you win then I'll be merciful. I'll render you unconscious and drown you in the marsh which is just a few yards out from where we are. You won't feel any pain. You won't be aware of the water when it fills your lungs. It'll be like dying in your sleep. On the other hand, if I win then you'll suffer just like all the other girls had to. I think I'm being more than fair after what you've put me through all these years. Now, if you'll turn around I'll cut that tape and then we can begin with Rock, paper, scissors."

Shelby gritted her teeth and pulled her hands apart, the remaining tape coming loose. If she displayed her hands now after he had offered to remove the tape, he might become upset and kill her on the spot. *No,* she had to keep him talking for a few more seconds in order for her to decide on her next move.

Laying the scissors on the rear fender, Harold ordered, "Turn around so I can release your hands. Then, we'll begin the game. I assume you know how to play?"

Shelby scooted back farther into the trunk and raised her voice, "I'm not going to play your stupid game. If you're going to kill me you'll have to do it all on your own without a decision from me!"

Instantly, Harold became angry, "But you don't understand! *You have to play the game!* You're the tenth girl. I cannot deviate from my plan."

Shelby shouted, "You're going to kill me anyway so just go ahead. You don't need your stupid game!"

Grabbing her by the hair he jerked her forward and yelled, "I am going to kill you, but it has to be on my terms. Now, turn around so I can free your hands so we can play the game!"

Bringing her hands to her sides, she mustered up every ounce of strength she could. Reaching up, she ripped Harold's left hand from her hair and swung her right fist into his face. She could feel the crunch of bone as her balled up fist connected with his nose. A sudden gush of blood squirted back onto her face. Harold, for a brief second seemed dazed. He couldn't believe what happened. Just as he was reaching for his broken nose with his left hand, Shelby swung again with her right, hitting him squarely in his mouth. He staggered backward and went down on one knee. Shelby quickly crawled out of the trunk and fell onto the ground as she looked for the scissors. Harold was blocking her from the side of the bumper where they were laying. Shaking his head, trying to get rid of the cobwebs that were flooding his mind from the two savage hits he had received, he raised his hands toward his face, but Shelby attacked with another blow to the side of his head. Struggling to her feet, she pushed Harold down to the ground and hopped to where the scissors were. Reaching for the scissors, she knew it was only a matter of seconds before Harold could recover. If he got back up and grabbed her before her feet were free she knew she'd be a goner. Any compassion that he previously had was now gone as he screamed, "You bitch! I'm going to kill you right here... right now!"

The scissors cut slowly through the tape but she was still not completely loose. Harold was awkwardly getting to his feet. "Come on... come on," Shelby yelled at the scissors. The final section of tape fell from her ankles as Harold rose to his knees. For a brief moment she thought to herself, *Just stab the bastard!* She couldn't bring herself to do it. She wasn't a killer. She just wanted to escape. Dropping the scissors, she ran off into the darkness, but tripped on a tree root. She went down hard and rolled. Just as she was getting back to her feet she felt Harold's hand wrap around her left ankle. Savagely, she kicked out and her right foot caught him on the side of his head.

He let go and screamed, "I'm going to kill you! You can't get away!"

Ignoring Harold's loud ranting, she got to her feet and staggered forward a few yards and fell down a slight slope into water. Turning, she saw Harold stumbling toward her, a flashlight held in his hand. Trying to get up, she slipped in the mud just below the surface. Reaching out, her hand hit the side of something wooden. Harold approached and the beam of light from the flashlight revealed a wooden boat with an attached motor. She stood up and slowly retreated further out into the water.

"You might as well give up Rebel," laughed Harold. "There's nothing out there except miles of salt marsh. I know every inch of that marsh. If you try to swim out, I'll run you down with my boat. It'll be a little more effort on my part, but you'll still wind up being number ten."

Shelby was far too tired to try and outswim Harold and his boat. Reaching into the rear of the boat she grabbed a wooden oar and held it in front of her in a defensive position and yelled, "Come on, you bastard. Come in and get me if you're man enough!"

Bending over, Harold laughed and tried to catch his breath. Wiping blood from his face with the back of his left hand she noticed the scissors he held. Clicking the scissors twice, he continued to smile and remarked. "You pack quite a wallop, there

Rebel. You should have killed me back there at the car when you had a chance. That's the difference between you and me. You're weak because you couldn't stab me to death. I'm strong because I won't hesitate for a second once I get close to you." Clicking the scissors again, his face took on an evil grin. "It's just a matter of time." Walking to the edge of the water he went on, "Do you really think you're a match for me? I'm in excellent physical condition, I'm quite the swimmer and my father trained me in hand to hand combat. A wooden oar against a skilled man with a pair of scissors. Come on, Rebel. Do you really think you have a chance?"

Holding the flashlight on her, he ventured into the water up to his knees and then stopped. Shelby stood her ground as she pointed the oar at his chest and stated with conviction, "You're right Harold. I was weak back there because I didn't kill you. I won't make that mistake again. Those nine girls you killed couldn't fight back; I can and I will! If you want to make me number ten, you're gonna have to work for it."

"So be it," said Harold. He walked out further until the water was at his waist. Shelby backed up slightly thinking the deeper they were the more difficult it would be for Harold to move. Harold laughed and pointed with the flashlight. "I know what you're doing and it won't work." Shining the light in his face, he smiled, clicked the scissors twice, then sank below the surface.

Shelby instantly worked her way to the opposite side of the boat, but then realized he could swim beneath the boat and take her by surprise. Quickly, she threw the oar into the boat and hoisted herself up and over the side. Crouching down, she held the oar in front of her and looked in every direction around the boat. Nearly a minute passed and she wondered how long he would stay under. The sound of the flashlight landing in the front of the boat caused her to turn. In that second, Harold leaped up on her right and rocked the boat at the same time slashing out with the scissors. The sharp bladed instrument nicked her right leg. Instinctively, she wheeled around and swung the oar wildly. The wide paddle end of the oar caught Harold on the side of his head forcing him sideways near the end of the boat, his head slamming into the metal motor. Harold held on to the side of boat and let out a low moan. Picking up the flashlight, Shelby shined it toward the rear of the boat. Harold was hanging onto the side, blood was running down the side of his face, his eyes were glazed over. Still, in a state of dizziness he tried to reach out and stab Shelby, the scissors plunging into the wooden rail of the boat. Slowly, he made his way hand over hand up the right side of the boat toward the bank of the marsh. Shelby, realizing she was dealing with a maniac, spoke out loud to herself, "Forgive me God, but I've got to put an end to this." Harold was weakened to the point where he rolled over onto his back, floating in the knee deep water as he held onto the side of the boat. Shelby took a deep breath and looked directly into Harold's eyes. Placing the oar on his heaving chest, she hesitated and had second thoughts, but then Harold spoke softly, "Don't let the authorities take me in, Rebel. I'd never survive in prison. You were the best thing that ever happened to me. Do me a favor now and end this... please!"

Shelby closed her eyes and shoved down on the oar, Harold's body sinking below the murky surface. She opened her eyes after a few seconds and shined the light down on the water and watched until the bubbles from Harold's labored breathing stopped coming to the surface. She didn't let up on the oar for nearly five minutes. She had to make sure Harold was dead. She wanted to reach down into the water and drag him out to make sure he was no longer breathing, but she could just imagine him rising up and pulling her under. "*No,*" she said loudly, "I'm leaving."

Taking the flashlight, she walked past Harold's car and shined the beam up a deserted road. She went back to the car and opened the door. The stench of old cigarette smoke made her eyes water. Besides that, the keys were not in the ignition. Driving the car was not an option. She'd have to walk out. She had no idea where the road led. It had to be somewhere between two and three in the morning. The sun would be up in four to five hours. She figured she was still on St. Helena Island. She'd just keep walking until the sun came up. Eventually she'd come to some sort of civilization. Walking slowly up the road she checked the wound from the scissors on her left leg. It was bleeding a little but didn't appear to be that bad. She wondered where Nick was at the moment. *Probably in bed sound asleep.*

Chapter Twenty-Three

CARSON SHOOK NICK'S SHOULDER VIGOROUSLY. "NICK... get up!"

Nick, in a deep sleep, sat up as if he didn't know where he was. Focusing his eyes, he looked at Carson and asked, "What time is it?"

Carson looked at his watch. "Just after five in the morning. You sleep out here on the deck since I left?"

"Yeah, is that a problem?"

"Well, you're still here, so no, it's not a problem."

Nick, rubbing his tired eyes, asked, "Did you see your friend?"

"Yes, I did." Holding up a bag of groceries, he motioned toward the lower quarters. "Got us some breakfast: eggs, bacon, juice and some cheese Danish. I'll give you some of the details of the plan while we're eating."

Making a nasty face, Nick spit over the side and remarked, "I feel like crap. I don't suppose you've got a shower on this boat?"

"No shower. If you want to freshen up, it's over the side for you. I've done it a number of times this time of morning. There's no one around. I gotta tell ya. There's nothing like jumping into the Beaufort River naked as a Jaybird. Go on. You'll feel better. I'll lay a towel out for you."

Watching Carson disappear down into the lower deck area, Nick stripped off the deck shoes and sweat suit and climbed down a ladder leading into the dark river. Despite the fact he had spent the better part of the previous night in the ocean swimming for his life, the warm river water felt refreshing on his bare, tired body. Slipping beneath the surface, he came back up and rubbed his hands over his face and through his hair. He could have used a few more hours sleep, but at the moment felt surprisingly revived.

Back on the boat, he toweled off, dressed and walked down the steps to the lower level where he found Carson busy frying bacon on a hot plate. Carson, pointed a spatula across the cabin and commented, "The juice and Danish are over there on the table."

Nick poured a glass of juice and sat on a built-in cot next to the wall and asked, "From what you said up top I assume you talked with your friend about your plan?"

Flipping the bacon, Carson answered, "I did and if everything falls into place the way I think it will this whole thing could be over by tomorrow."

"So who is this friend of yours?"

"You don't need to know that just yet. Like I said if everything works out, you may meet them later tonight."

"What about this plan? Can you tell me what that's all about?"

Placing the bacon on a plate, Carson broke an egg and placed it on the hot plate. "I can't divulge the entire plan, because a lot depends on how Carnahan reacts in the next few hours. I can tell you this. I'm going to contact him and offer him a deal. In short... we're going to con a con!"

Swallowing some juice, Nick gave Carson a strange look. "Con a con. What does that mean?"

Placing two more eggs on the hot plate, Carson explained, "Carnahan is nothing less than a shrewd con man. What we are going to attempt to do is con *him*. We're going to give him his seven million dollars, but in all actuality we're not going to give it to him. I know that probably doesn't make a lot of sense, but the secret to a good con is that after the deal is completed that the mark... in this case, Carnahan, doesn't even realize they have been conned. It's a fine line and with a man like Carnahan we have to be careful. On a daily basis he deals with some of the most unscrupulous individuals you can imagine. He knows how to deal with those who are untruthful because he is untruthful. He knows how to deal with dishonest men, because he is a dishonest man himself. He didn't get to where he is because of stupidity. The idea behind our con is to let him think he has won."

"How do we do that?"

Handing Nick a plate of bacon and eggs, Carson smiled and answered, "You don't need to know that just yet. You just go where I tell you and do what I say and you'll stand a better than average chance of getting out of this mess. Eat your breakfast."

Carson fixed a plate for himself and within less than a minute devoured the food, stood and stretched, "I'm going to drive over to Fripp. That's the first part of the con. You're going to remain here on the boat. I'll return in a few hours, hopefully with good news. Try and get some rest. If things work out the way I've planned we could be up late tonight."

The sun was just coming up as Nick watched Carson walk across the wharf. A few more hours sleep sounded good to Nick. Back down in the lower level, he stretched out on the cot and closed his eyes as the boat rocked gently from the low waves from the river.

It looked like another sweltering day in the lowcountry as Carson drove down the Sea Island Parkway across St. Helena Island. Turning the air-conditioner on high, not paying attention he almost ran into a pedestrian walking along the side of the road.

By the time the Fripp Island Bridge came into sight, Carson had gone over the plan he had devised a number of times. Stopping at the guard shack he was approached by a security officer who noticed him. "Good morning. Mr. Pike. I thought by this time of the day you'd be out fishing."

"Nope, not today," said Carson. "Got a lot of errands to run. With any luck I should be heading back over to Beaufort within the hour." Waving at the guard, Carson smiled. "Have a good day."

Driving slowly down Tarpon Boulevard, he went over his plan one last time to make sure he wasn't overlooking anything. If he was going to succeed in conning Carnahan, he had to think like the man, he had to be two to three steps ahead of him. He was going to have to appear honest, but at the same time be dishonest. The first part of the plan was to contact one of Carnahan's men. He was hoping Carnahan still had men watching Nick's house.

Sure enough, across the street perched in a golf cart sat Charley Sparks. The cart was partially concealed by a stand of Palmetto trees next to a home that at the moment appeared to be unoccupied. Pulling into the driveway of Nick's house, Carson got out and walked across the yard and the street toward Sparks without the slightest hesitation. Walking toward the cart, Carson raised his hands indicating that he had no weapon. Sparks, who had a revolver laying on the passenger seat raised the gun, pointing it at Carson as he approached.

Carson, relaxed, waved his arms acting like the gun pointed directly at him was of no importance. Stopping two feet from the cart, Carson spoke, "No need for the gun Charley. I'm here to make a deal with Carnahan. If I was you I'd put that gun up and pay attention. If Carnahan finds out there was an opportunity to get his money back and that you screwed it up... your boss is going to be pissed."

Without being invited, Carson walked around the front of the cart and climbed in. Sparks still held the gun on Carson and was about to make a call on his cell phone, but was interrupted by Carson. "Before you contact your boss you might want to listen to what I have to say."

Sparks gave Carson a look of skepticism, and then spoke, "All right Pike. I'm listening. But keep in mind. You try and pull anything funny and I'll plug you right where you sit. Is that clear?"

Showing no fear whatsoever, Carson propped his feet up on the dash and smiled, "Perfectly clear."

Sparks remained skeptical. "What's this deal you mentioned?"

"Well, first of all Nick Falco is tucked away. Neither you nor Carnahan will be able to get to him. But, that's beside the point. Falco has grown tired of this business his grandmother dumped on him. He doesn't have any idea where the money is. The truth is; Amelia was honest with you when you initially contacted her. She knew about the money and that it was hidden somewhere in the house, but she didn't know where. Her grandson, Nick is in the same boat. He has been told about this money but has never seen it nor does he know where it's hidden." Sitting back and placing his hands behind his head in a relaxed fashion, Carson stated confidently, "I have the money. I found it at the house and removed it before Falco moved in. It is presently in my possession. I'm willing to turn the money over to Carnahan if he's ready to call off the dogs; meaning you, Simons and whoever else he's got down here. It's simple: I turn the money over to you, you in turn, deliver it to Carnahan and Falco is off the hook, never to be bothered again by the organization. Think about it. You could wind up being a hero in Carnahan's eyes. Just think how pleased he'll be when you hand the money over to him."

Without waiting for Sparks to react, Carson continued, "All you need to do is call Carnahan and tell him I want to speak with him. Like I said before. You don't want to blow this for the organization. As you are well aware. They are not all that forgiving. So, do I get to speak with Joseph or not?"

Sparks hesitated, then punched in a number and spoke, "This better be on the level, Pike. You screw me over and you're dead!"

Carnahan was enjoying his breakfast on the upper deck on the yacht when the call came through. Mark picked up the call. "Who've I got?"

Sparks immediately demanded, "It's Charley. I need to speak with Joseph."

Handing the phone to Carnahan, Mark announced, "It's Charley. Says he needs to talk with you."

Setting down a freshly made Bloody Mary, Carnahan cleared his throat, then answered, "Sparks... what's up? This better be good news."

Looking over at Carson, Charley explained, "I've got Carson Pike here with me. He wants to talk with you. Says he has a deal for you."

"Put him on."

Charley handed the phone to Carson and reminded him, "Don't forget... I'll have this gun on you the whole time."

Taking the phone, Carson began, "Joseph, good morning!"

"Cut the crap, Pike. I have the strangest feeling you know where the Falco kid is."

"I do know where he is and we want to make a deal."

"I'm listening."

"Good news... bad news," emphasized Carson. "I've got your money but it's a little short of what you're expecting. There never was seven million. It's more like in the vicinity of 5.8 million. I've got it in two suitcases hidden here on Fripp. I'm willing to turn the entire amount over to you if you agree to go back to New York and let Falco be. He has nothing to do with any of this. He just wants to be left alone to live here in peace in his grandmother's house."

"Sounds all well and fine," remarked Carnahan, "but there seems to be a few loose ends you haven't mentioned; like when and where I receive the money."

"Here's the way I figure it," said Carson. "Falco and I are going to head on over to his house after dark tonight. You can send two of your men to the house just after midnight. Actually, I'd prefer Sparks and Simons. I know both of them and I prefer to hand the money over to someone that I know is employed by you. It'd be nice if you dropped by to pick up the cash, but I know you like to distance yourself from these sort of situations. How's the deal sound so far?"

"I'm still listening. What takes place at the house after my men arrive?"

"Simple; I hand over the two suitcases of money, Sparks calls you from the house and verifies it's in his possession, they leave and that's the end of it. Where should I tell them to meet you with the money?"

"One thing at a time, Pike. If I do go along with this deal of yours it won't be over until *after* I receive the money and it's counted. If the count is correct, then Falco is off the hook... for good. If you try to screw me in any fashion, both you and the Falco kid die... understood?"

"I understand completely, Carnahan. But here's the thing. You can't afford not to take me up on this offer. Sure, you can eliminate both myself and Falco, but then there would be no reason for you to purchase the house after Nick's death because the money will not be there. If you kill me, you'll never find that money. You agree to my deal and by tomorrow you'll have your millions."

There was a moment of silence on the other end and then finally Carnahan spoke, "Okay Pike, the deal is on. The crew of men with me and myself are going to sail up to the Charleston Harbor where we'll dock. If we leave now we'll be up there before it gets dark. After Sparks has the money in his possession, he is to give me a call. He will then drive up to Charleston and deliver the money to me. We verify the count and then and *only then,* you and Falco have nothing to worry about. Now, let me speak with Sparks and I'll give him the rundown. It's nice doing business with you, Mr. Pike. Big Ed always said you were a good man. His grandson owes his life to you."

Handing the phone back to Sparks, Carson stepped out of the cart and saluted. "I'll see you and Derek tonight around midnight. Come prepared to pick up nearly six million. Your boss will fill you in."

Walking back across the street Carson thought to himself, *So far, so good! Carnahan took the bait.* Climbing back into the Land Rover, his next step in the plan was to drive back to Beaufort and fill Nick in on how things went.

Passing the guard shack, Carson waved at the officer on duty and sped across the bridge spanning Fripp Inlet. It wasn't even nine o'clock in the morning and the temperature felt like it was already in the nineties. Carson turned all the vents on the dash in his direction and checked to see if the air-conditioner was on high. Wiping his face with a handkerchief, he smiled and thought there was a very good probability that the situation with the organization's money would come to an end by tomorrow. Stopping at Barefoot Farms, he purchased an ice cold peach tea and was on his way once again.

A short line of cars was congregated on the southern end of the Harbor Island Bridge, the bridge's middle section swung out as a fishing trawler slowly made its way beneath the structure. Carson sat back and allowed the coolness from the air-conditioner to blow directly in his face. Taking a drink of the refreshing tea, he went over the next part of his plan. Once, back in Beaufort, he'd return to the boat and update Nick on how the con was going so far. Then, he had to meet with his friend again and set things up for the upcoming evening at Nick's. Carnahan was extremely intelligent, but his greed looked like it was going to overshadow his ability to see through Carson's plan.

The bridge finally swung back and the line of cars in both directions began moving. Not even two miles in on St Helena Island, Carson noticed a girl walking on the side of the road. She stumbled slightly; nothing that seemed like a problem but it was enough for Carson to notice. Besides that, it was the same girl he had nearly run down on his way to Fripp. The girl had been walking the entire time he was on the island. Pulling into a side dirt road, he turned around and headed back down the highway.

Passing the girl, he pulled over a few yards in front of her and got out. The girl approached and didn't seem to display any emotion that he had stopped. As she got closer, Carson noticed that she looked the worse for wear: her shorts and top looked wrinkled and filthy, her hair was sticking out in every direction. When she was close enough, he noticed that her face wore a look of great fatigue.

The girl stopped just short of his vehicle and took a deep breath as if she wanted to just sit down and rest.

Carson took a step forward and asked, "Didn't I see you earlier, about an hour or so ago walking down the parkway? As a matter of fact, I nearly ran you over. You were walking pretty close to the edge of the road. Do you need a lift somewhere?"

The girl looked Carson up and down and then answered, "Yeah, I could use a ride out to Fripp if it's not out of your way."

"Just came from Fripp. Actually, I live there. I was on my way into Beaufort when I saw you. You look exhausted. Hop in. I'll have you on Fripp in less than ten minutes."

The girl walked to the passenger door and climbed in the Land Rover and plopped down in the seat. Carson climbed in and seeing that she was nearly overheated, turned the air-conditioner vents on her. "There, how's that feel?"

The girl remained silent but nodded her approval of the cool air and brushed her hair from her face. Wiping the top of the bottle off with his shirt, he offered her the tea. "Here, drink this. It'll make you feel better."

Pulling out onto the highway, Carson looked across at the girl and asked, "You live on Fripp? I know most everyone who lives on the island. I don't recall ever seeing you around."

Drinking all of the tea in four deep swallows, the girl belched, smiled apologetically and answered, "No, I don't live on the island. I'm just visiting a friend. I've been staying there for the past week or so."

Carson was getting the strangest feeling and stared out the front windshield as they passed Johnson's Creek. Looking across the seat at the girl, he made a confused face and asked, "I might be way out in right field here, but you wouldn't happen to be Shelby Lee Pickett... would you?"

Amazed, the girl replied, "I am... how would you know that?"

Gesturing at the passing restaurant, Carson explained, "You were having dinner with Nick Falco last evening when I called him. I'm Carson Pike!"

Shelby, though tired, managed a smile and commented, "Yes, I remember that. You were supposed to meet with Nick at his house around ten. I was told that I couldn't be there. It's strange. I've been trying to call Nick for hours and his phone is dead. So, how did your meeting at the house go?"

"It didn't. Nick never showed up. He was kidnapped last night."

Shelby was instantly upset, but Carson reassured her, "Don't worry, he's all right. He managed to escape."

Shelby turned in the seat, her feeling of being tired disappearing. "Where is he? Do you know where he is?"

Carson reached out and patted the side of her face. "Don't worry yourself none. I know exactly where he is. He's safe for now. I've got everything under control and this whole mess could be over by tomorrow morning."

Shelby was talking so fast, Carson could hardly understand her, "I know all about the hidden money. You have to take me to Nick... now! There's something I need to tell him. It's really important. It doesn't have anything to do with his kidnappers. Can you take me to him?"

"Slow down, child! You're going to pop a vein if you don't cool it! I'm going to turn this heap around and take you to Beaufort. You'll be seeing him in less than thirty minutes."

Looking in the rearview mirror he made a U-turn on the highway and headed for Beaufort. "When's the last time you had something to eat? You don't look so good."

Shelby laid her head back in the seat, the cold air blowing across her upper body. "The last time I ate was yesterday about six in the morning. I've been so busy chasing the RPS Killer that I really didn't think about food."

Carson shot her an odd look and suggested, "I'm going to stop in Frogmore and grab you a couple of cold waters and something to munch on." Jokingly, he laughed, "It won't do you any good to go to Beaufort if you die on me on the way."

Shelby managed a weak smile and nodded her approval.

Ten minutes later, Shelby wolfed down an egg and sausage breakfast sandwich and a small blueberry pie, then finished up by gulping down one of the two waters Carson had bought. Pulling back onto the highway, Carson motioned up the road in the direction of Beaufort. "Ol' Nick thinks quite a bit of you. You guys have been hobnobbing now for what... a week or so?" Not waiting for Shelby to answer, he went on, "I remember the afternoon Nick and I ran into each other over at the Bonito Boathouse. That was just prior to his first date with you. He said he had a dinner engagement with a girl and didn't even know her name. Putting aside the fact that he could have been killed last night, it surprised me how concerned he was over your welfare. He couldn't call you to warn you about the men after him *and* possibly you because his cell phone was confiscated. He didn't know your cell number or exactly where you were staying on Fripp, so we decided to run over to your apartment in Savannah. There were some men watching your place. So, when we get to the marina in Beaufort to my boat, you're going to have to hide out until this thing is over after you talk with Nick."

Placing her hand over her mouth, Shelby yawned. "I do have to admit that meeting Nick Falco on that beach a few days back and reluctantly going to dinner with him, has turned into the most exciting summer I've ever spent on Fripp. I'm glad he's okay."

Thinking for a moment, Carson backed up his conversation to something Shelby had mentioned earlier. "You said you were busy following the RPS Killer. Nick mentioned to me that you two were in the process of following a man you thought might be the killer. I'm going to give you the same advice I told him. Forget that. That's police business. Anyway, we've got more important matters to attend to."

Shelby could have easily explained that hours before she had not only tangled with the RPS Killer, but had killed him. At the moment, and for the past few hours hiking across the island, she had been rolling around in her mind whether or not she was going to report her encounter with Harold to the police. She needed to talk with Nick first. She had so much to share with him and from what Carson had explained, Nick as well, had experienced a rough night.

Making a left on Bay Street, Carson decided to park farther on down the street west of the marina in case they had been followed. Carnahan was no slouch when it came to conning people. He had told him the deal was on, but he had to be careful that Carnahan was not running a con of his own.

Looking in the rearview mirror, he spoke to Shelby, "Here's what we're going to do. You need to get out and walk casually back up the street to the marina. My boat is down on the left. You can't miss it. It has an Atlanta Braves flag on the bow. When you get to the boat step on board. Nick will either be up top or down below. I'm going to wait a few seconds after you get out and I'll follow. See you in a few minutes."

Shelby climbed out and looked both ways up the street. Everything seemed normal. Business people opening their shops, another person sweeping the sidewalk. Once at the marina, she turned and saw Carson twenty yards behind her. Carson gave her a nod indicating for her to continue. Walking out onto the wharf, she immediately saw the bright red and black flag Carson had told her about flapping in the river breeze.

Carson hesitated and watched Shelby Lee walk down the wharf and board his boat. Sitting on a bench, he scanned the area for anyone who appeared suspicious. It appeared to be a typical morning at the marina. Three teams of draft horses were being hitched up to tour wagons, a few cars were pulling into the lot, a couple, nodding at Carson walked out to their anchored boat.

Shelby walked the length of the boat then decided to go beneath. There Nick stood with his bare back to her as he gulped down a glass of juice. Silently, Shelby sat on the cot and then spoke, "Hey there, sailor!"

Nick, taken by complete surprise, turned, his face beaming with a broad smile. "Shelby Lee. How did you know where I was?"

Shelby crossed her legs and answered, "Carson picked me up over on St. Helena Island. I was walking back to Fripp—"

The conversation was interrupted when Carson appeared in the small doorway. Shelby stopped talking immediately.

Carson apologized, "Didn't mean to butt in on your conversation, but we have to make plans for tonight." Walking across the enclosed room, he opened a closet and removed a revolver and a spear gun. Tossing the gun to Nick, he handed the spear gun to Shelby. "I'm sure you two have quite a bit to talk over. I'm going into town and meet with my friend. I should be back late afternoon. When I leave I'm going to hang around in the parking lot for a few minutes to make sure you don't get any unwelcome visitors. Whatever you do. Do not – I repeat – do not leave the boat. If Carnahan, Sparks, Simons or anyone else tries to board in my absence you can defend yourselves with those weapons. I don't think you'll have any problems, but don't let your guard down. I'll be back in a few hours. I'll be bringing dinner back with me. Seafood sound good?"

Shelby stared at the strange weapon in her hand and answered, "Sounds great!"

Carson no sooner was up the steps and off the boat, when Nick threw on the sweat shirt and sat on the cot next to Shelby. "Why in the world were you walking back to Fripp. That doesn't make any sense, especially since you planned on starting your day in Savannah."

"I did start out, just the way we planned with me staking out the gas station. Our boy showed up and I followed him out to the suburbs, waited all day for him to get off work, then followed him out to Tybee Island where he dropped by that bar Chester owns. I stayed outside, hoping to follow him home to find out where he lives, but he must have come up on me from behind when it got dark and hit me with that damn stun gun." Pulling up her top, she displayed a slight burn on her side.

"Then it was him," said Nick." All the girls he abducted were hit with a stun gun according to the police. But, that still doesn't explain why you were walking down the road toward Fripp? You must have escaped?"

"I did, but not until after I refused to play Rock, paper, scissors with him. He got so upset. He told me everything about why he killed those girls and how he had been abused as a young boy. He had every intention of killing me, but I managed to free my hands and punched him unexpectedly in his face. He chased me into a salt marsh somewhere on St. Helena where we tangled. I was lucky. I hit square in the head with an oar and he banged his head on the motor of a boat. Then, it happened. He was dazed and I shoved him under. I drowned the man... I killed him!"

Reliving the horrible experience brought Shelby to tears as she buried her face in her hand, stood and walked to the other side of the room. Turning, she repeated herself, "I killed him, Nick... I killed the man!"

Going to her side, Nick hugged her and tried his best to console her. "It's all right. Sounds to me like he didn't give you a choice. After what he's done, no one is going to view you as a killer. You did what you had to."

Shelby stomped her foot angrily and looked up into Nick's face. "You don't understand! It was Harold... Harold T. Benjamin and I killed him."

Confused, Nick let go of Shelby and repeated, "Harold... Harold, where have I heard that name before?"

Shelby walked back to the cot and sat. "Harold was that boy on the beach I met ten years ago over near Charleston. The military cadet I met on Foley Beach. You remember. We talked about him when we were at the Dockside."

Suddenly, it hit Nick. "Harold, the father of your daughter, Kirby is the RPS Killer?"

"Yes, I killed my daughter's father!"

Sitting on the cot next to her, Nick asked softly, "I can't even imagine the way you must feel. I take it you haven't gone to the police yet."

"No, I haven't and I have no intention of doing so. You're the only one who knows any of this. Pike doesn't even know. I know you trust him, but no one can ever know what happened out there in the marsh last night. Eventually, someone will discover Harold's body. There's enough clues around there that they'll figure out he was the killer. Besides that, the murders will now stop. Kirby must never know the RPS Killer was her father. This whole sordid situation will eventually go away. Over the next few days, months, maybe even years I'll have to deal with what happened out there in the marsh. Kirby doesn't need to know. She's only nine years old. If I have to I'll take the secret of the RPS Killer to me with the grave." Clutching Nick's hand, she pleaded, "Promise me... you'll do the same. No one must ever know."

Chapter Twenty-Four

SHELBY LEE SAT NEAR THE BOW OF THE BOAT AND GAZED out over the river while Nick finished up his two-hour long explanation of his adventure from the previous night: "Carson brought me up to Beaufort to his boat. He said I would be safe here and that we weren't going to wait around. He told me he has a plan in mind and that we were going on the offensive. According to him, we're going to pull a con on Carnahan."

Shelby picked up the spear gun at her feet and pointed it at the gun laying at Nick's side and remarked, "I think we're operating way out of our league here. I killed a man last night; a man who has killed nine girls we know of, maybe more. You have eight men looking for you, with orders to kill you. This is insane. All I wanted to do was spend a few peaceful days on Fripp, and you, well you just wanted to live out your dream of living on Fripp." Holding up the spear gun, she went on, "Here we sit like James Bond and one of his sexy female sidekicks ready to take on the evil Joseph Carnahan and his men."

Nick laughed at her analogy and commented jokingly, "I hadn't dated a woman in five years when I arrived here. Now, I find myself sitting across from a *sexy female sidekick.*" Standing, he picked up the revolver and tucked it into his sweatpants, placed his hands on his hips, puffed out his chest and mimicked the famous character, "Bond... James Bond!"

Shelby didn't find his attempt at humor amusing. "This isn't something to joke about, Nick. We're lucky to be sitting here. Harold could just as easily killed me last night and that creature, Derek came within a few seconds of drowning you. Here I sit with a damn spear gun, and according to Pike, I'm supposed to defend myself if need be, when where I really need to be is on Fripp with my nine-year-old daughter."

"So what you're saying is that you're sorry we met on the beach that day. I never meant for any of this to happen. I just wanted to have a nice dinner with you. To tell you the truth, I wish I would have never crossed paths with the likes of Ike Miller, Sparks,

Simons and Carnahan. I'm also sorry that you had to butt heads with Harold T. Benjamin. These past few days have unfolded into somewhat of a nightmare situation. I apologize for dragging you into this mess. You're right. You should be with your daughter; not sitting here with me on this boat; me with this stupid gun and you with that spear gun, looking like you're on an old episode of Sea Hunt. *We are* out of our league, but I've got to see this thing through to the end... whatever that may be. When Carson gets back, I'm sure he'll be glad to run you down to Fripp so you can be with Kirby. He never wanted you to be involved with my problem of this so-called money that the organization is demanding I give them. I should have never told you about that. All I did was put you in danger and for that... I'm sorry."

Shelby got up and walked across the deck and without a word embraced him, kissing him squarely on the lips. The kiss over, she looked into his eyes and stated firmly, "Look Mr. Falco, I happen to like you quite a bit, so stop apologizing. I'm in this, as you say... to the end."

The intimate moment was interrupted when they heard Carson's voice, "Maybe I should come back at a more appropriate time."

Shelby, slightly embarrassed, walked over to the spear gun, picked it up and held it at her side and smiled. "No, come on board. I'm just waiting to run one of these spears up Carnahan's ass!"

Stepping down onto the deck, Carson remarked, "Well then, I'm glad I'm not Joseph Carnahan." Holding up two different sacks, he continued, "I've got dinner for us." Throwing one of the sacks toward Shelby, he explained, "I dropped by the local Walmart and picked you up a few items. I've never had a wife or daughter so I'm not all that good at figuring out what sizes are, so I hope that stuff fits okay. There's a pair of shorts and a top. I got you a pair of undies also. I thought about getting you a bra but that's beyond my comprehension. There's some deodorant and some shampoo in there. I don't know all that much about you females but I figure you'd like to get cleaned up a bit. Got you a swim suit too so you can jump in the river and wash your hair and the like. I'm going down below and set up dinner."

Shelby motioned to Nick with the sack and said, "Don't just stand there. Go on down and give him a hand while I get cleaned up."

Ten minutes later, Shelby, standing at the bottom of the steps in the cabin, cleared her throat getting both Carson and Nick's attention. When they turned she placed her hand behind her wet hair and went into what she thought was a professional model pose as she displayed her new outfit. "I'm famished. Is dinner ready?"

Carson gestured at a small fold out table and responded, "Yes, dinner is served. We've got salmon patties, white fish, coleslaw, fries and apple pie for dessert. All we need is three beers and we're set." Opening a small refrigerator, he removed three bottles and announced, "Let's eat!"

Shelby grabbed a paper plate on which she placed a round piece of salmon and some fries. Taking one of the beers she sat on the cot, stuffed a fry in her mouth and asked, "Carson. While you were gone Nick filled me in on everything that's happened. He said you had a plan... something about conning this Carnahan character."

Cutting into a piece of fish, Carson explained, "That's right. The plan has already been set in motion. Tonight around midnight Nick and I are meeting with Sparks and Simons at the house on Fripp. We are going to turn over to them two suitcases which contain all of Carnahan's money. After they inspect the contents then they are to call Carnahan to verify they have the money. They, then drive up to Charleston and deliver the money, Carnahan counts it, and we're all off the hook. That's it."

Shelby bit into her salmon and spoke, "I'm confused. If we give Carnahan his money and he lets us off the hook, as you say, where does the con come in? It sounds more like an agreement than a con. Carnahan gets what he wants and we no longer have to fear for our lives. Where's the con?"

"Part of the con will actually take place at the house, but you won't be there to witness what takes place. As it is, I'm uncomfortable with you knowing about the money, but apparently Nick trusts you. I'm okay with that, but none of this business can go any further than this boat. The plan is simple but it could backfire. When Nick and I meet with Sparks and Simons there's a chance things could go awry. I don't want you anywhere near the house. As a matter of fact, we're going to drop you off at your friend's house on Fripp on our way over. As soon as Sparks and Simons leave with the money we'll give you a call to let you know we're all right. That's the way it has to be... understand?"

"Yes, I understand, but I have a question. Where is the money?"

Getting up, Carson walked to a closet, slid open the door and displayed two large suitcases. Right here."

Nick nearly choked on a mouthful of fries. "Do you mean to tell me the entire time you've been gone the seven million dollars has been right here?"

"Yep, that's what I'm saying."

Shelby got up and walked over and placed her hand on one of the cases. "Seven million dollars! Are you kidding me? I can't even imagine having that much money. I've always wondered what a million dollars would look like. But this... this is seven million! Can we look in one of the cases?"

Carson swallowed a drink of beer and opened his wallet. He extracted a number of bills and tossed them on the end of the table. "There's ones, fives, tens, twenties and I think maybe even a fifty there. The only thing you're going to see if you look in one of those cases is a whole lot of these. It's just money... a lot of money, but still, just money."

Shelby, feeling a little ridiculous admitted, "What the hell. There's no sense in looking at something I'll never have. Just sayin'."

Carson smiled and returned the money to his wallet. "Here's the plan for the rest of the evening. It's now just three o'clock. After we eat we'll just relax here on the boat." Tossing Shelby his cell phone, he suggested, "You probably need to call your friend's house and let her and your daughter know that you're all right. Tell them you'll be coming home about nine o'clock or so tonight. After Nick and I drop you off we'll head on over to Nick's house and wait for Sparks and his sidekick to show up. If everything works out the way I planned, later on tomorrow evening we'll all be having dinner at the Bonito Boathouse without a care in the world."

Nick hoisted his beer and announced, "Here's to success!"

Carson pitched his empty beer bottle in a nearby cardboard box, walked to the bow of the boat and looked out at the river. Looking at his watch, he ordered, "All right, it's almost nine. Time to head out to Fripp." Picking up one of the suitcases he motioned toward the second case. "Nick, grab that case. We'll put them in the back of the Rover. You need to take that gun I gave you along. When we get to the house you need to get Edward's gun out of the cookie jar. We may need both of them. Let's get over to Fripp and get this show on the road. Curtain call should be around midnight."

Pulling up in front of Shelby's friend's house on Fiddler's Trace, Carson reminded her, "Don't call us... we'll call you when it's over.

You should be hearing from us between twelve-thirty and one o'clock in the morning."

Standing in the front yard, Shelby gave Nick a kiss as she held his hands and smiled. "I'm looking forward to our dinner at the Boathouse. If you get killed and screw that up, I'm really gonna be pissed... you hear me?"

"Everything's going to be fine," assured Nick. "I'm looking forward to meeting Kirby."

Back in the Rover, Nick pulled the gun from his sweat suit pants and asked, "Is this thing loaded?"

Pulling out, Carson answered, "Full load!"

It was just short of ten o'clock when they pulled in Nick's driveway. Nick started to get out, but Carson pushed him back in the seat. "Let's wait until it's completely dark."

A half hour passed when Carson looked at his watch and ordered, "Let's go. We'll take the cases in the front door. I'm sure Carnahan has someone watching the house. I want to make sure they see both cases."

Nick grabbed one of the cases and followed Carson across the front yard and up the steps where Carson unlocked the front door and stepped inside. Gesturing at the surrounding walls, Carson smiled, "Home sweet home!" Walking down the hallway toward the kitchen, he suggested, "We'll wait for our visitors in the living room."

Setting the case he was carrying next to the couch, he walked back to the kitchen and grabbed a beer and asked Nick, "You thirsty?"

"Yeah," said Nick, "but I think I'm going to go with something a little stronger." Walking to a built-in liquor cabinet next to the fireplace, he opened the cabinet and removed a bottle of Jack Daniels. Back in the kitchen he opened the refrigerator and grabbed some ice cubes and a coke. Taking a glass down from a cabinet, he dumped in the cubes, coke and a full measure of Jack. Taking a long swig, he commented, "Normally I don't drink the hard stuff, but right now I need a stiff drink. What do we do now?"

Carson picked up the second case and walked into the living room, placing it next to the first. "We wait for our guests to arrive. Just try and relax. You need to give me the gun. Everything is going to work out... believe me."

Handing the gun over to Carson, Nick sat in an easy chair and put his drink on an end table. "Your friend who you went to see in Beaufort. I can only assume they helped you work out this plan."

Carson held up his drink and affirmed, "That they did."

"If I recall, you said that I might get to meet them tonight."

"All in time, my friend."

Changing the subject, Carson asked, "How did things turn out with Ike Miller. I know you tangled with him and you said Shelby was going to break things off with Miller. How'd that work out?"

"Actually, quite well. He's in the hospital right now, but the word is when he gets out he's moving to Florida."

"Was he in an accident?"

"Let's just say he ran into some people that were a tad bit meaner than he is. It's for the best. He was really a pain in the ass! I'm glad for Shelby Lee that he's decided to move on."

Carson smiled. "And it would appear from the way she kissed you back there on the boat that you're moving right in!"

"Well, I do have to admit she's quite the girl. I haven't known her all that long. She had a rough start right out of high school, but she seems to be a good mother... a good person."

Going in a different direction, Carson probed, "Ya know, it was strange to say the least when I picked her up while she was walking down the Sea Island Parkway to Fripp. She mentioned something about tracking down some man that you and she felt might be the RPS Killer. Just like I told you... I told her to let it go. I didn't just fall off the back of a turnip truck. I could tell from the way she looked when I picked her up that she had a bad experience last night. She didn't offer much info and I didn't push. I'm sure during my absence back there on the boat that she no doubt filled you in. Is there anything you want to tell me?"

"No, not really. She did tell me what happened. She asked me to keep it a secret and I intend to honor her request. If she, at some point decides to tell you about last night, then you'll know; but it has to come from her. I'd rather talk about what we're faced with when Sparks and Simons show up."

"I can't tell you how they're going to react after they arrive. We'll just have to wait and see. My advice to you is try not to worry. All of the pieces of the puzzle will fall into place and I think you'll be amazed when the biggest part is snapped in place. You'll know soon enough."

At 11:45 Carson stood and looked out the picture window at the back of the house. "Let's go over everything one more time. I know you don't know everything that's going to go down in the next hour or so, but when it starts it'll go quick. You need to let me do all the talking and don't be surprised when things don't go the way you think they should. Everything is not as it appears."

Nick finished up his second mixed drink of the evening, stood and joined Carson at the window. "I sure wish it was tomorrow evening at the Boathouse... and this was all behind us."

"Patience, my son," remarked Carson. "In a few minutes Sparks and Simons are about to have a wakeup call. They'll arrive thinking they are in control, that they have the upper hand, but here's some advice for you to remember for the future. He who thinks he knows all, soon finds out that he knows not! Now, why don't you go back to your chair and try to look relaxed for our friends when they arrive. I'm gonna grab another beer."

The grandfather clock next to the fireplace began the melodious chiming at the top of the hour—midnight. Relaxed, Carson sat on the couch, both suitcases at his feet and listened to the pleasant chimes. "I always liked that clock. There was many an evening that I sat here in this room with your grandparents and listened to that clock announce the time."

The clock wasn't even finished chiming when Sparks appeared framed in the arched walkway that led into the kitchen, Derek looming in the shadows behind him. Nick was taken by surprise, but Carson remained calm. "Gentlemen, right on time. Please come in and have a seat." Standing, Carson went right on, "I believe you both know Mr. Falco here, so I think we can forgo any introductions."

Sparks entered the living room with his gun drawn. Derek followed, a gun in his large hand as well.

"What's all this," said Carson. "I was under the impression that this was to be a friendly negotiation. Perhaps you should dispense with the armor. In other words, if you do anything to piss me off and this deal falls through and Carnahan does not receive his money he's not going to be a happy man. I know you both think you're hot shit, but tonight you're nothing but Carnahan's messenger boys. You are to pick up the money and deliver it into his hands... nothing else. Now, why don't we put the guns away?"

Charley agreed and Derek followed suit as they both tucked their guns in their pants. With that, Carson offered the two men seats on either side of the fireplace. Carson sat back down on the couch and spoke, "I'd offer you both a drink, but I'm sure you're anxious to receive the money and be on your way."

"That's right," said Charley, "so let's get on with it."

"First," pointed out Carson. "Let's make sure we're all on the same page. It is to my understanding that you are to inspect the contents of the cases and then call Carnahan in Charleston here from the house, telling him the money is in your possession. You then leave, drive to Charleston and deliver the money to him. He counts the money *and* I assure you the count will be correct to the penny. The end result is that Nicholas here is off the hook, never to be bothered by you people ever again. Am I correct?"

Sparks nodded. "That's what Mr. Carnahan explained to us. He said there was to be a total of 5.8 million."

"That's correct," said Carson. "5.8 mil."

Sparks looked at the case and asked, "I assume the money is in those two cases?"

"It is." Carson stood and dragged both cases across the hardwood flooring and placed one each in front of Charley and Derek. Backing away, Carson grinned, "Merry Christmas boys. That'll buy you a lot of toys... or I should say it'll buy Carnahan a lot of toys. Once again, you're just the messengers... nothing more!"

Charley stared at Carson as if he didn't understand, while Derek wrestled with the latch on the case, his large fingers having difficulty opening the top. Finally he succeeded. He raised the leather top and much to his surprise, stared down into folded newspapers. Charley, seeing the contents of the case, quickly opened the second only to observe the same thing—newspapers. Charley reached for the gun in his waistband but Carson beat him to the punch as he leveled his revolver directly at both men. "Keep your hands clear if you want to walk out of here tonight gentlemen!"

Derek was livid as he objected, "You're dead, Pike! And so is the kid!"

Charley sat back in his chair and spoke calmly, "You must be nuts, Pike. Do you have any idea how Carnahan is going to react when I show up without the money?"

"That's your problem, not mine," pointed out Carson. "Right now you're going to give your boss a call just like we planned and tell him you have the money."

"I'm afraid I can't do that. I don't have the money."

"You and I know that, but Carnahan doesn't."

"I'm not making that call. When Joseph discovers that I don't have the money, he'll kill me!"

"If you don't make the call, I'll kill you, Sparks!"

"Here on Fripp Island. I doubt that very seriously."

Carson turned to Nick and ordered. "I need you to walk over to the cupboard and get your grandfather's gun out of the cookie jar. Make sure it's loaded, then stand by the fireplace and keep them covered for a few seconds."

Nick reluctantly got up, walked into the kitchen, opened the cabinet and withdrew the gun, then walked across the room and nervously leveled the gun at both men. Meanwhile, Carson pulled a silencer from his pocket and attached it to the barrel of his gun. Pointing the gun at Sparks, he ordered again, "Nick, you can return to your seat. I'll handle everything from here on out."

Nodding at the gun in his hand, Carson explained, "A silencer comes in handy on occasion, like right now where we don't want to disturb any of our neighbors with loud gunfire. Make the call, Sparks!"

Charley refused and crossed his legs. "I think you're bluffing, Pike. Let's just say you kill Derek and myself. That still leaves Carnahan and his entire organization that you'll have to deal with. I wouldn't wish that on anybody."

Carson got up and walked across the room, stopped in front of Derek, aimed the gun at his right leg and pulled the trigger. Derek yelled in pain as his knee cap exploded in a mass of blood and muscle tissue. He crumbled to the floor, rolling in pain.

Carson put the gun to Charley's head and stated firmly, "Does that look like I'm bluffing?"

Nick sat perfectly still, his hand wrapped tightly around the gun in his own hand. Carson looked across the room and reassured him, "Take it easy, Nick. This will soon be over."

Much to Nick's surprise, Sparks held his ground and refused to make the call.

Carson shook his head in disbelief and remarked in a joking fashion, "You just can't get through to some folks." He turned, pointed the gun at Derek's head and pulled the trigger. Derek's eyes rolled back into their sockets, he took a final breath and was dead, a pool of blood forming on the floor. Carson raised his hand to Nick. "Stay calm... just stay calm. This could get worse before it gets better."

Jamming the gun roughly into the side of Charley's head, Carson remarked, "You have less than three seconds to make up your mind."

Charley raised his hands. "All right... all right, I'll make the call. What do I say?"

"You make the call, short and sweet... businesslike. When Carnahan gets on the phone you tell him you have the money in your possession and that you and Derek are leaving immediately for Charleston. You'll see him in a few hours. You don't give him an opportunity to ask you anything. You hang up."

"I'll make the call like you say Pike, but I still don't understand how you think you can get away with this."

Carson handed Sparks his cell and ordered, "Let me worry about that. You just make the call."

Charley took the phone, stood up and punched in the number. Within seconds, it was obvious from what Sparks said that Carnahan was on the other end. "Joseph, this is Charley. Derek and I have the money. We're leaving right now and driving up to Charleston. See ya in a few hours." He then hung up.

"Very good," complimented Carson.

Sparks sat back in his chair, crossed his arms and asked, "Now what, Pike. Do I just walk out of here without the money?"

"It's not up to me if you walk out of here. That's someone else's decision." With that, a woman appeared in the kitchen door. Nick was at a loss for words as he stared across the room at their newest guest. Carson spoke up, "Nick, this is the friend I've been telling you about."

The woman looked at Nick and spoke softly, "Good evening, Nicholas."

Nick stumbled for the correct words, "Grandma...! Amelia... I can't believe it! You're not dead... you're alive! How can this be? I spread your ashes out over Ocean Point over a week ago. I must be dreaming. This just can't be!"

Amelia displayed herself and commented, "As you can plainly see... I'm alive and well! We'll have plenty of time to clear all this up for you later. I'm sure you'll have a million questions for me. But, for now we have some loose ends we need to tie up." Walking across the room, she took the revolver from Carson and walked over to where Sparks was seated.

Charley seemed to be in a state of shock, but he did manage to speak, "Amelia. You played us all. Big Ed taught you well."

"Edward, my beloved husband was killed by the organization you work for. Someone has to pay for that."

Charley pleaded, "You can't blame me for something the organization did."

Nick walked toward Charley and shook his head in disgust. "Yeah, well that's where you're wrong, Mr. Sparks. Last night over on Pritchards Island when Derek was trying to drown me, he told me he was going to enjoy killing me just like he and you did when you drowned my grandfather."

Amelia patted Nick on the shoulder. "I had a feeling it was Sparks and Simons but I could never be sure until this moment." Turning her attention back to Charley, Amelia tapped him on the side of his head with the gun. "Mr. Sparks, if I recall, the last time we talked in Beaufort you told me the next time you saw me it wasn't going to be pleasant. Well, that time has arrived and you were right. It's not going to be pleasant... for you." She fired the gun directly into the side of Charley's head. He slumped forward and down onto the floor. Amelia dropped the gun to the floor as a tear came to her eye and she spoke gently, "And that was for Big Ed."

Nick was beside himself. He bent over and vomited on the floor. Amelia went to his side and placed her hand on his back. "It'll be alright. This will all be over... soon."

Carson interrupted her conversation and sprang into action. "Look, there'll be time for this family reunion later. Right now we have to get this mess cleaned up. Nick, you need to help me bundle these two up in some old carpet that I put in the front room earlier today. We need to put them in the Rover. I'll run them over to the marina and load them into my boat. Then, I'll head out about twenty miles or so into the Atlantic and dump them. They'll never be found. Meanwhile, aside from getting this mess cleaned up, you and Amelia have a lot to talk about. I'll be back in a couple of hours, then you and I need to drive over to Charleston and pay Mr. Carnahan a visit. That will conclude the final stage of the con."

Nick raised his hands in confusion. "I don't understand any of this!"

Amelia took her grandson's hand and explained, "You have to trust Carson and me. We know, believe it or not, what we're doing. Now, let's get these hoodlums loaded up."

Nick stood in the darkness of the front porch and watched as Carson pulled out, the bodies of Sparks and Simons wrapped in old carpet in the back of the Rover. Still not believing what had happened and what was still happening, he walked back in the house to the living room where he found his grandmother with a bottle of heavy duty cleanser and a rag, wiping the blood stains from the back of the chair Sparks had sat in. Noticing Nick when he walked back in the room, she held up the rag and gestured toward the kitchen. "There are some more rags under the sink. The bloodstains on the floor and walls should be easy to clean up. I'm not so sure about these stains on the chair fabric. You might have to have both chairs reupholstered."

Nick couldn't believe how cold and indifferent Amelia was reacting to the situation. Sitting on the couch, he spoke strongly, "Wait a minute, just wait a minute! Things are moving along way too fast for me right now. Carson told me earlier not to try and figure any of this out. You're right, I do have a million questions for you. I don't even know where to start." Running his hand across his face, he recanted, "No, I do know where to start. How in the world did you pull off the fact that you died. That's just not believable!"

Amelia stopped her cleaning and placed the rag on the back of the chair, stood and removed a paper towel from a roll and started to clean some blood off the front of the grandfather clock. "Staging my death was easy. When Carson and I realized after Sparks approached me in Beaufort and informed me the next time he saw me it wouldn't be pleasant, we knew he meant to kill me, just like he killed Edward. So, at that point we decided to eliminate me from the equation by staging my death."

Running the towel down the front of the clock, she continued, "The day that I *supposedly died* Carson dropped by the house and we used make-up to make my face appear ashen... deathlike. He then, called the county coroner and told him that he had discovered me in bed... dead. Just before the coroner arrived, I laid in bed. The coroner showed up and pronounced me dead."

"That doesn't make any sense! How could the coroner pronounce you dead if you weren't?"

"Simple... we paid him off. The county coroner is a member of the country club and a longtime friend of myself and your grandfather. A person will do many things for a half million dollars. He called Fripp Island Security. Ol' Jeff Lysinger came over to the house and when the coroner flipped up the covers and said I was dead, Lysinger took one look at me and agreed. He went into the adjoining room and filled out his report and left. We didn't have to pay him anything. And then there was the mortician, another friend of the family. There was a time, years ago when our mortician friend lost his wife. He took it pretty hard and after a period of time his business started to flounder. Big Ed and I stepped in and helped him not only financially but we were there for him. He recovered and told us that if there was ever anything...

anything we ever needed to give him a call. In short, he owned us a favor. When we asked him to go along with my false death, he didn't even question us. He agreed."

"But I spread your ashes... or at least I spread something on the water out there on Ocean Point."

"That was a combination of fireplace ashes and old sand."

"But what about the memorial service we had for you. All those people... your friends who came and said their goodbyes to you."

"That was the hardest part for me, but we had to make it appear real in order to make the organization back off, at least for a while."

Nick stood and walked to the picture window. "Where have you been living all this time, and if you gave everything you owned to me in the will, how have you been able to survive?"

Joining him at the window, Amelia placed her arm around his shoulder. "Remember when Carson told you I sold him the home Edward and I had up in Canada? Well, Carson drove me up there and I've been staying there. As far as how I survived goes. I've lived quite well. There never was seven million dollars, but there was 6.4 million. The 5.8 million that was supposedly in those cases was moved to Canada and invested in off-shore accounts and stocks and bonds, not to mention a hefty bank account in a number of banking institutions in Canada. I have plenty of money."

Walking back to the chair, she started cleaning once again and continued speaking, "Nick, no one can ever know that I'm alive. It's part of the con. Later today, I'll be flying back to Canada and you're life living here on Fripp will continue."

Nick couldn't believe what he was hearing. "I can't just accept that. I thought you were dead and now I find I have you back and now you're telling me that I'll never see you again?"

"That isn't what I said, Nicholas. You can come visit me up at the lake house in Canada anytime you want... and I hope you will. I suppose I could meet you here in the United States from time to time, but I can never return to Fripp or even Beaufort County."

Wiping the back of the chair, Amelia changed the subject, "Carson tells me you're seeing a young lady."

Nick didn't want to stop talking about the mysterious life his grandmother was now living but realized she wanted to talk about something else, so he answered, "I wouldn't exactly say that I'm seeing her. She's a nice girl... actually she reminds me of you. She's kind of a tough bird. She has a nine-year-old daughter that I'm looking forward to meeting when this is all over."

Amelia stood and faced her grandson. "Nicholas, you know that I love you more than life itself. I would never do anything to hurt you. This was the only way out of this mess. When Carson told me Derek nearly killed you, I thought I'd never forgive myself. I never meant for you to be harmed in any way. You've got to believe me. I'm asking for your forgiveness, if you can find it in your heart."

Nick went to Amelia and gave her a hug. "There's nothing to forgive. I figure you had to do what you thought best. This has been quite a shock to me, but I'll get over it and things will get back to normal." Taking the rag from her, he grabbed the bottle of cleanser and stated, "Let's get this place cleaned up."

The grandfather clock chimed the time at four in the morning when Carson walked in the front door. He found Amelia and Nick seated in the darkness of the living room. Seating himself, he yawned and spoke in a very tired voice, "Sparks and Simons were dumped far out at sea. They'll never be found. If everything here is in order, then I say we leave for Charleston. We'll drop you, Amelia off at the airport, then Nick and I will contact Carnahan and complete the con."

Chapter Twenty-Five

PULLING UP AT THE DEPARTING FLIGHTS DROPOFF AREA
at the Charleston International Airport, Amelia hopped out of the
back of the Rover with a small carry on piece of luggage. Leaning
in the window, she reached in and caressed the side of Nick's
face. "Remember, you're welcome anytime up at the lake house.
It's beautiful up north in the Canadian woods. I'm really going to
miss Fripp Island. I want you to keep an eye on Genevieve. She
was always such a great friend to Edward and I. If there is
anything she needs that you can't help her with give me a call.
Carson has my number. Maybe you can come up for Christmas.
Now, get out of here. You and Carson are almost at the finish line.
I'll give you a call tomorrow to find out how everything went down.
Love you."

Leaving the airport, Carson handed Nick his cell phone.
"Remember, we're supposed to call Shelby Lee after we left the
house. Tell her everything went just as planned and we'll be back
on Fripp later this afternoon."

Nick punched in the number and Shelby answered on the first
buzz tone. "This better be you, Nick!"

"It is," laughed Nick. "Who else would be calling you before the
sun's up? Listen, I'm all right. I have to make this quick. I'll see
you tonight at the Boathouse over dinner. Don't worry,
everything's fine. I'll call you when I get back on Fripp."

Giving the phone back to Carson, Nick suddenly realized
something. "I really can't tell her everything that went on at the
house, can I?"

"No, you can't," agreed Carson. "You can't tell her that
Sparks and Simons were killed or that your grandmother is
alive. You simply tell her Carnahan fell for the con. Tell her we
gave them some of their money, but not all of it. That was the con
as far as she knows. Shelby strikes me as a sharp girl. We don't
want her to figure any of this out, at least completely. As long as
you're safe and everything returns to normal, I think she'll be
satisfied. Now, it's just after six o'clock. We're going to stop and

grab some breakfast while I explain the final part of the plan to you."

Walking out of the diner, Carson stretched and looked at his watch. "Okay, let's head toward the marina in Charleston. From here it's only about a half hour drive. You do everything like we discussed in the diner and we'll pull this off just fine."

Once in the Land Rover, Carson handed Nick the cell phone and reminded him, "Carnahan's number is logged in the phone from when Sparks called him. All you have to do is call the man and explain why you and I are on our way to see him. It's now seven-fifteen. If Sparks and Simons would have left the house with the money between twelve thirty and one o'clock, that means they would have arrived at the marina somewhere around three-thirty to four o'clock, which is when we left Fripp. Right now, Sparks and Simons, at least in Carnahan's eyes are over three hours late. He's probably beginning to get a wee bit impatient right about now. It's the perfect time for a call. The call has to come from you. It'll be more believable. I've known Carnahan for years. Deep down, I know he doesn't completely trust me. But you, an innocent painting contractor from Cincinnati, I think he'll trust. Now, make the call. Do you remember how to answer any questions he has?"

"Yes," replied Nick. "Just keep the conversation simple and act surprised when Carnahan starts talking about how his men haven't shown up with the money yet." Holding up the phone, he punched in the number and said, "Here goes!"

The call was answered on the second ring, "Who am I talking to?"

"This is Nick Falco. I need to speak with Mr. Joseph Carnahan."

"The voice on the other end, confirmed, "This is Carnahan. I was just getting ready to call your friend, Pike."

Nick looked across the seat at Carson as he explained the reason for the call. "The reason I'm calling you is because after Sparks and his friend left, I found six hundred thousand dollars Carson Pike overlooked when he found the money in my grandmother's house. I wanted to square things with you, so I thought Carson and I would drive over and give you the rest of your money. Combined with the 5.8 million Sparks and Simons delivered to you that should put the total at 6.4 million."

Nick hesitated for effect and just like Carson figured, Joseph came back with exactly what he figured he would say. "I'm getting a little nervous. So far I haven't received one red cent let alone 5.8 million. My men are over three hours late. They should have arrived here at the marina with the money around four o'clock at the latest. Something stinks Falco and I don't like it."

"This doesn't make any sense to me. I was there in the house when Sparks called you and I watched when he and Derek walked out of the house with the two cases of money and drove off. Maybe they had car troubles or something."

Carnahan was getting more irritated as the conversation went on. "Let me speak with Pike!"

Nick handed the phone to Carson who answered, "Joseph, I take it there's some sort of problem."

"You bet your ass there is! I don't have my 5.8 million and now Falco tells me he's bringing me another six hundred thousand."

Carson winked at Nick and Spoke into the phone. "Tell you what Joseph. We'll be at the marina in twenty minutes or so. Who knows, by then maybe your boys will show up with the cases. See ya in a few." Carson closed the phone and the call ended.

Looking across the seat, Nick asked, "What do you think will happen when we arrive?"

"That depends on how good of an actor you can be. Like I said, just keep things simple and Carnahan will go right down the road we want him to go."

Carson no more than pulled into the parking lot at the marina in Charleston, when they were approached by a man who signaled for them to roll down their window. The man leaned in the window and asked, "Pike and Falco?"

Carson answered, "That'd be us."

Pointing at a parking spot a few yards on the right, the man ordered, "Pull in there, then come with me. Carnahan is expecting you."

It was a short walk through the parking lot and then down a long wharf to where Carnahan's yacht was docked. Boarding the lavish boat, Carson and Nick were greeted by Joseph who was smoking a large cigar and had a drink in his hand. "Welcome aboard." Giving Nick an uncomfortable smile, he added, "I believe Nick here is already familiar with the layout of my yacht from the previous evening."

Nick, carrying a briefcase stopped and spoke directly to Joseph. "Mr. Carnahan, I'd like to clear the air if at all possible right now before we go any farther. I apologize for dumping you over the side, but I was fighting for my life. I really didn't have much choice, but I am sorry."

Carnahan laughed and pitched his unfinished cigar over the side. "Not to worry, my friend. That was quite a feat you accomplished. Swimming all that way and avoiding all of my men. You remind me of myself in my younger days. I figure you had to do what you had to in order to survive. Believe me, I've been in some rough situations in my younger years, where I had to think on my feet. It wasn't anything personal at the time. My giving orders that you be killed was just simply business."

Joseph offered his guests seats and asked, "Care for something to drink?"

Nick who had been instructed by Carson to do most of the talking, spoke up, "No thank you, I'd like to get down to business and finally close the book on this entire situation." Taking his seat, he handed the briefcase to Carnahan and continued to speak, "In there you will find six hundred thousand dollars that Carson somehow didn't discover when he found the money at my grandmother's house. The thought never even entered my mind about keeping this money, because it doesn't belong to me. Call it good upbringing, I don't know, but here's the rest of your money. When Sparks and Simons show up with the 5.8 million we gave them, you'll have a new total of 6.4 million. I just wanted to square things with you. It seemed like the right thing to do."

Carnahan opened the briefcase, picked up one of the stacks and flipped it through his hand. "You could have kept this money and I would have never known the difference. Honesty in the business that I'm in is quite rare to say the least, but we still have a looming problem and that's the 5.8 million that I have not received as of yet."

Nick shrugged as if he didn't understand. "Mr. Carnahan, I sat right there in my grandmother's living room and watched Sparks and Simons open those two cases. I saw the money myself for the first time. I was there when Charley made that call to you, explaining that he and Derek were leaving immediately with the money and that they were driving over here to deliver it to you. If I remember correctly, they said they'd see you in a few hours. I assume you took the call." Holding up Carson's cell phone he pointed out. "I actually have a record here on the phone when the call was made. They should have been here by now. I don't understand what could have happened."

Nick had done a great job of putting Carnahan in the casket, now it was time for Carson to nail it shut. "If I may," said Carson. "It's a known fact that I don't particularly care for Sparks and Simons. I know they have worked for you for years, but myself, I never trusted either one of them."

Joseph, downed the remainder of his drink and gave Carson an odd look and asked, "What exactly are you trying to say, Pike?"

"I'm not saying anything. I'm just trying to point out that 5.8 million dollars is more money than Sparks and Simons will ever earn in their lifetime." Lying, Carson continued, "I remember when they opened the cases, how they reacted. Derek was like a little kid in a candy store; running his hands through the stacks of bills and Charley making a comment about how a man could go a long way with this kind of money. Let me ask you this, Joseph? Did you, or have you considered the fact that they could have taken off with the money?"

"I've already thought of that possibility, but that would be a stupid thing to do on their part. There isn't anywhere they could go in the world where I couldn't eventually track them down. I have connections everywhere."

"Speaking of stupid things to do," remarked Carson. "Don't you think it would be stupid for Nick to drive all the way over here to Charleston to give you an additional six hundred thousand dollars if he felt he was in any danger? I mean, let's face it. You tried to kill this young man and he sits before you. That has to stand for something even in the world you exist in. And another thing I just happen to remember. At the time it didn't strike me as odd, but now, looking back, it was. When they got up to leave, Derek held up the case he was carrying and stated in a very cocky way, 'This could change a man's life!' If you want my opinion, I think you've been had by your own employees. They could well be on their way to Florida. If they manage to get out of the country, you'll play hell catching them. I could be wrong. But, from my own past experiences if I find that something seems wrong, it normally is. I've got a question for you, Joseph. Despite the fact that you said we would not be off the hook until you saw and counted the money, when you consider what seemed to have happened... are we good?"

Joseph lit up another cigar and sat back in his chair as he eyed both Carson and Nick. "I've always considered myself a pretty good judge of character. Big Ed always said you were a good man, Pike, and as far as Mr. Falco here is concerned, I believe he is on the up and up, so yes, for now, we're good. I'm not happy that I don't have all my money, so we'll just wait and see what happens. I'll put some feelers out across the country. If Sparks and Simons, as you say, are on the run with my money, eventually they'll have to deal with me." Joseph stood and extended his hand to Nick. "Nick, I appreciate you bringing me the money you found." Reaching over, he shook Carson's hand. "I offered you a job a number of times in the past. You always refused, claiming that you like to work alone. My offer still stands. If you ever find the need for employment, give me a call."

Carson, realizing that this was a polite way of ending the meeting, stood and spoke, "Well, I guess we best be getting back over to Fripp. I have a number of friends around the country myself. If I hear of anything regarding Sparks and or Simons I'll give you a jingle."

Carson waited until they were a block and a half down the street from the marina before he started to celebrate and even then was somewhat subdued. Thumping the steering wheel, he looked over at Nick and announced, "Well, it would appear that you deserve an academy award for your brilliant performance back there on the yacht. Carnahan bought into the concept of being ripped off by Sparks and Simons. As the days wear on without their appearance with the money, Carnahan will begin the process of a statewide and eventual countrywide search for those two. He'll spend a lot more than the six hundred thousand dollars we gave him trying to locate Sparks and Simons. That's the problem with greed. Carnahan will spend all the money we gave him and more in order to locate the 5.8 million he thinks two of his own employees stole from him."

"Do you think this is the end of it?" asked Nick.

"Yeah, I do. You did a great job back there. You almost had me convinced that you were on the up and up, as Carnahan put it. We won't hear from them again. There's no reason for them to contact us again. Now, here's the thing. The only people that can ever know what really happened back there at the house are you, I and Amelia. Is that understood? You share what we did with the wrong individual and believe me it can come back on you."

Once on the highway, Carson handed Nick his phone and suggested, "Why don't you call Shelby Lee and invite her and Kirby over to the Boathouse tonight for dinner like we planned. I'm gonna bail for tonight. I was so confident that we'd be successful that I went ahead and booked a reservation for three tonight. I'm going to go home, take a shower, load up my boat with enough beer and grub to last a week, and head out for an extended few days of relaxing fishing."

Nick drove the '49 Buick over to the Boathouse where Shelby agreed to meet him with Kirby at seven o'clock. Following a long shower and a change of clothes at the house, he was looking forward to a relaxing dinner.

Shelby had already arrived and secured a window table facing south in the direction of Skull Inlet. Nick walked in and after speaking to a hostess, was guided to their table. Kirby was cute as Shelby had described her: long blond hair, deep blue eyes and most definitely, a southern bell, lowcountry accent. After he was seated, Kirby reached out and shook Nick's hand. "You must be Mr. Falco, my momma's new friend. She talks about you all the time."

Nick returned the compliment. "Yeah, but I bet it's not near the amount of time she talks about you. Did you know your mother told me where you go to school over in Savannah? And, another thing: you can call me Nick if you'd like."

Brushing long blond locks from her face, Kirby grinned and stated, "One of my teachers last year told my class that when you use a person's first name that it's a sign of friendship."

Before Nick could respond, the little girl was off in another direction. Grabbing a menu, she turned to Shelby and announced, "I'm starving. I do hope they still have that fish sandwich I like so much." Changing the subject again, she went on without so much as taking a breath, "Momma, would it be alright if I went over to the other side and watched the boats come in?"

"Yes, but make sure you're back over here at the table in about ten minutes. We'll be ready to order by then."

Nick watched as Kirby ran across the room, her pink and yellow summer dress and white sandals the perfect outfit for a nine-year-old young lady. She jumped up on an unoccupied bench and gazed out the large windows. Turning his attention back to Shelby, Nick complimented her, "I can tell you've done nothing short of an excellent job of raising Kirby. She seems sharp as a tack. In a few years you're going to have your hands full fighting off all the boys who'll desire her company."

"I know, but thank God, that's still down the road aways." Taking on a more serious tone, Shelby remarked, "By the way, you haven't said all that much about what happened over in Charleston this morning."

"There isn't that much to tell, except for the fact that Carnahan bought into the con. He accepted a lot less money than what Amelia had and is no longer going to be a burden to me, you or Carson."

"That's it?"

"Well, there's more to it than just that, but Carson would just as soon keep what went on between he and I."

In a manner that suggested she didn't like Nick's response, she asked skeptically, "So, what went on is a secret?"

"Now, just hold on a minute before you go off and start judging Carson. You and I share a secret about what went on out there in that salt marsh on St. Helena Island. You told me you don't want anyone other than you and I to know what happened, so why should Carson feel any differently?"

Seeing Nick's point, Shelby shrugged her shoulders and agreed, "I guess you're right—"

Their conversation was interrupted by none other than Jeff Lysinger who approached their table, removed his hat and took an uninvited seat. "Hey guys! Have you heard the latest on the RPS Killer?"

The fact that they had just been discussing Shelby's unknown encounter with the fateful killer caused her to remain quiet, but Nick responded by stating, "No, we haven't heard anything new. What's up?"

"The news is all over the island. People are buzzing from Beaufort all the way over to Savannah. They found another body out in the marsh."

Confused, Shelby asked, "Another girl?"

"No, that's the strange part. It was a man."

"What's the body of a man found out in the salt marsh have to do with the RPS Killer? All of his victims were female."

"They don't think the man was killed by the RPS Killer. They think there's a pretty good chance that the body *is the RPS Killer!*"

"What brought the authorities to that conclusion?"

"From what the coroner reported, the man's head had been hit by an oar that was found lying in a boat next to the body. The coroner also stated that the man died from drowning, not from being hit with the oar. There were also a number of clues: like a pair of scissors stuck in the side of the boat and some electrical tape laying on the ground a few yards from a car in the marsh. The car itself reeked of cigarette smoke. If you'll recall, the girls the killer let go all agreed he was a chain smoker. He fit the

description the girls gave us: tall, slim. There were two sets of
footprints in the area just up from where the apparent struggle
took place. One can only assume that one set of prints probably
belongs to the person who killed the man."

Nick could tell Shelby was doing her best not to appear nervous
as she asked, "Do you think they'll follow up and try to determine
who killed the man?"

"If the man turns out to actually be the RPS Killer... I doubt it.
What point would there be? Most folks would probably agree that
whoever killed that bastard, if he is the RPS Killer, should receive
a metal. Oh, and one other thing they found. In the glove
compartment they found a driver's license and registration. It
looks like the car belongs to an individual by the name of Harold T.
Benjamin. Apparently, he comes from a wealthy family over in
Charleston. That's about all we have so far. Listen... gotta go! In a
way I hope this Benjamin character was the RPS Killer."

After Chief Lysinger left the table, Shelby leaned over and
whispered, "You don't think they'll find out I was there... do you?"

"I don't know," said Nick. "But you heard what the Chief said.
You'd be viewed as a hero. Besides that, it was self-defense. Harold
is dead and the killings will stop. I think we've both had our share
of misfortune these past few days. If you want my two cents I say
we forget all this for now. I don't know about you but for the past
few days I haven't exactly enjoyed my time here on Fripp. I'm
ready to get back to a normal life... my new life on Fripp Island."

Suddenly, Kirby was back at the table as she joyfully explained
what she had seen. "I saw lots of boats out there. I just love it here
on Fripp, Momma. I enjoy it so much when we get a chance to
come here." Resting her chin on her elbows, she looked up at the
ceiling as if she were making a wish. "Momma, do you think we'll
ever get to live here on Fripp Island?"

"I love it just as much as you do darlin'," commented Shelby.
"The houses here on Fripp are quite expensive and it cost a lot of
money to live here." Without thinking, Shelby blurted out in a
comical fashion, "The only way we would wind up living here is if
we found a man with a lot of money."

Kirby looked at Nick and stated, "My Momma says that you
live in a big house on the beach. Do you have a lot of money, Nick?"

"Kirby... please!" said Shelby. "That was not nice. You
shouldn't ask people those kind of questions."

Nick reached across the table and placed his hands over top of
Shelby's and looked deep in her eyes. "I do have a lot of money."

Shelby sat back in her seat and gave him an odd look, thought for a moment, then smiled and spoke, "Please don't tell me this is a repeat performance of that awkward day we met on the beach when you asked me to dinner. Please don't tell me this is your way of asking me to marry you?"

Nick released her hands, sat back, smiled, and held his hands out to his side, winked and then stated, "Just sayin'."

About the Author

Gary Yeagle was born and raised in Williamsport, Pa., the birthplace of Little League Baseball. He grew up living just down the street from the site of the very first Little League game, played in 1939.

He currently resides in Arnold, Missouri, with his wife and three cats. He is the proud grandparent of three and is an active member of the non-denominational church The Bridge. Gary is a Civil War buff, and enjoys swimming, spending time at the beach, model railroading, reading, and writing.

Also from Gary...

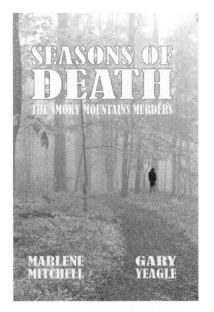

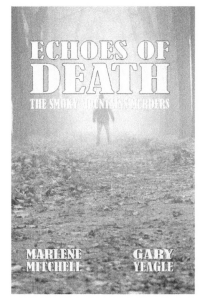

at www.blackwyrm.com

Also from Gary...

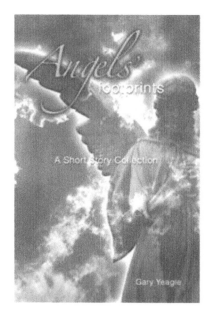

at www.blackwyrm.com

CPSIA information can be obtained at www.ICGtesting.com
Printed in the USA
LVOW05s0152041014

407177LV00002B/3/P